PLAYFUL LOVERS

Laura felt very brave and reckless. Despite a sprinkle of damp patches from flying droplets of water, Blake hadn't really managed to get her wet at all. She didn't know he was holding back purposely. With a wild cry of exuberance she dashed at him, cupping her hands together and spraying out a huge shower of water. Blake yelled in shock as the torrent hit him full in the chest, plastering his shirt to his skin.

"Why you little vixen! I'll get you for that!" he roared in mock ferocity.

Laura stood frozen at the unexpected havoc she had created. Her hands flew to her mouth, and she rocked with laughter at the sight. Her eyes grew wide with apprehension as she watched Blake quickly unbutton his shirt and tug the tails of the sodden material out of his waistband.

Suddenly he stepped toward her and put his arms gently around her waist. "Surrender?" he asked, his grin mocking her.

"Only to you," she replied. "Only to you. . . ."

TEXAS ROGUE
La Ree Bryant

ZEBRA BOOKS
KENSINGTON PUBLISHING CORP.

ZEBRA BOOKS

are published by

Kensington Publishing Corp.
475 Park Avenue South
New York, NY 10016

First printing: March 1987

Printed in the United States of America

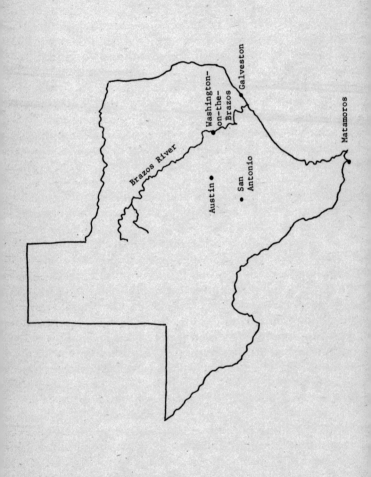

Chapter 1

1846

"You're an extremely lucky young woman. Bernard Arbuckle has spoken for your hand in marriage, and I have given my consent."

Laura sat in stunned silence before her uncle's massive oaken desk. Marry Uncle Henry's business associate? The man's image flashed in her mind: a balding, short, florid-faced man of somber attitude, his portly belly always encased in foppishly embroidered vests under expensive broadcloth coats.

Her breath caught in her throat as she remembered how he had clutched at her hand with fat little sausagelike fingers at their last meeting, his palm damp and clammy against hers. But it had been his eyes that bothered her most. Those slightly protuberant watery blue orbs had perused her with such intent that she had stuttered her excuses and fled from the room at the first possible opportunity.

Marry Bernard Arbuckle? Impossible! Her fingers gripped the arms of the chair in alarm.

"But, Uncle Henry . . ."

"Bernard has offered to handle all the arrangements, which is very generous of him in light of your circumstances. Such a fine opportunity for you. With Bernard's wealth and standing in the community, you'll want for nothing."

Laura watched mutely as he pushed himself ponderously out of the deep leather chair. Clasping his hands behind his back, he paced the room, magnanimously enumerating the many amenities she would enjoy: the fine house she would live in, the carriage, the servants, the generous clothing allowance. None of it was comprehensible to Laura's stunned mind.

"Yes, all in all, I'd say you're a very lucky young woman." Uncle Henry stopped his pacing and turned to Laura, his heavy-jowled face positively beaming with satisfaction.

Laura's head spun. How could this be? She hardly knew the man. Oh, he had called on Uncle Henry over the years concerning business matters. And lately those visits had been more frequent. But Laura had never done more than exchange a polite word or two with him until he began coming to dinner once a week several months ago.

Why, being married meant living in the same house, sleeping in the same bed! She shuddered, fighting the sick feeling in the pit of her stomach. She knew little of the man-wife relationship, but her girlhood dreams of such matters had always secretly centered on William Stratford. Sharing such imagined intimacies with Bernard Arbuckle was unthinkable.

Desperation gave her the bravery to protest—something that *no one* in the house ever did, not Aunt Mary, not Cousin Cynthia, and especially not Laura.

"But I don't want to marry Mr. Arbuckle."

Uncle Henry's mouth fell open in astonishment. "You don't want to? What a foolish thing to say." He waved a hand in arrogant dismissal of such a thought. "Of course you do. Any young woman would be thrilled at the thought of an alliance with one of the town's most prominent citizens. You're just nervous."

"No, y-you don't understand," Laura pleaded. "I can't marry him."

His eyes narrowed. "Now, listen, Laura. I'm quite sure a bit of apprehension on the bride's part is perfectly natural, but I have no intention of indulging any of your foolishness. The bargain has been made."

She flinched at the anger in his voice, but desperation drove her on. "But, I *can't* marry him," she repeated, groping for a reason that would sway her uncle's determination. "I can't marry him because I . . . I don't love him."

Uncle Henry snorted derisively. "Love! Humph! What does that have to do with it? Look what *love* got your mother! Two children and an early death, that's what. If my sister had listened to me, she would still be alive. And I wouldn't have been saddled with the responsibility of rearing her offspring without so much as a dollar's worth of inheritance for their care."

Laura cringed at the sting of his words. "But Anthony has been sending money . . ."

"Anthony," Uncle Henry sneered, his heavy jowls fairly quivering with indignation. "I don't want to hear your brother's name in this house! That ungrateful young pup—sneaking out and running off to Texas after all that I'd done for him." He stormed to the sideboard and poured a generous dollop of brandy in a glass. "You think that paltry sum he sends monthly has made up for the embarrassment he put me through, much less what I've spent for your care during these ten years? Humph! It's cost me a pretty penny, it has! Why, you've enjoyed the same treatment as my own daughter. Haven't I provided you with a good home?"

11

"Yes," Laura answered meekly.

"And clothing? Not just the necessities, mind you! You're as fashionably dressed as the other young women of your station, aren't you?"

"Yes."

Yes, he'd provided all the material necessities and even a good many luxuries. But she would have traded them all for the dimly remembered love of her parents, the laughter and contentment of their small home.

"And schooling. Didn't you attend the very same school as Cynthia?"

"Yes," she answered wearily. She drew a deep breath, her heart thumping painfully. "But . . . but, I overheard you tell Aunt Mary that the sums Anthony's been sending the last two years are really quite generous. Surely those helped . . ."

Uncle Henry's face purpled with rage. "A pittance! A mere drop in the bucket! As if *anything* he could send would make up for his ungrateful behavior."

"Well, whether the amount was small or not, it certainly didn't stop you from accepting his money," Laura retorted before thinking. Her hands flew to her face in horror. Crimson stained her cheeks as she waited for a reaction to her reckless words. It wasn't long in coming.

Uncle Henry stormed across the room to tower over her quaking figure. "We are not here to discuss your brother's reprehensible actions! You had better get such foolish thoughts as love out of your mind. Any man worth his salt is looking for an alliance with someone of wealth or social status. After all, *you* have nothing to contribute to the union except your pretty face. If you don't realize just how grateful you should be for Mr. Arbuckle's offering, then at least consider the wishes of your dear aunt and myself. We have cared for you diligently over these years, and we know what is best for you."

Laura rose to follow the imposing figure across the room. Her aching throat worked to swallow the icy lump that lodged there. "How can you know such a thing? How can you know where my affections lie? Perhaps there's someone else that I care for."

"And just *who* might that be?" Uncle Henry demanded in an incredulous voice.

Scarcely aware of the audacity it took to make such a bold statement, Laura blurted out a name. "W-William Stratford."

"And has he spoken to you about such matters?"

"No, but—"

His harsh laughter rang out. "Nor will he. You're indulging yourself in foolish female delusions! Oh, he's certainly willing to escort you and Cynthia to a party or two, but you can rest assured that William Stratford's affections will be earned by money and social status, not love. He's no fool."

Laura knew her pleas were hopeless against his granite determination. Uncle Henry *always* had his way. Her eyes shone with unshed tears as she fought to maintain her composure.

"You will *not* subject me to humiliation in this community as your brother did! You're going to wed Bernard. And with proper gratitude for such a privilege. I have done my duty by you, and now you will do yours. I've given my consent, and the matter is closed." He turned his back on her, signaling the end of the discussion.

With a sob, Laura whirled and ran from the room. She gathered her full skirts high, stumbling up the stairs to her room, almost blinded by the hot tears that coursed down her cheeks.

The slam of her door reverberated through the hall. She threw herself across the canopied bed, burying her

13

face in the ruffled pillows, sobs shaking her slender form.

Mere moments later the door creaked slowly open and Cynthia's blond head peeped around the corner. "Laura?" she called quietly. "What's wrong? I heard Father shouting."

Laura pushed herself up slowly, clutching a tear-drenched pillow to her bosom, the misery on her face so acute that Cynthia feared she was in actual physical pain.

"Oh, Laura, are you sick? What's the matter?" Cynthia flew to her cousin's side, putting her arms around her to soothe and console. "Shall I get Mother? The doctor? Oh, dear! Whatever is wrong?" she pleaded as Laura's tears began anew.

"It's Bernard Arbuckle . . ." Laura managed through the sobs.

"Mr. Arbuckle?" Cynthia repeated in bewilderment. "Whatever did he do?"

"Uncle Henry says I have to marry him," Laura wailed.

Cynthia's mouth fell open, her Dresden blue eyes growing wide in astonishment. "But he's . . . he's an old man!"

"Yes, I know!" Laura's tears fell harder.

"But why would Father do such a thing?"

"I don't know." Laura hiccupped softly. She gave a great sigh, trying very hard to control the sobs still rising in her throat. "S-something about duty and obeying his wishes."

"Oh, my. I suppose he gave you no say in the matter?"

Laura turned wide eyes on her cousin. "*Uncle Henry?*" She shook her head. "He just kept saying what a lucky young woman I am to be marrying such a fine man. He wouldn't even listen to my side at all."

"No, I suppose not," conceded Cynthia, chewing softly on her lower lip.

14

"I . . . I even tried to tell him that I loved William—"

"Oh, Laura, you didn't! What did he say?"

"He laughed at me." Laura turned stricken eyes to her cousin. "He said that William might squire me around but that in the long run he would care more about money and social status than love—just like any smart man!"

Cynthia gasped. "Do you really think so?"

"Of course not! William is sweet and kind and . . . and, well, he's not at all like people think he is."

"What are you going to do?"

Laura plucked nervously at the corner of the pillow clutched in her arms. "I don't know. But I'm not going to marry that man! Maybe . . . maybe Aunt Mary will talk to Uncle Henry."

"*Mother* stand up to Father?" Cynthia's shocked voice betrayed her feelings about *that* desperate suggestion.

Laura swiped angrily at the tears that still trailed slowly down her cheeks. Her back stiffened and her firm little chin rose obstinately. "Well, I won't marry that man. I won't!" Her eyes blazed with determination. "There's *got* to be a way out of this predicament! I'll think of something. I must!"

Chapter 2

The sun-streaked deck of the *Star Republic* swayed gently beneath Laura Nichols's feet as she eagerly searched the horizon for her first glimpse of Galveston. The gusty wind, sharp with the clean tang of the Gulf, tugged at her unbound hair, tumbling the rich brown curls in riotous disarray. The dark-blue skirt of her sea spray-dampened gown billowed around her ankles as she clutched the mahogany bow railing in nervous anticipation.

Would Anthony be at the dock to greet her? she wondered, quelling a feeling of trepidation. How had he reacted to the news of her rebellious flight?

"You must have been here since dawn."

Laura jumped in surprise at the softly spoken words. "Oh, Mrs. Martin! You startled me." She gave a small laugh. "Actually I've been up since *before* dawn. I was much too excited to sleep." Her deep blue eyes twinkled delight at the arrival of the prim little woman who had become her friend during the long voyage.

"I understand perfectly, my dear. A little excitement about this strange new land and perhaps something a bit more disconcerting about your brother's reaction to your arrival?"

16

"I simply must believe that he'll help me," Laura said, brushing wind-tossed curls out of her eyes with slender fingers. "Anyway, he can't send me back immediately. Surely, after I explain the circumstances, he'll understand."

Mrs. Martin patted her arm affectionately. "I'm sure he will. I wish you the best, Laura. You're a very brave young lady. And if there's anything these Texans respect, it's bravery."

Laura flushed. "Well, some might call it desperation or stupidity rather than bravery, I suppose. But I simply had no choice."

She remembered her first desperate plan. It had hinged on pleading with William to take her in, hide her until Uncle Henry gave up his crazy idea. She blushed in remembrance of even considering such a brazen move, very thankful that she had been saved from that embarrassing plot by the fact that William had left town and she had no idea how to get in touch with him.

"Anthony was the only person I could turn to. And I had to come to him. There simply wasn't enough time for him to come to Philadelphia before Uncle Henry forced me to marry that horrible man."

"Of course, my dear, I quite agree. I just wanted to remind you that our invitation stands. If your brother isn't here to greet you, Mr. Martin and I will be more than happy to have you stay with us for a few days. We can leave word at the ship line office and the post office to let him know where to find you."

"But I sent my letter over a month ago. Surely he's received it by now." Laura's brow furrowed at the disquieting thought.

"Mail is notoriously slow in Texas, dear. And sometimes a letter simply never makes it to the less populated areas. Between the weather and the roads and an occasional raid—"

"Oh!" Laura turned bright eyes on her small friend. "You mean Indians?" she questioned, with something akin to awe in her voice.

Mrs. Martin gave a small delighted chuckle as she fastened her fashionable bonnet a bit more securely against the sea breezes. "Actually, the Indians raid further west. We've had more problems lately with the Mexicans."

"The Mexicans? But why?"

"Some of them—the new government, in particular—simply never accepted Texas's independence, much less her statehood. They frequently run small skirmishes across the border and occasionally as far as Austin. Some say they're trying to work up nerve for a full-scale war. With Zachary Taylor and his troops now at the mouth of the Rio Grande, they just may get their wish."

"Oh," murmured Laura, pondering the possible impact of this new development on her precarious position.

The tinge of apprehension in Laura's voice caught Mrs. Martin's attention, and she reached to pat her arm affectionately. "There, there, my dear. Everything's going to be just fine. Don't you worry."

Laura smiled tremulously and turned her attention to the horizon once again. "Oh, look! There it is! Galveston, at last!" Her eyes sparkled at the tumultuous scene drawing nearer and nearer.

The harbor teemed with a vast array of sailboats, some at anchor and others, sails billowing, tacking across gray-blue swells toward the open ocean. A steamboat tooted in the distance, smoke pouring from its stack in great gusts as it maneuvered majestically past the teeming wharves.

"Isn't it wonderful!" Laura's voice trembled with excitement as she watched the bustling crowds along the docks, the clamoring sounds carrying on the spicy wind. "It's much busier than I expected," she exclaimed, turning eyes large with amazement on her companion.

"Well, it has every right to be busy. A large portion of all the goods coming to Texas are shipped to this port— everything from clothing, tools, weapons, and food to extravagant imported furnishings. The cotton goes out and the goods come in. Mr. Martin is only one of the many merchants in this town. Although we've done quite well in the business, many others have made their family fortunes in shipping."

"Anthony wrote about growing cotton. That's how he got started. He's trying something new now. Cattle— longhorns, I think he calls them."

"Yes, seems like quite a few people are thinking about putting money into cattle. But cotton's still big business in Texas. See those big stacks of bales on the end of the far dock?"

Laura shaded her eyes and peered in the direction Mrs. Martin indicated. "They're so large," exclaimed Laura, her voice filled with excitement at the intriguing activity on the wharves.

Laura gave a big sigh, her brow wrinkling in consternation. "There's so much to see, to learn about! I never dreamed what I was missing. Why, the teachers at Mrs. Peabody's Ladies Academy told us absolutely nothing at all about these wonderful things. All they cared about was teaching us to oversee the household help and sew fine handwork. I do believe they'd have passed over reading and writing if the young ladies hadn't needed them for keeping household records after they married."

"Well, believe me," Mrs. Martin said with a laugh, "Texas will be a whole new education for you. Come along, my dear. You must ready your bags for unloading. We'll be docking soon."

Laura lingered a moment, her eager glance sweeping the breathtaking panorama one last time before she turned to hurry to her cabin. She wanted to be back on deck when the gangway was lowered. Would she recognize Anthony? After all, it had been over ten years since she'd seen him.

Less than an hour later Laura hung precariously over the railing of the ship to search the kaleiodoscope of colors and activities below. Her heart beat an excited tattoo as she surveyed one gentleman after another in the milling crowd.

She frowned as she studied a buckskin-clad man, his gingery beard and straggling hair almost hiding his face. Certainly not! Anthony was a gentleman of means, according to his letters. Perhaps one of them, she thought, as three men in black frock coats and hats strolled into view. But it was impossible to tell at this distance if any of them favored the tall, thin lad she remembered in her heart.

Other passengers bustled about her, calling greetings to their friends in the crowd below or giving stern instructions about the handling of their baggage as they anxiously shuffled toward the gangway. It was all so busy, so very big.

Suddenly overcome with the uncertainty of her situation, Laura collapsed onto her trunk, oblivious to the damage she might do to the forest-green traveling costume she had so carefully donned just minutes before.

Oh, Anthony, Anthony, please be here! she prayed, her fingers anxiously kneading the soft fabric of her reticule.

"There she is, Samuel." Mrs. Martin tugged impatiently at her husband's arm, hurrying him across the deck in Laura's direction. "She looks absolutely lost, poor child! Oh, do hurry, Samuel!"

Mr. Martin followed meekly in her wake, a small smile of resignation on his face. He knew it was useless to protest when Mabel was on one of her crusades. She had taken the girl under her wing at the beginning of the voyage, and he knew Mabel certainly wouldn't abandon her until she was positive Laura had been taken care of.

"Any sign of your brother, Laura?"

"Oh, Mrs. Martin! I'm so glad to see you!" Laura hugged her in relief. "I don't know if he's here or not. I don't recognize anyone," she replied, dismay in her voice. She brushed nervously at a smudge of dust on her skirt, her eyes large and anxious. "I suddenly feel so foolish."

"Now, listen to me, my dear. We'll simply wait until the crowd thins out. That should give him a chance to ask the captain or some of the crew about you, if he's here. And if he's not, you're coming home with us. No arguments. Right, Samuel?" She folded her hands determinedly across her plump little stomach and gazed up at her tall husband sternly.

"Absolutely, Miss Nichols," he assured in a booming voice. "We have plenty of room. And you'll be doing me a favor. I'll be very busy seeing to the new shipments at the store for the next few days. You'll be company for Mabel. And perhaps she won't be so apt to nag me about my long hours away from home," he added, with a twinkle in his eyes.

"Samuel! You know very well I never nag. Now, see to the bags, Samuel. I'll stay with Laura." With that stern reprimand, Mrs. Martin returned to clucking over Laura.

Mr. Martin ordered the driver to take the long way home so that Laura could be treated to a tour of the more interesting parts of Galveston. The carriage wound its way first through the commercial center surrounding the wharves while Mr. Martin happily pointed out the town's leading merchants; then they drove out to Galveston College, where students were tutored in subjects ranging

21

from intellectual philosophy to astronomy to modern languages. They passed the temporary pavilion where the New York Circus was to perform as they made their way to the Tremount Hotel, reputed to be the finest in the state. Mrs. Martin proudly pointed out the Episcopal church which had just last year received a fine-toned organ from Antwerp for use in their Sunday services. Their last stop was a small foundry, the first to be successfully operated in Texas.

Laura was charmed and delighted with the many sights and very grateful to the Martins for being so kind to her.

"I know you're disappointed that Anthony wasn't at the dock, Laura dear. But you mustn't worry. Samuel left word at all the necessary places. Your brother's sure to learn of your whereabouts upon his arrival. In the meantime, I hope you'll be comfortable here with us." Mrs. Martin ushered Laura through the doorway of the guest room.

"Thank you. You're both very kind. I'm sure I will be." Laura gazed with pleasure around the cheery room. "I just hope I'm not imposing on you too much."

"Nonsense! We're more than happy to have you. Now, I want you to stop worrying. If you haven't heard from Anthony in a few weeks, we'll send another letter and let him know that you arrived safe and sound."

"A few weeks?" Laura repeated with dismay, sinking onto the rose chintz bedspread. "Oh, no. I couldn't possibly impose on you for that long. There's got to be another way. After all, I got this far on my own. Surely there's a way to get to the town near his ranch?"

"Well, yes, of course," Mrs. Martin assured her, masking her disappointment at the thought of losing Laura's company. "There's always the stage line. It's rather uncomfortable and dreadfully slow. And the roads

22

are quite deplorable at times. But I suppose it would do if you insist on continuing your journey—"

"Oh, yes! I must. You see, the sooner I get to Anthony's, the sooner he can help me untangle this mess I'm in. And I wrote to William—about where I'd be, I mean. There might be a letter from him waiting for me at this very minute."

Her face flushed at the thought of just how William might have responded to her brash declaration of love. No! she admonished herself. Even if it hadn't been the proper thing to do, she mustn't regret her actions. If she achieved her heart's dream, the happiness she would gain for the remaining years of her life would justify her rather brazen conduct during the last two months.

"Do you think he's had time to receive your letter and reply so soon, my dear?"

The quiet question interrupted Laura's reverie. "Well, I can only hope that his family forwarded my letter immediately. But I suppose it still might be months before I hear from him," she admitted with a wistful smile, her heart aching at the possibility that she might *never* hear from him.

"Laura, are you sure you want to undertake such a long journey unchaperoned? That area of Texas is not nearly as civilized as Galveston. I . . . uh." Mrs. Martin fidgeted a bit, not wishing to sound like she was chastising the girl. "It really is a bit . . . ah . . . inappropriate, my dear," she finally managed to say.

Laura gave a small strangled laugh. "Mercy, if I'd worried about what was appropriate, I'd have never made it out the door of Uncle Henry's house."

She shook her head at the memory of sneaking into the study late at night and helping herself to enough of the household funds to finance her reckless plan, justifying her actions with the thought that it would only be a small portion of what Anthony had sent over the years.

Heavens! The trouble she'd had thinking of an excuse to get out of the house long enough to purchase her ticket, and the story she'd concocted when she was almost caught bribing the stable boy to take her luggage to the station! She could almost see Uncle Henry's apoplectic face when he opened his strong box at the end of the month to pay the household bills.

"No, I have to get to Anthony. He's my only hope," Laura declared.

"I hesitate to pry, my dear, but I've been wondering about something . . ." Mrs. Martin's voice trailed off in embarrassment.

"What is that?"

"If things were so bad at your uncle's, why didn't you join your brother before? Did he never consider sending for you?"

"He did mention it in his letters from time to time. But his first desire was for me to finish school. You see, I was only seven when our parents died. Anthony was fourteen. He and Uncle Henry never did get along. We'd been there about two years when they had a big fight— I can remember standing outside the study door and listening to the angry voices. Anthony left that night. I remember him waking me in the middle of the night and hugging me, telling me to be a good girl, that he'd write when he could."

Laura recited the tale in the nonchalant manner she had mastered over the years, but it was plain to Mrs. Martin that the girl had been devastated by the loss of her brother. Mrs. Martin watched compassionately as Laura rose and fumbled with the buckle of her smallest valise. She waited patiently for Laura to continue the story as she began to unpack small articles of her clothing and place them in the cherry-wood chest of drawers.

"And he did write. The letters came sporadically at first. And, oh, how I treasured those letters!" She

24

whirled to face Mrs. Martin, her face aglow with childhood memories. "I'd draw pictures of Texas, pretending that I knew just what it was like. And, as I remember, those pictures were usually filled with wild Indians." She chuckled at the thought.

"For several years I hoped that he would send for me any day. But he had to work hard for a long time, and he put almost all he made into building the ranch. When he'd finally made his fortune and built the big house—when he was finally secure and settled—and I could have come to him, I was quite in love with William and wouldn't have dreamed of leaving."

Laura sighed deeply as she mused on the whimsical nature of life.

"And now, here you are in Texas, finally fulfilling those childhood dreams," stated Mrs. Martin.

"Yes, here I am," Laura replied with a merry laugh.

It pleased Mrs. Martin no end to see Laura regain her usual spunky attitude, to hear the silver ripple of her laughter once more.

A young boy swept lackadaisically at the rough wooden planking in front of the stagecoach station. He did little more than stir dust into the golden beams of sunlight splashed across the silver-gray boards. Laura and Mrs. Martin stood beneath the sheltering overhang of the porch as they watched Mr. Martin check the bindings, which secured Laura's trunk to the stage, one more time.

"Laura, are you really sure you want to do this, my dear?" Mrs. Martin plucked nervously at the dainty lace edging on the linen handkerchief clutched in her hand. "You know you're more than welcome to continue staying with us."

"I really do have to go. Please don't worry about me," Laura admonished, giving her a brave smile. "Mr.

Martin's been so kind in making all the arrangements. I should have absolutely no problems. When I reach Washington-on-the-Brazos, I'll send a message to Anthony. I have enough funds for a boardinghouse. I'll be fine, really."

The thud of booted footsteps interrupted their conversation, and Laura glanced up as two gentlemen crossed the porch to the stage. As the older man nodded in their direction, doffing his hat politely, the boy scooted off the platform and up to the stage roof. Laura hardly noticed the man's polite gesture; her attention was drawn to his tall companion. He was the most handsome man Laura had ever seen.

He walked with a magnetic, rhythmic saunter, his obviously eastern-tailored clothes snugly encasing powerfully muscled thighs and massive shoulders. His broad chest tapered to a narrow waist. Softly bronzed skin was drawn over high cheekbones; eyes of deepest brown were fringed with heavy dark lashes. His jaw was strong and slightly square with just the hint of a dimple in the firm chin. A luxuriant mustache, several shades darker than his hair, shadowed his full lips. As he moved from the shadows of the porch, the sunlight caught in his tawny hair and it gleamed like old gold.

He tossed his heavy bag up to the boy with ease, following it with his companion's valise. He watched the boy secure the bags, rolling his broad shoulders as if to settle the well-cut coat more comfortable across their breadth before turning back toward the porch.

Laura unconsciously flicked the tip of her tongue across her bottom lip, gazing in innocent fascination as he ascended the wooden steps. Each movement pulled the fawn-colored pants tightly across his thigh muscles.

The man paused at the edge of the porch, and her startled gaze flew to his face. Scarlet stained her cheeks as she became aware of the fact that she had been staring at him in a most unladylike manner. What was worse, she knew he was very much aware of her perusal.

His mouth twitched in amusement. With a slow, deliberate motion he tugged at the brim of his hat, never taking his eyes from hers. "Ma'am."

A slow liquid heat spread through her veins. She could hear the pounding of her heart in her ears, feel its frantic beat in the soft hollow of her throat. Her hand flew to cover the revealing flutter above the modest neckline of her plum-colored dress. She wished heartily she had not allowed Mrs. Martin to talk her into foregoing the matching jacket in deference to the warmth of the sunny spring day. Frantically, she spun back to her companion, thankful to find her unaware of the disturbing exchange and still prattling about the weather.

"Morning, ladies," spoke the dapper older man. "Bound for Austin, are you?" he inquired in polite conversation as Samuel joined them in the shade of the porch.

"No, just our young friend here. She's traveling to Washington-on-the-Brazos," replied Samuel, offering his hand in friendly greeting. "Samuel Martin's the name, sir. May I present my wife, Mabel, and our friend, Miss Laura Nichols."

"Jonathan Taylor, at your service, sir." He gave a quick little bow toward the women. "And my business associate, Blake Saunders."

The golden man inclined his head. "My pleasure." He straightened slightly for just a moment before returning to his deceptively casual lounging position against a weathered post, a position which just happened to give him an unobstructed view of Laura.

Laura returned Mr. Taylor's smile, then nodded quickly in Blake's direction, carefully avoiding any contact with those disturbing brown eyes.

"The young lady is traveling alone?" inquired Mr.

Taylor in a concerned voice.

Mrs. Martin sighed deeply. "I'm afraid so. I haven't been able to talk her into postponing her visit to her brother for a while longer—"

"Now, Mabel," admonished Samuel. "We've had the pleasure of Laura's company longer than she planned to begin with. She's anxious to find her brother."

"Yes, Samuel, I'm well aware of that," Mabel replied in a slightly piqued voice. She turned to Mr. Taylor. "May I impose on your sense of chivalry, sir, and ask that you watch over Laura?"

"No imposition at all, ma'am. We'd be absolutely delighted to see to her well-being during the trip. Wouldn't we, Blake?"

Blake maintained his silence, simply nodding slightly.

Laura glanced surreptitiously at the golden man's immobile countenance, then flushed with apprehension as she became aware of the almost wicked sparkle in his eyes. She took a deep breath, fighting to conceal the confusing whirlwind of emotions that swirled and swooped in her stomach.

"Is this your first trip to Texas?" inquired Mr. Martin politely.

Mr. Taylor flicked his gaze quickly at Blake. He nodded almost imperceptibly as Taylor began the recital of their prearranged story. "I've made the trip several times, but this is Blake's first visit. It looks as if cattle's going to be big business here. We thought we might purchase a few thousand acres before all the good land's snapped up."

"Shrewd thinking. There's many a man making his fortune hereabouts just that way. In fact, Laura's brother has a large ranch near Washington-on-the-Brazos."

Blake and Mr. Taylor exchanged another quick glance. "That's interesting," Mr. Taylor commented, slipping an elaborate gold watch from his vest pocket. He snapped it open and peered at the face. "Looks like it's just about

28

time to leave, if they run on schedule."

Just then the driver came out of the office, clumped across the wooden porch, and climbed onto the high seat of the dilapidated stagecoach. He threw a small strongbox under the seat and spat a stream of tobacco juice over the side. "Let's go, folks!"

The ticket master hurried after him to open the door of the stage, lowering the steps for Laura's convenience.

"Oh, dear!" moaned Mrs. Martin. There was a catch in her voice as she admonished Laura once again to be careful and write as soon as she arrived. "Oh! Don't forget your basket, Laura. You never know what they'll feed you at the way stations." She thrust a massive woven basket at Laura, its brimming contents carefully covered by a snowy linen napkin.

"Umph!" snorted Mr. Martin, trying to dislodge the sudden lump in his throat. "Have a pleasant journey, Laura, and do let us hear from you."

Laura rose on tiptoe to place a kiss on his whiskered cheek, then turned to embrace Mrs. Martin one last time.

"Thank you for all your kindness," she whispered, tears gathering in the cerulean depths of her eyes to pool and cling to her lashes like sprinkled diamonds.

"I'll write and let you know all about my trip. And perhaps I'll be seeing you again soon. After all, I'll have to come this way to return home when I hear from William." She smiled bravely and swiped quickly at a teardrop that threatened to escape.

Samuel placed a consoling arm across the shoulders of his wife while she dabbed at her eyes with the lace-edged hanky.

Laura tilted her chin bravely, took a deep breath, and placed her foot on the bottom of the suspended steps.

Swiftly Blake was at her side. He reached to steady her, his large hand grasping her upper arm firmly.

"Allow me," he said, his voice deep and velvet edged.

29

He relieved her of the heavy basket, enabling her to duck through the small doorway with ease. She scooted across the narrow opening between the seats and sat down in the far corner, primly tucking her full skirt about her. She murmured a small "thank you" without quite meeting his eyes.

The basket was handed in to her, and she placed it on the seat beside her, unconsciously erecting a barrier between herself and the man's disturbing presence. But it wasn't long before she wondered if she'd done the right thing. He took the seat directly across from her.

Laura's eyes flickered nervously away from his gaze. Quickly she turned to poke her head through the small window, leaning out to wave diligently at the Martins until the swirling dust obscured their shrinking figures from view.

Settling back in her seat, she reached to tuck a windblown curl back in place. She patted her hair, smoothed her dress again, shifted the basket a fraction of an inch, and finally looked up. Those mahogany eyes were still watching her.

"And where are you from, Miss Nichols?" Mr. Taylor's question broke the suffocating silence.

Laura gratefully turned her attention to the pleasant older gentleman, and they were soon engrossed in conversation.

Blake spoke little, letting John carry their end of the discourse for the most part. But each time Laura let her guard down and looked his way, his gaze held her still.

The coach swayed and jolted over the rutted road, and Laura was soon worn out from holding herself tense in an effort to keep her knees from bumping Blake's at each bounce. A sheen of perspiration dotted her upper lip, and she patted delicately at it with her hanky.

"I'm afraid you're getting too much sun." The rasp of Blake's voice startled her after his many miles of silence.

He leaned forward, his bronzed face coming closer and closer. He reached out his hand, and for a breathtaking moment she thought he was going to touch her. But he only clasped the window shade and adjusted it carefully, shading her from the heated rays of the sun, which poured in through the opening.

"Thank you," she managed to whisper, those mesmerizing eyes so close that she could see golden flecks sprinkled in their mysterious brown depths.

She suddenly had a very troublesome feeling that this was going to be a long, long three days.

Chapter 3

Laura, her head and shoulders stuck comically out the window, braced herself against the rock and sway of the stage as it made its precarious way down the riverbank. She smothered her feelings of apprehension by watching the spokes of the wheels disappear as if by magic as they rolled slowly through the murky water, stirring up the muddy bottom and creating a dirty brown trail in their wake. Small waves lapped at the bottom of the stage as it jolted to a sudden stop. Nervously she watched the reflections on the swirling waters below as Blake and Mr. Taylor readied the long poles carried for use during river crossings.

"Steady," the driver instructed over his shoulder to the two men balanced precariously behind him. "On my call, give it your best."

"Ready," they called out in unison, bracing against the small railing on top of the stagecoach.

"Yehaw!"

The shout rang out, and the driver slapped the reins against the backs of the straining horses. Blake and Mr. Taylor put their shoulders to the poles, pushing as hard as possible. The stage held stubbornly, and then the wheels pulled free of the muck and lurched forward once more.

"Almost there!" shouted the driver.

Laura craned her neck to peer quickly ahead as they neared the bank. Pulling her head back inside, she breathed a sigh of relief that they had not been condemned to spending the entire day in the middle of the broad shallow river. She held tight to the window frame and braced her other hand against the leather seat as the stage bucked its way up the bank, finally coming to a stop under a canopy of huge trees.

Soft thuds and scrapes came from above as the poles were secured in place once again; then the coach rocked slightly as the two men scrambled their way down from the roof. Laura looked out once more at the sound of Blake's hearty laughter.

He clapped Mr. Taylor on the shoulder and said in a teasing manner, "Some fun, huh, John?"

John eyed him with amused tolerance and continued to wipe the beads of sweat from his red face with a large linen handkerchief.

Blake stood, legs planted far apart, hands braced against his slim hips as he threw back his head and took a deep breath. He rolled his shoulders, working the tension out of the slabs of hard muscle that bunched and slid under the clinging white cotton of his shirt.

And once again Laura was caught. A warm flush crept up her throat as Blake looked her way. She tossed her head in agitation when he headed toward the coach.

"We mustn't forget Miss Nichols," he remarked, the deep rumble of his voice rolling across the small clearing. He approached the vehicle with fluid strides and opened the door. In resignation she extended her hand, but he only smiled that wicked smile of his and grasped her about the waist, swinging her out and down with ease.

Mere inches separated them. His spicy male aroma assaulted her senses. It was seconds before she realized

33

that they had not moved since her feet touched the ground. Her hands still rested lightly against the sun-warmed expanse of his shoulders; his were still balanced lightly against the soft swell of her hips. She stepped back quickly, stumbling a bit in the process. He caught her arm and steadied her. She whispered, "Thank you" and hurried away.

What was it about the man that bothered her so? She stalked to a fallen log and flounced down upon it, her skirt billowing around her ankles. After all, he hadn't really *done* anything. He had been scrupulously polite, even doing many small things to ensure her comfort. Each gesture epitomized the behavior of a proper gentleman.

But there was something disturbing about him—something she couldn't quite put her finger on. Didn't his hand grip hers just a smidgen longer than was really necessary each time he handed her down from the coach? And she wondered if his long fingers had *really* brushed against the side of her breast when he took her arm yesterday to escort her to the way station.

She told herself she was getting in a muddle over nothing; that she would simply have to compose her mind, dwell on more serene thoughts, concentrate on the sweet memories of William's dear face. Then she would be able to ignore the man. Good heavens, just *what* was it about him that tugged at her mind with such persistence?

Oh, granted, he was immensely good looking. That tall, muscular physique would draw any woman's attention. But weren't William's dark good looks and clean-shaven face preferable to Blake's toasty gold coloring? And wasn't William's aristocratic bearing more appealing than the overpowering strength and raw maleness that Blake exuded?

She sighed deeply, wishing the trip was over and she was already safe and secure at Anthony's ranch. The crunch of footsteps across the pine needle-strewn ground

34

caught her attention, and she looked up to find Blake towering over her.

"Drink of water, Miss Nichols?" He held the waterbag and a slightly battered tin cup. She was tempted to refuse. But it was quite warm and a cool drink would be refreshing before she was forced to return to the confines of the coach.

"Thank you, Mr. Saunders," she replied with as much dignity as she could muster, taking the proffered cup from his hand.

He loomed over her, those cinnamon eyes studying her quietly as she sipped at the liquid. The harder she tried to ignore his gaze, the more impossible it became. She felt like a young schoolgirl again, trying to put on her best party manners at her first social outing, frighteningly conscious of each and every movement she made, praying that she looked graceful and aloof and sophisticated—and terribly afraid that she didn't.

Her hands began to tremble, and she quickly thrust the cup back at Blake, suddenly fearful she might clumsily pour its contents in her lap. His fingers grazed hers as his large hand wrapped around the cup. She snatched her hands back, clasping them tightly in her lap. But she could not drag her eyes from his as he turned the cup and placed his lips where hers had so recently been, slowly draining the remaining contents.

"Better get going, folks," called the driver, spitting the inevitable stream of tobacco with the precision of a sharpshooter. "It'll be nigh on dark 'fore we get near town as is. Any more delays and we may have to camp for the night." He hitched his baggy pants up and stumped back to the coach.

Heaven forbid! thought Laura. She was ready for a long soaking bath in hot water after three days of cold sponge-offs. And the thought of sinking into a big, cushiony featherbed for hours of undisturbed sleep was even more alluring. She jumped up quickly, snagging the hem of her skirt on a protruding branch. She took but a step or two before being jerked back.

"Oh!" she exclaimed, casting a startled glance back and giving her skirt a series of small, useless tugs.

Blake smiled that slow, provoking smile and bent to release the fabric, plucking it easily from the fallen tree limb.

"Thank you," muttered Laura stiffly.

She hurried to the coach and accepted Mr. Taylor's assistance with a grateful smile, taking a seat quickly and trying to compose her features in some semblance of tranquility.

Blake grasped the door frame and swung lazily up, blocking the opening for a moment with his huge frame. Ducking his head, he maneuvered in the tiny area and took the seat beside her again. Laura sighed softly. It was debatable which was worse: having him ride across from her where those devilish dark eyes could watch her for hours on end, or having him beside her where the sway of the coach jounced the hard length of his thigh against hers with maddening frequency.

"Yehaw! Git up, there!" came the driver's shout, and the coach jerked and rattled its way back to the rutted road.

The sun hung lazily in the sky, a blazing golden orb in the deepening blue of the late afternoon. Laura leaned her head wearily against the back of the seat, more fatigued from these past few days than after the long weeks of her sea journey. Her eyelids fluttered shut, lashes casting dusky shadows on her rosy cheeks. The coach bounced softly. Her head rolled loosely against the seat and then came to rest lightly against Blake's broad shoulder.

Blake turned his head to watch the sleeping girl from shuttered eyes, annoyed at the feeling of protectiveness

36

she aroused in him. She was not his type at all.

She fit neither category of women he was used to dealing with: the sparkling but prim and proper belles he escorted to the glittering Washington parties or the more sophisticated ones willing to indulge in more than mere flirting, but always with the understanding that mutual satisfaction was the aim, *not* marriage.

He had never allowed a woman to monopolize his thoughts as this one was doing. And he had no intention of letting any female interfere with his life. He could spot Laura's type from a mile off: the ones who wanted a *proper* relationship. *She* certainly wouldn't be satisfied with the tinsel gaiety of society. It was equally obvious that she would be horrified at the thought of a lusty romp with *anyone* but her duly wedded husband.

No, her dreams would center on home and family. And, for Blake, the thought of settling down to such a dull, routine existence, cooped up day after day in some stuffy office, going home every evening to some simpering, clinging female, had never held any appeal. He'd always laughed and said that he was "married to the department." He liked the excitement and occasional danger of his position and could not comprehend giving it up for the likes of *any* woman.

So why was he playing this game with Laura? Why did he search out every opportunity to touch her, to provoke a reaction—any reaction—from her?

The rasp of a match broke his reverie. Blake flicked his gaze to John as the tang of sulphur wafted through the air. Laura stirred slightly, sighing softly in her sleep, and Blake's attention was drawn back to her. She looked so young, so innocent and so very vulnerable.

John held the yellow flame to the end of his long thin cigar, rolling the cylinder between his fingers in absentminded ritual. He drew deeply on the cigar, savoring the taste in his mouth for a long while before exhaling a long blue plume of smoke. He studied the glowing end intently for a moment, then his gentle gray eyes shifted to Blake.

"Nice girl," he commented with a slight nod of his head in Laura's direction.

"Yes," came Blake's carefully casual reply.

"The folks in Galveston sure thought a lot of her."

"Yes."

"Imagine that brother of hers does, too."

"Imagine so," agreed Blake, keeping his voice soft and nonchalant.

John lapsed into silence, once again rolling the cigar between his short fingers, studying the growing gray ash with seeming fascination.

"All right, get it out of your craw. Just what are you leading up to?" prodded Blake.

John raised his eyebrows quizzically, a look of pure innocence bathing his ruddy face. "Me? Not a thing, son. Not a thing."

Blake frowned in irritation. John was about as subtle as a sledgehammer, at times.

A sudden explosion of shots rang out. The stagecoach swayed sharply as the driver whipped up the horses, his harsh urgings for speed mingled with angry curses. The coach lurched drunkenly over the deeply rutted road, throwing the passengers from one side to the other like so many rag dolls.

Laura gave a startled cry as she woke in alarm. "What's happening? What's wrong?" she wailed, clinging to Blake's arm as they were whiped crazily from side to side.

John grabbed the window frame, steadying himself as much as possible to peer through the billowing dust at the riders pounding after them.

"Bandits! Looks like a half dozen or so," he managed to shout over the rumble of the wheels.

A violent lurch shook John's hands loose, sending him skittering across the slick leather seat. Blake braced his long legs against the opposite seat frame and held onto Laura as they bounced wildly about the coach's interior.

"What now?" yelled Blake, trying to hold Laura and reach for his gun at the same time.

"Pray he can outrun them! Couldn't hit anything now! If we stop, it means a shoot-out."

Laura screamed again as they were jolted so hard the top of her head struck Blake's chin, clacking his teeth together like demented castanets.

Another volley of shots filled the air.

"They're getting closer!"

"Son of a bitch!" Blake swore softly, feeling the wheels of the coach slide sickeningly as the driver tried desperately to maneuver a bend in the road. Blake held his breath, praying that the wheels would regain their grip on the corduroy surface.

"Here they come!" yelled John.

And suddenly the driver gave a sharp cry. The reins flew from his hands. He clutched at his chest and slumped into the footwell. The stage swayed violently as the panicked horses reacted to the total loss of control. They bolted straight ahead, dragging the stage closer and closer to the edge of the jumble of brush and rocks at the edge of the road.

The wheels thudded from rock to rut in a crazy destructive dance. Branches whipped at the sides of the coach, sending torn leaves swirling madly in the maelstrom created by its violent passage. The front wheel crashed into a large boulder, and the coach tipped crazily onto two wheels, hanging suspended for an eternity before giving a great shudder and crashing to the ground. The fierce jerk dislodged the locking pin of the traces, and the horses broke free, stampeding wildly out across the scrub-covered ground.

Blake felt it coming. He had just enough time to wrap his arms protectively around Laura, his hands cupping the back of her head. He twisted quickly, throwing her down against the seat cushion, shielding her with his body.

Laura screamed shrilly. Blake's head slammed against the door frame, and they went down in a mad tangle of arms and legs.

The stage lay like a great dying animal, the upper front wheel broken, the spokes protruding in jagged disarray. The back wheel turned lazily in the air. The body of the driver was draped drunkenly over the outcropping of rocks that had been his vehicle's undoing.

The thunder of hooves sent the dust whirling madly again. The riders sawed savagely at their reins, sliding to a stop in the road across from the wreckage. The horses reared and pranced, heavily lathered from the frantic chase.

Four men quickly dismounted as the leader looked on from a safe distance. One of the men clutched the reins of the horses, pulling them to the side and out of the line of fire should anyone in the coach be in any shape to defend himself. The other three advanced carefully toward the stage, guns at the ready. They stopped roughly six feet from the broken behemoth, eyes flickering nervously. The wheel continued to turn slowly, a nerve-jangling squeak piercing the heated afternoon silence with each revolution.

"*¡Sacan los de coche!* Get them out of the coach!"

The menacing softness of their leader's voice whipped them into action. The boldest hunched over and ran to the shelter of the overturned coach, banging loudly against its underside with the butt of his gun.

"Out! All of you! Get out or we fill this thing full of holes!" he shouted in broken English.

Laura's soft, frightened sobs were barely discernible

40

in the jumbled interior. Blake lay in a heap on what had been the side wall of the coach, a crumpled figure almost lost in the gloom. She struggled to free herself from the deadweight of his inert limbs. John pushed himself to his feet, clutching the window frame above for support.

The heavy thudding began again. "Out! Do you hear me? Or you die where you lie!"

"We're trying!" shouted John, grasping Laura's arm and pulling her up.

"Oh, my God! What are we going to do?" she whispered hysterically.

"Sounds like Mexicans, Laura. No telling what they're after. Just get out. Keep quiet and hope for the best. Give them the money, jewelry, whatever they want."

"Wh-what about Blake?"

"He's hurt." John glanced down at the still form, Laura's gaze following his. There was an angry red swelling on Blake's forehead. "We don't dare try to move him. Besides, our friends out there don't sound too patient."

"But—"

"But nothing!" he whispered fiercely. "We've got to get out of here before they make good their threat. We can't help Blake if we're shot all full of holes!"

"Oh," Laura replied meekly, her eyes filling with tears again.

"Now, brace your foot against my knee. I'll boost you up."

Laura did as she was told, placing her hands against his shoulders for balance.

"Push the door open."

She grasped the handle and pushed against the heavy weight. It rose slowly and then fell crashing against the side of the coach.

"I'm afraid," Laura wailed softly.

"I know you are, Laura, but we've got to obey them,

41

and quickly, too. Grab the sides of the opening and pull yourself up as I push."

Laura followed his instructions, grasping the edges of the doorway and levering herself up as best she could while John struggled to brace her legs, push her up, and avoid being smothered by her layers of petticoats. If she hadn't been so terrified at what awaited them outside, she would have been thoroughly embarrassed by her predicament.

She managed to get her upper body out, scrabbling for a hold on the slick siding with her hands and then her knees as John gave one last desperate push. At last! She lay gasping against the wildly canted surface. Then John levered himself up and out.

Using the railing and roped-on baggage for handholds, he worked his way down to the ground and then helped Laura descend. More than anything she longed to be back in the relative safety of that crazily tilted coach. She cringed as angry shouts rang out again, a strange, almost incomprehensible mixture of English and Spanish.

"Stay behind me. Be very still and don't make any sudden moves," John instructed quietly. He began to move slowly around the wreckage. Laura clutched at his arm, her pulse pounding madly.

As they stepped into view, three pairs of eyes snapped their way. The lower halves of the men's swarthy faces were covered with ragged bandannas. Laura jumped at the deadly click of a hammer as the guns were quickly leveled at them.

"¡Arriba las manos!" shouted the man closest to them, his words muffled by the dirty kerchief. He motioned threateningly with his revolver.

Laura didn't understand what the man was saying, but she caught on quickly as John thrust his arms skyward. With eyes large and filled with fright she raised her arms and watched the men come closer.

42

"*¡Registen los!* Search them," called the bandido leader from the back of his huge black horse, the velvety rasp of his voice somehow even more menacing than the harsh shouts of his men. His aristocratic bearing and well-tailored clothing emphasized his vast contrast to the ragged bunch that scampered quickly to do his bidding.

John blanched. His eyes darted to the leader. "See here, that's not necessary," he called out. "We'll give you all our valuables. Just leave us in peace."

The tallest bandido stepped to the side, keeping his revolver trained squarely on them. Flat black eyes watched them without a flicker. The other two advanced menacingly toward the two helpless figures.

"*Es muy bonita,*" said the fat one as he reached out and twined a lock of Laura's disheveled hair around a grubby finger. "*La padriamos llevar con nosotros.*"

Laura flinched in revulsion as the finger was drawn across her cheek and down the soft ivory column of her throat. She choked back a sob, instinctively stepping nearer to John.

"What's he saying?" she pleaded, not at all sure she wanted to know, as the leering eyes continued to rake her form.

The deep voice of the leader cracked out. The dark horse pranced nervously, the bridle jingling as the man pulled him sharply back. "*No hay tiempo para tonterias.* Do as I say!"

"Wh-what did he say?" pleaded Laura, backing desperately away from the dirty, probing hand.

"That one," said John, nodding his head toward the leering fat man hovering over Laura, "wanted to take you with them."

She gasped in alarm. "Oh, no! Please, don't let them take me!"

"Don't worry. The leader vetoed his plan."

Laura quivered against the underbelly of the coach,

43

her arms held stiffly at her sides, hands clutched so tightly that her nails bit into her palms. She could retreat no further to escape the unwashed stench and questing hands of the clearly disappointed robber. Reluctantly he lowered his hand and demanded the purse that hung by a cord around her wrist. Almost gratefully she jerked it off and thrust it at him.

The dirty fingers greedily parted the opening and scrabbled at the contents. Furious that it held so little of value, he crumpled the bills in his fist and then threw the purse angrily to the ground, blazing eyes once again devouring the prize he really desired.

Laura's head jerked at the loud scrape of metal. The third bandit had found the strongbox under the driver's seat. His mask had slipped awry in his haste to get to the prize, and avarice contorted his features. He balanced the box precariously against the lopsided wheel, muttering under his breath when the lock refused to open under the sharp blows of his gun butt.

"You're wasting time! We'll take it with us," shouted the leader as the man continued to struggle with the stubborn strong box. "*¡Aprisa!* Search the man."

Laura turned frightened eyes on the dark figure astride the huge horse. She could see nothing of the man's face. The wide brim of his hat shadowed what the bandanna did not cover. It was impossible to judge his height atop the huge, prancing horse. But she knew instinctively that the dandified appearance and soft sibilant voice belonged to a man much more dangerous than the ill-mannered ruffians he ruled.

The fat man's eyes narrowed. His rusty spurs jangled as he advanced, dirty fingers groping for the golden watch chain draped across John's disheveled waistcoat. John knocked his hand away, scrambling to pull the watch from its confining pocket, and then he quickly tossed it to the angry man. Fat hands plucked the prize

44

out of the air, deposited it quickly in the sagging pocket of his dirty trousers, and then reached again for the lapel of John's coat.

"Get your hands off me!" John demanded. "I'll give you my money." He jerked his wallet free of his pocket, opening it quickly and spilling the bills out. Some tumbled to the hot, dusty ground. Others were swept up by an errant breeze. Angered at this action, the fat man grabbed the wallet. John struggled with him, trying to maintain his grasp on it.

"Bring it here," the dark man instructed. "There must be something of great interest for him to protest so much."

The fat man stomped over to him. His eyes blazed angrily at the loss of his hard-earned loot, although he dared not protest. He flicked the wallet up to the leader, who caught it easily and then casually opened it and withdrew a sheaf of papers. "¡Madre Dios! ¡Agento del gobierno! A government agent!"

And suddenly the sights and sounds blended in a whirlwind of madness as John lunged for the gun still pointed menacingly at him by the fat man's companion. The gun exploded in fiery thunder. Laura screamed, her hands flying to her mouth as John sank slowly to the ground, crimson spreading across his chest.

Laura's screams continued as the men argued violently in Spanish. The leader's harsh shouts finally subdued their rebellion, and they quickly gathered up the strongbox and the scattered bills and hurried to their horses.

The leader shot one last hungry look at Laura. She was so beautiful. His loins burned with a depth of desire he had not felt in a long time. He was very tempted to take her for himself. But he didn't dare. The hold he had over his men was tenuous at best. He knew with every fiber of his being that, if he took her, he would not want to share.

No. He could not take a chance at losing control now— not when he was so close to his goal.

"¡*Aprisa*! ¡*Regresen al Valle Fuego del Sol*!" the dark man finally shouted. The men vaulted to their horses' backs, whipping them into a gallop.

The thundering hooves stirred the thick red dust. It swirled around Laura, shielding her from the horrible sight of John's motionless body for a moment. Her hot tears left dirty streaks down her flushed cheeks as she watched the riders disappear around the bend of the road.

Chapter 4

Blake's eyes fluttered open. At first he had no idea where he was or how he came to be lying in this strange jumbled space. His head throbbed. Slowly he raised his hand to his forehead, gingerly fingering the tender lump on it.

He winced and, willing his mind to sink into sweet oblivion again, closed his eyes against the dim light that started anvils pounding in his head. It was so much more pleasant to snuggle his head into the softness that cushioned it than to continue the throbbing torture of trying to make sense of the muddled thoughts pushing at his consciousness.

Something soft and cool caressed his brow. He sighed and snuggled closer to the cushioning warmth beneath his head.

"Mr. Saunders, please wake up," came a soft velvet voice from far, far away. "Mr. Saunders, please!"

"Ummm," he moaned, reluctant to obey. The voice called to him again. Finally, he forced his eyes open, flinching as the hazy light once again stabbed at his brain.

He squinted, probing the deepening haze around him with little result. Slowly the figure above him swam into focus, haloed against an amber haze of light.

"Ahhh, an angel of mercy. Must have died and gone to heaven . . ." he muttered softly.

"Oh, Mr. Saunders, thank goodness!" Laura gulped back tears of relief, quickly dipping the torn scrap of cloth in water and once more gently bathing the head cradled in her lap. "I thought you'd never wake up."

Loath to have the gentle ministrations end, Blake closed his eyes again.

"Oh!" Laura exclaimed in worry, leaning over to search his face with frightened eyes. "Please don't go back to sleep, Mr. Saunders . . ."

"Blake," he instructed.

"Blake, yes, yes, Blake—oh, please, stay awake!"

"I'm awake," Blake assured her in exasperation. "Please stop wiggling. I'm afraid my head is going to explode if you don't."

Laura froze. "I'm sorry."

Reluctantly Blake pushed himself up on his elbows and shook his groggy head. He looked around in bewilderment at the topsy-turvy interior of the stage, then understanding dawned in his eyes.

"The bandits! What happened? Where's John?" he questioned, jerking into a sitting position. He groaned as a sharp pain stabbed through his shoulder at the sudden movement.

"Be still!" Laura instructed in a frightened voice, brushing aside the splintered pieces of wood he had been lying on. "There's blood on your coat. Here, let me see—"

"Never mind that now. We've got to get out of here." He struggled to his feet, swaying against Laura in the crazily tilted confines as she scrambled to stand beside him. "Now, how do we manage that?" Blake muttered as he surveyed the door opening that hung suspended just above his head.

"Mr. Taylor boosted me up before," Laura offered

48

softly. "I got back in without too much trouble. But I couldn't get you out by myself—"

"By yourself?" He scowled at her in the dim light. "Where's John?" he demanded again.

Tears pooled in the deep blue of Laura's eyes. "He's dead," she answered, her voice so small and quiet that Blake could barely hear her. She watched the play of emotions on Blake's face with frightened eyes, from disbelief to apprehension to sorrow.

"Damn!" he swore softly, the quiver in his voice betraying the depth of his feelings. Raggedly he pushed his fingers through his disheveled hair. He winced as he grazed the tender swelling at his temple, the pain returning his attention to the task at hand. "All right, let's do it John's way."

Laura braced her foot against his rock-hard thigh as he boosted her upward. Blake's great height made it much easier for her to pull herself out of the opening this time. She scooted to the side and turned to offer help to Blake, but he quickly levered himself out and onto the lopsided coach. They were soon safe on the ground.

Blake turned troubled eyes toward Laura. "Where did . . . uh . . . where's John?"

"On the other side of the coach."

Slowly Blake made his way around the broken vehicle and over the scattered luggage to gaze sadly down at the crumpled body of his partner and friend. His broad shoulders slumped sadly, and once again he raked his hands through his hair.

"Tell me what happened," he instructed with deceptive calm. His eyes sparked with savage emotion as she told him of the dark man and his ragged band, of John's defiance and death.

"And you weren't hurt when the stage overturned?" he questioned with concern.

"No. You pushed me down and . . ." She blushed in

memory. "You shielded me with your body. It must have cushioned me against the fall."

He remembered clutching her tightly against him, feeling the heated softness of her body, then wedging his head and feet against the sides of the coach as he cradled her in his arms.

With Laura's help he moved John's body and the driver's into the lee of the stage roof and covered them with a tarpaulin. They both felt a little better when this task had been completed.

The sun barely rimmed the horizon, casting deep rose and purple fingers across the darkening sky. Blake set Laura to constructing a makeshift pallet from the scattered contents of the trunks beneath the sheltering underbelly of the stage. He gathered brush, piling it within easy reach of the stage, then knelt to start a comforting fire. Finally satisfied that he had done all he could to protect them against the night, he sank wearily onto the bedding.

"Thank heavens for Mrs. Martin's basket," Laura said with a tremulous smile. "We won't go without supper tonight anyway. There's still cheese and bread and quite a lot of fruit."

Blake's dark eyes followed her movements as she knelt beside him to spread the napkin and place the remains of Mrs. Martin's feast upon it. She filled the battered tin cup with water, and they shared it as well as the food. Afterward Laura bundled the leftovers back into the basket and then tucked it into the space under the broken wheel.

Blake leaned tiredly against the stage, his face contorting as his shoulder bumped painfully against the hard surface.

"Oh, your shoulder!" Laura exclaimed. "I forgot. Let me look at it." She scrambled quickly to his side, her face lined with concern.

"It's okay, probably just bruised." He brushed aside her worries.

"No, it's not. There was blood on the back of your coat." Her fingers trailed down the fabric, coming away sticky and damp. "See there! You've got it bleeding again. You *must* let me look at it. At least let me try to stop the bleeding."

He smiled slightly at the stern figure she cut, her diminutive form drawn to the fullest possible height as she knelt over him, arms akimbo in exasperation at his reluctance.

"All right. I give up," he finally conceded with a small chuckle, struggling to his knees to remove the torn coat and shirt. He cast them aside and sat down once again, his back to the soft glow of the fire.

Laura peered intently at the broad slab of muscle and sinew, running her hand gingerly over the wound. "I think it's just a very deep scratch," she finally said. "You were very lucky. The thickness of your coat must have kept it from being any worse."

"Fine," he growled, reaching for his bloodstained shirt. The feather touch of her fingers had stirred feelings in him more alarming than mere pain.

"Oh, no, you don't," she insisted. "I'm going to wash it off first. You certainly don't want it to get infected, do you? And you need a clean shirt to protect it from dirt. You just sit still."

She busied herself gathering rags and clean water again while he scowled at the disquieting quiver in the pit of his stomach.

The leaping flames bathed his broad back, turning it to molten gold in the darkness. Gently she bathed the hard expanse of muscle, washing away the crusted blood to reveal two ragged scratches running diagonally across the breadth of his shoulder. She scolded him softly when he wiggled like an impatient child at her touch, placing a

51

gently restraining hand on the rounded bulge of his arm to hold him still.

The heat of his skin caressed her palm, seeping through her fingertips to flow like warm honey through her veins. Softly, slowly she continued to stroke the molded bronze of his back with the damp cloth, mesmerized by the awesome strength that rippled under her ministrations. Her free hand shifted ever so slightly, then trailed lightly across the massive shoulders to the tender vulnerability of his nape. The tips of her fingernails grazed his skin like tiny daggers piercing his soul. Her fingers skimmed the tousled curls, and he jerked away, scrambling swiftly to his feet.

"Thank you," he managed to say in a strangled voice. "I'd better . . . uh . . . get a clean shirt. Like you said."

He hurried to the luggage he had stacked at the back of the stage, rummaging wildly through his valise. Like a drowning man he clutched a shirt to his chest, then quickly slipped his arms into the sleeves and drew it protectively around himself.

Laura watched from her kneeling position on the pallet, the dancing flames alternately lighting and shadowing the disoriented expression on her startled face. She drew a deep breath, struggling to analyze the gamut of perplexing emotions that whirled in her mind.

"We'd better try to get some sleep. I'm afraid tomorrow is going to be a long day," Blake declared.

"All right," Laura agreed softly. She lay down on her side, propping her head on her arm. Firelight flickered in the navy blue of her eyes as she watched Blake pound a lump of clothing into pillow shape and then stretch out on his back mere inches from her. He sighed deeply, eyelids half shuttered against the glow of the flames.

"What are we going to do tomorrow?" Laura's soft whisper broke the quiet of the night.

"Walk. Now go to sleep."

52

Laura obediently closed her eyes. Soon Blake heard her soft, even breathing. Mulling over their predicament long into the night, he watched the star-sprinkled sky. Far off a coyote howled, and Laura whimpered softly in her sleep.

"Shh, little one, it's all right," Blake soothed, turning to stroke her arm tenderly. Laura murmured incomprehensibly and then snuggled against Blake's warmth, sighing with contentment. He froze for a moment, knowing he should move away from her. But she was young and afraid and much in need of comforting after the turmoil of the day.

And, yes, he badly needed comforting, too.

He scooped her to him spoon fashion, nestling her softness against the hard length of his body, nuzzling the sweet woman smell of her hair as she cuddled her head into the hollow under his chin. He draped his arm protectively over her, cupping his hand around the delicate shape of her midriff. With each soft inhalation her rib cage swelled, raising his hand a mere fraction of an inch so that his thumb barely grazed the soft swell of her breast. The gentle rhythm of her breathing and the comforting warmth of her nearness soothed Blake's troubled mind. Soon his eyes closed wearily.

And they slept entwined through the warm spring night.

Chapter 5

A mockingbird perched precariously on the swaying branch above the stagecoach, busily feeding its nest full of fledglings. Blake grumbled as the incessant chirping grew louder, the noise finally penetrating his sleep-shrouded mind. Bright shafts of early morning sun speared through the leafy lacework of the towering oak to dapple his face with warmth as he hovered in that delicious space between sleep and waking.

Laura stretched languorously, then scooted closer so that Blake's bulk shadowed her face from the offending sun. She nuzzled against the comforting strength of his broad chest like a sleeping baby.

Slowly her eyes opened, her scope of vision narrowly confined to a bewildering harvest of crinkled gold upon a bronzed meadow. She squinched her eyes up, lying very still while she tried to decipher this mystery.

Suddenly her eyes flew open and crimson stained her face. It couldn't be! But it was. She had her nose practically buried in the thick mat of gilded hair on Blake's chest.

Ever so carefully she tried to extricate herself from his grasp, almost frantic to gain her freedom before he awoke and became aware of their intimate position. He mumbled sleepily and tightened his grip. Laura frowned in exasperation.

Gingerly she eased her arm free so that she could grasp a portion of his sleeve in her hand. Carefully she pulled the fabric upward, lifting the heavy weight of his arm from her body while slowly rolling out of his embrace. Just another inch or two and she'd be free. The pink tip of her tongue worked at the corner of her mouth as she concentrated on her efforts.

Almost done! She let her eyes flicker to his face, positive she had not disturbed Blake's slumber—and found those devilish dark eyes sparkling with amusement at her contortions, his mouth quirked up at the corner in a roguish grin.

"Oh!" she exclaimed in embarrassment, flinging his dangling arm away from her body in irritation. Quickly she scrambled to her feet, smoothing her sleep-crumbled skirt nervously and then raking her fingers through her tangled curls.

Blake smiled up at her, his teeth flashing white against the bronze of his skin. "Good morning, Laura."

"Morning," she mumbled.

"Well, I feel a little better this morning. How about you? Did you sleep well?" Blake's eyes watched her every move with intent interest.

"Uh, yes. Yes, of course. I slept very well, thank you." Heat bathed her face as she wondered just how much of the night she had spent in Blake's arms. She was completely out of her element dealing with this man.

Just how did one react after waking up in such a compromising position? Back home her reputation would be ruined after such an episode. All it would take was the mere hint of suspicion and tongues would wag with malicious zeal. A young woman placed in a situation of that sort could only hope that the gentleman would marry her and save her from a life of ignominy.

55

Marry! Her eyes flew to Blake's face. Good heavens, where did such a thought come from? William was the only man she wanted to marry. Thank goodness he was too far away to learn of her humiliating predicament.

Blake watched the emotions flicker across Laura's face with something akin to penitence, almost ashamed of his continued ploys for her attention. Quickly he rose and crossed the small space separating them. She studied the ground intently. Slowly he reached out, placing his finger under her chin, tilting it upward until her wide, bewildered eyes met his.

"I'm sorry. I didn't mean to upset you."

"It's . . . it's all right."

His hand dropped softly to her shoulder and he shook his head, the golden curls dancing in the bright morning light. "No, it's not. Things have been rough enough without my thoughtlessness. I'm sorry. I shouldn't have teased you like that."

"Really. I'm all right." Her voice trembled a bit, but she smiled up into his eyes to prove that it was true.

He gazed down into the brave innocence of her eyes and the world dimmed around him, shutting out all but Laura. He searched her face, cataloging its every feature: the sparkling sapphire depths of her eyes, like twin pools of star-studded midnight sky; the soft arch of brow over lashes so thick they cast dusky shadows on the blush of her cheeks; the pale apricot of her skin; a sprinkling of tiny golden freckles across the bridge of her nose so intriguing that he longed to taste their sweetness upon his tongue; enticingly full lips the color of a red summer rose, trembling ever so slightly with the effort of her smile.

And suddenly he had to taste the beguiling, glistening softness of those lips. Slowly, slowly his head dipped toward hers, and of their own volition her lips rose to meet his.

56

At first there was only the warmth of his breath, the barely perceptible brush of his mustache against her lips. Then softly his lips grazed hers. So softly, so sweetly gentle that she wasn't sure it was even happening. His hands were feather light against her shoulders, giving her the freedom to move away from him should she so desire.

But the strange fluttering awareness building in the center of her being was too new, too intriguing, too delicious. She thought only of savoring this new feeling, of relishing the honeyed heat beginning to flow through her veins.

Slowly, timidly she raised her hands to rest lightly against the broad expanse of his chest. She could feel the tom-tom beat of his heart beneath her fingertips. His hands slid from her shoulders, splaying against the fragile plane of her back, pressing her to him as he sipped at her mouth, running his tongue fleetingly over the moist inner softness of her bottom lip, teasing at the tiny even row of teeth, probing and retreating softly, slowly, until her lips opened to his joyous exploration. And as he searched each honeyed crevice, the sparks became a flame.

Instinctively her arms encircled his neck, her hands threading through the riot of curls at his nape, clasping, grasping, sealing his mouth to hers with heated abandon. His mouth claimed hers hungrily, devouring its sweetness with increased intensity. His hands explored the soft hollow of her back, the gentle swell of her hips, then clasped her tightly to him, pulling her up on tiptoe to mold the tender contours of her body to the demands of his own.

The frightened nicker of a horse exploded the velvet fog that surrounded them. Blake's head snapped up. He was instantly alert, his eyes wide and searching at the sound.

Intoxicated with the fiery emotions he had aroused,

Laura struggled to comprehend his sudden withdrawal. She gasped for breath, her legs trembling so much that she was afraid she'd fall if he released her from his embrace. She leaned her head against the broad expanse of his chest and tried to make sense of her whirling emotions.

"What . . . what is it?" whispered Laura, giving her head a little shake to clear the heated mists.

"A horse. Close by."

"They've come back," she almost sobbed, her voice thick with fear.

"No, I don't think so. Listen."

The soft nickering came again.

"Hear that? Only one horse, I think. But I'd sure settle for one at this point."

Laura turned in his arms to peer in the direction he was scrutinizing.

"There!" she called excitedly, pointing at a mere shadow in a thick tangle of trees and brush across the road. "See it?"

"Yes. Here, take this," Blake instructed, handing her his gun. "Stay here. I'm going to check it out."

With stealthy footsteps he made his way across the rutted surface, carefully holding aside branches and tangled vines as he worked his way into the dense foliage. Laura grasped the gun with both hands, holding it straight out in front of her, still afraid it might be the bandidos.

"It's all right," called Blake from the shadows.

Laura sighed with relief, gratefully allowing the gun to drop down by her side. She shielded her eyes against the sun, edging closer and closer to where Blake had disappeared into the thicket. The bushes snapped and rustled with his efforts.

"What is it? What are you doing?" Laura questioned.

"It's one of the stage horses. She's been dragging part

of the shattered harness rigging. Lucky for us she came back. The traces got all tangled up in this brush, and she couldn't get away."

The branches parted, and Blake appeared leading a bedraggled roan mare.

"You won't be walking after all," he said with a grin. "I heard a stream a little further back in the woods. Let's get this harness off of her so we can get through there easier. I think we could all use a cool drink and a chance to wash up a bit."

Blake led the mare to the stagecoach and hitched the reins over the broken wheel. The horse stood quietly, weary from its night's sojourn in the wilderness. She cropped eagerly at the tender shoots of grass within reach of her strong white teeth. Blake went to work untangling and removing the remnants of the traces and chains.

Laura finger-combed the horse's tangled mane with trembling hands, removing leaves and twigs from the snarled hair. She darted covert glances at Blake as he worked, his attention completely absorbed by the chores at hand.

He seemed totally unruffled by the tumultuous embrace they had shared just moments ago. How could he forget so quickly, so easily? *She* certainly couldn't. Perhaps he was so used to women abandoning themselves to his charms that he could turn his emotions off at will. He obviously was not suffering from the whirling emotions that still assailed her senses.

She tried to convince herself that she would have stopped him, that she had only been sampling the tantalizingly new experience, that she had been in complete control of her emotions and body. But the thought of that tall form against her own, the memory of muscle and sinew straining for an ever closer bonding sent tingles running through her again.

No. She had to admit the truth. She hadn't been in

control—not from the first touch of his hand. It was almost as if he had cast some sort of spell over her from the very first time their eyes met at the stagecoach station in Galveston. Not love, certainly, for she loved only William. But *something* about Blake's nearness drove all reasonable thought from her mind. His touch set her soul afire.

Gratefully she leaned her head against the mare's neck, knowing full well that only the horse's fortuitous arrival had saved her. *He* certainly had no compunction about taking advantage of her innocence. And her own body had suddenly become a stranger with a mind of its own, leaving her unable to even think straight, much less rebuff his advances. In the future she was going to have to stay far, far away from Blake Saunders.

"Sort out some clean clothes and something to dry with," Blake instructed as he made the final adjustment by cutting the horse's long reins to riding length. "I'm going to pack everything else up and stack it in the shelter of the stage. They'll have to send someone out from town to bring it all back."

He surveyed the scattered baggage, the overturned vehicle. His eyes clouded as he thought of his friend. There was nothing he could do for John now except perhaps pile a few more stones on the tarp for protection from scavengers until the two bodies could be taken into town.

He sighed in bitter resignation. It would have been different somehow if John had died as a result of their assignment, in the service of their country. But this needless, sad ending angered Blake. While he pursued the government's work, he vowed to also be on the lookout for information about the marauding Mexican band that had attacked them.

All he had to go on was Laura's confused description of the men and the few jumbled words of Spanish and

60

English that she recalled. But it was something. God willing, it would be enough.

"Make sure you pick something comfortable," he called to Laura as she rummaged through her trunk. "And forget about a corset and all those petticoats. You certainly don't need them astride a horse."

Laura looked up with a start. Good heavens! The man had absolutely no sense of propriety. The very idea of discussing a lady's underthings! She bit back a caustic retort and returned to her task, finally choosing a simple blouse and skirt and a comfortable pair of slippers.

Blake waited for her to finish repacking her clothing and then placed her trunk alongside the pile of stacked baggage.

"Let's go."

Laura positioned herself a safe distance behind the mare—or was it the emotional "kick" of Blake's nearness she feared rather than the rather doubtful danger of the tired horse's hooves? She quickly pushed this thought from her mind as she followed Blake across the road.

It was much easier to make their way through the trees, now that the horse had been freed of the snagging harness parts. A surprisingly short walk found them beside a fast-flowing creek that broadened, becoming almost a pond, before looping back on itself and disappearing off through the woods.

"We'll get washed up and water the horse real good. She ought to be rested enough by late afternoon to head for town. That way we'll miss the worst of the heat."

Laura simply nodded, clutching her bundle of clothes to her breast as she glanced first at Blake and then back to the creek.

"Well?"

"Yes?" she snapped, her voice betraying her lingering irritation at his cavalier attitude during the past hour.

"Bathing is usually easier if you get a little closer to

61

the water."

"Oh! Yes . . . uh . . ." Again her eyes darted around the clearing.

Blake sighed in exasperation. "Those bushes should make a good enough screen. You can bathe on that side. I'll tether the horse so she can graze, and then I'll use this side."

He frowned at the shocked look on Laura's face.

"But people will think—"

"There're no people here to think anything, Laura." He spoke with the tone of a weary adult to a small, petulant child. "This is not the time to worry about superfluous formalities. We're both tired and dirty. It's still a good ways to town. It's important to be rested and feeling our best before we start out."

He grasped her shoulders, turning her toward the lush green bushes that divided a good part of the clearing before marching into the water.

"The bushes make an adequate screen. You'll be on that side. I'll be on this side. I am not in the habit of dashing through the brambles to force my unwanted attentions on women." He gave her a small push toward her side of the hedge. "Now, be a good girl. Just go over to the other side, take your clothes off, and get in the water."

Laura smothered a horrified gasp, then jerked away from his touch and hurried away so he couldn't see the heat rise in her face once again.

Honestly! she thought to herself as she viciously shoved the branches aside and struggled through a narrow opening in the dense foliage. He's the most irritating man I ever met!

"Just take your clothes off," she mimicked under her breath as she angrily shed all but her dimity chemise and pantalets. "Ha! I bet he'd like that just fine. Doesn't have to force his attention on the ladies, huh? The conceit of the man!" She waded into the dark blue waters. "I'll bet he thinks all he has to do is snap his fingers and I'll swoon over him just like all his fancy women! Well, Mr. high and mighty Blake Saunders, this is one woman who's immune to your charms! I wouldn't let you within arm's distance of me again if you were the last man on earth!"

"What'd you say?" called Blake. "I can't understand you."

"Nothing! I didn't say a thing," she shouted in mortified denial, arms clasped protectively across her bosom as she bolted quickly into the sheltering depths of the water as if the very devil were after her.

Blake secured the horse near a lush blanket of sweet grass, then stomped back across the clearing, muttering heated curses as he went. He stripped quickly, tossing his clothes to the ground in irritation.

"Ought to have my head examined for ever kissing her! Now she'll be getting all sorts of silly female ideas. Just exactly what I deserve," he berated himself. "What else would you expect from a 'lady'? Always knew there was a good reason for avoiding that particular species of female!"

He sloshed angrily into the creek, the water swirling around legs brown and firm as tree trunks, over the sleek bulge and clinch of buttock muscle, until he stood waist deep in its sun-warmed depths.

The emotions warring inside him were beginning to wear him down. He simply couldn't understand his pendulum swings from tenderness and concern for Laura to total exasperation with her. There was something very wrong with him lately—if he could just figure out exactly what the problem was.

Anyway, he'd have to be very careful in the future. Just because she had the face of a saint and the body of a sinner, he wasn't going to become snared in her silken trap.

No, sir! Not Blake Saunders! He was smarter than that.

The sound of splashes carried to him on a teasing breeze. He groaned inwardly as visions of Laura blossomed in his head. He knew what she felt like through the prim layers of clothing. Now he dreamed of his hands on the bare satin of her skin, slick and cool from the caress of the undulating waters. He could almost see the diamond droplets of water clinging precariously to the pert tips of her lush breasts. Would those tips be dusky rose or perhaps pale, sun-kissed coral?

And not even the swirling blue waters could cool the heat of his loins.

Chapter 6

Laura shook the crumbs from the slightly bedraggled linens, then folded them and tucked them back inside the empty hamper along with hers and Blake's dirty clothing. The last remnants of Mrs. Martin's generous basket had been their meal. At least they wouldn't undertake the trip into town on empty stomachs.

She checked the level of the water in the canteen and then capped it tightly. It would be all they had for the next several hours unless they came across another stream.

Laura glanced up and caught Blake watching her, his eyes dark and brooding.

"You about ready?" he questioned, needlessly checking the mare once more.

"Yes," she replied, tossing her head nervously as her hands went to her head once again to fluff her still damp hair.

He watched the sun play over the long tresses, intrigued by the sight of the velvety brown length cascading down her back. Until now it had always been confined in a ladylike chignon. Burnished highlights danced through the curls with every movement of Laura's head.

"Well, let's get going, then," he said gruffly.

She stiffened at the sting in his voice. "Very well. I just want to put the basket back with the other things."

Her chin rose obstinately as she hooked the handle over one arm and gathered up her skirt. Without benefit of the copious petticoats, it hugged her form in the most beguiling manner. The hem brushed the ground, slightly hampering her steps as it snagged and caught on the brush. She hitched her skirt higher and picked her way determinedly across the clearing and through the surrounding woods, leaving him to stare after her.

He shrugged and clutched the reins in his hand. His gaze followed the tantalizing sway of her hips under the clinging fabric back to the stage, where he watched her place the basket carefully among the pile of abandoned luggage.

"I'm ready," she declared, turning back to face him, hands primly clasped in front of her.

Blake tethered the mare and bent over to lace his fingers together. "Put your foot in here and I'll boost you up."

Laura almost protested, then bit her tongue. She could stand his touch one more time. After that she'd be high above him, safely astraddle the horse.

She raised her skirts enough to clear her foot and placed a dainty slipper into the cradle created by his hands. Blake boosted her up and onto the horse's broad back, catching a heart-stopping glimpse of trim ankle and supple calf in the process. He swallowed convulsively and reached down to snatch up the reins.

"Thank you," said Laura coolly, reaching a hand out to accept the lines, her hauteur returning a bit now that her elevated position protected her somewhat from his disturbing nearness.

But Blake didn't relinquish the reins. He simply clutched them and a handful of mane in his left hand and placed his right on the horse's rump. And suddenly he was astride behind her.

"Wh-what are you doing?" Laura spluttered.

"What does it look like?" Blake retorted. "Getting on the horse so we can go into town."

"But . . . but, won't two people be too heavy for the horse? I mean . . . I thought—"

"Well, I'm not walking if that's what you thought. Two riders won't bother her if we go slow. It'll take us a little longer, but we'll make it. All we have to do is follow the road. Giddup," he called softly, flicking the reins gently against the mare's neck until she settled into a steady walk.

And Laura found herself encompassed by two invincible bands of steellike muscle and sinew. Blake's strong, sun-browned hands were held disturbingly near her stomach as the rock and sway of the horse jostled him against her back with each and every step.

She closed her eyes and breathed very deeply, trying to still her outraged mind. And the very act of that tranquility-seeking gesture wrecked more havoc as her air-filled diaphragm expanded and pressed the heated skin of her midriff against his hands. She heard his startled gasp. From then on she inhaled only in tiny sips, scarcely daring to move for fear of further contact.

The roan moved placidly down the rutted road, hooves clopping softly against the grass-barren surface, each slow step rocking the broad back in tantalizing rhythm. Little puffs of red dust swirled at each foot fall as they wound through the hilly, wooded land. Cypress, juniper, and oaks bordered their path, arching overhead at times to offer cool tunnels of respite from the golden southern sun.

A flirty little breeze ruffled Laura's unbound tresses, dragging soft wisps across Blake's throat like a caress. If he leaned forward just a few inches he could bury his nose in the sweet-smelling curls that cascaded between her ramrod stiff back and his chest.

Lord! He wished she had bound it up properlike. It might make it easier for him to remember that she was a lady—and definitely off limits. What was the matter with him? He hadn't been so consumed with bawdy thoughts since adolescence. But the riotous mass of curls continued to shimmer and shine in the hot afternoon sun, dazzling his eyes and heating his blood. Lips pressed in a tight, thin line, he tried very hard to concentrate on the winding road before them, searching the wildflower-strewn land for a sign of civilization.

Laura struggled to hold herself as far away from Blake as possible. She was soon utterly exhausted from their long ride. Her thighs were beginning to cramp from the hours of clutching desperately at the horse's sides for balance. Would they *never* get to the town?

She slumped tiredly, wishing she could allow herself the dangerous luxury of leaning against his broad chest for just a moment. With great effort she straightened her aching back, her leg muscles clenching convulsively as she tried to hold herself away from the seductive rasp of Blake's inner thighs against her hips.

The horse scrabbled up a small incline, and Laura hurriedly grabbed a handful of mane. There was only a tiny amount of distance between their bodies, but she fought to maintain it. It was useless. Slowly, fraction by fraction, she slid back, her softly rounded bottom inexorably coming to rest smack against the vee of his legs.

The heat of his chest burned into her back. The hard

strength of his groin was imprinted against her backside. She wriggled almost imperceptibly, trying to inch her body away from his. Her squirmings brought a sharp gasp from his lips.

"Jesus, Laura!" he barked desperately. "Sit still!"

And in his torment he wished he *had* walked.

Chapter 7

The road wound through a dense stand of post oak, blackjack, and hickory and then dropped through a cut in the tall, red-clay banks of the Brazos. Laura sighed with relief when she spied the ferry roped in at the edge of the broad river. She was hot and tired and aching from the long hours of self-imposed, rigid posture. She sagged gratefully when Blake dismounted, too tired to even complain when he reached up to help her, circling her waist with his strong hands and pulling her close to him as he eased her to the ground.

"Howdy, folks," greeted the ferryman, eyeing the couple curiously as he rose from a rough wooden bench and hitched up his trousers. He'd been at this post for many years and had seen some mighty peculiar folks come through town during the time that Washington-on-the-Brazos had been the capital of Texas. But this bedraggled pair definitely whetted his curiosity.

Sure a pretty little thing, Amos Hall thought, rolling a frazzled matchstick from one corner of his mouth to the other. He accepted Blake's quarter, made change, and watched them board the ferry.

Lady looks plum tuckered out. Not even one bag between them. Strange. No saddle and riding double.

Couldn't have come too far like that. Must have had a bit of a tiff, too, he mused when Laura moved as far from Blake as she could.

"How far into town?" Blake questioned as the ferry made its slow way across the reddish muddy river.

"Up the rise and then just a piece down that road. Runs you right into Ferry Street."

"Who's in charge? Sheriff? Marshal?"

"'Spect Thomas Matthews is the man you need to talk to. Justice of the peace. Just go straight down Ferry Street. His office's right there on the corner of Main and Ferry."

"Thanks." Blake turned his attention to the approaching rich, red-clay bank, its stature dwarfed by the majestic height of trees stretching their lordly limbs, bowerlike, over the river.

He wondered if he should tell Mr. Matthews the truth. No, it would probably be better to leave things just the way they were. There were rumors of unrest in this part of Texas, and he could check them out a lot easier if people thought he was nothing more than the land speculator he professed to be.

Blake turned back to the ferryman. "Is there a hotel or inn in town?"

Laura's attention was snatched away from the gently swirling waters by Blake's question. A hotel? What a wonderful thought! A bed. Clean sheets. A bath in the privacy of a real room. No more fitful dozing in the stagecoach. And thank goodness there wouldn't be another emotion-torturing day like today. She cut her eyes at Blake under a veil of thick lashes, wishing she knew what was behind that inscrutable bronze face.

"Yep. Just look for the two story log building. Right on the main road. Can't miss it."

The ferry bumped softly against the shore. Amos Hall tipped his hat politely as they disembarked, then stood

71

gazing after them, matchstick dancing from side to side in his weathered face.

The man and woman plodded up the steep bank, the weary horse trailing behind; soon they were out of his sight. Amos wondered how they came to just appear out of the wilderness with only a horse and the clothes on their backs.

Well, it'd make for an interesting piece of conversation when he got home, anyway. Things had been pretty dull since the capital had been moved back to Austin in February. But it'd sure put Gertie in a right good mood if he could go home with the whole story. Maybe he'd learn something more about them when he made his nightly stop at the saloon. Amos shoved his hat back on his head and headed for the twin bench on this side of the river.

Laura braced herself against the incline of the road, which climbed steeply for a while, then evened out at the top of the bank. It felt good to walk after the hours of riding, to stretch her tired muscles. A breeze ruffled her hair, and she absently raised a hand to lift its heavy weight off the back of her neck, holding the curls in a jumble against the top of her head so that the refreshing gusts could cool her heated skin.

Blake quickly pulled his eyes away from Laura's slender form, trying hard to ignore the way her proud, firm breasts pulled and rounded against the confining bodice of her dress, forcing away thoughts of how the soft vulnerability of her nape would feel under his lips. He breathed a sigh of relief when she dropped the long tresses to shield her eyes against the bright rays of the setting sun that knifed through the spreading branches of a huge pecan tree.

He peered through the deepening dusk at the approaching cluster of log and frame buildings.

"Must be the hotel there," stated Blake as they neared a structure that matched the ferryman's description. He hitched the mare to the post and took Laura's arm as she stepped up on the boardwalk. He propelled her hurriedly through the doorway, a grim look on his face.

Wondering at his sudden haste, Laura eyed him sharply. He studiously avoided her gaze while trying to suppress guilty feelings of relief at the thought of placing her in the care of others—and out of the all too tempting proximity they had shared over the last four days.

"Evening, folks," greeted the proprietor. "Welcome to Fox's Hotel. Nathaniel Fox's the name. How can I help you?"

"We need two rooms."

The man's bushy eyebrows rose quizzically. Laura pushed an errant curl out of her eyes and smoothed her skirt nervously as the man's gaze flickered to her ringless left hand.

"I can fix you right up. That be all?"

"No, the lady would like a bath brought up to her room, please. I'll be out for awhile, but when I return I'll be needing a bath, too."

"Yes, sir. Right away. Shall I have your baggage fetched in?"

"I'm afraid we don't have any. It's all back at the stage."

"The stage? Y'all had some trouble?" The man's voice rose in concern as he glanced hurriedly toward the doorway. "Where's ol' Pete?"

"If you mean the driver, he's dead," Blake answered grimly.

"Dead? Lord-a-mercy! What happened?"

"Could we get the lady settled first? And then I need to see Mr. Matthews. Arrangements need to be made for the bodies—"

"Bodies?" Fox exclaimed. "Who else—"

"It's a long story, friend. First, let's take care of the lady." There was just a touch of steel in Blake's voice.

73

"Oh . . . sure. 'Lizabeth!" Fox bawled loudly, fairly trotting around the rough-hewn counter.

A tall, sturdy-built woman of indeterminate age poked her head through a door at the back of the room. "Stop shouting, Nat. I'm right here."

"Sorry, honey. This here's the missus," he explained, turning back to Blake and Laura with the woman close behind him. "These folks . . . uh, I didn't catch your names . . ."

"Pleased to meet you, ma'am. This is Laura Nichols. I'm Blake Saunders."

And this time Mrs. Fox's eyebrows rose in interest.

"Right. Miss Nichols and Mr. Saunders. Let's put the lady in the first room on the right upstairs," Fox instructed his wife. "Mr. Saunders can have the one next door. The lady wants a bath . . ."

"Blake," whispered Laura, tugging at his sleeve.

"Yes?"

"Well . . . uh . . . what about after the bath?"

He looked at her questioningly, exasperation clear on his face.

Heavens! Why was he so dense at times? "Clothes," she whispered vehemently.

"Oh, yes." Was there just a hint of his old wicked smile? "Is there a store nearby where we could obtain a few necessities until we can get our baggage brought in?"

"Well, sure. Harrison's is just down the street. We'll get the little lady all settled upstairs and then Elizabeth can run down and pick up what she needs."

"Thank you." Blake pulled out his wallet and withdrew a sheaf of bills. "This should take care of the rooms and whatever Miss Nichols needs. I'll stop by the store on my way back from Mr. Matthews's office."

"Fine, fine." Fox glanced quickly at the bills and then stuffed them into his trouser pocket. "Matilda!" he bellowed, and a young black girl came scurrying through the door.

"Yassir?"

"Put on some hot water for the lady's bath, then help Miss Elizabeth get the gentleman's room ready."

"Yassir." She bobbed her kerchiefed head and scuttled back through the door.

"Come along with me, dear," instructed Mrs. Fox. "We'll have you settled in no time."

Laura followed her to the stairs, then turned abruptly. "Oh, Blake, I almost forgot. We need to send a message to Anthony right away."

"Anthony?" questioned Nathaniel, finally connecting the familiar name. "Anthony Nichols?"

"Oh, do you know my brother?" Laura's eyes sparkled hopefully. "Can you arrange for someone to ride out to his place?"

"Sure, I know him. Everyone around here does. Good man. Got him a real fine spread several miles southeast of town. Well, I'll be durned. Anthony's sister." The big man shook his head in amazement. "I'll take care of it. I can get someone to ride out first thing in the morning."

"Thank you," Laura replied gratefully, feelings of relief washing over her.

"I'll go along with Mr. Saunders to show him the way," Fox informed his wife, who knew full well that it was more curiosity than common courtesy that prompted her husband's offer.

"Now, don't you go messin' around for too long, Nathaniel Fox," she scolded halfheartedly. "There's plenty to be done right here."

"Yes, dear," Fox muttered as he ushered Blake hurriedly out the door.

Laura listened until the clack of Blake's boots receded into the deepening night.

"Right this way, Miss Nichols."

Laura responded slowly to the sound of Elizabeth's

75

voice, finally turning her attention back to the woman. "Oh, yes. Of course. I'm coming." She clutched her bedraggled skirts and hastened to follow the innkeeper's wife up the stairs.

Elizabeth threw open the door at the head of the stairs, standing back for Laura to enter. "Not too fancy, but nice and clean and comfortable."

Her pride in their establishment was evident in her voice. Nat might be the charmer in the family, always able to jolly a customer into a good mood, but it was the long hours of cleaning and cooking that Elizabeth put in, that really made the inn what it was.

Laura smiled gratefully as she gazed about the pleasant room. The soft glow of the lantern was reflected in the waxed sheen of the plank floors; a homey rag rug covered the space between bed and dresser. She breathed a sigh of pure delight as her fingers tested the fluffy feather-filled mattress, and then she gasped in dismay as she caught a glimpse of herself in the mirror.

"Now, don't you fret, deary. A nice hot bath and a good night's sleep'll do wonders," Elizabeth assured Laura, all the while thinking to herself that the girl was a real beauty—even with the tangled curls and sweat-stained clothes.

A loud knock sounded on the door. "Miz Lizbeth!" came Matilda's voice. "I's got the water!"

Elizabeth opened the door, then hurried across the room to move aside a folding screen that revealed a porcelain tub positioned on yet another thick-braided rug. Matilda scurred behind her, two buckets of water sloshing alarmingly with each step. Misty tendrils of steam rose alluringly as the water splashed merrily into the tub. It took Matilda two more trips to fill the tub sufficiently, then she bobbed politely in Laura's direction and scampered from the room.

"Now," instructed Elizabeth, "you get right into that

tub. I'm going down to Harrison's and I'll be back shortly with a nightdress and a change of clothes for tomorrow."

"Thank you," Laura called after her as the door closed softly behind Elizabeth.

Gratefully she shed her clothing, leaving it in a tangled heap on the floor beside the screen. She braced her hands against the edges of the tub and tested the water by gingerly waggling her toes just below the surface before stepping in.

She lowered herself slowly into the steamy depths, then sighed and slid as far down as she could, leaning her head wearily against its back as the soothing warmth soaked into her bones. The water had begun to cool before she roused herself sufficiently to soap and rinse her hair and body thoroughly.

Laura's fingertips were puckered and pruned by the time she stepped from the tub and wrapped one of the big fluffy towels around herself. Elizabeth's timid knock came just as Laura was beginning to rub her long tresses dry with another towel.

"It's me, Elizabeth. I have your things."

"Come in," Laura called, retreating modestly behind the screen.

The door creaked open, and Elizabeth's soft footsteps echoed across the room. She thrust a paper-wrapped parcel over the screen. "Here's your nightdress. I thought you might just want to be comfortable and slip into it. I'll hang the dress in the wardrobe for tomorrow."

"Thank you." Laura untied the string and pushed aside the rustling paper to lift out a white cotton gown. She slipped it over her head, and the soft fabric floated to the floor. Gentle gathers were caught at the neck and wrists with tiny blue ribbons.

She padded on silent bare feet around the edge of the screen and across the room to perch on the side of the bed, her weight sinking into the soft mattress. The lantern light cast ruby shadows in her hair as she continued to fluff and rub it dry with the towel.

There was a knock at the door again. "That'll be Matilda," Elizabeth explained. "I had her fix you a tray."

Matilda balanced the overloaded tray carefully, edging across the room to place it atop a small table in front of the window. She bobbed again and retreated.

"Come over here and sit, dear. A bite to eat will help you sleep better."

Laura obeyed happily, casting a dimpled smile and nod of thanks in Elizabeth's direction as she seated herself in the small straight-back chair. The aromas wafting from the covered dishes set her mouth to watering.

Blake trudged back toward the hotel, a parcel of clean clothes from the general store clasped under his arm. He'd been relieved to find Tom Matthews was no simple country bumpkin but an intelligent and well-organized man who listened quietly and attentively to Blake's full story before posing any questions of his own. Matthews's bushy brows had furrowed in concentration when Blake repeated the few fragments of conversation Laura had relayed to him yesterday.

Blake had finally left Nat to repeat the tale for what seemed the dozenth time to the growing crowd of men at Matthew's office. He'd done all he could at this point. They would ride out in the morning to retrieve their belongings and bring the bodies in for burial.

He quickly pushed that thought from his mind. He was bone tired, mentally and physically. All he wanted now was to fall into bed. He felt as though he could sleep forever.

A flicker of movement caught his eye. His gaze was drawn to a silhouette in the window high above his head. Then a sudden breeze tugged at the edge of the curtains, and for an endless sliver of a second Blake caught a glimpse of Laura's slim form, shadowed sweetly, beguilingly against the mellow glow of lamplight, her unbound hair a smoky mist about her shoulders.

He stood mesmerized in the quiet dark of the street, the sheen of the moon turning his golden curls to silver. He swallowed convulsively, his feet leaden, his eyes glued to the window. That strange aching heat swirled in the pit of his stomach once again.

And he knew there'd be no restful sleep for him that night.

Chapter 8

Anthony's brows furrowed at the thunder of hooves coming up the road. He glanced at his pocket watch, confirming his suspicion that it was very early in the morning for visitors. After one last swallow of coffee, he pushed his breakfast dishes aside.

He hurried across the dining area and arrived in the reception hall just as Rosita swung the huge door open to admit a rangy, tousle-haired youth. Anthony could see his winded pony tied at the rail out front. The boy had been riding hard.

"Mornin', Mr. Nichols," the lad gasped, sweeping his dust-covered hat from his head.

"Mornin', Ben. Somebody light a fire under you?"

Ben grinned, then the words began to tumble from his mouth. "Yes, sir. You might say they done just that. Mr. Matthews told me to fetch you right quick this morning. Him and most the men from town done gone way out by Tyler's Creek with the stranger, and the lady's waiting at the hotel, and—"

"Whoa, boy." Anthony laughed, holding up his hand as if to stop the flood of words. "Back up just a bit. What stranger? What lady?"

"Why, the ones that rode into town last night just

'bout dark. 'Pears they was ambushed on the stage. Ol'
Pete was killed, and the man's partner, too. Now the men
have all gone out to bring in the bodies and the stage if
they can . . . took a wagon for the baggage if'n the
coach's too badly damaged. And the lady is waiting for
you at the hotel right now, sir."

"And what lady would that be, Antonio, *mi amor?*"

Anthony's eyes darted upward to meet the sultry gaze
of his bride's dark eyes. As always, the sight of her
brought a catch to his breath.

"I'm sorry, darling. Did we wake you?"

Her ruby red lips pouted seductively. "Darling
Antonio, only the dead could sleep with all the chattering
going on down here." The throaty velvet of her accent
caressed his ears.

She stood at the top of the mahogany staircase, a lace-
trimmed dressing gown clutched modestly at her throat.
It fell in soft ripples to the floor, hugging the lush curves
of her body. Anthony's pulse quickened at the sight. A
dainty hand rose to cover a yawn, then moved upward to
push a mass of tumbled black curls from the ivory
perfection of her forehead. Even freshly risen from bed,
hair disheveled, eyes clouded with sleep, she was
beautiful.

Anthony's heart swelled with pride, and he marveled
again that fate had been kind enough to bestow such a
jewel into his care. Fate in the form of an invitation last
February to a ball being held in San Antonio in
celebration of Texas statehood.

There he had met Maria Francesca Luisa Del Gado, the
niece of his old friend Don Jose Santiago. The Santiago
family had lived in Texas for decades and had chosen to
remain loyal during the fight for independence, declaring
themselves Texans first, in spite of their Mexican
heritage, as had many other Mexican families.

Over the past few years, other members of the family,

sponsored by the kind and benevolent Don Jose, had made their way to Texas to escape the political upheaval in Mexico. Maria had been the newest arrival. Anthony never quite believed that a man such as he could have been lucky enough to win the heart of this daughter of Mexican aristocracy.

He had been content with his life. He took pride in the fact that during a ten year period he had clawed his way from a hard-scrabble existence as a runaway youth to the life of a landed gentleman. He was secure in the knowledge that he was well liked and respected in the local community, pleased that he had helped in guiding Texas from independence to statehood. Although he had been urged by some political friends to run for public office, he had been happier working in the background during Texas's long struggle for admittance to the Union.

His life had been full with the work of planning and building the grand house he had always dreamed of, as well as slowly moving his main business from cotton to cattle. Occasionally he had squired Cletus Moore's daughter Olivia to the local functions, but he had long ago vowed to abstain from any thought of taking a wife until he had the big house built and the ranch well on its way to stability. Memories of his own turbulent childhood drove him in pursuit of security in its highest form.

He had thought himself a man with everything, and then Maria had come into his life like a whirlwind. Maria, with her fire and spirit. Maria, with her declarations of unexpected and overwhelming love within days of their first meeting. Maria, who clung to him and set his soul afire, until he could no longer bear the thought of returning to the ranch without her. Maria, who made him blind to all else.

"I'm still waiting to hear about the lady, Antonio, darling." Her red lips turned down in a little pouting smile, and her black eyes flicked momentarily at the boy.

Ah, thought Anthony, what a lucky man I am. Who would ever imagine such a marvelous creature being jealous of me?

Ben dragged his awestruck young eyes away from the tempting sight above him and back to Anthony. "Your sister, Miss Laura Nichols," he hastened to explain.

Anthony's mouth dropped open in shock. "My sister! But . . . but she's back East."

"Well, she ain't no more. She's right back there in Mr. Fox's hotel, just waiting for you." Ben grinned hugely, white teeth flashing in his boyish face.

Anthony bounded up the stairs, grabbing Maria about the waist and swinging her around and around.

"Isn't that wonderful, darling?" He gave her a resounding smack on the lips. "I can hardly believe it! I've got to go get her." He released Maria so quickly that she stumbled. Then he leaned far over the elegantly carved handrail.

"Rosita!" he bellowed, and the plump little woman hurried into the hallway, wiping her hands on her apron as she came. "Tell Pedro to hitch up the buggy and follow me into town just as fast as he can!"

"*Si*, senor," she replied and bustled back the way she had come.

He turned back to Maria. "I'll ride on in with Ben. Go back to bed, honey. It'll be afternoon before we get back." He gave her another exuberant hug and kiss and clattered back down the stairs to grab his hat and gun.

"Let's go, boy!"

"Yes, sir." Ben nodded his head in Maria's direction. "Good day, ma'am." He clapped his hat on his head and bolted through the door after Anthony.

Maria's eyes narrowed. What had brought Anthony's sister to Texas? And just what effect would this sister's arrival have on Maria's plans?

"Miguel," she whispered. "I must tell him about this." And she whirled in a froth of silk and lace and hurried to her room.

Chapter 9

Thick clouds of red dust billowed up and rolled across Ferry Street as Anthony and Ben galloped into town. A fine powder settled on the scattering of old men in front of Harrison's store. They stopped their whittling and checker playing long enough to look up and speculate on the men's haste.

Bright-eyed with curiosity, they watched Anthony dismount and throw a hurried loop of rein over the hitching post before bounding through the inn's front door, Ben close on his heels. When Anthony and Ben were out of sight they settled themselves again in the warmth of the golden sunshine and returned to their games and gossip.

The sound of boots clumping across the plank floor drew Nat's attention from his book work behind the counter. He closed the ledger with a thud and rose to greet his friends.

Anthony rushed to the counter, dragging his hat from his head. He slapped it nervously against his thigh, sending small puffs of dust swirling through the sunbeams.

"Where's she at?" he demanded in an eager voice.

"Upstairs, first room on the right," Nat answered. He and Ben grinned happily at each other as they watched Anthony take the stairs two at a time.

Anthony skidded to a stop in front of the closed door. *Laura!* He still couldn't believe it. His little sister—here—now. He anxiously slicked back the shock of unruly hair from his forehead, brushed off his clothes, and then knocked timidly.

"Come in."

Anthony swallowed a painful lump and gently eased the door open. He edged inside the room as the young woman turned from the window.

"L-Laura?" he asked hesitantly, not at all sure that the beautiful young woman before him was really his baby sister. There was a peculiar little squeak in his deep bass voice.

Her heart almost stopped beating when she turned and realized that she knew his face—that she recognized him even after all these years.

"Anthony!" Laura cried happily, flying across the room to throw her arms around him. "Oh, I've missed you so much!" She hugged him exuberantly.

"My God, Laura! Is it really you? Are you all right?" Anthony questioned.

"I'm fine. Really." Tears of joy misted her eyes as she gazed up into his concerned face.

Hands on her shoulders, he held her out from him and searched her face with wonder. "You're all grown up." He shook his head. "What happened to your pigtails?" he asked, yanking gently on the tumble of curls which fell across her shoulder.

She laughed with delight. "Same thing that happened to the scraped knees and snaggle teeth."

"What in the world—"

"Tell me all about—"

86

Their words tumbled over each other. They laughed and hugged once more.

"Are you sure you aren't hurt? I mean, I heard about the ambush. It must have been an awful experience for you—"

"Anthony, stop worrying. I'm just fine."

He gave her one last searching look and then said, "Come on, let's go down to the dining room. We can talk easier down there. Have you eaten yet?"

"Yes, Elizabeth brought a tray up earlier. But I'd love to have another cup of coffee."

Anthony opened the door and ushered her through, tucking her hand possessively in the crook of his arm as they descended the stairs.

How strange, thought Laura, to be almost as tall as Anthony. She only had to tilt her head a few inches to return his smile. The year that he'd left Uncle Henry's she hadn't even come up to his shoulder. She had thought him so tall, so brave, so invincible.

Ben jumped to his feet as they entered the lobby, appreciatively eyeing the lovely young lady who had been the prime topic of conversation throughout the whole town this morning.

"Need me to do anything else, Mr. Nichols?" he questioned, turning his hat round and round in his hands.

"Would you watch for Pedro? He should be gettin' in pretty soon. Tell him to load Laura's baggage, I guess. We'll be in the dining room for awhile."

"Anthony, my bags aren't here. I think Mr. Saunders went out to the stage with some men from town. I guess they'll be bringing our luggage back in."

"I'll take care of it, sir," assured Ben, clapping his hat back on his head. "Bye, Nat." He waved and left as Anthony and Laura went through the swinging doors into the dining room.

The room was clean and cheery. Gingham cloths covered the half-dozen small tables scattered about the floor. Matching gingham curtains were pulled open, allowing the bright sunshine to spill through the windows. Anthony slid one of the small wooden chairs out from a table, waiting for Laura to settle herself comfortably before taking the chair to her right.

Elizabeth bustled through the kitchen door carrying a heavy blue-speckled coffeepot and two mugs.

"Well, I see you managed to find her," she said with a smile as she placed the cups on the table and filled them with the fragrant brew. Steam wafted from the heavy stoneware mugs. "Sugar?" she questioned.

"Yes, please," replied Laura.

Elizabeth carried a bowl of sugar from the sideboard to the table. "Would you like something to eat? I just took a new batch of biscuits out of the oven."

"Oh, no, thank you, I'm still full from breakfast," Laura answered, stirring her coffee slowly as she appraised Anthony.

Somehow Laura felt very relieved that the man across the table from her still looked so much like the loving big brother she remembered. She'd been so afraid that she wouldn't recognize him after all these years.

Oh, he was a little stockier and his unruly brown hair was now sprinkled with gray. But the impish smile and the twinkling blue eyes that peered at her from the sun-weathered face were the same.

"No, thanks, Lizabeth. I was just finishing breakfast myself when Ben got to the house."

"Well, you two just take your time. I imagine you've got lots of catching up to do."

"Yes, we do." Anthony nodded his head, still a bit dazzled by the fact that Laura was actually sitting across from him.

"Guess I'd better get busy and finish up the cooking.

Folks'll be coming in for dinner before long. I'll be in the kitchen if you need anything," said Elizabeth, and she left them alone.

"Well." Anthony cleared his throat nervously. "Where do we start?"

"I . . . I guess you want to know what I'm doing here?" Laura questioned hesitantly, frowning a little as she tried to settle her thoughts. She wondered just what Anthony would think of her story.

"Well," he said with a grin, "it *was* quite a surprise."

"But I wrote you a letter. Didn't you get it?"

At the look of dismay on her face, he reached to pat her hand and hastened to add, "No, honey, but that doesn't matter. I'm thrilled that you're here. I'd just about given up hope of ever seeing you again."

"Oh, Anthony, I know just how you feel! So had I. I kept hoping you'd come back sometime, just to visit—"

"Uh! No chance of that." Anthony shook his head vehemently. "Once I got out from under Uncle Henry's thumb, I vowed I'd never go back again."

"I know. I was old enough to realize some of what was going on. Lots of times Cynthia and I heard him shouting at you."

"Yeah, that seemed to be his favorite pastime. I just never could seem to please him, no matter how hard I tried. I didn't want to go off like that—leave you alone—but I had to get out of there. I just couldn't take it anymore." Anthony searched her eyes, worry heavy in his. "God, you don't know how I hated doing that. Laura, did you . . . uh . . . did you resent me for deserting you like that?"

Laura gripped her cup with both hands, sipping slowly at the hot liquid. She lowered her eyes, remembering the sorrow she'd felt at the loss of her brother, the last link to the mother and father she barely remembered.

"Oh, I did a lot of crying those first few months. But I

89

knew I was too little to go on the road with you. I think I was more scared what might happen to you than I was afraid of being left alone. After all, Uncle Henry never treated me the way he did you. And you were right; he did mellow a bit after you were gone."

"I wasn't sure when you were little, but your letters over the past couple of years have led me to believe that you were fairly happy there. Were you?"

"Yes, I suppose so. I was well provided for. And, for the most part, I was happy. Aunt Mary was always good to me, and Cynthia will always be my dear friend. She even helped me plan my escape—"

"Sweet, quiet little Cynthia?" Anthony questioned incredulously, remembering the tiny, timid blond child of ten years past.

"I think she was really terrified that Uncle Henry would find out, but she helped me anyway. I couldn't have done it without her."

"What about Uncle Henry? Did he do right by you?"

Laura shrugged. "Mostly he just ignored me. But then, he ignored Cynthia, too." She sat the cup down carefully. "At least until just before I left."

Anthony's eyes grew stormy. "What did he do? If that bastard hurt you—"

"No, no. It wasn't like that," Laura assured him.

"Well, what did he do?"

"He picked out a husband for me—a business associate of his. His name was Bernard Arbuckle." She gave a small shudder.

"I don't recognize the name. I guess I wouldn't after all these years."

"No, Mr. Arbuckle and Uncle Henry have only been doing business for two or three years. Anyway, I couldn't bear the thought of marrying that man, and Uncle Henry wouldn't even listen to me. He said I had no choice—that I had to do what I was told, that he knew best. Oh,

Anthony, I couldn't marry that man! I just couldn't! Please don't make me go back there!" Laura clutched at Anthony's hand.

"Now, now, honey, I'm not gonna do that." He patted her hand reassuringly. "You're welcome here, you know that! We'll work it out, don't you worry."

"Oh, Anthony, thank you," she said, slumping with relief. "I was so afraid you wouldn't let me stay."

"Well, you can quit worrying about that. My home will always be your home, too. Now, what in the world happened—something about an ambush? Ben only knew a little about the trouble. He said some man brought you into town—"

"Yes, Blake Saunders. He was traveling with me—" Heavens! That didn't sound right. She certainly didn't want Anthony—or anyone—getting the wrong idea. It was bad enough that she'd undertaken such a trip all by herself. Perhaps she'd better wait awhile to tell Anthony about William; things are confusing enough already. "Uh, not *with* me . . . I mean just traveling together in the stagecoach." Laura fidgeted in her seat.

"Who else was on the stage?"

"His friend Mr. Taylor was with us, too."

"Ben said something about someone getting killed. Is he the one?"

"Yes, and the driver, too."

"My Lord, Laura, what happened?"

"Well, this band of men chased after us—they just seemed to come out of nowhere. There was shooting and finally the coach crashed. I don't know if the driver was shot or killed when the stage overturned. Mr. Taylor said the robbers were Mexican. He seemed very upset about it."

"That's strange. Oh, we still have quite a few Mexicans in Texas—people who chose to stay here after independence. Why, Pedro's been with me for years, and I have a couple dozen working out on the ranch right now. But they're all loyal Texans. I haven't heard of any outlaw bands around here, especially this far from the border. Was Mr. Taylor killed in the accident?"

"No, that was later. The robbers shot him . . . they were arguing about something they found in his wallet. Oh, I don't know. It's all such a jumble. I was so scared!"

"Of course you were, honey. It's okay. Anyone would be." Anthony searched her face worriedly. "You're all right? You didn't get hurt?" He half rose from his chair. "Maybe I should get the doctor—"

"Oh, no, Anthony. I'm fine. Really." She caught at his hand and pulled him back down in his chair again. "Blake—I mean Mr. Saunders—well, when the stage turned over . . . he . . . uh, protected me. He kept me from getting hurt. Actually, he got a bad bump on the head because of shielding me. That's why he was unconscious when Mr. Taylor was shot."

"But how did y'all get into town?"

"Blake found one of the coach horses. We rode it."

"Well, thank the good Lord for that man. I hate to think what might have happened to you if he hadn't been along. Why, those ruffians might have . . ." Anthony swallowed convulsively. The thought of what could have happened to Laura set his stomach to churning. "I'll have to be sure to thank Mr. Saunders for his help."

"Yes, we surely must do that," Laura said nervously. "After all, he'll probably be leaving town right away. He was headed for Austin, I think. Looking for land. He's going to raise cattle, too—just like you."

Laura Susan Nichols, she told herself, if you don't stop prattling about the man, Anthony's going to know something's amiss! Quit talking about him. Quit worrying about him. He'll be gone before long.

"Do you suppose I might have another cup of coffee, Anthony?" she asked, anxious to get his mind off of what happened after the ambush. Maybe he'd never realize that there was still some time unaccounted for—that she and Blake had spent the night alone.

"Why, sure, honey. I'll just call Elizabeth." He bolted from his chair and went through the kitchen door.

Soon their cups were full again, and Laura searched for another ploy to change the subject. "Tell me all about the ranch. I'm just dying to know what's been happening. I hadn't had a letter in four or five months."

"The ranch is fine. The big house is finished—it's really beautiful. You'll love it. But the best news is that I got married!" Anthony beamed with pride.

"Married?" Laura's mouth dropped open in shock. "But . . . but, you never said anything in any of your letters—"

"No, it happened too fast. I met her in San Antonio just this February. We were married the next month. I never believed in love at first sight before, but . . ." Anthony grinned sheepishly. "Well, she's beautiful . . . and . . . aw, you'll see what I mean when you meet her, honey."

"I'm sure she must be wonderful or you wouldn't have married her. I'm so happy for you!" Laura leaned over to give him a hug.

"How 'bout let's have a bite of dinner, and then I'll walk you around town—show you the sights until Mr. Saunders gets back. How does that sound?"

"Perfect."

"Oh, Laura, I can't wait till you meet Maria. You'll just love her." His eyes shone with pride. "And I know she'll love you. Just think, I'll have my two favorite people with me. How lucky can a man get?"

The old men stopped their checkers again when Anthony walked down the boardwalk, his lovely young sister on his arm. Anthony was proud to stop and introduce her to them. Then they continued on their way, Anthony intent on showing off his town.

Among other businesses, Washington-on-the-Brazos boasted three general stores, a carpenter's shop, a gunsmith, and a doctor.

"And what's that big building?" Laura asked as they neared a very plain two story frame building at the corner of Ferry and Main.

"That's Independence Hall, where the 1836 Convention assembled to write the Declaration of Independence for the Republic of Texas. It wasn't even finished at the time of the convention, but it was the only building large enough to hold the delegation. They rented it from Byars and Mercer for one hundred and seventy dollars, but they never got their money because it wasn't used for the whole three months they contracted for. When Houston sent news of the fall of the Alamo, rumors spread that the Mexican army was approaching town. The delegates hurriedly completed their work, and then most of the town's residents fled. But the Mexicans never arrived. The townspeople returned to find little if anything disturbed. It's a public hall now—used mostly for meetings and balls."

"It's thrilling to think that such an important historical event took place right here," Laura exclaimed. Each day she loved Texas more, and she eagerly soaked up all the fascinating tidbits concerning its glorious past.

"We even have a famous person or two in town. Anson Jones, the fourth and last president of the republic lives here. His home, Barrington, is just outside of town. I'll take you by to see it sometime."

A commotion of people up the street drew their attention.

"Looks like Matthews and his men made it back to town. Guess we'd better hurry up. I want to know what they found out." Anthony looped Laura's arm through his, and they walked toward the hotel.

Chapter 10

Much to Laura's dismay, Blake and Anthony liked each other immediately. They each sensed something in the other that they could relate to and admire: a certain strength, a sense of adventure, a feeling of kindred spirit.

Laura perched nervously on a small Hepplewhite chair in the hotel's parlor, forcing herself not to fidget as she waited impatiently for their visit to come to an end. Her gaze flicked back and forth between the two men across from her. They were such a contrast.

Anthony was the shorter of the two, and although he was stockier built, it was clear that there wasn't an ounce of excess flesh on him either. The long years of planting and range work had honed him to a sturdy hardness.

His face was permanently browned from the southern sun except for the small white strip of virgin skin just beneath his hairline which had been protected by his ever-present hat. He sat on the edge of the sofa, back slightly bowed, arms propped across his jackknifed knees, dust-streaked hat dangling from broad, short-fingered hands as he and Blake conversed jovially about everything from cattle to cotton to the latest news about the unrest on the Mexican border.

Blake's tall form was sprawled casually in the corner of

the sofa, arm flung across the back. His crisp white cotton shirt was unbuttoned halfway to the deep U of the waistcoat which was pulled firm against the broad expanse of his chest, exposing a crisp wedge of golden brown hair. One muscular leg was nonchalantly crossed over the other, ankle to knee, the fabric of his form-fitting black trousers pulled tight across his thigh.

The tawny gold of his tousled curls caught and held the last rays of afternoon sun. His good mood was mirrored in his eyes, almost cinnamon colored against the bronze of his face and sprinkled with topaz highlights, no longer the velvet brown they turned when passions ran high. As she watched he reached with thumb and forefinger to stroke the bristle of sable mustache shading his mouth.

And Laura remembered how it had felt against her lips, feathery soft, not at all prickly like she expected. She dragged her gaze away from him, hurriedly turning her attention to the first thing that caught her eye. She was intently studying the delicate swirls in the black marble tabletop when Anthony's words shocked her back to reality.

"But I insist, Blake," Anthony said. "After all you've done for Laura, it's the least I can do. I hate to think what might have happened to her if you hadn't been there."

Humph! thought Laura. He'd do better to worry about what almost happened because Blake *was* there.

"That's awfully kind of you, Anthony. I'd be delighted to accept your offer. Provided, of course," he said, with a smile in her direction, the tiniest hint of mischief tugging at the corners of his mouth, "that Laura hasn't grown weary of my company."

Laura's heart skipped a beat, and then began to thump painfully against her ribs. Blake's gaze held hers, almost daring her to protest. She lowered her eyes in consternation. Why did he enjoy baiting her so? He knew she had no choice in the matter, being not much more than a guest herself. Besides, to speak up now would only pique Anthony's curiosity.

She had been so certain that today would be the end of this strange ordeal, that at last she'd be safe at the ranch and Blake would be on his way to Austin. She'd been almost giddy with relief at the thought that the emotional tension she had lived with since first climbing aboard the stage in Galveston was about to end.

She'd just been contemplating what heaven it would be to be able to move and talk without the almost crystalline awareness of Blake's perusal of her every gesture and word! Then Anthony had startled her with his invitation, offering the ranch as a base of operations while Blake surveyed the surrounding territory for possible land investment.

Her gaze darted back to Blake's face. She knew immediately by the amused gleam in his eyes that he was going to accept Anthony's offer.

"Why, Laura'd love to have you, too. Wouldn't you, honey?" Anthony prodded eagerly.

"But, of course I would," Laura assured her brother. She shot Blake a look of wide-eyed innocence. "My heavens, why ever would I be tired of your charming company, Blake? And how could a lady refuse hospitality to someone who's done what you have?"

Blake smiled roguishly, recognizing the double meaning of her words. He could hear the edge of irritation in her soft voice, while Anthony heard only the polite concurrence of his own words. He watched her smile sweetly at her brother, then flick an accusatory glance back in his direction when Anthony wasn't looking. He merely smiled, tipping his head slightly in recognition of her mute protest.

The skirt of Laura's pale blue gown rustled beguilingly as she shifted nervously in her chair to reach for her teacup. Blake silently cursed his body for its instan-

97

taneous response to the way her breasts strained against the fabric of her bodice as she raised the cup to her lips.

His mouth was suddenly dust dry as he watched the beguiling way the thick fringe of her lashes cast half-moon shadows on her cheeks as her eyelids shuttered down. He liked the way she'd fixed her hair: pulling it back from her face and catching a mass of curls at the crown of her head with a splash of crimson ribbons that dipped and twined in the profusion of tresses streaming down her back. His fingers ached to touch it.

He watched her lips settle on the rim of the cup and remembered the way they had tasted. When she tilted her head to sip, the sweet ivory column of her throat was bared to his gaze. Under his perusal the tiny pulse beat quickened in the tender hollow.

Blake knew she was wishing he'd tell Anthony no. Whatever it was between them, she was feeling it, too. Laura didn't trust him, and she didn't trust herself with him—and Blake knew it.

He also knew that for his own good he ought to thank Anthony politely for his invitation and then get on the first stage and get the hell out of town—and away from Laura. But he couldn't.

Oh, he could justify his actions all he wanted to by telling himself it would allow him to pursue John's murderers and perhaps learn more about the rumored Mexican uprising. What could be more perfect than the opportunity to come and go without suspicion? And there was no doubt that Anthony could provide him much more information about the local people than he could ever pick up on his own.

It was the perfect cover for the real reason he was in Texas. Didn't his mission take top priority? When he thought of it like that, he really had no choice. Did he?

But the fact of the matter was he didn't want to leave Laura. Not yet. Not while the thought of her burned diamond bright in his mind and fire hot in his belly.

Surely, after a few weeks, he would find her as empty headed and boring as the other women who had caught his eye over the years, and he would be able to erase her from his thoughts.

"Then the matter's settled," said Anthony, rising from the sofa. "I'll tell Pedro to load your trunk, too." His work-weathered boots thudded across the floor as he left the room in search of his ranch hand.

Laura's cup rattled noisily against its saucer as she thumped them down on the table and jumped up. "I'd best finish my packing," she said, never once meeting Blake's eyes. Her hand flew nervously to her hair. "Oh, yes, and I must tell Elizabeth good-bye and thank her for all her kindnesses."

She clutched her full skirts and scurried from the room like the fiends of hell were on her heels, leaving Blake to stare after her with mixed emotions.

"What do you 'spose they're up to now?" questioned Oscar Fields as the old men again watched the bustle of people in front of the hotel.

"'Pears the city dude's going out to the ranch with Anthony, too." Eli White hooked one bony haunch on the porch railing and leaned out to spit a stream of tobacco juice into the dusty street. He wiped at his chin with a faded red bandanna, tucked it back in his pocket, and commenced whittling again.

"Wonder what Miz Nichols gonna think about all this company," mused another.

"Don't reckon she'll mind the feller . . . he'll just be someone else for her to shine up to. But I'd bet my last dollar she won't take too kindly to the sister. Pretty as that little gal is," Oscar said, with a nod in Laura's direction, "I'm afeared she'll be ruffling Maria's tailfeathers a mite. Anthony spoils his missus, he does. She's too used to being the center of attraction. Nope, I don't believe she'll be too fond of sharing his attention."

With sage noddings of heads, the old men watched Blake climb onto the wagon, bracketing Laura between himself and the driver. Anthony's horse pranced nervously beside the wagon, as if sensing they were headed for home. Pedro flicked the reins over the horse's back and they rolled out of sight.

Chapter 11

The wagon followed the rutted road out of the river bottoms and over the beautiful rolling hills of the surrounding blackland prairie. Meadows of dense grass, some of it waist high, were sprinkled amongst the thick stands of pecan, oak, and pine that bracketed the trail. A profusion of wildflowers blanketed the fields, and Anthony called out their names—primrose, wine-cups, bluebells, snow-on-the-prairie—to Laura as they rolled through the carpet of rainbow colors.

"It's all so beautiful, Anthony," she exclaimed, her eyes sparkling with curiosity as she wiggled this way and that upon the wagon seat, eager to see everything.

Laura felt a strange affinity for this wild, beautiful land that was so unlike the busy, cosmopolitan city she had grown up in. She reveled in the clear view of the deepening blue sky, snowy clouds billowing high above the vibrant green treetops. How clean and bright everything was, with no factory smoke to spoil the clarity of the air or dust gray cinders over the leaves.

Anthony smiled at her enthusiasm. "Keep a lookout, Blake. Sometimes you can catch a glimpse of black bear or cougar, although not as often as you could a couple of years back. Too much traffic around here now. Scares

101

'em off. Still lots of deer, though."

Anthony's horse tossed his head, prancing sideways as a startled dove broke cover, flying up and out of sight in the late afternoon sky. He reached to pat the sleek neck, tightening his hold on the rein. "Easy, Dancer."

The wagon jounced over a tumble of stones, throwing Laura against Blake's shoulder. She clutched at the first thing she touched to regain her balance, then snatched back her hand as if it were burned when she realized she had braced her hand against Blake's rock-solid thigh.

"Pardon me," she mumbled, a flush of pink rising up her throat and across her cheeks. She clutched her hands together in her lap, holding her back ramrod stiff. She rode the next mile in painful silence while Anthony and Blake carried on their animated conversation.

Why, if she was so eager for Blake to be gone, was she experiencing butterflies in her stomach simply because the warm bulk of his shoulder had been snugged against hers for most of the trip? How on earth could she be in love with one man and still be so affected by another?

All the crazy emotions she was feeling were totally foreign to Laura. There was certainly no similarity between the strange stirrings that Blake generated and her long-felt affections for William. Surely he'd only stay a few days at Anthony's—surely she could handle the situation for that long.

"Not much further now," called Anthony. Dancer jerked his head with a snort, nostrils flaring wide. Home was close and he was anxious to be back in his stall in the barn. He snorted again, bumping his nose impatiently against the other horse.

The wagon crested a ridge and then slowly passed down into a broad shallow saucer nestled protectively inside a ring of rolling hills. A creek wound its way through the surrounding meadows, circling behind the barn and corrals to pool in a deep pond at the far side of the house.

Large oaks towered over the buildings, majestic branches outstretched to shelter the sprawling complex.

Built of foot-thick cottonwood logs, hewed and counter hewed until they were smooth as glass, the imposing two story house beckoned from a haven of cool green shade. A broad veranda ran the full length of the front and around both sides. Huge beautifully polished posts of solid walnut supported the deep overhanging balcony, standing out strikingly against the pristine whitewash of the walls. Chimneys of sandstone from the Brazos River stood guard at each end, towering over the roof of oak shingles. Floor-length multipaned windows marched across the imposing facade and down the sides, some thrown open to allow easy entry to the cool evening breezes.

Scattered at some distance behind the main building were the barns and storage sheds, smokehouse, wash shed, several small cabins, and two long, low buildings which housed the workers' living quarters. Several men were working around the barn and corrals, obviously completing the last of the evening chores.

"My heavens, Anthony! I certainly never expected such a grand place," exclaimed Laura, eyes round with surprise as she swiveled her head, trying to take it all in. "It's so lovely."

Anthony beamed with pride. "Thank you, honey. I'm glad you think so. See there, Blake, I told you there'd be plenty of room. Maria and I just rattle around in that big ol' place all by ourselves. You're welcome to stay for as long as you like."

"I can't thank you enough. You don't know how much easier this is going to make things for me," Blake said sincerely. "And I must confess, this is much more appealing than a lonely hotel room."

The wagon covered the final distance to the house, rolling to a stop in front of the broad porch. Anthony dismounted and tied Dancer loosely to the back of the wagon. He and Pedro began unloading the baggage, placing it on the bottom step for the time being.

Blake jumped lithely to the ground and then turned to help Laura down from the wagon, placing his strong hands familiarly around her waist as he swung her down. Very much against her will her gaze met his, her breath catching in her throat as the last rays of the sun reflected amber highlights in the stormy depths of his eyes.

Her feet touched the ground and, almost imperceptibly, his fingers cupped the soft curve of her hips, exerting just enough force to tilt her body toward his ever so slightly. Another minute, another ounce of pressure and their bodies would touch. The warmth of his breath caressed her cheek as he exhaled and then drew a deep breath before dropping his hands to his side.

Laura stood mute for a moment, then she managed to whisper, "Thank you," in a strangled voice.

"You're welcome," he replied and reluctantly turned away from her as Anthony's voice broke their reverie.

"Pedro, take Dancer on out to the barn. Be sure to give him an extra handful of oats."

"*Si*, senor." Pedro clicked his tongue to the horse, and the wagon rolled on around the house and down to the barn, Dancer following docilely behind.

The front door swung open, spilling golden lamplight over the porch. Rosita bustled out, followed by two gangling boys.

"Senor Nichols, you're home at last. The senora was beginning to worry about you. Your supper is getting cold," she scolded sternly.

Blake bent to pick up his trunk, and Rosita scampered to stop him.

"No, no, senor. The boys will take care of the luggage. *Por favor*, you must all go in and have your supper." Rosita shooed them toward the open door with a flap of her crisp white apron.

"Might as well do as she says," Anthony said with a grin, putting his arm around Rosita's plump shoulders and giving her a teasing hug. "Rosita's the real boss around here."

Rosita gave a little squawk and launched into a stream of Spanish. Anthony threw back his head and laughed. Blake joined in.

"What did she say?" questioned Laura, intrigued at the sight of Anthony's easy camaraderie with his servant after the years of observing Uncle Henry's stiff disposition with the household help.

"Well," answered Blake with a chuckle, "my Spanish isn't near as good as your brother's, but I think he just got told that he had no more manners than a certain mule down at the barn."

Laura smothered a giggle behind one hand as they followed Anthony through the entryway, leaving Rosita issuing instructions in nonstop Spanish while the boys scurried about gathering up the baggage.

"Come on in the parlor. I want you both to meet Maria. Then I'll show you to your rooms so you can clean up before we eat."

The men's booted heels thudded pleasantly across the planks as they crossed the hallway. Laura gaped at the lovely carved balustrade of the staircase, the colorful woven rugs scattered around the gleaming oak floor, the clay pots spilling over with bright red blossoms that stood sentinel beside the parlor door. The house was a curious blend of American and Spanish that came together to create an aura of comfort and easy elegance.

The parlor was lit with an abundance of lamps and candles. It was furnished with leather-covered chairs and couches and a scattering of small carved tables. It had a comfortable hominess to it. The windows were open onto the front porch, and a soft caressing breeze stirred the heavy drapes that had been left open. A massive chest graced the wall between them. Atop it were several decanters and a tray of crystal glassware. A large natural stone fireplace dominated the adjoining wall. The dining room could be viewed through the open double doors at the back of the room.

With a graceful, fluid movement, Maria rose from her chair. "Antonio, my love, I was beginning to feel neglected. You have been gone so long." Her voice was a throaty purr, the Spanish accent soft and alluring.

The satin skirt of her garnet-colored dress rustled seductively as she glided across the floor to drape her arm possessively through Anthony's. She was much shorter than Laura, coming barely to Anthony's shoulder. A fringed silk shawl was draped casually across her shoulders, framing rather than covering the soft swell of her bosom. The rich cream of her skin was highlighted in the flicker of the candle flames, shading to molten gold in the shadowed cleavage of her full, proud breasts.

"We had to wait for Mr. Saunders to return," Anthony explained, placing a kiss on the pouting ruby lips Maria turned up to him. "Laura, this is my wife, Maria." Anthony grasped Laura's hand and pulled her to his free side. "Darling, this is my sister, Laura."

Maria's midnight black eyes studied Laura across the expanse of Anthony's broad chest. There was just the slightest hesitation before her lips curved in a smile that didn't quite reach her eyes. Then she stood on tiptoe and placed a silken cheek against Laura's.

"I am so pleased to at last meet one of Antonio's family. *Bienvenidos a nostra casa.* Welcome to our home."

"Thank you, Maria," Laura replied softly. "I'm very happy to be here."

"And this is Mr. Blake Saunders," Anthony said. "He was kind enough to care for Laura after the ambush and see that she got safely into town. I've invited him to stay with us while he conducts his business in this part of the state."

"But, of course, you must stay with us as long as possible. We are so pleased to have you, Mr. Saunders," Maria said. She tilted her head up to smile into Blake's eyes. A chignon of thick black hair nestled low against her nape, its heavy lushness accentuating her slender throat. She extended a tiny hand, and Blake enveloped it in his, bending over it politely.

"Call me Blake, please," he murmured.

"Blake," she repeated, purring his name softly. Her fringed shawl slipped even lower.

Laura felt sparks of indignation as she watched Blake's eyes flicker over Maria. And she wasn't sure *what* was fueling her irritation: the fact that her brother's wife was being so attentive to Blake or that Blake was enjoying it so much.

But why should it bother her at all? Maria was certainly loving and attentive to Anthony, hanging on his arm and gazing up at him with those dark smoky eyes. And Blake was certainly no concern of Laura's. Besides, Maria was probably just trying to make Blake feel welcome. It was probably only her sultry accented voice that made the words sound so seductive and alluring. Anthony hadn't even turned a hair at the exchange, so obviously Laura was overreacting to the whole incident.

"I'm going to show them to their rooms, darling, and take the time to clean up a bit myself. Then we'll all be back down to join you for supper."

"Very well, *mi amor*, I'll tell Rosita." Maria offered her lips to Anthony once more, then turned and crossed the room toward the dining area in a slow, seductive walk, her hips swaying beguilingly with each step.

Laura's chin tipped obstinately as she watched Blake's observance of Maria. She dragged her attention away from his bemused face, turning quickly to Anthony and forcing a happy smile as he tucked her hand through his arm.

"Come along," called Anthony, heading back through the entryway and up the grand staircase.

Blake followed them up the stairs, across the elegant landing, and then down a broad hall. Anthony stopped outside the first door on the right, pushing it open and standing politely aside so that Blake could enter.

"Blake, this is your room. There's fresh water and towels. You just take your time. We'll see you back downstairs when you're ready."

Blake nodded his thanks and disappeared into the room. Anthony and Laura continued down the hall to the second door.

"Here you are, Laura. I think you'll be comfortable in this room. Your bags have already been unpacked. Join us downstairs when you're ready."

"Thank you." Laura hugged Anthony quickly. "Oh, I'm so glad to see you—to be here. I-I hope Maria doesn't mind—"

"Nonsense! She's as thrilled to have you here as I am," Anthony assured her. "Now, you quit fretting about such things and get yourself all prettied up."

He bestowed a kiss on her cheek and then retraced his steps down the hall. Laura watched his tall figure disappear around the corner before closing her door.

Her room was more than comfortable. It was quite spacious and elegantly furnished with a huge bed, an ornately carved chest, and a small writing desk and matching chair.

It was evident that Rosita, or someone, had been very busy. Laura's clothes had already been unpacked and her dresses put away in the massive wardrobe. The washstand was ready for her use.

A soft evening breeze stirred the lace curtains covering

the open window. Laura crossed the room to draw the heavier drapes before undressing to wash and change her clothing. She dallied as long as she could at these tasks, almost reluctant to finish up and make her way back downstairs.

She should have been completely happy. She had completed her trip, achieved her goal. She was at last safe and sound in the protective care of her much beloved brother. And Anthony was obviously delighted with her arrival. There seemed very little reason to still fear that Anthony might send her back now or at any time in the foreseeable future. She would have plenty of time to wait for word from William or to plan other measures if her letter had not done its work. And thank God she was out of Uncle Henry's—and that horrible Bernard Arbuckle's—reach!

So what was it that was bothering her?

First of all, even in her wildest imagination Laura couldn't call the reception she'd received from Maria overwhelming. Perhaps it was only that Maria was a little shy with strangers. She paused at this thought, brush poised at mid-stroke in her wind-tangled hair. Maria? Shy? No, shy certainly didn't seem quite the right word to describe Maria. Then just what was the problem?

Maybe Maria simply resented guests being thrust upon her with no warning. After all, Maria and Anthony were practically still newlyweds. Certainly it would be a little disconcerting to any bride to know she was going to have to share her new husband with some unknown relative who just appeared out of the blue to take up what might be a rather prolonged residence in their home. And the fact was that Anthony had brought home not one, but *two* unexpected guests—that had to be a little disconcerting.

Which brought her to Blake. Laura eyed the separating wall between her room and Blake's warily, guiltily envisioning his ablutions as he went about the task of washing away the dust of the road and donning clothing more suitable for the evening meal. The fact that he was a mere matter of feet from her brought flutters to her stomach. And the fact that he might be there for days—or even weeks—intensified those flutters into quakes.

Just what had happened to her since that fateful day in Uncle Henry's study? She was certainly no longer the demure, unprotesting girl she had once been.

Had the mere fact that she had chosen to defy her guardian in the first place planted some strange seed of change within her? Had it been further nurtured by her brash undertaking of a journey that few young ladies—even chaperoned—would have undertaken? What about her brazen disregard for propriety in taking pen to paper to declare her love for William? And to make matters worse, how in the world could she explain the strange yearnings that Blake caused?

Laura's brush clattered angrily against the polished surface of the chest. She tossed her hair back in irritation and stalked to the wardrobe, searching impatiently for the gown she wanted to wear.

Well, it was certainly too late to start worrying about such things now. All she could do was put them from her mind and go on with her life.

Things would work out.

Somehow, some way, she'd make them work out.

Chapter 12

Blake stripped off his shirt, tossing it on the end of the bed as he crossed the room. He poured water from the large blue china pitcher into a matching bowl and bent to wash, bathing his face, arms, and chest.

He splashed his face and then cupped the water in his palms and ran them around the back of his neck and across his shoulders. His gilded hair darkened with the dampness, curls springing tighter. Tiny droplets fell and caught in the burnished hairs on his chest as he straightened up and reached for a towel. Before they were swept away, the liquid beads reflected the dancing candlelight like tiny diamonds upon a field of spun gold.

It was time to make some decisions.

His first reaction to Anthony made Blake want to tell him the truth about his mission. There'd been only one other man in this thirty-four years who had inspired such instant trust and friendship—John Taylor. And now John was dead.

Now Blake had two goals. First, he must get the information that Washington had commissioned him to obtain. And then he was going to find John's murderers. Someone was going to pay.

Blake had toyed all afternoon with the thought of

confiding in Anthony. The urge was strong, but something held him back. Something very gut level, very primal made him decide to wait.

Perhaps it had been nothing more than the revelation of Anthony's total infatuation with his wife. Anyone who could be taken under someone else's spell that completely might be susceptible to influence in other matters also. The none too subtle way in which Maria had appraised Blake had triggered an alarm deep in his mind. Her calculating eyes had awakened disturbing feelings of caution.

It bothered Blake that Anthony had simply stood there, worshipful smile on his lips as he proudly presented his bride, and obviously never felt the flow of tension in the room. If he could be that gullible about her, perhaps he had failings in other areas. Blake couldn't take the chance.

And something about Maria had disturbed Blake. She had seemed almost wary, trying almost too hard to be charming. Something about her made him feel that she was not completely at ease. But the question was, what was causing that apprehension? Was it the unexpected company? Was it jealousy of Laura, who was sure to take up a good portion of Anthony's time and attention?

Maybe she was simply the type of woman who required a man's admiration—any man's. Perhaps all she wanted was a steady flow of gratification for her ego from any male within her range of vision. Blake had come across women like that before. Attention was a tonic they craved like some men craved strong drink. Anyway, *something* about Maria disturbed him, and he had learned long ago to follow his gut instincts. He wasn't about to stop now.

While Anthony might have been oblivious to his wife's behavior, Blake knew Laura had sensed something was amiss. He didn't think she knew just what she was

112

reacting to, but he was sure that Laura had felt the strange aura of unrest in Maria, too. He was also fairly certain, because of Laura's intense loyalty to her brother, that she had blamed her feelings solely on the undue attention Maria had paid to another man. He doubted that Laura had recognized the subtle undercurrent of tension for anything other than that.

And another teasing thought crept in around the edges of Blake's subconscious mind. Could it be that Laura was just the tiniest bit jealous of him because he had paid too much attention to Maria? Not that she'd even recognize her reaction as jealousy. She was fighting her attraction for him—fighting it hard. And as young as Laura was and as sheltered as she had been, she probably didn't even recognize the whirlwind of emotions that had enveloped them for what it was.

Blake knew what it was.

Sheer physical attraction. There could be no other explanation. He'd certainly been around enough to recognize the symptoms. Oh, this time it had happened faster. This time the desire had sparked brightly inside him at first glance and had left a smoldering flame in his belly that threatened to reduce him to ashes. This time the desire was stronger than anything he'd ever experienced before.

But that's all it was. Wasn't it?

After all, it was perfectly human for a man to desire a beautiful woman. And Laura was certainly beautiful.

He was even pretty sure that "nice" girls were occasionally subject to such emotions. Why else did doting parents shelter them so strictly and marry them off at the first opportunity? To protect those sweet young things from falling prey to their own very human emotions, of course. What other reason could there be?

So what was he going to do about Laura?

As a gentleman he should leave her alone. But as a

113

man—could he?

Blake angrily jerked a fresh shirt from the wardrobe. He thrust his arms hurriedly into the sleeves and emitted a soft curse as the buttons refused to obey his fumbling fingers. He raked his fingers through his hair and stormed toward the door.

He couldn't worry about Laura now. He had other more important issues to concern himself with. He'd think about it later. Yes. Tomorrow. Perhaps then he could clear the smoke of desire from his mind and think rationally.

Supper was a pleasant affair despite the earlier undercurrents. Everyone did their best to be charming and entertaining. Maria was so sweet and attentive to Anthony that Blake almost wondered if he had been mistaken about his earlier feelings.

Rosita hovered over them like a guardian angel, spurring the serving girl to even greater speed with whispered snatches of Spanish as the girl covered the table with a multitude of dishes.

Laura immediately liked the biting flavor of the strange dishes that were so very different from the food back East. She especially liked the spicy frijoles, and there was a great deal of laughter and joking when Anthony showed her how to roll them in the strange flat bread called tortillas.

"The cook's knowledge of traditional American cooking is a bit limited, I'm afraid. We have native dishes most of the time, but I could ask her to prepare something else if you'd like," Anthony offered.

"Oh, no. Please, don't do that," Laura protested. "I think this is all delicious. And I'm enjoying the chance to try new things. Uncle Henry certainly never gave us the opportunity to do so. He was so set in his ways. If the cook put anything but the barest spices in the food, he threw a fit. He said it aggravated his gout."

"I quite agree with Laura. The food is delicious," Blake said.

"Well, we have Maria to thank for all this. If she hadn't sent for some of the servants from her home in Mexico after we married, we'd certainly be dining on something a little more boring." Anthony's large square hand enveloped Maria's dainty one. He smiled at her as he gave it a little squeeze. "Actually, nothing about this house would run as smooth if it weren't for Maria and her people."

"Now, Antonio, you flatter me too much. I only do what any good wife would do," Maria said with an indulgent smile in his direction.

"No, it's true. You see, I'd finally finished the construction of the house just a few months before Maria and I married. I hadn't even furnished all of it. But, like most died-in-the-wool bachelors, I was content to have things stay just like they'd always been. I was still using the meager amount of help I'd had in the old house. It wasn't until Maria's people came that I realized how lackadaisically things had been run around here. Yep, this little lady sure made some changes in my life." Anthony raised her fingers to his lips.

"I noticed you have quite a few Mexican ranch hands, too," Blake said, pushing his plate away as he leaned nonchalantly back in his chair.

"Yes, I do. When Maria sought refuge in San Antonio with her uncle, Don Jose Santiago, she brought some of the family servants with her. She knew of others who were desperate to escape the political turmoil of Mexico, and she sent messages back to them soon after our marriage. About half the workers I have came from Mexico seeking a new life in Texas. I certainly couldn't turn them away. If the unrest doesn't get any worse, I'm

115

hopeful that the men will be able to send for their wives and families soon."

"No offense meant, ma'am, but I'm curious about something," remarked Blake with a gentlemanly nod in Maria's direction before he addressed his question to Anthony. "I can't help but wonder if it creates any special problems, having Mexican workers here when the United States and Mexico are at such odds."

"No, it really doesn't. If there's anything grand about Texas, it's the fact that people are accepted for what they are here. Texas is a real hodgepodge of nationalities anyway. There're settlers from all over the United States here and even a thriving German community. Besides, the Mexican influence is still strong in Texas; it always will be. There were many loyal Mexican families who chose to stay here after the fight for independence. After all, the Mexicans really forced the issue of independence themselves."

"What do you mean?" Blake asked.

"There was no doubt that Texas was loyal to Mexico—everyone who came into the country accepted Mexican citizenship and pledged their loyalty to Mexico. The people had no argument with that; most of them had no thought of independence. All they wanted was to be treated equally as well as the other Mexican states. Texas was lumped together with Coahuila, placing the seat of government many miles from the population. Texans had little or no voice in national or regional affairs. There were no provisions for education or much needed improvements on the roads. The convention in San Felipe in 1832 drafted a petition asking for separation from Coahuila and full Mexican statehood for Texas. That's all the people wanted."

"But, Anthony, do you mean that Texas really didn't want independence?" Laura questioned, slightly confused by the political talk.

"Not at first. Even in the petition of 1833, Texas was still only asking for full statehood and the accompanying authority to govern itself. Stephen Austin took the petition to Mexico City himself and tried for months to negotiate some sort of settlement. Even after Santa Anna had him arrested and thrown in jail, Austin urged patience and peace. But it was useless. Finally, in November of 1835, Texas was forced to make a decision: whether to fight for full Mexican statehood or complete independence. I'm afraid the people had lost faith that Mexico was ever going to do right by Texas, so they voted for independence. You know the rest of the story."

"And a lot of the Mexican people chose to stay in Texas?"

"Yes. It was a choice of leaving their homes and everything they had worked for to move to Mexico or supporting Texas in its fight for independence."

"And how did you feel about the issues?" Blake asked with quiet deliberation.

"I didn't come to Texas until after independence had been won. I'm not sure how I would have felt. I hate to see bloodshed of any sort. I guess it's a shame that Mexico never tried to settle the issue peacefully. But that's all over and done now. We have to move on into the future."

"You're right," Blake agreed, nodding his head sagely. "Now, if the people can only continue to work together."

"I have faith that they can. I guess a lot of it is because we've all had to stick together to whip first the wilderness, then the Indians, and finally Santa Anna. These people are strong. They can handle whatever they have to."

"Shall we adjourn to the other room?" asked Maria, rising from her chair. She smiled sweetly, masking her irritation at what she considered slurs against her beloved homeland. Some *Americanos* were so boastful,

117

so impudent. They were as raw and rankling as the scheming, greedy country they came from. They had no appreciation for the great things her country had accomplished—could still accomplish in the future if guided by the right person. "We'll be more comfortable there." There was no hint of her inner turmoil in her gentle voice. Her satin gown swished softly as she passed through the doorway and into the parlor. The others followed.

The ladies settled themselves on the two opposing sofas in front of the fireplace. Blake waited until Laura was settled, then nonchalantly took a seat on the other end of her sofa. Anthony crossed the room to the carved chest.

"Would you like a brandy, Blake?" Anthony questioned.

"Yes, I believe I would."

Anthony poured two glasses of amber liquid and handed one to Blake.

"Thank you."

Anthony turned toward the two women. "Darling, would you like a small sherry perhaps? Laura, how about you?"

"Yes, thank you, my love," said Maria.

Laura nodded her agreement, feeling quite wordly. Uncle Henry had seldom allowed Cynthia and Laura to drink wine at home. Anthony handed the women their glasses and then joined Maria on the sofa. Laura sipped at the deep red liquid, savoring the heady taste.

"Anthony, this Santa Anna you spoke of—I seem to recognize the name, but I'm not sure why," said Laura.

"Probably from hearing about the Alamo and the Battle of San Jacinto. I'm sure that was news back East, too. You were really too young when all that went on for it to have made much impact, though. It was still big news when I arrived in Texas, but I was too late to get in on any of the fighting."

"The Alamo," mused Laura. "Yes, I remember the name, but I'm not sure why it was so important."

"It was really the rallying point in the fight for independence. It's a little mission in San Antonio. A small group of Texans—something less than two hundred—were holding it under siege. Bowie, Travis, and Crockett among them—you probably recognize their names. Santa Anna had over four thousand troops surrounding it. He gave no quarter, and all of the Texans were slaughtered on the morning of March 6, 1836. 'Remember the Alamo' became the rallying cry for the state."

"You mean he killed *everyone?*" Laura asked in horror.

"Just about. The only survivors were a handful of women and children and Travis's slave, Joe."

"That's terrible. They were vastly outnumbered. Why didn't they surrender?"

"Santa Anna had sent word that there would be no leniency for anyone, so they knew they'd be shot anyway. They chose death on the field of battle over the firing squad. It was a matter of honor. But there's more to the story. Few people know the other reason the Alamo sparked such passion in Texans. Just four months before that final battle, the tables had been turned. Some three hundred Texans had defeated Santa Anna's brother-in-law, General Cos, at the very same site. Cos surrendered over eleven hundred men to the Texans. Burleson, the commander of the Texas forces, accepted a pledge from Cos that he would never again fight Texas, and he let all of them go."

"You mean he just turned them free?"

"Yep, that's exactly what he did. Why, he even provided Cos and his troops with enough weapons and powder to protect themselves from Indian attack before he sent them marching back across the Rio Grande."

"I see," said Blake. "The Mexicans were allowed to surrender with honor and return home. But Santa Anna refused the same privilege to the Texans. It certainly *was* a matter of honor."

Maria turned to Anthony, placing her hand gently on his arm. Her head was pounding from the pent-up tension. Much as she hated Santa Anna herself, she'd heard all she wanted to hear. "Antonio, my love," she said, struggling to keep her voice normal, "this is such a depressing subject. You know how I hate to be reminded of the troubles between our countries. Can't we talk of something else?"

"Of course, darling. I'm sorry." Anthony stopped long enough to light a long, thin cheroot. Blake declined the offer to join him. "Let's see, what else do we need to take care of now that we've got you both settled in your rooms? I suppose the first thing we need to do is pick out horses for the both of you." He paused in thought a moment. "You can ride, can't you, Laura?"

"Oh, yes. Uncle Henry gave Cynthia and me riding lessons. I even tried it without the sidesaddle—although Uncle Henry would have had a fit if he'd known," she replied with a chuckle.

"Well, that's good because I'm afraid there are none available hereabouts. You'll have to do with a regular riding saddle. Maria, we'll have to find a riding skirt and some boots for Laura."

"Of course, Antonio. I'll have Rosita take care of it." Maria genteelly tipped her crystal glass for another sip. A tiny drop of wine trembled on her full bottom lip, and she darted the tip of her pink tongue out to catch it, like a cat licking up the last drop of cream.

Anthony's face was animated. "I want to show you all around the ranch, Laura—just as soon as you feel up to it. And you, too, Blake. You're welcome to come with us."

"Thank you. I'd enjoy that very much."

"Have you made any plans yet—about your business, I mean?"

"Your kind offer of a horse has simplified matters for me. I think I'll just do some scouting around for awhile, get the feel of the land before I try to do any actual buying. Any suggestions where I might start looking?" Blake stretched his long legs out in front, balancing his glass against his flat, hard stomach.

"There's good land further east. The neighbors are scattered about rather randomly—Cletus Moore and his family to the east, the Wilsons and Donaldsons back toward town—but there's still a lot of open range. Now, north—"

"No, surely not north, Antonio. It's so barren and deserted that way," Maria spoke up quickly. "Southeast, you must look that way, I think. It's the prettiest land around." She smiled most charmingly.

Blake tossed down the last drops from his glass. "Thanks for the recommendation. I'll try that way first," he said agreeably.

Laura smothered a yawn. The good food and the wine on top of all the day's excitement had made her sleepy.

"I fear we have kept our guests up too long, Antonio," Maria commented. "They must be very tired after the long trip from town."

"You're right, my dear. Let's call it a day. We have lots of time ahead of us for visiting."

Anthony let Rosita know they were retiring for the night. As they left the room the little woman was busily snuffing candles and straightening up. The four of them ascended the stairs.

At the top of the landing, Anthony bent to place a kiss on Laura's cheek. "Good night, Laura, dear. I'm really so pleased to have you here."

"Thank you, Anthony," she replied softly, reaching to

give him a hug.

"See you in the morning, Blake. Hope you rest well." Anthony clapped Blake heartily on the shoulder.

Anthony and Maria turned toward the left wing. Blake and Laura went down the right-hand hall.

Blake paused at his door, hand on the knob, until Laura opened her own door. For a moment his gaze held hers. A spark flared in the dark depths of his eyes.

"Good night, Blake," she said softly.

"Yes, good night," he replied with a small sigh, watching her door slowly close.

Chapter 13

Morning dawned bright and beautiful. After breakfast, Laura and Blake followed Anthony down to the barn to pick out their horses. Laura had guiltily suppressed a surge of relief when Anthony told them that Maria usually preferred to sleep late and therefore would not be joining them for the meal.

Now she would not have to share Anthony's attention with anyone other than Blake. And perhaps, she finally admitted to herself, she was the tiniest bit glad she'd have Blake's full attention also.

Laura had been surprised and pleased when Rosita had knocked gently on the door of her room before breakfast. She had offered Laura a split riding skirt and a pair of soft leather boots. Rosita had scurried about the room, fussing and fixing, chattering all the while in her charming broken English, while Laura eagerly donned her new clothes. Laura was brave enough to ask a few questions and found out that Rosita had been with Maria's family since Maria had been a baby. From the little woman's rambling, effervescent discourse, it was obvious Rosita doted on her charge and had been relieved and happy to be able to join Maria in Texas, sure that no one could care for her as well as Rosita herself. Rosita had only the kindest things to say about Anthony and how good he was to her little Maria.

When Laura was ready, she quickly thanked Rosita again and left her still bustling about the room while she hurried to join Anthony and Blake.

There was an almost wicked feeling of freedom in having her legs unfettered by the cumbersome petticoats she had always worn, Laura decided, as they ambled down the path toward the barn. Life on the frontier certainly had its advantages. No more stuffy matrons and pompous people to worry about—what luxury! She was going to enjoy every minute of her visit while she waited to hear from William.

Blake thought Laura looked very fetching in her new outfit as he strolled along slightly behind the other two. She had caught her hair at the nape of her neck with a bit of bright blue ribbon, and the golden morning sun set ruby highlights dancing in the curls. The high heels of the boots put a tantalizing little sway in her walk.

Blake reluctantly pulled his attention from Laura and turned his mind to the problem at hand. He needed to find out more about the people in this area and how they felt about the current unrest. If there really was a surprise uprising being planned by Mexican factions in Texas, there had to be some proof somewhere. And some of the hottest rumors had come from this very area. Perhaps he could make friends with some of Anthony's Mexican workers. Although they evidently were all loyal Texans, there was always a chance they had heard something.

The barn smelled of fresh hay and horses. Anthony stopped in front of each stall, proudly showing off his stock. He finished the impromptu tour by ducking through a back door. At the back of the barn, in a separate large corral, a magnificent black stallion pranced and snorted, long mane rippling in the wind as he tossed his elegant head to acknowledge their arrival.

"This is Midnight."

"He's superb, Anthony," said Blake. He watched with the obvious pleasure of a lover of good horseflesh as the majestic animal paced around the enclosure, sleek muscles bulging under the jet-black velvet of his skin, proud tail held high.

"Yes, I think so, too. I'm counting on him to sire some great foals. Nothing a Texan likes better than horse racing, and Midnight ought to produce some dandies."

"I don't suppose I can choose this one," Blake said jokingly.

"Not on your life," Anthony replied with a hearty laugh. "Midnight's only for special occasions."

The two men draped their arms over the top bar of the corral and continued their discussion of racing and breeding. Laura stood to one side, a slightly perplexed look on her face.

"Well, y'all ready to pick out the horses you want?" asked Anthony, turning back toward the barn.

"Sure," replied Blake, following in his wake.

They had almost reached the barn when they realized that Laura was not behind them. Anthony turned to find her still standing at the corral fence. She was staring at Midnight with a strange, bewildered expression on her face.

"What's wrong, Laura?" he called.

"Wh-what? Oh . . . uh . . . nothing. I just had this funny feeling . . ."

"What feeling? What do you mean?" Anthony hurried to her side. "Do you feel all right?"

Laura gave her head a little shake and laughed in an embarrassed manner. "I'm fine. I really don't know what it was. Just a funny little feeling about . . . about . . . oh, I really don't know. I was just being silly, I guess." She linked her arm through Anthony's. "Come on, let's go find that horse you promised me."

They headed back toward the barn again. Just then a man came out of the shadows.

"Oh, Miguel, glad you made it back. Come meet my guests," called Anthony.

The man stepped from the darkness, and the sunlight speared off of his dashing Mexican-style clothing. Silver toggles laced the front of his short black jacket across a white shirt and cravat. Silver buttons danced down the side seams of his tight-fitting pants. A wide gray sombrero shadowed his face.

"Did you have a good trip? Were you able to find those relatives you were looking for?" Anthony asked as the tall imposing figure neared them.

"Yes, my trip was most enjoyable. Thank you. I did find the people I was seeking. And I was able to accomplish what I'd set out to do."

"Glad to hear it. Oh, Miguel, this is my sister, Miss Laura Nichols, and this is Mr. Blake Saunders. They'll be staying with us for awhile. Would you be sure all the men know they're here and see that they're available to help them in any way?"

"Of course, Senor Nichols."

"Blake, Laura, this is Miguel Hernandez," Anthony explained. "He's a distant cousin of Maria's. He's my foreman."

Miguel was devastatingly attractive. Tall, broad shouldered, slim hipped. His skin was sun-kissed bronze. A thick black mustache was etched above his sensuous lips. His piercing black-eyed gaze moved warmly over Laura before he clicked his heels and bowed politely over her hand.

"I am honored to meet you, senorita." His voice was soft and melodic. A small smile barely tipped the corner of his sultry mouth. Laura blushed prettily as his black eyes again traveled with slow deliberation over her face.

It seemed forever before Miguel's beguiling eyes released her, and he turned to nod in Blake's direction. "And you also, senor. You will excuse me, please. I must prepare for the workday."

Laura watched the tall, regal figure walk away. And Blake watched her watch him.

"*He's* your foreman?" Laura said with a touch of awe in her voice. Miguel's deeply accented, beautifully resonant voice had raised tingles up and down her spine, and he was out of sight before the strange feeling subsided, leaving a puzzling sense of restlessness in its wake.

Anthony laughed. "I know he doesn't look the part. He's from a very high-class family in Mexico. According to Maria he fell from grace with the current government because he spoke up for Texas independence. It wasn't safe for him to stay there any longer. Maria asked if we could help him out. Naturally, I had to find a position suited to his social status. It's worked out quite well, really. His family had a very large spread in Mexico so he had experience. And the men respect him a lot. He's doing a good job."

"I can see how it would be beneficial to have him in a position of authority—especially since so many of your men are Mexican," commented Blake, watching Laura with hooded eyes while she still stared after the man.

"Yes, it takes a lot of responsibility off my shoulders. I've been spending a fair amount of time working for the government the last couple of years—helping work toward statehood in the past and, more recently, working with the governor on the problem with Mexico. With Miguel being a relative of Maria's and all, I don't have to worry about her or the ranch while I'm gone."

"That's interesting. I didn't know you were involved in politics," remarked Blake as they moved back into the shaded interior of the barn. "How did that come about?"

"Well, I guess it was when Sam Houston moved the capital to Washington-on-the-Brazos late in '42. I'd met Sam many times over the years, and we just naturally struck up our friendship again. I was asked to sit in on some fairly important committees and discussions. Several times he's even tried to talk me into running for public office, but I'm more comfortable working behind the scenes."

"Why did they move the capital again? Washington seems like a real nice little town."

"Western factions just wouldn't accept the move. The government archives were never allowed to leave Austin. With annexation and statehood, the capital was moved back to Austin the first of the year. Washington-on-the-Brazos sure has quietened down since then."

"I guess that means you do some pretty regular traveling since you're still involved with the political scene," Blake mused aloud.

"Yes, I do. Since Henderson's election as the first governor of Texas, I've been going to Austin fairly often. The government really wants to avoid a confrontation with Mexico, but I'm not so sure they can."

"Just exactly what is the problem?"

"Oh, it's been going on for years. Mexico has never formally recognized Texas—not as a republic, and certainly not as a state. There've been skirmishes every year or so since the thirties. In 1842, Vasquez crossed the Rio Grande and occupied Goliad, Victoria, and San Antonio. He didn't really do anything—just raised the Mexican flag, inspected the defenses and then withdrew. But some of the hotheads in Congress issued a declaration of war. Houston vetoed it and kept us out of war. Then in September of '42, Woll captured San Antonio. A troop of volunteers drove him out." Anthony paused for a breath and then continued. "Some of them stayed to patrol the Rio Grande, and about three hundred of them crossed the

128

river and attacked the Mexicans on Christmas afternoon. The Mexicans had set up an ambush, and the Texans who weren't killed in the battle were taken back to Mexico, where they were either imprisoned or executed. Been bad feelings on both sides for a long time."

"Do you expect trouble, now that General Taylor and his troops have been sent to guard the Rio Grande?"

"I don't know. Mexico's been fired up ever since annexation. They claim it was a direct act of hostility by the United States to make Texas a state. They still consider Texas as rightfully Mexican territory. And they're arguing about the Rio Grande being the border. They claim it should be the Nueces River."

"What do you think the chances are for settling all this peacefully?"

"I wish I knew. Ever since the new government came into power in Mexico the first of the year, they've been threatening to retake Texas. I guess the government of the United States must be taking the threat seriously since they sent Taylor out here. And I guess if the Mexicans start it, we'll just have to go in and finish it. Well, enough of this talk. We must be boring Laura to tears. Come on, Laura, honey," he turned and called back to her. "Let's go get those horses, and we'll go for a ride."

"Ummm?" she asked absently. "What? Oh, yes. The horses. I'm coming, Anthony." She hurried to catch up with the men who were already studying the occupants of each stall and discussing the merits of each available horse.

Thirty minutes later they were saddled up and ready to go. Anthony boosted Laura into the saddle and then he and Blake mounted up.

As the three figures rode away, a lone man stood very still in the deep overhanging shadows at the side of the barn. He watched them until they faded away against the distant horizon, his inscrutable face masking the turmoil of feelings in the pit of his stomach.

The three riders reined in their horses at the top of a hill overlooking a broad, sunny meadow filled with rangy longhorn cattle. Laura pulled her hat from her head to allow the cool breeze to ruffle her hair.

"Oh, are they *all* yours, Anthony? There're so many of them!" Laura exclaimed.

"Yep, they're all mine. Lots of them were just here for the taking. All you had to do was round them up and brand them and then keep an eye on them so they don't stray too far off. But the grazing's good around here. I don't have too much problem with that."

"Is all the land hereabouts rolling hills like this?" asked Blake. His saddle creaked pleasantly as he turned and braced his hand on the horse's rump, swiveling his head to view the land behind him.

"Most of it. Got a few boggy places where the river dams up in the bottoms. Toward the west it gets a little flatter. Out past my property line on the far north it's real hilly. Used to be pretty thick Injun country out that way. In fact there's one secluded valley some say is an old Injun burial ground. The old folks call it 'Sunfire Valley.' Bad medicine to mess around with it; sacred ground or some such thing. Don't know as I believe in all that hocus-pocus stuff, but folks around here mostly just let things alone and stay away from it. No sense in riling up the spirits—if there's any such thing—I guess," Anthony said with a laugh.

Blake chuckled along with him and then asked, "What made you get out of cotton and into cattle?"

"Too many rumblings about the slavery issue. I didn't like being dependent on that in order to survive. Oh, most slaves are very well treated, but from what I hear the North is raising more and more hell about the slavery question. That was one of the problems that delayed Texas's annexation. Northerners didn't want it coming in as a slave state. We might have gotten statehood in '44 if it hadn't been for the slavery issue."

"You're right about that. There is a lot of arguing going on about slavery. And I agree—it can only get worse as time goes on."

Anthony gave Dancer a little nudge with his heels and turned him around. Blake and Laura followed. They rode in comfortable leisure down the gentle slope of the hill, back toward the dry, rutted road at the bottom. It led through a thick stand of trees, over the backbone of another ridge of hills, and then back into the valley where the house stood.

"Anyway," Anthony continued as they rode side by side at an easy pace, "you can't farm cotton without slaves—it just isn't economically feasible. I'd worked too long and too hard for what I had. I didn't want to pin everything on something that's really under fire. So several years ago I started getting away from the cotton and moving into cattle. I've never regretted it."

"Looks like you made a good choice," Blake commented. Laura had nudged her horse slightly ahead of the two men on the road. Blake was finding it hard to keep his attention on cattle while he watched the alluring way Laura's firm little backside bounced in the saddle. The embers in his belly were fanned to bright coals. He shifted uncomfortably in the saddle, finally dragging his gaze from the intriguing sight and forcing his attention back to Anthony.

"I hear that longhorns are hearty animals."

"Yes, they are. But lately I've been thinking about crossbreeding. I think the longhorn is a great range animal, but I believe something can be done to improve the beef yield. The right crossbreed would give us stamina plus weight. It's something I'd like to try."

131

Blake was surprised at the far-reaching plans Anthony was considering. The longer Blake was around Anthony, the more he respected him. It was obvious he was an ambitious man, a hard worker, a man loyal to his land and his country. He wished he could put his finger on just what it was that kept him from confiding in Anthony.

After all, Anthony's government connections might come in handy during Blake's search for the truth. He'd just have to bide his time and see if Anthony was really all he seemed to be. Blake certainly hoped so.

Anthony shielded his eyes with his hand, peering into the cloudless blue sky above. "'Bout time for the evening meal. Guess we'd better head back to the house."

They kicked the horses up into a trot and, plumes of dust rising from the red dirt road, they headed for home.

They had no sooner gathered around the table for the evening meal than a rider thundered up the road. There was the sound of quick footsteps across the porch and a heavy pounding on the door. Rosita scurried to open the door.

As Anthony started to rise from his chair to go see who it was, a burly man stormed into the room.

"Sorry to interrupt your supper, Anthony," the man apologized. He was a big man, a good deal older than Anthony. His iron gray hair was ruffled by his hurried ride. Worried eyes looked out of a weather-etched face.

"That's all right, Cletus. What's going on?"

"Just got news in town that Mexican troops crossed the Rio Grande and attacked Taylor's army. He drove them back, but things are really riled up down there. Henderson wants us to come to Austin. They're waiting for word from President Polk."

"The United States isn't going to like this at all, I'm afraid," Blake said. He pushed his chair back and got up to join the men.

"Forgive my lack of manners. In all the confusion I didn't even introduce you to my guests, Cletus. This is Mr. Blake Saunders. And that's my sister, Laura," Anthony said with a nod of his head in Laura's direction.

"Howdy ma'am," the man said, bobbing his head first in Laura's direction and then Maria's. "Miz Nichols."

"This is my old friend, Cletus Moore. His spread borders mine to the east."

Moore thrust out a work-roughed hand and pumped Blake's vigorously. "Pleased to meet you."

"Would you like me to go to Austin with you, Anthony? I'd be happy to. Perhaps I could be of some help," Blake offered.

"Thank you for the offer, Blake. But I'd appreciate it if you'd stay here and entertain Laura for me while I'm gone. That way she won't be confined to the house. You can take her out riding—let her see the country a little bit." He turned toward her. "I hate to run off and leave you like this, honey, but it's important that I get on back to Austin."

"I understand, Anthony, but I'll be perfectly fine if you need Blake to accompany you," Laura tried to assure him. Heavens! The last thing she needed was to be put back in Blake's care. Look what had almost happened last time.

"No, I'll really feel better if he stays here. Maria, darling, will you excuse us?"

"Of course, Antonio. Laura and I will finish our meal. You go on about your business." Maria lifted her knife and cut a small portion of meat, then raised her fork daintily to her scarlet lips.

The sound of booted feet echoed through the house as the three men quickly left the room.

"Blake, you stay and tell Cletus what you told me earlier about what's going on back East while I go pack a few things. I'll be right back down," Anthony instructed, leaving the other two in the parlor as he hurried toward

133

the stairs.

Laura could hear the muffled sound of baritone voices as Cletus and Blake continued their discussion. She glanced surreptitiously at Maria, who continued to eat her meal as if nothing was amiss.

Laura sighed, resigning herself to the thought of Anthony's absence. Maybe it would be a good thing that Blake was staying. At least she wouldn't have to stay in the house with Maria all the time. Surely he'd behave himself while Anthony was gone. At any rate, she'd just have to see to it that she kept him in his proper place at all times. That shouldn't be too hard to do.

Should it?

Laura turned restlessly in her bed. It was a warm night, and she just couldn't seem to get comfortable. She threw back the covers and crossed the room on bare feet. Perhaps a little fresh air would help, she thought, opening the window and leaning out to breathe deeply of the pine-spiced night.

A sudden movement caught her attention. A shadowed figure scurried from the shelter of the house and across the cleared ground that surrounded it, disappearing into the blackness of the thick trees.

Strange, thought Laura. Who would be out at this time of night? And whoever it was hadn't even carried a lantern to light the way in the darkness. She watched a while longer but the figure did not reappear.

Laura finally shrugged her shoulders, dismissing the incident. Maybe one of the servant girls had slipped out to meet her beau. Yes, that was probably it. Laura covered a yawn with her hand and padded back across the room to her bed. She snuggled into its downy softness and was soon fast asleep.

Chapter 14

The horses' bridles jingled softly as Blake and Laura made their way along the trail. There was a lazy feeling to the late afternoon atmosphere, and they were content to let the horses slowly pick their own way across the land. A hawk circled overhead, gliding on the soft currents of the wind far above them. Fluffy white clouds piled high across the turquoise of the sky.

"Thank you for taking me riding," Laura said.

"You're welcome. I would have taken you yesterday or the day before if you had just said something. All you had to do was let me know you were ready to get out for awhile."

"I know, and that's very kind of you. I just thought I should spend some time with Maria—maybe have an opportunity to get better acquainted with her." She gave a little sigh. "I'm afraid it's going to be harder than I thought. She's so . . . so . . ."

"Yes? So what?" prompted Blake.

"I'm not sure. I can't quite put my finger on it. She's very polite to me. She always says the right things at the right times. But somehow I feel that underneath it all she wishes I weren't here." Laura turned troubled blue eyes on Blake. "Have I done something wrong? Something to

135

provoke her in some way?"

"No, I'm sure it's not that."

"Well, whatever it is, I just can't seem to get beyond the surface. I don't think she wants to be friends at all. Oh, and I had so hoped that we would be. It would please Anthony so very much."

"And that's the important part, isn't it? To please Anthony? You love him very much. I can tell."

Laura's eyes shone. "Oh, yes, I do. When Mother and Father died and we went to live with relatives, Anthony was all I had left in the world. Maybe it wouldn't have been so hard if Uncle Henry and Aunt Mary had been a little more loving—but they weren't. Uncle Henry never was, and Aunt Mary was afraid of her shadow when he was around. Anthony was so much older than me—seven years—that he became my parent in a way. He was the one I turned to with scraped knees and bruises. He was the one who kissed away the hurts and cuddled me and told me bedtime stories."

Blake swallowed the lump forming in his throat. He didn't like to think of Laura young and alone, with only Anthony to protect her and give her love. "That must have meant a great deal to you."

"Yes, it did. I thought my heart would break when he left."

"Were you very upset with him for doing that?"

"No. Even as young as I was, I knew there was really bad blood between Anthony and Uncle Henry. I think Anthony reminded him too much of our father. He'd never forgiven Mother for marrying someone he considered beneath her social status. He never knew how wonderfully happy we all were in that little house he refused to set foot into."

"Maybe he did. Maybe that's what angered him so," Blake said softly.

Laura's gaze darted to him. "You're a very perceptive

136

person. I never thought of it like that. Maybe you're right." She ducked an overhanging limb as the horses ambled through a cluster of trees, working their way deeper into the thicket.

"What happened?"

"They had a big fight one day—much worse than any before. That night Anthony came into my room very late and told me he was leaving. He said things would be better if he did. I didn't understand at the time, but I think he was right. Uncle Henry did act nicer to me after Anthony was gone. I think Anthony left for me as much as for himself."

"I think you may be right."

The horses broke into a small clearing. A broad rippling creek meandered gracefully between banks of lush green grass sprinkled with colorful wildflowers.

"Ah," said Blake, "the horses smelled the water. I should have guessed. Why don't we give them a rest? It's nice and cool here."

"All right. I think I'd enjoy a little rest, too," Laura replied with a grin.

They reined in their horses at the edge of the stream. Blake dismounted and walked around behind Laura's horse to help her down. This time she welcomed the feel of his strong hands around her waist as he swung her down to the ground. The hours they had spent together during the afternoon had been pleasant and tranquilizing. It had been easy to push thoughts of the past from her mind and simply dwell on being friends instead of opponents over some strange unknown antagonism.

Her hands settled naturally against the hard strength of his shoulders as he eased her to the ground, then slid lightly down to rest against the broad plane of his chest for the briefest moment.

She tilted her head back and smiled warmly up into his eyes. "Thank you."

"My pleasure," he said. His cinnamon eyes held her gaze for a long moment, and then his mouth quirked up into a smile, wiggling the luxuriant brush of his mustache in the most beguiling manner.

He stepped casually away from her and took hold of the reins to her horse as well as his own. "I think they could use some water." He led the horses a few feet down the bank to the sparkling creek and dropped their reins, ground-tethering them so they could drink and graze.

Blake unhooked the canteen from the saddle horn and walked back up the bank to where Laura still stood. "You could probably use a drink, too," he said, uncapping the flask and offering it to her.

"Thank you." She tilted it gratefully, allowing the cool, quenching liquid to trickle into her mouth for a long drink before handing it back to Blake.

He raised the canteen to his lips, head back, bronze column of throat working as he swallowed. Her gaze traveled down the twin lengths of strong cord in his neck, down to the open vee of his shirt, down to the field of crinkly gold hair on his chest. She remembered the way it had felt against the soft skin of her cheek that morning in the shelter of the stage: so crisp, so vital, so alive to her touch.

A blush crept up her cheeks. "I-I feel a little warm myself." She went to the creek and dipped her handkerchief into its cooling depths, rubbing the wet linen slowly over her face and throat.

"I know what'll cool you off even better," Blake said, a mischievous tone to his voice.

"Oh? What's that?"

"Let's go wading."

"Wading?" she asked in surprise.

"Sure, pull your boots off. You can tuck your skirt up."

He threw himself down on the ground and hurriedly

pulled off his soft leather boots and socks, quickly rolling his pants legs up to just below his knees. His legs were covered with the same golden down as his chest. The sun glinted off the silky hairs momentarily before he scrambled up and spashed into the water.

"Come on! It feels great!" He reached down to dip his hands into the water and playfully splash some in her direction.

Laura laughed with childish abandon. "Oh, no, you don't!"

She quickly sat down and pulled her boots and stockings off, throwing them in a jumbled heap on the ground. Scrambling up, she grabbed the tail of her gingham skirt and pulled it through her legs, securing it firmly in the tight waistband. She said a silent word of thanks that she had once again abandoned her petticoats in favor of comfort and convenience.

Blake's gaze feasted hungrily on the sight of her legs: the slim white curve of her calves, the trim turn of her ankles, the soft beguiling sculpture of her knees. He cupped the water again, spraying it in Laura's direction, careful to come very close without actually wetting her.

Her laughter rang out in delight as she quickly entered the water and began splashing the water back at him. He was agile enough to stay just out of her range, and he tempered his splashes so that they fell harmlessly short of their target.

Laura felt very brave and reckless. Despite a sprinkle of damp patches from flying droplets of water, Blake hadn't really managed to get her wet at all. She didn't know he was holding back purposely. With a wild cry of exuberance she dashed at him, cupping her hands together and spraying out a huge shower of water. Blake yelled in shock as the torrent hit him full in the chest, plastering his shirt to his skin.

"Why, you little vixen! I'll get you for that!" he roared

139

in mock ferocity.

Laura stood frozen at the unexpected havoc she had created. Her hands flew to her mouth, and she rocked with laughter at the sight. Her eyes grew large with apprehension as she watched Blake quickly unbutton his shirt and tug the tails of the sodden material out of his waistband.

Quick as a fox he whipped the shirt off and pitched it to the bank, advancing menacingly toward her. She gave a squeal and bolted for land, Blake in hot pursuit. Their laughter rang through the woods as she scrambled desperately up the grassy slope with Blake close behind her.

"Got you!" he cried triumphantly as his hand closed around her slim ankle. She screamed in mock fear and struggled to free her foot. Blake crawled up the bank and gently tugged her down onto the ground, cushioning her fall so that she wouldn't be hurt in the playful battle.

They rolled and struggled, pushing and pulling with pretend ferocity, laughter ringing out with their jubilance in the innocent charade. Finally Blake threw himself across her body and pinned her to the ground.

"Surrender!" he demanded.

"No! I won't! Not ever!" she cried amid delighted giggles.

He growled fiercely and burrowed against the tender juncture of neck and shoulder, nipping playfully at her earlobe.

"Oh!" she squealed. "Stop, Blake! Stop! That tickles!"

"Good," he murmured against her throat and growled threateningly again.

"No, no! I surrender," she cried again as he began his assault on the sensitive place again.

Laura ceased her struggles, collapsing tiredly against the ground. Blake's hands still secured her wrists at either side of her head. He lay limply across her, his head tucked into the hollow of her throat, his breath as ragged as hers from their exertion. She chuckled softly, and her warm breath ticked his ear.

"What's so funny?" he murmured.

"You're all wet. I'm going to be as wet as you are if you don't move."

And suddenly he was aware of the dampness of her clothing, soaked from his nearness. The soft lush fullness of her breasts pressed against him; each deep breath she took caused them to brush across the copper nodules buried in the thick mat of hair on his chest in the most agonizing manner.

The drugging woman scent of her filled his nostrils. He sighed and breathed deeply of the tantalizing aroma, mixed with the sweet perfume of wildflower blossoms they'd crushed in their tumble. He moved his head very softly to rub his cheek against the spill of silken hair that fanned across the ground.

The laughter died, and they lay very quiet for a long, long moment, each caught up in a strange magic that seemed to suspend them in time.

Laura could feel the heavy pounding of Blake's heart against her breast. It was a very strange feeling to have another's heartbeat mingle and blend with her own. Each thud echoed in her ears, building and building until reality dimmed and faded, until there was nothing but a strange timeless throbbing in her veins.

Blake slowly raised his head. His gaze held hers, boring into her very soul. She watched him in stunned silence, her dazed mind somehow etching a picture of every particle of his being on her memory: the tumbled mass of tawny curls, sunlight streaming through an opening in the overhanging branches above them to create a misty golden halo around his head; the dark slash of his mustache over slightly parted lips that seemed to struggle to suck in enough air for his laboring lungs; the tick of

141

his heartbeat under the soft vulnerability of his temple, his face so close that she could see the fine grain of his bronze skin; the deep brown velvet of his eyes that gave back the wide-eyed reflection of her own face from the obsidian depths of his dilated pupils.

His face loomed closer and closer, and then his lips claimed hers. Softly, softly. Then harder and more demanding as she met him with growing ardor. His tongue gently caressed the seam of her lips, then moved to stroke the silken flesh of her mouth, darting to trace across the tiny even rows of teeth, delving into each and every secret recess.

Hesitantly she dared to touch her tongue to his, indulging only in tiny flickering touches at first, then growing braver as she thrilled to the intriguing prickly way his mustache felt as she ran her tongue caressingly over his lips. When at last she thrust her tongue between his lips, he gave a half sob and ground his mouth against hers, sucking gently at the sweet tool of his torment.

His hands released their hold on her wrists. His arms swept around her, crushing her against him, desperate to hold her softness against the raging heat of his body. Her arms wound around his neck, her fingers buried in his hair, pulling him closer, closer, ever closer.

His mouth slashed across hers, ravaging, plundering. He rained kisses across the line of her jaw, down the sweet ivory column of her neck as she arched it in offering. Gently he eased the length of his body across hers until his heated loins were nestled in the sweet cradle of her body. He claimed her mouth again, delving deeply, thrusting with his tongue until she moaned softly under him.

He freed one hand from beneath her body and slid it seductively up the sweet slope of her ribs until he possessed her breast. His fingers molded it, gently kneading, caressing, tormenting. His hand slid away, and she muttered a little cry of protest against his lips.

Quickly he found the row of tiny buttons, forcing them through their holes, desperate to feel the warm weight of her against his hand again. He thrust the fabric aside until only the thin cloth of her chemise separated them. His fingers trembled as he untied the tiny blue ribbon, baring one sweet breast. He lifted his head to savor the view like a starving man before a banquet table.

His fingers traced the circle of coral that crowned the lustrous pearl-white globe, then plucked at the enthralling pout of nipple. Heat coursed through his veins as he watched it respond and harden to his ministrations. He cupped the fullness of her breast, forcing the rich weight of it upward. His lips descended. His tongue retraced the course his fingers had just taken, then he took the tiny puckering bud in his heated mouth.

A tiny moan of pleasure escaped her lips, driving him to greater efforts. As he suckled the sensitive peak, a small tugging began in the depths of her being, swirling outward, stronger and stronger, like the ripples on a pond. She threw one bare leg over his, arching her back, her desire-drugged body seeking only to mold itself against his.

Blake ran his hand down the sweet curve of her hip, cupping around the soft flesh of her thigh, sliding into the tender hollow at the back of her knee to pull her even tighter against him. His body rocked in ageless rhythm against her answering warmth. His fingers blazed a trail to the firm roundness of her buttocks, provocatively glazing over the thin fabric of her pantalets, then flexing softly against the jut of hip bone before lightly trailing across the satin skin of her belly, down, down to cup the heated warmth of her womanhood against his palm. Mindlessly she tilted her body, raising herself sweetly against his searching fingers.

"Sweet Jesus!" Blake cried explosively, thrusting

143

himself up and away from Laura. "I can't do it, I can't do it," he said, his voice a ragged sob. He drew his knees up, laying his arms across them and bowing his head wearily, struggling to fight back the rage of desire that coursed through his body.

Laura lay dazed just as he had left her, arms outflung, skirt a tangled mess about her legs. The red mists slowly cleared from her mind, and her eyes once again focused on the world around her. Her breath came in great ragged gasps. Her body continued to burn with a strange yearning. She propped herself up on her elbows, only to be confronted with the sight of Blake's bare back.

And the desire turned to shame. It was bad enough that she had behaved in such a wanton manner, that she had succumbed so completely to whatever strange hold Blake held over her. But worse, oh, so much worse, was the undeniable fact that he had turned away from her. He didn't want what she had so innocently offered.

Hot tears gathered in Laura's eyes. She sat up, pulling her skirt down over her legs, twining her arms about her knees and burying her face in the sheltering fabric.

"I-I'm sorry," Blake whispered, his face a study of agony, which Laura failed to see. He reached to touch her gently, and she flinched away from his hand. "Please don't worry. It won't happen again. I promise."

He moved away, walking to the other side of the horses, keeping his back turned while she refastened her buttons and smoothed the tangles from her hair.

They didn't speak on the ride back to the house.

Miguel saw Blake and Laura when they rode in. He noted the nervous flutter of her hands and the high color in her cheeks. He watched with great interest as she refused Blake's offer of help and then dismounted quickly by herself, stumbling a little in her haste. She practically ran toward the house.

144

Miguel's black eyes narrowed suspiciously. What was wrong with the lovely senorita? he wondered, suppressing a flash of irritation. Laura finally disappeared into the house, and then Miguel swung his attention back to the barn. Blake was still inside.

A small kernel of anger formed in Miguel's belly. If the gringo had harmed her— The thought went unfinished. With the grace of a panther Miguel moved across the field and into the barn.

"There has been some trouble, senor?"

Blake jumped in surprise at the sound of Miguel's voice. "No! No, what makes you think that?"

"The senorita—she looked upset."

Blake gave a small nervous laugh and continued to rub down the horses. "No, you're wrong. She's just . . . uh . . . tired from our long afternoon out. That's all."

Miguel broodingly noted that Blake looked almost as upset as Laura. "Very well, senor," Miguel finally replied, but he continued to watch Blake dubiously. He paced slowly across the barn and leaned one shoulder against the rough post of Blackjack's stall.

Blake wished fervently that Miguel would leave him in peace. What the hell did he want? He had no right to question Blake about anything! Blake bent to his task, turning his back to Miguel, altogether unsure of how long he could maintain his facade of composure.

My God! Why didn't the man go about his work? Surely he had more important things to do with his time. The last thing Blake needed was to have Miguel standing there with that look on his face like some dark avenging angel.

Laura lay in the enveloping darkness, heavy salty tears sliding silently down her face to pool wetly in her tangled hair. What was wrong with her? What flaw did she have that a man who had surely known the pleasures of dozens

145

of women would be so repelled? And why was she so weak of spirit that she succumbed to his touch each and every time? Deep down was she one of those bad women she had heard whispered about? Would she respond so wantonly to any man's caress? Or was it only Blake who could set her afire?

She didn't know the answers. She wasn't even sure she really wanted to know.

Blake lay quietly upon the bed in the wee hours of the night, hands behind his head. He could have had her. Just one more minute and all his frustrations would have ended. The woman he wanted more than anyone before in his life had lain beneath him, warm and willing. What was wrong with him? Why couldn't he take what she offered?

Was it because he knew she had been helpless under his hands? Was it because she was so obviously innocent? Was it because he knew she had been starved for loving, for touching, for tenderness for a great part of her childhood, thus making her all the more susceptible to a rogue such as he?

Or was it because she meant more to him than he wanted to admit?

Chapter 15

A loud knock sounded at the hotel room door. William Stratford jumped in fear, his hand jerked, and the whiskey he was pouring splashed against the edge of the glass and puddled on the tabletop. His breath caught in his throat and he stood very still, his aristocratic face pale under the shock of ebony hair that hung haphazardly over his high forehead. Perhaps they'd think he wasn't in if he were very quiet. Maybe they'd go away.

"William! Are you there, man? It's me, Tom."

William expelled a shuddering breath. His trembling hand sat the decanter down with a thud. He hurried to the door, opening it just a sliver to peer with pale blue eyes through the narrow gap before opening it wide enough to allow the man's entry.

"I came to warn you about Franklin."

"My God, I know about Franklin." William laughed a trifle wildly. "I thought you were Franklin's men." He ran his long thin fingers through his hair, rumpling it even more than it already was.

"Well, I'm afraid they're not far behind me. Franklin wants his money. You'd better do something quick."

"You know I don't have that much money here. I need time to make arrangements. I think I can get some money from my mother if I just have a few more days. I can't get it any sooner. I have to have more time!"

"I'm afraid the time's run out. Franklin's been boasting all day that he was going to collect the bet one way or another tonight—money or your hide—and that it didn't really matter to him which it was."

"Damnation!" muttered William, pacing the room in agitation. He grabbed up his glass and tossed down the whiskey, then refilled it to the brim.

"Why in the world did you play cards with that man, anyway? You know his reputation! I've never known you to lose like that before."

"That's precisely why I played. Because I thought I could win! Why the hell else would I do it?" William snapped at his friend. "I needed a new stake. Father's angry with me for that little escapade last month. He's cut off my allowance. I had a deuce of a time calming him down. He warned me if I made one more slip before my birthday, he wouldn't relinquish control of my inheritance until I turned thirty. My God, man, I can't afford to have that happen! Five more years of waiting? Impossible!"

"Well, you'd better come up with a plan quick. If Franklin sets those thugs of his on you—"

"Will you be quiet? How do you expect a man to think?" William exploded.

William's eyes roamed the room desperately. Franklin would laugh at the paltry amount of money he still had. Except for the small roll in his money belt—just enough to fund his escape from the dreadful situation he found himself in—all he possessed was the handful of scattered bills on the dresser. And he still owed for his room.

The clerk had drawn his attention to the bill once again when he picked up his key last night, looking suspiciously at William through the little glasses perched ridiculously on the end of his bulbous nose. Of course,

William had sneaked out the back door of better places than this; he could certainly do it again if he had to.

"Tom, old man, could you—"

Tom threw his hands up. "No use, William. I'm scraping bottom, too. You'll have to think of something else. Maybe you'd just better leave town. The sooner, the better."

"And where would I go? I certainly can't go back home. Father's still in a foul mood, and besides, Franklin would just come looking for me there. No. No, it's got to be some place farther than . . . that . . ." William's words trailed off as he spied a slip of blue paper on the dresser. He snatched it up. "Maybe the gods have smiled on me after all, Tom, old man," he said with his old familiar devilish grin.

"What are you talking about?"

William waved the paper under Tom's nose. "A plea for help from a lady of my acquaintance. It was sent on to me a couple of weeks ago. I'd forgotten all about it, but I think this might be a fortuitous time to look into the matter. After all, the little lady has shyly expressed her love and admiration for yours truly. That should be reason enough to join her in her place of sanctuary on her brother's big ranch. Thousands of acres, she says here. She should be very glad to see me, don't you think?"

"Aha, and that ranch means money," said Tom, nodding his head conspiratorially. "Hope she isn't ugly as a mud fence. 'Course, if there's enough money, I doubt that would matter much."

"That's certainly not the case. She's a pretty little thing, all right."

"Then how did you manage to let her slip through your fingers before?"

"Oh, I squired her and her cousin around a bit. But she was always on the quiet side, rather prim and proper. Not

149

exactly my type," he said, elbowing Tom in the ribs.

"What you really mean is she wouldn't have agreed to a tumble or two, right?"

"Exactly. She was definitely the marrying kind."

"And that didn't interest you either."

"Not hardly. You see, she lived with a guardian, her uncle. He certainly wouldn't have come up with a proper dowry for the girl. Not with a daughter of his own to worry about. No, if I'd have been of a mind to pursue a wife, I'm afraid I'd have had to look toward her cousin, Cynthia. Old Henry just might have come across for her—but certainly not for Laura."

"Always looking out for yourself, aren't you, William?" said Tom with amusement.

"But, of course." William smoothed the crumbled paper and scanned the delicate penmanship. "Yes, this ought to work out perfect. This'll be far enough away to discourage Franklin."

"Are you planning on staying permanently? You sure can't come back East until you pay Franklin off. He's going to be mad as a hornet."

"Maybe," William answered with a wicked grin, "when I get back, I'll have enough money to pay him off with interest."

"And just where is it you're headed, William?"

"Texas, Tom, old friend. Texas."

The band of renegades thundered over the hill in a swirl of dust and gunshots, taking the convoy of supply wagons by surprise. It was over in a matter of minutes.

The dark man shouted instructions to his bandidos from atop the spirited black horse. Three of them quickly dismounted and tied their horses to the backs of the wagons before pulling the tarps back so their leader could survey the plunder.

150

Good! Guns and ammunition, medical supplies, foodstuffs—all bound for the border—all destined for use against Mexico. The dark man smiled grimly, a smile that never touched his eyes. Yes, they'd certainly be used against the Mexicans—but not in the way that had been expected.

"All right! Cover it back up. Let's get out of here!" he shouted.

The men hastily tied the tarps back in place and then climbed onto the wagon seats and took up the reins. The wagons lumbered off, bouncing and jarring their way across the rolling hills toward their rendezvous with fellow believers.

Soon there was nothing left to tell of their coming except for a smudge of dust on the horizon and six bodies sprawled in the red Texas dirt.

Chapter 16

Blake vowed to be up and gone by sunrise. He tossed and tumbled the rest of the long night away, sleeping some, but mostly trying to sort out the jumbled mess of his mind. One thing was obvious: He had no business spending any more time around Laura until he could get his thoughts straight.

Besides, his first obligation was to the government. He had never let personal situations impinge on his work before, and he had no intention of doing so now. He and John had been sent to Texas to obtain some very important information for the department, information that might now be vital to the war effort. It was up to him to see that the assignment was completed satisfactorily—for John's memory, if nothing else.

Blake had always been able to lose himself in his work before; the department had always been uppermost in his mind. It would just be a matter of time and discipline until it was that way again. Yes, work would be the best thing for him.

He flopped over onto his stomach, squirming to get comfortable in the tangled covers. Perhaps he should take the time to get to a telegraph office and let Washington, D.C. know of John's death. They might even have new orders for him.

No, he finally decided, that would require a trip of considerably more than a week—far too time consuming. It was more important to do a little surveying and see if he could pick up any pertinent information that could be included in his first dispatch. He really didn't like the idea of reporting in until he had a better idea of whether or not there was any truth to the rumors they had received from their man in Mexico.

Hours later, Blake heard the faint crow of a rooster and crawled gratefully out of the tumbled bed. He cursed softly when he stubbed his toe against the chest as he edged across the room in the dark. His fingers scrabbled over the smooth wood surface, finally finding the matches.

After two unsuccessful attempts he managed to light a candle. The small golden flame cast long wavering shadows in the dark corners of the room. Blake padded softly over to the pitcher and basin, splashing water on his face. His beard felt scratchy, but he didn't care. Shaving seemed too monumental a task even to contemplate in his surly mood.

Right now all he wanted was out—out of the room and out of the house. The sooner, the better. He dressed as quickly and quietly as possible, very conscious of Laura's presence in the adjoining room.

The door creaked as Blake eased it open, sounding very loud in the silent house. He froze, listening to see if he had disturbed anyone. He heard nothing but the soft groanings of new timber as the house settled more comfortably about itself. Carefully he closed the door behind him and tiptoed down the hallway.

At the bottom of the steps he heard the very faint chatter of female voices from the back of the house. Relying more on memory than sight in the near dark, he edged across the entryway, and then through the parlor.

When he reached the dining room, he spied a tiny line of light under the door leading to the kitchen. He sidled carefully around the large carved dining table and chairs and pushed open the door.

The sound of Blake's boots clacking across the floor interrupted Rosita's happy chatter, and she jumped in alarm.

"Aye! Senor, you give me a fright!" she scolded, placing a plump hand against her very generous bosom. "You are up much early."

"Good morning, Rosita," Blake said, smiling at the pleasant little woman and nodding in the cook's direction. "Yes, I suppose I am. I thought I'd get an early start this morning. I've got a lot of ground to cover."

"*Si*, senor. The coffee is ready, but I'm afraid it will be a little while before the breakfast is done. Juanita is just beginning—"

"That's fine, Rosita. I'll just have a cup of coffee and be on my way."

Rosita hurried to pour Blake a big mug of the potent brew.

"Gracias. Thank you," he said when she handed it to him. And she smiled in a pleased manner. He took a careful sip of the hot liquid.

"The senorita is going with you?"

"No," Blake answered sharply. Then, ashamed of his gruffness, he went on the explain, "Not this time. I'm just going out to look over the land for a little business deal I might try."

"You will return for the noontime meal, senor?" Rosita asked.

"No, it may even be after dark before I get back."

"Then you must take something to eat with you," she exclaimed. Despite his protests she packed a mountain of food into a knapsack. "I will fix this for you each morning that you ride out."

154

"You're very kind to do so, Rosita. Thank you," said Blake, accepting the overstuffed bag. He swallowed the last drops of coffee and put the cup on the table. Slinging the bag over his shoulder, he called out a good-bye to the two busy women and hurriedly slipped out the back door.

The early morning air carried the tangy aroma of wood smoke from Juanita's cook stove. It tickled Blake's nose pleasantly as he took a deep breath, allowing the rigidity of his body to slowly seep away, now that he was free of the house. There was a soft little breeze in the warm air. It plucked gently at the rich green leaves of the large oak trees overhanging the path leading away from the house as Blake started down it.

Blake reached the barn as the first rays of golden sun peeped over the rim of the hill, gilding the valley in variegated shades of gold. He saddled Blackjack and was starting to lead him out of the barn when he heard the soft crackling of footsteps over the hay-strewn floor. Reacting with pure instinct, Blake whirled, hand on the butt of his gun, and found himself face to face with Miguel.

"Can I help you with something, senor?" Miguel asked softly.

Miguel was dressed much as he had been the first time Blake saw him, and the thought crossed Blake's mind that Miguel could just as easily be coming in as getting ready to go out for the day. It was impossible to tell. His bronze face was inscrutable, showing no surprise at Blake's rather strange actions.

"No . . . uh . . . I thought I'd get out and look around a bit. I've a notion to buy some land around here if I can find what I'm looking for," Blake explained, although he was sure word of what he was supposed to be doing in Texas had gotten around to everyone on the ranch by now.

"And just what is it you are looking for, senor?"

155

Blake felt a little uneasy under the scrutiny of those midnight-black eyes. "Good cattle land," he finally managed to reply.

"There is so much good land throughout Texas."

"Yes, I'm sure there is. And if I don't find what I'm looking for here, I'll probably try somewhere else. I have plenty of time."

"I would think that the death of your partner would be a discouraging thing to you. Many a man would prefer to leave Texas and lay aside his plans under such unfortunate circumstances. Surely it will be very difficult to proceed alone."

Miguel's soft words rankled Blake. They almost sounded like a warning rather than a commiseration.

"Well, difficult or not, I intend to do just that. This is something John and I set out to do, and I'm going to finish the job."

Blake tried to subdue his irritation. Miguel had no way of knowing that Blake was really talking about something entirely different from the phony business about the cattle ranch. Blake knew very well he shouldn't be taking his frustrations out on other people. It wasn't Miguel's fault that he was in a rotten mood this morning. And there was really nothing wrong with what Miguel had said—a fact that further fueled Blake's unreasonable mood.

Blake reasoned that the tinge of bitterness he heard in Miguel's voice could be chalked up to the fact that Miguel was an exile from his own country. His fortunes were probably tied up in Mexico, and he might never again have the chance to own land himself. Blake had to admit he'd probably be angry, too, under those circumstances. Especially when some stranger was spouting about how he was looking to buy thousands of acres of prime land if the notion struck him. Yes, Blake could see how that would make a proud man like Miguel more than slightly bitter.

"Well, I'd best be on my way," Blake said, anxious to end the conversation and escape from the pressures bedeviling him. He needed space and time to come to terms with the confusion of emotions whirling in his head. And, he had to admit, he was in no mood to deal with Miguel at this time. Although Blake couldn't put his finger on a particular reason, the man made him decidedly uncomfortable.

"Perhaps you will find all that you are looking for—and more," Miguel commented in that soft, black-velvet voice of his, and then he turned and walked away.

Blake rolled his eyes in annoyance. What the hell was that supposed to mean? Was he overreacting again? Or was that simply Miguel's strange way of wishing him luck?

Blake gave a world-weary sigh and led Blackjack out into the misty morning. He mounted up quickly, anxious to be on his way.

It was long past dark when Blake returned to the ranch. He put Blackjack in his stall, taking the time to rub him down and give him an extra handful or two of oats. He felt pleasantly exhilarated from his long day in the saddle, although he hadn't done much more than reconnoiter the surrounding territory.

Blake had accomplished one small goal: striking up an acquaintanceship with some of the ranch workers. He had spotted a half dozen of Anthony's hands while riding through one broad meadow and had veered across to join them. Their English had run the gamut from broken to nonexistent, but Blake had managed to talk with some of them for a good while. They had all seemed pleasant enough, friendly and open in their conversation.

Although he didn't dare ask any outright questions,

they didn't appear to be aware of any strange goings-on around Washington-on-the-Brazos or the surrounding area. Blake had the feeling that they didn't get into town too often anyway, spending most of their time on the ranch and saving their money to send for their families.

He slipped in the rear door of the house and then through the door leading directly into the broad entry hall, hoping to reach his room without being noticed. All he wanted now was to be left alone so he could mull over the day's results. And, although he didn't want to admit it, he simply wasn't ready to face seeing Laura yet.

But his plan didn't work.

"Senor Saunders? Blake, is that you?" Maria called in her throaty manner.

"Damn!" muttered Blake, reluctantly taking his foot off the first step of the staircase. "Yes, ma'am." He pulled his hat from his head and walked reluctantly into the parlor, where the two women sat.

"Did you have a pleasant day, Blake?" Maria asked courteously. She rose from the big chair she had been curled in and walked over to the massive carved chest that held the whiskey decanters, her dark-green satin gown swayed seductively with each step. "Come, let me get you something to drink." Her hand was poised over the crystal containers. "What would you like?"

"I really should go upstairs first and clean up a bit, ma'am. It was a long, dusty day." He ran his hand self-consciously across the course stubble of beard that shadowed his face in a hint of the same luxuriant brown as his mustache.

"Of course, Blake. You do just that. But I insist that you join us afterward. It's so boring here with Antonio gone," Maria said with a sultry little pout. "We will be pleased to have your company to break up the monotony of our evening. Won't we, Laura?" And she smiled sweetly in Laura's direction.

Blake's gaze darted to the small quiet figure on the far end of the sofa. He had studiously avoided looking at Laura since he entered the room.

Her gown of rich blue shimmered in the soft amber candlelight. It was the exact beguiling color of her eyes. The gently rounded bodice dipped low on creamy shoulders, displaying a tantalizing view of the shadowy hollow between her breasts. The full skirt flared gently from her tiny waist, flowing in soft whispery folds to the floor, where the dainty toe of one small slipper peeped from under the hem.

She turned her head ever so slightly in his direction. Her chin tipped up in the beguilingly familiar manner he remembered so well, making his heart thump painfully against his ribs. Their eyes met and held for a long moment before she answered.

"Yes, of course, Blake. Please join us." She spoke so softly that he almost couldn't distinguish her words.

He forced a bright smile, reluctantly dragging his gaze back to Maria. "Well, in that case, I'll just have to hurry up. I could hardly turn down the company of two such lovely ladies, now, could I?"

"Rosita has bathwater heating," Maria told him. "I'll tell her to have the boys bring the things up to your room."

"Thank you," he managed to say and then bolted from the parlor, muttering silent imprecations all the way to his room.

Well, so much for his hope to postpone seeing Laura for a few days. He had thought this might enable the embarrassment of their last afternoon together to fade. But there was no way he could gracefully get out of Maria's invitation—not unless he wanted to raise her curiosity, maybe even to the point that she would say something to Anthony.

What an ugly mess it would be if Anthony even

suspected what had happened!

No, Blake had to carry on with a semblance of normalcy, no matter how difficult it was for him to be around Laura. Maybe, he thought ironically, this was his punishment for allowing his emotions to overrule his head.

It was just a matter of minutes after he reached his room before the boys who had taken care of the baggage on their arrival struggled through the door with a tin tub, then scurried out to quickly return with heavy buckets of water. As soon as they dumped the steamy liquid into the tub, they left again, closing the door firmly behind them.

Blake stripped off his clothing and stepped gingerly into the heated water. He hunkered down, his tall muscular frame almost overflowing the small tub. His knees stuck up comically, and he had to dip his head awkwardly between them to rinse the soap from his thick tawny curls.

With much splashing and twisting and turning he managed to complete his bath. Amid mutters and moans he vowed to visit the pond far behind the house next time. There was simply no dignified way for a man his size to wash in the dainty little tub.

Now Laura's slim supple body would fit in it just fine.

Stop that! he chided himself angrily. He couldn't allow such thoughts even to begin.

He struggled up out of the water, sloshing a good deal of it out onto the floor. "Hellfire and damnation!" he cursed as he grabbed a towel, quickly dried himself, and then knelt to mop up the puddles around the tub before they marred the glossy sheen of the highly waxed wood.

He crossed to the chest and readied his shaving things, standing naked in the soft warmth of the night while he peered intently into the mirror, pursing his mouth crookedly this way and that as he drew the razor across his face. The sleek muscles in his arms and across his

160

broad back bunched and slid under the golden texture of his skin as he raked away the raspy whiskers until his skin was soft and smooth again.

He turned to the wardrobe. The ladies were dressed elegantly, and good manners demanded that he do the same. He selected pale cream trousers and a crisp white shirt. He topped these with a cocoa-colored satin vest that was embroidered over with light stitching and a coat of rich brown, then sat on the bed to draw on Wellington boots of the softest leather.

Raking the brush through his tousled curls one more time, with great reluctance he went to join the ladies.

When he entered the room Maria smiled up at him in her most charming manner. "Ah, there you are. Are you hungry, Blake? I'm afraid Laura and I have already eaten. Would you like me to have Rosita fix you something?"

"No, please don't bother. She packed me a huge sack of food for the day. I'm fine, really."

"And how did your day go? Did you travel very far?" Maria asked, her eyes bright with interest.

"I really just spent the day getting the feel of the land. Tomorrow I'm going to ride out a little further, perhaps to stop to talk with some of the neighbors."

"Yes, that would be nice. We have some very nice neighbors." Maria's face brightened suddenly. "You will both have a chance to meet them soon. There is to be a ball in town next week. Everyone in the county will attend."

"Oh, how nice," said Laura. "Will Anthony be back in time?"

"But of course he will," replied Maria with an almost sullen downturn of her pretty mouth. "He knows how I love parties."

Blake barely listened to the ladies as he mulled the news over in his head. He was almost pleased at the prospect. It might work out very much to his benefit, he thought. It would give him ample opportunity to talk with a greater number of people than he could on his daily rides.

"Speaking of town, maybe I'll ride over to Washington in a day or two," he commented when the ladies finally fell silent.

"Oh?" His statement had caught Maria's attention.

"Yes, I thought I might talk with Thomas Matthews and see if he's heard any news about the ambush."

"Well, if that is the case, perhaps I can persuade you to take the wagon so that Laura and I can ride along with you."

"Oh . . . uh . . . sure, I guess so." Oh, great! Just what he needed! Here he was, trying to stay away from Laura, and Maria was thinking up this little shopping excursion—just one more stumbling block to overcome in his determination to stay away from Laura. Why hadn't he kept quiet about his plans? Well, it was too late now. There was simply no graceful way to get out of it.

Blake chanced a quick glance to see what Laura's reaction was, but she quickly averted her eyes before voicing her opinion.

"I . . . I really don't want to bother Blake. I'm sure he's much too busy," Laura said rather timidly.

Maria's gown rustled softly as she got up and poured herself another glass of sherry. "But, wouldn't you like a chance to go into town, Laura? Surely with the ball coming up, there are a few small things you need from the store."

"Oh . . . yes . . . yes, of course. That would be pleasant, but we shouldn't impose on Blake—"

"Nonsense. Blake doesn't mind. Do you?" Maria dimpled prettily in Blake's direction.

"No, of course not," Blake managed to say, all the while wishing he could throttle Maria.

"See there, Laura? We will have such a lovely time. I

very much miss all the parties and socials that were held in San Antonio. There was always something to do. It is so boring here most of the time," Maria said petulantly. She stopped, her mouth a round little O of surprise as she realized what she had said. She forced her mouth into the semblance of a smile. "But, of course, I would not trade my darling Antonio for all the balls in the state."

Maria gave a nervous little laugh and pushed restlessly at the thick mane of midnight-black hair that curled about her face and down her back. "But tell me, Blake, you dance, do you not? I am so looking forward to dancing with you. Antonio does not care for dancing very much. It will be very pleasant to have someone new at the party. You must show me all the new dances they are doing in the East."

Maria smiled at Blake in her sultry fashion, and Laura thought that she looked rather like a hungry cat peering at a grounded bird.

"Sure, I'd be happy to," Blake replied. Might as well make the best of a bad situation, he thought, trying hard to sound properly enthusiastic.

Laura's embarrassment at Blake's arrival was slowly turning to anger. All he'd done since coming into the room was fawn over Maria! And the thought of Blake and Maria dancing while Anthony quietly looked on really rankled Laura. A married lady ought to be happy to stay at her husband's side, not gad about looking for new dancing partners, Laura fumed.

Laura felt certain she could have disappeared in a puff of smoke for all Blake and Maria would care. They were so all-fired interested in discussing the silly old ball! Why, Blake hadn't said more than two words to her since coming in the room. He could at least be polite enough to include her in the conversation.

Well, she'd show him! She'd *make* him talk to her. She certainly wasn't going to give him the pleasure of

163

thinking that he bothered her in the least.

"I'm sure Blake will be more than pleased to show you absolutely everything he knows," Laura said in a voice like maple syrup. "Now, do tell us all about your day, Blake. We'd just love to hear about it." And she batted her eyelashes at him in the most provocative manner she could manage.

Blake swallowed uncomfortably, his eyes darting back and forth between the two women, feeling somewhat like a butterfly pinned to an exhibit board. He slipped a finger inside his collar, which suddenly felt too tight, and then cleared his throat twice.

Was there something more to the blue fire in Laura's eyes than simply what had passed between them the other afternoon?

Lord, he wished Anthony would come home.

Laura heard small sounds from Blake's room and knew he was getting dressed for another day away from the house. She almost wished he wouldn't go.

Oh, there was no doubt it was easier on her to not be around him so much. The time she had to spend in his company every evening, smiling and chatting pleasantly to keep Maria from realizing anything was wrong, was almost more than she could bear. But somehow it was worse when he was gone.

It was so quiet at the house with both Blake and Anthony away. And Maria never stirred from her room until almost noon. Laura couldn't understand how anyone could sleep so late every morning.

Laura might as well have had the house all to herself for all the company Maria was during the day. But come the night, Maria would descend the stairs, dressed in still another elegant gown. All she lacked was an appreciative audience—and she certainly had that as soon as Blake arrived every evening, Laura thought with irritation.

Laura had spent her free time roaming the house, inspecting the rooms. She had been happy to discover a stack of books in Anthony's office at the back of the house and selected several to carry with her to help pass the afternoon. But that wasn't going to be enough to keep her busy for long.

Laura wasn't used to such inactivity. When she and Cynthia didn't have lessons at Miss Peabody's, they were shopping or calling on friends or entertaining. And Aunt Mary could always find something for them to do—sewing or small lessons in cooking—things that any proper lady should know to run a home some day.

Late that morning Laura, bored, closed the book she'd been reading. She climbed the stairs to her room and put on her riding clothes, deciding that she could at least ride by herself in the broad valley surrounding the house. She should certainly be safe enough with all the ranch hands coming and going.

She stopped in the kitchen to let Rosita know where she was going and then made her way down the narrow path, grateful for the feel of the warm sun on her face after the gloom of the house.

In the barn her footsteps made funny little swishy sounds through the hay as she peered into the stalls, trying to remember which horse Anthony had said she could ride. She finally recognized the white blaze on Sugar's forehead when the horse thrust her long nose over the stall door and whinnied at Laura.

"There you are!" Laura exclaimed, rubbing the horse's velvety nose, suddenly very happy at the thought of escaping the quiet of the house. Then she realized that someone would have to saddle the horse for her. Blake had done it last time. "Oh, drat!"

There was nothing that she could do but go find one of the men to perform the chore for her. And she vowed to watch carefully this time so she could do it herself in the future. She patted the horse affectionately and went looking for help.

Laura exited through a small side door near the back of the barn, picking her way carefully past Midnight's empty corral as she searched for help. Fleetingly she wondered if Anthony had taken the magnificent stallion to Austin. There wasn't a soul in sight.

She retraced her steps, cutting back through the dusky interior of the barn. She still didn't see anyone when she walked out of the big double doors at the front of the barn. She was just about to give up and return to the house when she heard the muted sound of voices. She followed the rutted path around the far side of the barn. As she neared the back corner of the building, the voices grew louder. She hurried toward the sound, eager to find help and be on her way.

Just as she was about to turn the last corner, the bellicose tone of the man's voice slowed her footsteps. He was speaking in a mixture of rapid-fire Spanish and accented English, his voice low and filled with anger.

Laura hesitated, not sure whether she should interrupt whatever was going on. And then she was startled by the sound of Maria's voice.

How strange. She hadn't thought Maria had even come downstairs yet today. The tone of Maria's voice also betrayed her angry mood. It was obvious Maria was having quite an argument with someone.

Laura stood very still for a moment, thinking that she should turn around and walk quietly away. But her curiosity finally got the best of her, and she peeked around the edge of the weathered boards.

Two figures stood very close together in the shadows between the barn and a stand of large oak trees. Maria and Miguel.

Miguel towered over Maria's small form, his eyes

dark and stormy as he spit out fiery words. "*I* will be the one to decide! Don't you ever presume to—"

"Presume!" Maria hissed. "How dare you! If it weren't for me, you would have only dreams instead of an opportunity to make them come true!"

"No one is indispensable, Maria. You would do well to remember that." Miguel's voice was so soft that Laura could hardly distinguish the words, and as he uttered them he turned away, fury contained beneath his regal bearing.

Maria gasped and her small hands reached for him, plucking at Miguel's arm with something akin to desperation. He turned back, grasping her shoulders in both hands. He gave her a vicious little shake, and his head bent low over her upturned face as he softly issued another warning.

A gamut of emotions flowed over Maria's beautiful face. When she spoke again it was in Spanish, her tone gentle and cajoling. Her hands had been pinned against Miguel's chest when he grabbed her, and as her soft words began to work their spell, his hold gradually loosened. Maria reached to lay one tiny palm against the bronze sheen of his cheek.

Suddenly embarrassed at eavesdropping on the strange confrontation, Laura whirled away from the sight, her back flat against the sun-warmed boards of the barn. She gave herself a sound mental thrashing for being such a snoop and then hurried back toward the house, regretfully giving up the pleasure of a ride. Whatever was going on, it was certainly none of her business.

Nagging little questions dogged her hurried footsteps as Laura attempted to decipher what she'd overheard. Was Maria sorry that she'd prevailed on Anthony to give Miguel the job of foreman? Did Miguel's words mean that he was planning to leave Anthony's service to work for someone else? Or maybe he wanted to establish his own

167

place. Either way, Anthony would certainly be left in a bind. Heavens! It was all so very confusing.

Should she tell Anthony about the confrontation? No. Better not. He had enough to worry about, without the added burden of a family feud between his wife and her cousin.

Chapter 17

Indigo shadows crept slowly across the valley as Laura clucked to her horse, urging the mare carefully around the tumbled rocks that dotted the crest of hill she had just explored and then down the gentle slope of its side. She shaded her eyes against the blazing ball of light hanging low in the sky, its golden brilliance taking on shades of rose and lavender and pink as night approached. It was time to turn back toward home.

It had been so wonderful to escape the confines of the house the past few hours that Laura hated the thought of going back. But she knew she had put off returning as long as she could.

The ebbing rays of the sun painted violet and coral splashes across the high white billows of cloud in the deepening cerulean sky. Much as she wanted to prolong her pleasant amblings through the large shallow basin of land that cradled Anthony's home, she could tarry no longer. She'd be lucky to reach the house before nightfall as it was. And she really didn't want to be out alone after dark, even though she felt safe enough in the shelter of the little valley.

Laura gave a small sigh of resignation and prodded Sugar's flanks, turning her gentle mount toward the road. Swaying gently with the rhythmic roll of Sugar's broad back, she sat easily in the saddle as the horse plodded her way slowly homeward. The soft creak of leather, the fragrant aroma of fresh pine, new grass, and riotous wildflowers soothed Laura's spirit.

Like a child turned loose in a fairyland, she had eagerly ventured to the sun-dappled tops of the rolling hills to view the beauty of the surrounding countryside, and then through the beckoning shadows of the numerous scattered stands of timber that dotted the land. She had been amazed at the endless variety of foliage: ash, oak, cedar, and a dozen other trees she couldn't name; thick climbing vines, dense low bushes, wild scatterings of flowers of every hue and color. She had eagerly absorbed the new sights and sounds and smells, taking special delight in the infrequent glimpses of the small furry animals that populated the valley.

The trail she followed was little more than a beaten path leading across the northeast end of Anthony's valley, used occasionally by the ranch hands as they rode to the distant meadows in search of the lean, longhorned cattle that roamed freely over her brother's land. Laura knew there was little if any steady traffic through the area because the narrow path lacked the telltale three ruts created by wagon wheels and horses' hooves.

The road rounded one last small rise and disappeared into a broad thicket of trees and shrubs, skirting the edge of a large pond before angling back toward the house. The woods were thick and tangled, the setting sun barely penetrating the shadowy green world beneath the sheltering boughs. The powdery red dirt of the trail muffled the sounds of Sugar's hooves as she ambled along.

Laura smiled at the antics of a squirrel high in a tall pecan tree as he scampered from branch to branch, stopping occasionally to peer down at her, bushy tail held high. Shiny little shoe-button eyes watched her suspiciously, and he chattered sharply at her intrusion. Bright flashes of green and yellow and pale red marked the swift passage of wild parakeets inside the sheltered little grove. The tranquility was broken only by the soft sough of the wind, the chittering of the squirrels, and the pleasant melodic trill of the birds calling in the dusk.

The thick tangle of foliage thinned out a bit, and Laura could see a portion of the shimmering surface of the pond through a small leaf-fringed opening. She reined Sugar in, stealing one last moment of freedom, enchanted by the rippling reflections of the orange and rose and gold sunset on the mirrored surface of the water. It looked like a rainbow had been plucked from the sky and caught in the cool blue depths.

A small movement caught her eye. She brushed aside the low hanging branch that obstructed her view of the grassy bank. There in a little clearing at the edge of the pond stood Blake.

With quick leonine movements he shed his clothes and walked briskly toward the water. And in the space of a heartbeat Laura was lost to reality, caught up in a misty Edenlike time where only the fundamental naturalness of life reigned. There was no here and now, no right or wrong; only the pure innocent pleasure of viewing something of grace and beauty.

The dying rays of the sun gilded Blake's skin, sprinkling the fine silken hair on his body with gold dust. He might have been some beautiful pagan god descended to earth.

Laura's breath caught in her throat. Having never seen a naked man before, nothing in her sheltered world had prepared her for the strange feelings that welled up at the sight of Blake. Instead of being shocked or ashamed, she could only think that he looked magnificent, a thing of natural splendor, which belonged in the wild beauty of this place.

She marveled at the soft flow of muscles beneath the sun-kissed skin, the strength manifested in the broad shoulders and muscular legs, the sweetly vulnerable dip at the small of his back before it flared into firm buttocks.

His powerful, well-muscled body moved with easy grace as he walked across the clearing. Fascinated, she watched the satiny flex of his long sinewy legs, the intriguing clench of richly rounded haunches as he walked into the water.

Suddenly Sugar shifted her weight and a branch cracked under her hoof. Laura's heart slammed against her ribs as Blake's head snapped up at the sound, and he turned to stare in her direction. She scarcely dared draw a breath while those haunting dark eyes flickered over the woods that sheltered her. He paused a long moment, poised at the edge of the water: a magnificent male animal, head cocked slightly to the side.

A strange flame kindled in the pit of Laura's stomach, and its disturbing warmth slowly flowed through her veins. The shallow breaths she had been taking in an effort to remain silent were making her light-headed. She pressed the heels of her hands against her eyes and fought to still her quickening heartbeat. It's only the heat, she assured herself. She'd been out too long under the hot Texas sun. That's all. When she lifted her eyes again, Blake had entered the water.

When he was waist deep he gracefully executed a shallow dive, disappearing under the color-drenched water for a long moment. Tiny wavelets rippled across the mirrored surface, spreading across the pool to lap gently at the emerald banks.

A long-held breath whooshed from Laura's lungs as she gratefully realized she was safe from Blake's prying eyes. But would she ever be safe from the wild emotions that raked her soul because of the man?

With a trembling hand she pushed a stray tendril of hair away from her suddenly damp forehead. Thank goodness Blake hadn't been able to see her through the thick foliage! Laura tightened her hold on the reins in preparation to leave, but the stillness of the pond's surface bothered her. Hadn't he been down too long? Her worried gaze raked the mirrored expanse of the pond. Was something wrong? Eyes wide with concern, she anxiously searched for signs of Blake's underwater passage through the deep-blue depths. A flood of relief washed through her body when he surfaced far out in the center of the pond, tossing his head to fling diamond bright droplets of water into the air.

Tiny butterfly tingles flowed through Laura's veins, and she was shocked at the sudden overwhelming longing to shed her inhibitions along with her clothing and join Blake, to let the cooling waters wash over her heated skin.

She struggled with her warring emotions until finally good sense prevailed. Laura knew she must leave the grove or she would lose what small tenuous hold on decorum she still possessed.

Tapping her heels into the soft hollows of Sugar's sides, she tugged gently at the reins as the mare stubbornly continued to nip daintily at the lush green grass edging the road. Sugar flickered her ears, gave an irritated snort at being denied her snack, and finally turned her attention to the packed red earth trail.

Laura caught a last glimpse of Blake stroking through the shimmering waters toward the far bank. He looked blissfully unaware of her clandestine observance. Sugar had only to take a few steps and the pond was once again obstructed from Laura's view by the curtain of tangled green boughs.

Laura rode quietly, a curious mist fogging her mind. She probed at her conscience, mystified that a peculiar

173

longing far outweighed any feelings of guilt that pricked at her conscience. It seemed such a disconcerting contradiction to her upbringing.

Why did she desire this man so desperately when she loved another? She didn't begin to understand; she only knew that she did. Each moment alone with him heightened the addiction she felt to his kisses, his caresses. Unwilling and unable to decipher the strange feelings at this time, she pushed the disturbing thoughts deep in her mind, knowing only that she should avoid Blake at any cost—put him from her mind once and for all. But within moments her willful mind once again called up the memory of Blake at the pond: the magnificent golden beauty of his long, lean body. His wraith haunted her as she rode homeward, tormenting her with unknown desires.

The parlor seemed stifling to Laura. It had become too close, too confining the moment Blake had entered it. Her gaze turned longingly toward the tall open windows. How she wished she could escape—escape the overheated atmosphere of the room, escape Maria's silly chattering, but most of all escape the uncomfortable tension that seemed to pluck relentlessly at her nerves every time Blake appeared.

Laura cut her eyes surreptitiously at Blake, stealing small nervous glances in his direction far more often than she wanted to. Maria had managed to seat herself on the sofa next to Blake—much to Laura's relief at the time—and she had chattered incessantly throughout the evening, reaching with maddening frequency to lay a dainty hand upon his coat sleeve in punctuation of some brilliant bit of conversation. Laura had little to do throughout the evening but mumble an occasional "yes" or "no" when Maria managed to remember she was in the room and addressed some pointless remark Laura's way.

Laura had known immediately that she was in for a long uncomfortable night when Blake entered the parlor that evening, elegantly dressed and groomed. His hair was still damp from his dip in the pond, and Laura had quickly ducked her head, blushing furiously as vivid memories once again sprang into her mind. The guilt, which had been so strangely absent before, had descended on her full force. She'd barely managed to stutter a reply to his quiet greeting. The next time she had looked in Blake's direction, he'd been watching her intently, his dark eyes dancing mischievously.

Laura squirmed uncomfortably, the resulting rustle of her gown sounding alarmingly loud in the suddenly still room. Blake darted a quick glance in her direction. She dared not meet his gaze. What in the world would Blake think of her if he knew that she had seen him? Worse yet, what would he think if he knew the feelings that had raged within her while she watched him? And, Lord, what would William think if he knew what she had done—and felt?

Puzzling over the strange emotions that plagued her all through the uncomfortable hours in the parlor, she vacillated between almost total disregard for the other occupants of the room and a blazing awareness of Blake's presence and Maria's coy flirting.

Dredging up her feelings of love for William, Laura tried to picture his familiar form. She struggled to visualize his lean, aristocratic face, the aquiline nose, the dark locks shading his high smooth brow, but the picture was distorted, like the wavy image in a defective looking glass.

It was almost midnight when Laura could stand no more. "I'm exceedingly tired, Maria. I do hope you'll excuse me." Blake started to rise. "No!" Laura blurted. "Uh . . . please keep your seat, Blake. I wouldn't want to spoil the evening for you and Maria. I'll just slip off to bed."

"Bed sounds like a wonderful idea to me, too," he replied. Laura frowned at the almost amused tone of his voice. Was he teasing her again? "Good night, Maria." He bowed slightly toward his hostess and then followed Laura from the room.

Devastated that her ploy hadn't worked, Laura all but scurried up the stairs. It was no use. Blake's long legs kept up with her every step of the way. In her haste to escape the parlor she'd forgotten to bring a lamp to light her way. The darkness closed around the two figures like a velvet cape, relieved only slightly by the fluttering candlelight from the wall sconce at the end of the hall.

She was almost there. Laura quickened her pace. Her hand eagerly closed around the doorknob. Sanctuary! Another moment and she'd be safe in her room.

"Laura." Blake's whisper cut through the shadows.

She longed to fling the door open and slip through to safety, but her body refused to obey. Her skirt rustled loudly as she turned to face him in the indigo shadows.

He moved a step closer, and her heart thudded erratically against her breast.

"What . . . what do you want?" she asked hoarsely, afraid he'd tell her, afraid he wouldn't.

He leaned toward her. His breath fanned across her face. His hand came up to fondle the curl that lay against her cheek. "I just wanted to tell you good night."

"Oh." Her voice was a breathy whisper in the dark. Was there a tinge of disappointment in the softly murmured word?

"And to do this."

Mesmerized, she watched his lips descend toward her. Head tilted back on the slender column of her throat, her eyes fluttered shut. The gentle whisk of his mustache tickled the seam of her lips, and then his mouth captured

176

hers. His arms enfolded her, wrapping around her so tightly that she could feel the hard strength of his body through the restrictive layers of her clothing.

He pinned her against the wall, shifting his weight so that his legs bracketed hers. One hand swept down her back to the soft swell of buttocks so he could lock her even tighter against him. The other trailed its way from the nape of her neck, across her shoulders, to splay against the lush swell of her breast. She groaned in sweet agony as the nipple under his palm hardened with desire.

His lips found the pulse beat at the base of her throat, his tongue flicking down the satiny skin until he could nuzzle against the lace-edged bodice of her gown. Her back arched. Her body cried for the feel of his lips on her breast. Her hands tangled in the curls at the nape of his neck, urging him on in wild abandon.

A moan escaped her lips when she realized what she was doing. She slid her hands back down his lapels and pushed with all her might against the broad barrier of his chest. "Stop it!" she pleaded. "Don't do that. I don't want you to!"

"Liar," he taunted gently, raining kisses across her throat. "My sweet little liar."

"I'm not lying." Her words were a soft whimper. "I want you to leave me alone."

"Why deny it? You want me just as bad as I want you," he whispered against her throat.

"No," she moaned, shaking her head. "I don't. I don't." Her heart thudded painfully against her breast. Each breath seared her throat as she gulped for oxygen.

"I know better."

She eyed him with alarm. "How can you possibly say such a thing?"

Blake grinned wickedly. "I saw you."

"You . . . you what?"

"I . . . saw . . . you." The words were drawled out in

177

the most aggravating manner.

Laura's mouth dropped open. "You . . . you dirty rotten skunk! You have no more manners than an alley cat!" Her eyes glittered with blue fire. With an angry twist of her shoulders she quickly slipped out of his arms and through her door.

She could hear Blake's roguish laughter even over the resounding slam of her door.

"Hurry up, Laura!" Maria called up the stairs. "The wagon is ready and Blake's waiting on us." Her smartly tailored day dress swished softly against the golden planks of the hall floor as she paced restlessly.

"I'm coming!" Laura's answer was a bit grumpy. She knew she had delayed as long as she could. Gathering her skirts high, she ran quickly down the stairs. "My goodness, what's the hurry? We have all day." She plopped her bonnet on the mass of upswept curls, tying the blue satin ribbon in a pert bow at the side of her chin as she grudgingly followed Maria out into the early morning sunlight.

Blake leaned lazily against the wheel of the wagon, arms folded across his chest as he peered into the distance. At the click of their heels on the broad veranda, he pushed himself away from the wagon, standing almost at attention as they swooped down the porch steps. Laura's heart set up an erratic beat at the sight of him.

"We do *not* have all day to dally." Maria gave an irritated sniff and tossed her head. "I have many things to do in town, and I must allow enough time to visit my seamstress—my ball gown should be ready for a final fitting."

Maria stopped her complaining long enough to cast a sultry smile in Blake's direction. She extended her hand regally so he could help her into the wagon and then leisurely settled herself at the center of the wagon seat, smoothing her skirt and adjusting her saucy little bonnet with small, precise movements.

Blake turned to help Laura, and she frowned in irritation at the amused tilt of his mouth. Her embarrassed gaze slid away until it rested just to the left of his ear as he took her hand. She paid careful attention to the task at hand, as if hoisting her skirts out of the way and climbing onto the wagon were the most important challenges she'd ever faced. She breathed a little sigh of relief when Blake turned as soon as she was settled and made his way around the back of the wagon.

With easy grace he climbed up and took his seat, snatching up the reins and giving them a flick over the horse's back. "Giddup," Blake urged in a slightly strangled voice.

Laura darted an annoyed glance his way. Was he smothering a laugh? The wagon gave a small jerk and then rolled down the road. Grabbing for the side of the wagon, she bit back a most unladylike word.

It was a beautiful day. Their trip was pleasant and uneventful enough that Laura finally began to relax and look forward to the day in town. For the most part, she tried to ignore Blake and Maria, leaving them to their chattering. She spent her time agonizing over the drastic changes in her life during the past few months.

She had so hoped to hear from William by this time—rather unrealistically, so it seemed. The hazy dreams she had concocted back East had never progressed much further than a short time of sanctuary with Anthony in Texas and then a blissful return to her old hometown as William's betrothed. How foolish she'd been!

It rather hurt her pride to admit that she might never receive that longed-for letter from William. Despite this, she still stubbornly clung to the belief that she could have won William's heart and his name if Uncle Henry's

179

horrendous manipulations hadn't precipitated her hasty flight.

But it appeared that time and distance were going to snatch away whatever elusive opportunity she might have had. There were dozens of other girls in her circle of friends who also had swooned over William's tall, dark good looks. Any number of them could have set their cap for him by now, and there was absolutely nothing she could do about it.

Reality intruded on Laura's daydreams as the wagon bounced over a rough spot, and she was jostled against Maria's shoulder. Perhaps it was time to stop pinning her hopes of happiness on William and get on with her life. But what would that entail?

Well, whatever happened, she certainly had no intention of imposing on Anthony's charity for too long. Yes, she was definitely going to have to make some decisions about her future—a future that just conceivably might not include William Stratford.

Laura had no idea what a young unmarried woman might do in Texas to earn her own keep, but she supposed it was time to find out. Her schooling had been quite complete. She wondered if those skills could be put to use. Surely there was a great need for teachers in Texas, especially in the rural areas.

Were the children sent into town for schooling? Did the town already have a teacher? Could some sort of school be established at the ranch for those who lived too far from town? She sighed dejectedly when she thought of the vast distances between families where Anthony lived. Besides, she didn't relish the thought of moving into town just yet, even if they did need a teacher. She'd had so little time with Anthony. She hated the thought of leaving the ranch and being able to see her brother only infrequently.

What was it Anthony had said at dinner the night

before he left for Austin? Something about the book work at the ranch never getting done, never having enough time to see to all the tallies and accounts properly. Laura had excelled in mathematics at school, pursuing the challenge of figures with such enthusiasm that Mrs. Peabody had grumbled that it wasn't quite ladylike.

A surge of excitement rekindled her good spirits. She could at least offer to keep Anthony's books. That would help repay him for taking her in, and it would also alleviate the boredom and moodiness she had been experiencing lately. She squirmed restlessly on the hard plank seat, wishing Anthony would hurry home so she could talk to him about her idea.

The trip between Anthony's and the town seemed much shorter this time. Laura was flooded with memories when the road they were traveling came to a junction and then merged with another. She turned her gaze silently back down the left fork of the road, thoughts of the day she and Blake had traveled it together whirling in her head.

Lord, how things had changed since she left Galveston! Her whole life had turned topsy-turvy. She sighed and turned her attention to the road ahead once again. In just a matter of minutes the wagon dipped down the bank of the Brazos and rolled to a stop at the ferry landing.

Amos Hall scrambled up so quickly when they arrived at the ferry that his little bench teetered and then fell over with a resounding thud. He snatched his hat from his head.

"Howdy, Mrs. Nichols," he said and then bobbed his head politely in Blake and Laura's direction. His watery blue eyes widened considerably when he suddenly recognized them as the two bedraggled travelers he had ferried across just last month. His mouth fell open and his ever-present matchstick fell out.

181

Laura watched his reaction, remembering her first entry into Washington. Amos blinked twice and then quickly scrambled to help Blake load the wagon onto the ferry. Laura considered his response wryly, knowing what a sorry sight she'd been that day: wind blown and sweat stained from their bareback ride. No wonder Amos had been startled.

Laura carefully worked her way to the front of the ferry, where she watched the muddy red water lap at the edges of the craft. When Blake's deep voice cut into her reverie, she forced herself to continue looking straight ahead. But pictures of the days on the coach, the night alone after the ambush, the long ride into town swam in her head; and, much to her dismay, the prime focus of each was Blake Saunders.

Blake left the wagon and horse at the livery stable and escorted the women to the seamstress shop. As soon as they were inside the little store he disappeared to pursue his own endeavors.

"Please be seated," purred the delighted Mrs. Coggins. Maria was by far her best customer. She showed Laura and Maria to a little settee in the corner of the store and then began to drag out bolt after bolt of cloth. "Just look at the wonderful color of this satin! Isn't it marvelous? Such a rich, warm shade. It's just perfect for you, Mrs. Nichols." The seamstress scurried here and there, gathering bits of lace and trim for Maria's consideration.

Maria critically fingered each ribbon and swatch, discoursing endlessly with the prim little proprietress about the possibilities. Within minutes Laura was unbelievably bored with the whole process.

She endured the chattering of the two women as long as she could, smiling until her jaws ached, forcing the correct response to one inane question after another. There had been a time when such things as gowns and fashions had been of vast importance in her life also, but now those things seemed trivial.

How on earth could she worry if a swatch of material was exactly the right color or if velvet was preferable to satin, after having experienced the horror of the raid, the anguish of John's death, the terrifying hours when she'd been afraid that Blake would never wake up and she would be eternally alone?

"Maria, I believe I'll walk down to the hotel and say hello to Elizabeth. She was so nice to me when I was here—"

"Yes, of course," Maria said with an absent wave of her hand, and she returned her rapt attention to a pattern Mrs. Coggins was spreading across the counter.

They were so engrossed with their project that Laura doubted if they even heard the door shut. She hurried down the walk, inordinately pleased to be back in the pleasant little town. The clackety clack of her heels accompanied her down the weathered boardwalk as she passed the general store with its familiar cluster of old men out front.

"Good morning, gentlemen. Lovely day, isn't it?" She nodded and smiled at the group, her saucy little curls bobbing in matching staccato to her footsteps. They offered back a deluge of "howdy, ma'am's" and tipped their hats spryly.

Nat looked up in surprise when she entered the hotel. He shoved aside the papers he was working on and quickly dusted his hands against the seat of his trousers before rounding the counter to greet her.

"Why, Miss Nichols, what a pleasant surprise. We certainly didn't look to see you here so soon again. 'Lizbeth will be so pleased that you've come to visit us. She was talkin' about you just the other day. Anthony bring you to town?"

"No, he's still in Austin."

"Well, come along. 'Lizbeth's in the kitchen." He took

183

her arm and propelled her through the swinging doors and into the dining room. "'Lizbeth! 'Lizbeth, honey, look here. We got company!"

"Nat, you stop that caterwaulin'," Elizabeth scolded as she came out of the kitchen wiping her hands on the tail of her apron. "Why, Laura! How nice to see you."

"Thank you." Laura's mouth turned up in a broad, answering smile. She hadn't realized how lonely she'd been for female companionship until she was subjected to Elizabeth's enthusiastic hug.

"You come right on in this kitchen and let me get through with the noontime dishes. Then we'll have plenty of time to visit. Won't take me a minute."

"All right, but only if you let me help."

"Heavens no! You can't do that. You'll mess up that pretty frock," Elizabeth protested.

"Pooh!" replied Laura smartly. And nothing Elizabeth said could persuade her differently.

Between the two of them they had the kitchen chores finished in record time. Afterward they made themselves comfortable at a small table near the kitchen. The minutes slipped quickly away while they sipped tea, ate crusty golden biscuits and talked.

As the afternoon wore on, Laura followed Elizabeth on her rounds of the hotel. Together they changed linens and tidied rooms while Matilda swept and scrubbed the floors. And all the while they talked and talked and talked.

"You'll have a fine time at the dance," Elizabeth exclaimed with a hearty laugh. "There'll be so many fellas beatin' a path to ask you for a dance, they'll wear a rut in the floor."

Laura laughed in delight at the scene Elizabeth's preposterous statement conjured up in her mind.

"But I suppose you'll be saving most of your dances for that nice Mr. Saunders. If it weren't for my Nat I'd be seeing if I could steal a dance with that handsome beau of yours myself."

Laura quickly protested. "Oh, no. He's not my beau. We simply were on the stagecoach together."

Elizabeth stopped in the process of smoothing a snowy white pillowcase. She stood and gawked at Laura, hands on her ample hips. "You trying to tell me that that Saunders fellow hasn't taken a shine to you? Humph!"

A hot blush stung Laura's cheeks. "Well, no. I don't think so. Anthony just invited him out to the ranch out of courtesy. There's really nothing more to it," she finished lamely, scared that Elizabeth might see right through her meek protest and realize just what a tantalizing role Blake played in Laura's thoughts.

"That's what you think," Elizabeth muttered. "I've seen a passel of men in my time, and I know one that's got 'the look.'"

"My heavens!" Laura laughed nervously. "Whatever are you talking about? What 'look'?"

"Like a lovesick calf, that's what look."

"Ridiculous," declared Laura, although a little thrill tingled through her system.

"Just you wait and see. I can spot 'em a mile off. He's a goner, for sure." Elizabeth sternly patted the pillow into shape and smoothed the bright patchwork quilt.

Thomas Matthews's ancient chair creaked in protest as he leaned back, booted feet propped on the scarred desktop. He watched with quiet interest while Blake paced the length of his office in agitation. The news of two more raids—and apparently by the same band of renegades that had attacked the stagecoach—had upset him considerably.

Blake slammed his fist into the palm of his hand. "But who are they? And where in hell are they holing up in between times?"

"No one seems to know," Matthews replied. He swung his feet down to the floor with a thud. "I've sent word to all the surrounding area, but there's simply no news to be had."

"How can they just disappear like that?"

"Good question." Matthews shrugged his thin shoulders.

Blake stopped pacing long enough to stare at the justice of the peace rather belligerently. "Well, it appears to me that they've got to have some sort of local contact. They were after money when they robbed the stage. Now they're concentrating on stealing guns and ammunition, medical supplies, bedding—that kind of thing. Why? Now I ask you, just what kind of robbers would pass up money for such as that?"

Matthews shrugged again and waited for Blake to continue his angry tirade.

"It just doesn't make sense. And I'd be willing to bet that *someone* is helping them—providing food and shelter. They're sure not stealing those things for themselves."

Blake waited expectantly for Matthews's answer, wondering if the man had any inkling of the pro-Mexican activities Blake had been sent to verify. Blake was almost certain there was a tie between the bandidos and the rumors he'd been sent to check on. There was no other sensible reason for the raiders to be stealing those particular items.

Thomas Matthews nodded his head sagely. "I'm willing to concede that you might be right on that point. It seems pretty plain that they just might be gettin' help from someone."

"Then who the hell is it? Who's helping them? And why? There's more to it than a bunch of cutthroats out for loot! Who's behind all of this?"

"You've met quite a few of our local citizens. Would you be willing to hazard a guess as to which one might be a thief underneath his very respectable reputation—or even a traitor to his country?" Matthews's voice was calm, but it held an underlying edge of hardness.

Blake frowned and rumpled his hair in distraction. He slumped onto the wooden bench at the front of the sparsely furnished room, hands dangling between his widespread knees. "No," he finally said with an agonized sigh. "No, I couldn't do that."

"Well, I can't either. Not now, not yet." Matthews stood up and walked over to where Blake sat. He patted him consolingly on the shoulder. "I know you want to catch those fellas real bad. After all, you've got every right to feel that way after what they did to your friend."

"I just want them caught . . . and punished for what they did."

"I know you do. I'm workin' on it. Just be patient. They're gettin' too brave—too desperate maybe. It's almost like something's pushing at them. Just you wait and see. Someone will spill the beans somewhere along the way. They can't keep gettin' away with their shenanigans forever."

Blake laughed bitterly. "Patience has never been my long suit, but this is one time that I'm not going to give up. I'll get those bastards if it's the last thing I ever do."

When it was time for Elizabeth to begin preparations for the evening meal, Laura reluctantly made her good-byes. The two women exchanged hugs and assurances that they'd see each other soon at the ball, then Laura headed back to find Maria.

Once again Laura nodded pleasantly at the old men hunched over their endless whittling as she passed the general store in search of the seamstress shop.

They watched with interest as she crossed the street, commenting amongst themselves that Anthony's sister was sure a "nice little gal." Oscar Fields even went so far as to allow that she was "purty as a speckled pup." Then he shot a stream of tobacco juice over the rail and once again laid his knife to the willow stick in his hand.

Down the street, Laura stopped outside the store, hesitating with her hand on the doorknob. She finally bent slightly to peer intently into the interior of the small shop, watching Maria and Mrs. Coggins through the wavy glass.

My heavens! Had Maria been here all these hours? Laura might have just left the shop for all the difference she could tell in the two women's activities.

Laura could see the busy movement of their mouths although she couldn't hear their words. She could just imagine the conversation—still more endless discussions on what might or might not be fashionable for any number of functions. Maria's ramblings and exacting perusals of fabric and ribbon had left Laura quite bored that morning. She was loath to return to the shop for more of the same.

Stepping to one side so that she was carefully out of view of the window, Laura tapped a nervous finger against her chin as she contemplated what to do. Her gaze wandered up the short side street, and she spied Blake making his way toward the church. Elizabeth's words rang in her head, and it only took her a second to make up her mind. The temptation to test her friend's theory was too strong. Besides, even at his worst, Blake's company was certainly more appealing than Maria's. She hurried in his direction just as he disappeared from sight.

Raising her skirts higher, she hastened after him. She rounded the corner of the small clapboard church and started to call out his name. Her smile faded quickly when she realized with a shock that he was heading for the town's cemetery, a solitary plot of land surrounded by a small, weathered picket fence.

The sight of Blake standing quietly at the edge of a fresh grave brought her to a sudden stop. His tawny head was bowed, and his nervous fingers turned his hat round and round endlessly as he brooded over the raw mound of earth. John's final resting place.

A persistent little scratching began at the back of Laura's throat. Her eyes burned, and she swallowed hard to rid herself of the thick lump of emotion that lodged in her throat. There was something so forlorn, so heart-rending about the lonely figure before her.

She suddenly felt very guilty about the antagonism between them. What had happened was as much her fault as it was his.

The sad, slightly lost look on his face almost broke her heart. She longed to touch him, to somehow smooth the creases from his brow, to ease the pain he was so obviously feeling.

She wanted desperately to see his mouth curve up in its old familiar smile, see his dark eyes sparkle brightly, hear his laughter ring out. The desire to go to him was strong, but somehow she knew he wouldn't want anyone to see him this way.

She'd leave him alone now, but she vowed that from now on she'd try to be nicer to him.

She turned and slipped quietly away before Blake realized she'd been there.

Chapter 18

The hall was decked with garlands of evergreen twined about with wildflowers. Wooden crosspieces hung from the open rafters, serving as chandeliers. Candles were clustered on window ledges and small tables around the edges of the room, their wavering flames throwing tall dark shadows of the guests against the whitewashed walls. The pleasant scent of hot candle wax and honeysuckle hung in the air.

Two large tables graced one end of the long hall, laden with golden roasted wild turkey, slabs of venison, juicy berry pies, sourdough biscuit and bean sandwiches, and thick chunks of spicy cake. Huge bowls of punch were provided to quench the revelers' thirst, although many of the men would manage to find occasion to slip outside for a nip or two of something a little stronger as the evening progressed.

Two fiddlers, cherished instruments in hand, waited atop a raised platform at the other end of the room for word to begin the music. A group of boisterous young boys clutched clevis brackets and pins, most probably purloined from their papas' wagons, eager to offer their assistance during the more spirited renditions by beating out the time on their makeshift instruments with loud, ringing noise.

The large cleared space in the middle of the room was filled with a restless crowd. They were dressed in everything from satin to buckskin, and all were eager to begin the dancing, which would last until dawn.

"Line up for the Grand March!" called the host, and the people quickly scattered to obey his instructions. The single women, young or old, pretty or plain, were deluged with offers. The large surplus of men, so common to the frontier, framed the floor as they eagerly waited for their chance to dance.

Blake bowed slightly in Laura's direction. "Would you do me the honor?" he inquired and she dimpled prettily, thinking how magnificent he looked tonight in his black frock coat and snowy ruffled shirt. She accepted his hand, and they stepped into place behind Anthony and Maria just as the music began.

The fiddlers drew their bows across their instruments in a long melodic note and then broke into a lively tune. The long line of couples promenaded down the center of the hall, steps resounding smartly against the puncheon floor, and then they followed the leaders in a series of "double-backs" and "under-the-arches" patterns. The march ended with a rousing round of applause from the participants and the onlookers.

Blake escorted Laura off the floor to rejoin Anthony, Maria, Nat, and Elizabeth. As they waited for the music to begin again, Cletus Moore approached the group, a young woman a few years older than Laura trailing in his wake.

"Evenin' folks. I want Olivia to meet Laura. She's really looking forward to having someone close enough to home for occasional visits. I'm afraid it gets a little lonely for Olivia out at the house. Most times there's just me and the hands for company," Cletus explained, placing his arm proudly around the slender shoulders of his pretty daughter.

Laura was immediately drawn to Olivia. There was a feeling of instant rapport, and somehow Laura knew that they were going to be friends. Olivia's pale yellow gown enhanced her soft blond coloring and showed off the slender perfection of her figure. There was something about her that reminded Laura a little bit of Cynthia. But Laura felt quite sure that Olivia wasn't meek and quiet like Cynthia had been. There was a vibrant sparkle to her clear gray eyes, a self-confident tilt to her head. And when she smiled, deep dimples appeared in her cheeks.

"I'm so pleased to meet you," Olivia said, grasping Laura's hands firmly in her own. "Father and I don't live too far from Anthony's eastern boundaries. You must ride over some time soon."

"Oh, I'd love to," Laura answered with great sincerity.

Olivia squeezed Laura's hands in a friendly reassuring manner before releasing them. She cast a quick glance at Anthony and Maria. "Hello, Maria, Anthony. So good to see you again. What a lovely dress, Maria."

"How nice of you to say so," replied Maria, her eyes flickering restlessly about the room.

"You're certainly looking lovely tonight, Olivia," said Anthony, and Olivia's eyes flared brightly at his words. "You'll have to save me a dance."

"Yes, of course I will, Anthony." A rosy pink flush tinged Olivia's cheeks. Her hand fluttered at her throat for a moment.

"You'll have to excuse us, folks. There's Thomas. I need to talk to him about something," interrupted Cletus, waving a plump hand at the justice of the peace across the room to try to get his attention.

Olivia turned toward Laura, a sincere smile on her face. "Now don't forget, Laura, I'll be looking forward to your visit just as soon as you can come."

"So will I," Laura assured her, watching with great

interest the way Olivia's eyes flickered once again in Anthony's direction before she took her father's arm and walked away.

Laura was mulling over the strange scene when the host called out a polka, and young Ben practically bowled them all over in his haste to get to her.

"I'd be right honored to have this dance with you, ma'am," he managed to say in a slightly strangled voice, bobbing his head politely in Laura's direction.

Laura smiled in recognition of the gangling youth who had accompanied Anthony to the hotel that first day in town. Although every bit as tall as Anthony, his face still held the childish contours of boyhood. His eyes were wide with appeal, his downy cheeks highly colored with nervous anticipation. He was all decked out in a suit that would soon be too small for his growing frame, collar stiff and white against the dark material of his jacket. His shoes were polished to a high gloss and, except for a stubborn cowlick, his hair was slicked flat against his head.

"Why, thank you, Ben. I'd be delighted to dance with you," Laura replied sweetly, laying her hand on his shaking arm.

Ben swallowed convulsively, Adam's apple bobbing wildly as he managed to croak out a "thank you." He swelled with pride, cutting his eyes quickly toward a group of his peers to make sure they had noted his good luck. Squaring his shoulders and drawing his height up another good inch, he proudly led her out to the middle of the floor.

Anthony watched the scene and chuckled dryly. "I'm afraid Laura has made a conquest."

Nat surveyed the room, noting the eager eyes of a dozen other young bucks. "And I doubt that it'll be the last one." A smile creased his broad face. He beamed down at Elizabeth as she murmured her agreement, noting that she, too, looked like a fine specimen of womanhood in her dark-blue dress. "Ready for another try at it, Liz?" he questioned, and they moved out onto the floor to join the other dancers.

Blake couldn't help but feel a touch of pride in the attention that Laura was receiving. She deserved every bit of it, he thought, as he watched her with covetous eyes.

Laura looked absolutely ravishing. Her gown was pale lavender, shadowing to amethyst along the softly billowing folds of the skirt in the flickering candlelight. The beguiling expanse of flesh above the low-cut bodice of her dress had a vibrant glow, the soft swell of alabaster bosom shading from pearly pink to dusty rose in the tantalizing valley that dipped beneath the swath of tiny ruffles edging her dress.

Her hair was caught up on top of her head, the fragile nape of her neck bare except for a few wispy tendrils that escaped as she followed Ben in the energetic hippity-hops of the polka. Long curls were gathered high with a bunch of gaily colored ribbons, from deepest purple to palest orchid. Intertwined, they tumbled over her left shoulder and down her back.

Blake continued to watch Laura surreptitiously as one young man after another claimed her for a dance. He shifted restlessly from one foot to another, suddenly feeling stifled in the crowded room. He tried to shake the strange feelings that stirred in his breast, searching his mind for their cause.

Was it because of Laura's unusual demeanor these last few days? Is that why he felt strangely off balance, slightly out of step with the rest of the world? She had been very sweet and surprisingly pleasant each time she had come upon him. He had expected a longer reaction to the scene at the creek, not to mention the night he'd given into impulse and trapped her in the hallway.

This new side of Laura was something of an enigma, and he didn't quite know how to react to her behavior. Was she just being pleasant for Anthony and Maria's sake? Or was there another motive for her actions?

He struggled to feign indifference as she was enticed to the floor time and again to join the festivities, all the while uneasily watching her bestow those radiant smiles on each and every gentleman who partnered her. Blake scowled darkly when he heard the silver tinkle of her laughter above the rumble of the crowd and wondered what such a boring-looking man as the one who was dancing with her could possibly be saying that was so amusing.

In between handshakes and pleasant asides with the many townfolks, he managed to maintain his position at the edge of the floor so he could watch Laura as she gracefully followed her partners in a succession of reels and quadrilles and lancers. Even Amos Hall managed to escape his wife's side long enough for a dance with Laura.

Blake shuffled restlessly when one handsome fellow claimed her for a third dance. His brooding gaze was finally pulled away from the increasingly annoying spectacle of Laura in another man's arms when Maria was escorted from the dance floor by her latest partner and left at his side.

"Blake, you see how my Antonio is. He might just as well have stayed in Austin for all the company he is to me. Just back from a long trip, he gives me one dance and then disappears to talk politics with the men."

Maria tossed her head saucily in the direction where Anthony stood surrounded by a half dozen of the town's leading citizens. "Will you not dance with me? I am bored with old men and young boys. And I am bored with all this talk of war."

"But, of course, I'd be delighted to dance with you," Blake assured her. It was time to get his mind off Laura and back to business anyway. He stood at Maria's side until the next dance was announced and then led her out to the floor to join the lines for a reel.

Maria looked quite beautiful in her rich red dress, overlaid with black lace. Her raven tresses were pulled back in a luxuriant chignon that snuggled tantalizing against her delicate nape, topped by an ornately carved Spanish comb. She had a sultry beauty that drew the eyes of every man in the room. There'd been a time in the not too distant past when Blake would have been very susceptible to her volatile charms, perhaps even to the point of trying to seduce her into a quick tumble.

But, strangely, he seemed to have lost his taste for such shallow diversions. And somehow Maria came off a poor second best in comparison to Laura's fresh young beauty and sweet unaffected ways.

The caller's voice rang out over the wail of the fiddles. "Salute your partners!" The couples danced forward, bowed, and then danced back to their places. "Head couple reel the line!" he called, and Maria and Blake met in the center to link arms and swing each other before moving down the line to partner each of the other dancers.

At the end of the line, Blake took his turn with Laura. His arm bumped softly against the delectable swell of her breast as they linked up and spun in a circle, and his eyes flashed dark with frustration at the thought of any other man being so close to her. He looked down into her face, almost oblivious to the other dancers, noting how rosy her cheeks were, how bright her eyes glowed in the flickering candlelight.

Reluctantly he released Laura's arm and again took Maria's hands to form an arch. Laura and her partner skipped under their raised arms, parting once more on the other side and then doubling back to the end of the line.

Blake's eyes followed Laura's every move as the dance continued.

The reel ended and the fiddlers began another tune. Maria turned toward Blake, arms upheld and ready to accept his claim on her for another dance. Reluctantly he wrenched his gaze away from Laura's retreating figure and turned his attention back to Maria, placing his hand against her small waist as the music began. Bending his head in deference to her tiny stature, he determined once again to put the time to good use.

"Did Anthony learn anything new while he was in Austin? I haven't had much chance to talk with him since his arrival last night and I thought—"

Maria tilted her head back to gaze up at Blake, sultry eyes scanning his face. "Must we continue to discuss this war business?" Her ruby lips turned down in a quick pout, and then she smiled beguilingly up at Blake. "Can we not enjoy the party and put aside such unpleasant thoughts until tomorrow? I am sure that Antonio will be more than happy to tell you all about his trip. After all, there is little else of interest to him but this silly war."

"Does the thought of war bother you, Maria?" Blake questioned suddenly.

"What do you mean?" she asked, her black eyes narrowing slightly.

"The fact that your homeland and Anthony's might soon be at war."

"No, of course not. I came to Texas to escape the constant upheavals in Mexico. I do not regret my decision. I simply would prefer that matters were settled as soon as possible."

"It would almost seem that the Mexican people thrive on such strife. After all, there's been one revolution after another since 1821. Until the Federalists and Centralists settle their differences, I see no hope for a peaceful Mexico."

"What Mexico needs is a strong leader," retorted Maria, a husky zealousness to her voice. "Someone to unite the country under his leadership and restore it to its past glory."

"It was thought for awhile that Santa Anna would be that man. He has certainly surfaced on top of the political situation time and again over the years," Blake said as he whirled Maria across the floor.

"Humph! Santa Anna squandered his chances long ago. He has always been more interested in fine uniforms, money, and his multitude of women than in the welfare of Mexico," she said with more than a trace of bitterness.

Maria stopped her tirade long enough to nod pleasantly at a couple that whirled by. "Besides, he's in exile now. And since Paredes overthrew Herrera's government and installed himself as president, the country has been in a turmoil. Jose Herrera was not the right man to rule the country, and I doubt that Paredes will be an effective president."

"And who do you think would be?"

Maria tossed her head. "Who can say? There are many strong men in Mexico who could lead the country out of its problems. Time will tell."

"But perhaps Santa Anna shouldn't be discounted just yet. There were rumors back in Washington that he sent an emissary to President Polk in February. The gossip has it that he guarantees to negotiate peace with the United States if he's returned to power—and that he will agree to sell Polk the land that the United States wants for thirty million dollars. That would certainly settle the dispute over Texas once and for all."

Maria's eyes clouded momentarily, her face closed and secretive. "Then the United States is considering this possibility?" she finally asked.

"I don't know. I can't imagine Polk *not* considering

anything that might keep the peace." He watched Maria closely as she seemed to mull this news over in her mind. "And what do you think would happen if Santa Anna returned to Mexico?"

A wary glance was flashed his way. "Why, I cannot say. I am but a simple woman. I find all this talk of war and politics confusing and boring. My only interests are Antonio and our life together."

"What a lucky man Anthony is to have such a dedicated wife," Blake said gravely, striving for what he hoped was a proper tone of sincerity. But his mind was busily sorting the strangely disturbing feelings that Maria's words had created. And, despite her protests of ignorance and disinterest, he had a strange feeling that Maria knew much more about Mexico's political intrigues than she admitted.

Was there any chance that she was subconsciously mirroring Anthony's feelings about the situation? Could Anthony honestly be so blind in love with his wife that he was unaware of her antagonism toward the United States? Or did Anthony secretly feel an allegiance to Mexico because of his wife? What a disturbing thought that was, considering Anthony's personal connections with local government.

The music ended, and Blake's disquieting musings vanished as he spotted Laura standing with Nat and Elizabeth. He searched the crowd for Anthony, but he had disappeared. Blake scowled, wondering how he could graciously rid himself of Maria. For a moment he thought fate had sent him an answer, but his hopes for surcease were irritatingly dashed.

"Miguel!" Maria cried suddenly. There was delight in her voice when she spied the familiar form stepping through the doorway. "How lovely. I was so afraid he would be unable to come tonight."

"Oh?" murmured Blake.

199

"Uh . . . yes . . . the press of matters at the ranch. You understand. There is always so much work to do."

Miguel looked splendid in his dark suit, the candlelight bouncing brilliant sparks off his highly polished silver trimmings. Maria wasn't the only woman in the room whose covetous eyes followed his fluid progress across the floor. With feline grace he made his way to the group surrounding Laura and claimed her for a dance.

Blake was too caught up in his own reaction to this turn of events to notice the sudden pinched look around Maria's mouth or the blazing eyes that narrowed dangerously as she watched Miguel place his hand gently against the small of Laura's back and guide her to the dance floor.

Maria whirled and confronted Blake, her mouth turned down in a sultry pout. "Are you just going to stand here and let this lovely music go to waste?"

"No, of course not," Blake muttered, tearing his gaze away from Laura and Miguel. Once more he gathered Maria into his arms and began to move to the music. Suddenly his feet did not want to cooperate. He missed a step and then stumbled slightly when he tried to keep Miguel and Laura in sight among the dozens of swaying bodies. Maria shot him a look of pure venom. Blake cursed silently and valiantly struggled to regain his concentration.

In a far corner of the dim room, Miguel bent his head over Laura as they danced, his eyes never leaving her face as the soft music seemed to drift up and wrap them in a disquieting solitude. "You are the most beautiful woman in the room, senorita."

Laura's eyes widened in surprise at the honeyed sweetness of his words. She gave a small nervous laugh. "Why, Miguel, you'll have me believing you really mean that if you don't watch out."

"I speak only the truth," he murmured huskily, and

he tightened his arm around her waist. His gaze seemed to pour a slow liquid heat over her.

Miguel danced with the casual grace of a master, and Laura found herself wondering what his life had been like in Mexico—and just what catastrophe had caused him to flee to Texas. Did he greatly miss his homeland? Did he perhaps have a sweetheart waiting impatiently for him to send for her? There seemed to be a million unanswered questions about the mysterious, intriguing man who held her in his arms.

Blake and Maria managed to finish the dance without another misstep, but both were in a foul mood by the time the music ceased. As soon as Blake dropped his hold on her, Maria looped her arm through his and gave an insistent tug. "Come, we must go and say hello to Miguel."

Blake shrugged, more than willing to comply. Far be it from him to argue. He didn't care whether he deposited Maria back in Anthony's care or left her with her cousin. All he wanted to do was rescue Laura from Miguel's clutches before somebody else claimed her.

"Miguel, my dear, how good of you to come." Maria loosened her hold on Blake and moved to Miguel's side, curving her hand possessively around his arm. Her eyes snapped black fire for an instant when, despite her arrival, he continued to smile down at Laura.

With a slow, sensuous movement Miguel raised Laura's hand to his lips. His hot breath bathed her wrist, and then his lips barely grazed the back of her hand. "It has been a pleasure," he murmured before releasing his hold.

The very air around the little group seemed to ebb and flow in response to the turbulent feelings within each of them. Laura was slightly stunned by the force of Miguel's overpowering sensuality. Maria was suffering pangs of irritation at Miguel's apparent desertion. And Blake was quietly furious.

Maria tugged at Miguel's arm until she had his

201

attention. "Miguel, I'm so glad you are here. As always, Anthony is busy with his eternal politics. I'm terribly in need of a dancing partner." She tilted her head back to grace him with one of the dazzling smiles that always brought men to heel. The heavy wealth of her thick hair lay like a rainfall of black satin against the sweet slope of her bare shoulders.

Miguel barely glanced at her. Instead he reached to absently pat her hand where it lay against his arm. "Of course, my dear. The night is young. We'll have time for many dances." His black eyes finally left Laura's face to cut in Blake's direction. "Senor Saunders," Miguel murmured with a nod of his head.

"Miguel," Blake replied in clipped tones. Why did the man always raise his hackles? Blake quickly thanked Maria for the dances they had shared, but she barely acknowledged his words. She was too busy casting dark looks at her cousin.

Blake could have cared less about Maria's snippish manner. His attention was drawn to Laura like a moth flitting toward a golden flame.

Laura smiled nervously at Blake as he edged his way between Miguel and herself. "It's turning out to be a very nice party, don't you think?" she finally asked, hoping to break the icy silence. She gathered up the lacy fan that hung suspended by a satin ribbon from her wrist, flicked it open and waved it saucily, creating a small, erratic breeze that stirred the soft curls at her temples.

"Yes, of course. It's a very nice party," Blake muttered as he watched her brush a damp curl back from her forehead. He had a sudden inspiration. "Are you warm, Laura?" he asked. "Would you care to step outside for a breath of fresh air? I'd be happy to escort you."

"How kind of you to offer. That would be most refreshing." It would be a relief to escape the sullen looks

202

that Maria kept throwing her way.

Laura snapped the fan closed, smiled quickly at Miguel and Maria and then turned eagerly toward the door.

"How nice of you to devote your valuable time to entertaining Anthony's little sister," Maria said to Miguel with syrupy sweetness as she watched Laura and Blake walk away.

"Whatever do you mean, dear cousin?"

"Why, nothing. Just a simple comment."

"I thought dancing with her would be the polite thing to do. Would you have me ignore the girl?"

"Of course not. But what about me?"

"You seemed perfectly happy to be dancing with the dashing Mr. Saunders. For the third time, I do believe. Are you sure that your darling Anthony would approve?" Miguel retorted mildly.

"Anthony cares not one whit who I dance with—and you know it!"

"Then I suggest we stop wasting time and take advantage of the night. With the strain of war, it might be months before there's another opportunity for the frivolous pastimes you seem to dote on so highly." His fingers closed firmly around the tender flesh of her arm, and then he steered her unceremoniously to the floor.

Blake gave not one thought to the two people left behind. He simply followed Laura as she wound through the clusters of people gathered about the room, mesmerized by the graceful sway of her skirts, the proud straight line of her back, the saucy way the sable-brown curls bounced against the soft slope of her bare shoulder. His fingers itched to stroke the delicate curve of her neck and trace the beguiling line of her spine, down, down to the gentle swell of hip and thigh. He still remembered the satin feel of her skin under his hand.

He scowled, mentally chastising himself. Why was it his good intentions seemed to waft away like campfire smoke in a windstorm every time he got within touching distance of Laura?

They stepped out into the shadows. Blake gratefully drew a deep breath, pulling the cool night air deep into his lungs in the hope of extinguishing the embers that flamed in his blood. Hands in his pockets to still the trembling of his fingers, he followed Laura as they moved slowly away from the light and noise.

"I can tell *you've* been having a good time," Blake said, a touch of irritation tinging the tone of his voice. "I've given up wishing for another dance since I'd probably have to fight half the men in town for it. Including Miguel."

"Why, Blake," Laura said coyly, cutting her eyes up at him. "I didn't think you'd noticed. You were so busy with Maria."

"Oh?" he answered, his mustache quirking up at one corner as a grin tugged at his mouth. "And here I didn't think *you'd* noticed."

Laura's gown rustled pleasantly as they moved slowly over the grass. Blake adjusted his steps, matching the stride of his long legs more evenly to hers. The moon illuminated the snowy whiteness of his shirt and embellished his tawny gold curls with a silvery sheen. A playful breeze off the river stirred the leaves of the tall trees into a whispery dance.

"We could remedy the situation," said Laura as the fiddlers began again in the distant building, the melody of a waltz floating temptingly through the night air. She stopped and turned toward Blake, her mouth dry with a strange tingling surge of anticipation. Suddenly she wanted his arms around her, wanted to feel his comforting strength against her.

"How is that?"

"There's no one here but us. You certainly wouldn't have to fight for this dance." Her tone was lightly teasing, breathy, and so low he could barely hear her. She tipped her chin up and waited for his answer. The moonlight caressed her face, turning her eyes into deep sapphire pools sprinkled with a thousand stars.

Blake's breath caught in his throat. He hesitated for the briefest moment and then placed his arm around her tiny waist. He took her hand in his, drawing her much closer than he would ever have dared in the ballroom. They began to move to the faint wail of the fiddle, swaying and turning and dipping, floating over the soundless cushion of grass and wildflowers to the strains of the beautiful waltz.

Her body fit against his with utter rightness. There was a funny little constriction in his throat, a strange tightening around his heart. He sighed with something akin to triumph as he cradled her even closer.

The finely woven broadcloth of Blake's coat chafed comfortably against her cheek, the almost imperceptible rasp of his jaw grazing her temple. The heady aroma of magnolias and honeysuckle filled the night air. Laura closed her eyes and surrendered to the music and to the man.

The final quivering note of the violin hung in the air. Although their feet ceased the pretty patterns of the dance, Blake's arms held Laura just as close. Puzzled, she tipped her head back and gazed at him with star-sprinkled eyes. The moonlight spilled silver across her face and down the tantalizing swell of ivory bosom. A sweet, slow warmth spread through Blake's limbs, and with utter tenderness he bent toward her and pressed the gentlest of kisses on her ruby lips. They stood thusly for a long, long time, simply savoring the almost unbearable sweetness of their unity.

Finally Blake released her from his embrace and then tucked her hand tenderly into the crook of his arm. Neither of them alluded to the mystical communion they had shared. They merely turned to stroll aimlessly under the sheltering branches of the trees. A cool breeze from the river carried the spicy aroma of earth and woods and rushing water.

Laura's hand was gently ensconced between the hard strength of Blake's arm and the reassuring expanse of his body. Her fingers lay pleasantly against the firm musculature of his forearm. His great height imparted a satisfying feeling of shelter and protection as they picked their way randomly through the wildflowers. As their footsteps crushed the delicate blossoms, an illusive perfume swirled into the velvet night.

"Is your search for land going well?" Laura asked quietly. And in the back of her mind came the strangely comforting hope that Blake might find what he was looking for and stay in Texas.

She frowned slightly, watching her hem swish against the ground as she contemplated the alternative. Had Blake ever actually said what his long-term plans were? No, not really. Just the comments on the cattle business. But, even if he did find land to buy, did that mean he might stay in Texas and run the ranch himself? Or was he planning to hire someone else to take care of that job and eventually return to the East? Laura's heart gave a little twist at the thought.

True, she had known Blake only a short while, and for the most part they'd been at cross purposes. But their lives had somehow become entwined. Somehow, during the tedium of the trail and the strange heated tension between them and the danger of the ambush, a bond had been formed. Where once she had prayed for his departure, now the thought of Blake's leaving brought a chill to her very soul.

"Not as well as I'd hoped," he replied.

Her heartbeat quickened. "You're not giving up, are you? You . . . you're not . . . uh . . . going elsewhere to

206

look, are you?"

"No, it might take months to complete my work in this part of Texas."

"Oh . . . well . . . that's good," she said, striving for a nonchalance she didn't really feel.

"Why, Laura, I almost believe you'd miss me if I left."

"Well, I suppose I am sort of used to your being around. But don't let that swell your head," she bristled tartly. "As few people as I know here in Texas, I'd probably even miss Maria."

Blake threw back his head and filled the night with hearty laughter. "That's a backhanded compliment if I ever heard one. I'm not so sure I want to be put in the same league as Maria in your mind."

"Well, you certainly seem to like her well enough!" Laura sassed back at him, wishing she had never brought up the subject. "Now—back to your land—have you found any that you like?"

Blake sighed. He knew he had to keep up the pretense he had established as his cover. His daily rides into the countryside were undertaken in order to glean information; but Laura didn't know that. He almost wished he really was looking for a place to settle down. Somehow the thought didn't seem nearly as boring and confining as it had in years past. He had come to envy Anthony over the past few weeks—his ranch and the hundreds of head of fine cattle that grazed the verdant hills. How fulfilling it must be to look out over such holdings and know they were yours.

"I haven't located what I came after, if that's what you mean. I'll just have to keep looking." He paused a long while. "And what about you, Laura? You seem . . . oh, I don't know . . . changed, I guess is the word . . . different than you were when we first met. Does that mean you've found what you were seeking when you came to Texas?"

207

"I . . . I'm not sure. Maybe I have. I left for reasons that are hard to explain. And some of them seem less important now than they did at the time of my departure. I had thought of Texas as a very temporary measure, but I've grown to love this land."

"You really do love it here, don't you? It's not just because of Anthony, is it?"

"There's something really special about this land and its people. It weaves a spell around you. I've found a sense of contentment here. That's more than some people ever have in a whole lifetime. Perhaps my destiny is not at all what I once thought it was." She shrugged slightly. "If so, I'll just make the best of what life brings."

Blake chuckled softly. "Somehow, I doubt that you'd let a little thing like destiny slow you down." He shook his head in amusement. "No, my girl, I can't see *anything* stopping you."

Chapter 19

Laura awoke slowly, peeping through slitted eyelids to view the unfamiliar surroundings in mystified wonder. Then she remembered they had all stayed at Nat and Elizabeth's hotel after the dance rather than make the long journey home at the crack of dawn. She stretched languorously and then snuggled back into the warm tangled covers for a time to savor the delicious memories of the night before.

Although certainly not a wallflower back home, she had never been the subject of as much adoration as she had gleaned last night. What fun never to lack for a partner, to pick and choose from among the clamoring males in attendance, to let them scurry and scamper to bring her cups of punch and tasty morsels from the table. It was a heady experience to realize that she'd had the two most handsome men in the room vying for her attention—much to Maria's chagrin.

Perhaps the best part had been the knowledge that Blake had been aware of her every move during the early hours of the evening.

Laura wanted to save the tantalizing thoughts of Blake's struggle and capitulation for the last, so she reviewed the confidences she and Olivia had managed to share between dances, pleased that her first intuition about their friendship had proven to be true. With Maria so aloof and cool, it would be lovely to have Olivia within riding distance.

Laura pondered the brief flickers of hidden emotion she had glimpsed in Olivia's eyes whenever Anthony had been close by. Could it be possible that there had been something between them at some time in the past? The thought seemed rather unlikely, since Anthony seemed to treat Olivia much as he did Laura: joking and teasing in good-natured fashion.

But Laura was certain that there was something more than friendship in the fond looks that Olivia cast at Anthony over the course of the evening. After all, who knew about unrequited love better than Laura herself? And what about Maria's attitude toward Olivia? Laura was sure that Maria didn't care much for Olivia—and vice versa—despite their genteel words. Of course, Maria didn't seem to care much for any female, so it was possible that Laura had misread the situation.

Laura pushed the perplexing thoughts concerning Olivia and Anthony aside and allowed herself to go on to more pleasant memories, smothering a little giggle when she remembered the stormy depths of Blake's eyes as he watched her throughout the early hours of the evening, and the way he had quickly averted his gaze each time she looked his way. Despite his attempts at subtlety, she'd known each and every time he'd been watching her. Tiny little shivers had traveled up and down her spine despite the heat of the room. Butterflies had fluttered around her heart, causing it to skip and quiver in the strangest fashion. Yes, there was no doubt she had been highly aware of his perusal.

Miguel's arrival had provided the necessary catalyst to force him to make his move. Laura curled kittenlike into the downy nest of the featherbed, almost purring with ambrosial contentment as she thought of their escape from the heated room, the long, slow dance under the stars, the wonderful sweet agony of the kiss they had shared in the moonlight, the feelings of contentment and peace that had enveloped her as they walked and talked, the tender attention he had heaped on her as the evening progressed.

She was certain he had been as reluctant to return to the jostling crowds in the hall as she—and just as certain that part of his reluctance stemmed from the fact that Miguel was still very much in evidence. But Maria had monopolized Miguel's time for the remainder of the evening, thus preventing a recurrence of that first disturbing dance. Although Laura had danced with others after their return, Blake had claimed her as his partner every few dances with such charming persistence that the other men had finally given up, and she had spent the last hour of the dance enfolded in his strong arms.

Oh, if Cynthia could have seen her! Or William. Laura frowned slightly. William? This was the first time she had thought of him in days. He hadn't even crossed her mind last night. Not once had she compared his suave aristocratic manners to the raw vitality of the men who had partnered her at the dance. And not once, while Blake held her in his arms, had William's memory crept in to steal her attention.

Strange, she thought, that he should slip so easily from her mind after all these years. Just days ago she'd been anguishing over the fact that she still hadn't heard from him; now the thought only stirred a remote little sting of annoyance.

Was it time to put aside her girlish dreams and get on with her life? Was her heart trying to tell her something that her stubborn head had refused to acknowledge?

Her disturbing thoughts were interrupted by shouts

from the street. She slipped quickly from the warm coziness of the bed and ran to peer out the window. A dozen men were gathered in front of the hotel. Others were hurrying down the boardwalks and across the street to join the jostling throng.

She could pick up a word here and there amidst the loud murmurs of the crowd: "Congress" and "President Polk" and "Matamoros." The crowd swelled and the rumble grew louder.

Laura turned away from the window, removing her white cotton gown and leaving it in a careless heap on the floor. She hastily washed her face and brushed her tangled curls, then slipped on a simple gingham dress and shoved her feet into the lavender satin dancing slippers that lay discarded on the brightly colored rag rug.

Pulling the door to her room open, she skipped quickly down the stairs. She hurried across the vacant lobby and pushed her way out the front door of the hotel. Threading her way through the growing crowd, she raised up on tiptoe every few steps as she went, peering over the heads of the jostling crowd toward the source of all the commotion.

A little thrill of relief ran through her when she spotted Blake's taffy-colored locks towering over the others. Struggling through the press of bodies, she finally managed to work her way to his side.

"What's going on?" she asked breathlessly.

"War," Blake replied grimly. "Word just arrived that Congress declared war on Mexico. President Polk signed the papers. The United States is calling for volunteers. Troops are marching toward Texas from a dozen states to join Zachary Taylor at the Rio Grande. The country's ablaze with war fever!"

"War!" gasped Laura, her eyes large with alarm. "But . . . but, what will this mean? What's going to happen?" she asked worriedly, her voice barely audible over the mad babbling of the crowd.

Blake glanced down into deep blue eyes filled with apprehension. "Come on, let's get out of here." He took Laura's hand and pulled her behind him as he threaded his way back to the hotel entrance. When they were safely inside, he escorted her to the sofa in the lobby and sank down upon it, his hand still clasping hers.

"Please don't worry. There shouldn't be any effect on this part of the state." He pushed aside the persistent thought that his statement might not be so true if the rumor he was tracking for Washington turned out to be valid. Almost absentmindedly his fingers clutched her hand, his thumb brushing a nervous pattern across her palm as if he disliked breaking the contact between them. Her heart beat faster with each brush of his fingers.

"Right now," he explained in a gentle tone, trying to soothe her concern, "the fighting is taking place around Matamoros—right on the border. We're a long way from there. If they can keep the fighting from spreading northward, Texas as a whole should be relatively safe. And I'm sure the United States is going to do everything in its power to move the fighting into Mexico, to keep them on the defensive."

Laura's cheeks were tinged pink with high emotion. Her wide eyes watched Blake's face carefully while her small even teeth absently worried her bottom lip. "But, what about—"

Laura's question was interrupted by the clatter of boot heels on the stairs. Anthony burst into view.

"Blake!" Anthony called out in relief when he spotted the couple sitting close together on the far side of the lobby. "All that commotion woke me up. What on earth is going on?" He hastily finished stuffing the tail of his shirt into his trousers and then combed his fingers raggedly through his hair.

Blake realized with surprise that Laura's small hand

was still securely held in his own, and he sheepishly dropped his hold to stand and greet Anthony. "Word just arrived. The United States declared war on Mexico."

"Oh, my God!" Anthony said huskily. "I was afraid this was going to happen. I just kept hoping that it could be settled peacefully. Tell me all about it—all the news—everything they're saying."

The sounds of the crowd grew louder outside the entrance to the hotel. Blake frowned at the incessant rumble.

"Let's go into the dining room. It'll be quieter there, and we can get a cup of coffee while we talk," he suggested, raising his voice so he could be heard above the growing commotion. He turned toward the swinging doors that led to the dining room. Anthony and Laura followed behind.

Soon they were seated at a small table toward the back of the blessedly empty room, steaming cups of coffee in front of them. Blake took a sip from his cup and then began to recite what he had overheard. Elizabeth hovered nearby, shirking her duties in the kitchen for an opportunity to listen to Blake's discourse.

"President Polk signed the papers on May thirteenth. He's issued a nationwide call to arms. People in the States have taken up some crazy phrase about 'manifest destiny' and are beating down the doors of the recruiting offices. Everyone is eager to whip Mexico and push the United States one step closer to ruling the whole continent. Good Lord, man, even Walt Whitman is calling for the thorough chastisement of Mexico!"

"Who's that?" questioned Elizabeth as she leaned to refill their cups.

"A very renowned poet," Laura explained quickly before turning her troubled eyes back to Blake. "Surely, you can't mean even that gentle, intelligent man wants

214

this war?"

"Sure sounds like it, doesn't it? And it appears he's not the only one. Seems like everyone has taken up the cry," Blake said with a worried shake of his golden head.

"Have they said how Taylor is doing? What about arms? Supplies?" questioned Anthony.

Blake fiddled with his cup, turning it round and round aimlessly on the bright gingham tablecloth as he considered how best to answer Anthony's question. He didn't want to scare Laura, but he also wanted to give Anthony all the facts he could.

"Apparently they think he can hold out until the volunteers reach him. He's equipped with five regiments of infantry. And he has a mobile unit of 'flying artillery' under Major Ringgold—those new lighter, carriage-mounted guns made of bronze."

"I believe I heard something about that flying artillery last time I was in Austin," Anthony said.

"Could be. Ringgold's very well thought of in military circles. I've heard it said he can really handle those guns. And they have the old eighteen pounders as well. As long as Taylor keeps his supply depot at Point Isabel and the road leading from there to the fort across from Matamoros defended, he should be fine."

Tension etched deep lines in Anthony's sun-browned face. "I think I'd better go back upstairs and wake Maria. We'd best get back to the ranch."

"You don't expect trouble around these parts, do you?" Blake was quick to ask. Was Anthony aware of something that Blake had been unable to uncover?

"No, of course not. But it'll take me at least a day, maybe two, to put things straight at home, and then I've got to return to Austin as soon as possible. Governor Henderson's going to need all the help he can get."

"Um, you're probably right. I hadn't planned on doing

this quite so soon, but I'd like to go with you—if you don't mind, that is. I'd like to spend a day or two in Austin and see how things are going there, and then I need to go on into Louisiana. I've got to get to a telegraph office. I need to get work back East to the . . . uh . . . to my business associates."

"Fine. I'll be glad for the company. I'll be in Austin several days anyway, and then if Governor Henderson wants me to, I'll head on down to Matamoros. He may want some firsthand reports." Anthony pushed his chair back. The discordant scraping sound reverberated in the deserted room. "Laura, you'd better get your things together. Maria and I will meet you downstairs as soon as we're ready."

"Yes, Anthony." Laura rose from the table, poised to follow him.

"Oh, Anthony," Blake said before they could move away. "I'm going to stay in town for awhile. I'll be back at the ranch sometime tomorrow. I need to tie up a few loose ends before I telegraph the . . . uh . . . office." I have to make one last sweep of the area to see what everyone's reaction to this latest news is before I telegraph the department. Even the smallest scrap of information could be helpful now, he thought to himself.

"All right. I won't be leaving until the day after tomorrow at the earliest. We'll see you later." Anthony strode to the swinging doors and pushed his way through. Laura, eyes wide with barely suppressed alarm, threw one last apprehensive glance back at Blake, and then quickly scurried through the portal after her brother.

Blake watched the two retreating figures, his mind already on other matters. Now his mission to Texas would be doubly important. If there really were renegade factions of Mexicans anywhere in the state, it was going to be vital to find out what impact they could have, now that war had been officially declared.

The United States would be desperate to avoid fighting in Texas itself, if at all possible. They simply couldn't allow anyone who was evenly remotely sympathetic to the Mexican cause an opportunity to strike from behind the lines of battle.

As soon as he was sure he had all the information he could glean at this time, it was imperative that he get word to Washington as quickly as possible. It would take several weeks to make the trip, await word of his new orders, and return to Washington-on-the-Brazos.

Blake tossed down the last swallow of tepid coffee and frowned at the thought of how long the trip would take. He hated to think of both his and Anthony's being away from the ranch for so long. But surely Laura would be safe. After all, the fighting was far away, at the very bottom tip of Texas. There really wasn't much chance of danger from the battles.

And what else could possibly happen while he was gone?

Laura quickly gathered up her clothing, wadding her party gown into a rumpled ball, which she stuffed in her small bag, tossing in her brushes and personal items in hodgepodge disarray as she struggled to subdue her troubled thoughts. She wasn't afraid for her own safety. She knew the battlegrounds were hundreds of miles away. But Anthony's words kept ringing in her ears. What if the governor sent him on to Matamoros?

She'd only just recently found her brother, and the thought of losing him again was like a cold hand clutching her heart, the icy fingers of fear chilling her to the bone.

And what about Blake? Although he'd be headed in

217

another direction, was there any chance that he would be in danger? *That* rumination brought a quick catch to Laura's breath.

She swallowed the growing lump in her throat and scanned the room for further articles. Finding none, she grabbed up her bag and hurried from the room.

Chapter 20

Maria was oddly silent all the way home, replying in absentminded monosyllables to anything Anthony or Laura said, her eyes stormy and remote, lips pressed tightly together. As soon as the wagon rolled to a stop at the front steps of the big house, she gathered her skirts high and took off, disappearing around the corner of the house in a flash. Anthony barely noticed her hasty departure as he issued orders to Pedro in rapid-fire Spanish.

Laura glanced quickly at Anthony and then dismissed the incident. She had little doubt that Maria had gone straight to Miguel with the news of the war. Of course that wasn't really such an unexpected thing for her to do, Laura decided. Miguel and Maria probably had dozens of relatives still in Mexico. Who else would she turn to but her own countryman, the only blood relative she had near? Who else would understand her feelings? After all, Maria had every right to be upset by the turn of events.

Laura couldn't imagine how it might feel to know that your loved ones were possibly under gunfire at this very moment. Her brows drew together, tiny worry lines furrowing her forehead. If Governor Henderson agreed to Anthony's plans, she might know very well, indeed, just how it felt. Anthony could be in the thick of the fighting within days.

And Blake—what about Blake? Laura paused in her ascent, right foot poised on the edge of the top step. She knew with utter certainty that he would be right in the middle of the battle if he went with Anthony. There'd be no cautious viewing from the back lines for a man like Blake.

But maybe he'd just go to Louisiana like he'd said and then come straight back to the ranch. The thought of having Blake around was strangely soothing.

Laura gave a small self-concious laugh at her morose mood. It was just the thought of the war that made her uneasy about Blake's leaving. After all, Blake had seen her through several traumatic episodes, and she'd just feel a little safer with him around. Perfectly natural. She mounted the last step and moved slowly across the porch as her thoughts continued to whirl. Maybe she could say something—do something—to insure his quick return.

Her mind was nibbling at the edges of this intriguing thought when she climbed the stairs to her room.

The rest of the day was hectic with activity. Any time the household staff passed within speaking distance, quick snatches of worried-sounding Spanish would punctuate the silence of the big house. Most of the ranch hands were sent to bring the cattle in to a closer pasture. Those left at home busied themselves with checking supplies, mending fences, and generally securing the place.

Assured that things were going as well as possible at home, Anthony saddled up and rode out to relay news of the war to those neighbors who had not been in town that morning.

Laura felt positively underfoot as the day progressed. She felt very isolated with Anthony gone. She hadn't heard a word of English—except the ones in answer to her own meager questions—since he rode out. She tried to offer her help in the kitchen, but Rosita and Juanita only shooed her out of the way and then went back to their anxious chattering.

Laura suffered from a growing sense of uselessness as she wandered about the house, trying to stay out of everyone's way while they scurried about in what seemed to her a rather senseless frenzy. Bored to distraction, she finally slipped into Anthony's study in the late afternoon in search of a book.

The haphazard stack of journals and papers littering Anthony's desk triggered the memory of her earlier determination to broach the subject of applying her excellent schooling to Anthony's record keeping. She brightened considerably.

There *was* something she could do to help! She smiled in contemplation of Anthony's returning from his tiring trip to Austin to find his desk immaculate, and all his records up to date and filed neatly away. Cheered by the thought, Laura clapped her hands in anticipation.

Anthony had barely set foot in the house that evening when Laura eagerly cornered him in the hallway and began to outline her plan in a breathless, excited tumble of words, pleading that the time spent working on his books would help to fill the long, quiet hours.

"Are you sure you want to tackle that mess, honey?" Anthony asked.

"Oh, yes! It'll make me feel ever so much better to be helping. I was very good in mathematics at school, Anthony," she assured him. "I promise I won't let you down."

He put his arm around her shoulders and gave her a quick, reasuring squeeze. "I'm not worried about that, honey. I don't see how you could make it any worse, no matter what you did. Maria's been handling some of the book work since I've been in Austin so much lately. She doesn't mind placing orders for supplies, but she forgets

221

to follow through afterward. I don't know if it's because she's having a little trouble dealing with U.S. currency or what, but frequently expenditures and purchases don't match up, and I've just been too busy to dig through those mountains of paperwork to sort it out. I kept putting it off, and I'm afraid it's a real mess now."

"Oh, I don't mind," Laura quickly assured him. "I just know I can find the problem. Please! I'd really love to have something to do. I can't spend every day out riding."

"All right, Laura, the job's yours!" Anthony agreed, touched at her desire to help and even a little relieved that someone might be able to sort out the mess his bookkeeping had become since he'd been spending so much time away from home.

Laura rose the next morning full of excitement about her new project. She ate a hasty breakfast alone at the big table and then happily hurried to Anthony's study to begin her work. She spent the rest of the day sorting and stacking the mounds of paperwork in a somewhat reasonable order. When she refused to come out for the noon meal, Rosita brought Laura a plate, which she consumed quickly while sitting at the desk so she could continue scanning the pages of a journal.

It would take days, maybe weeks, to actually complete the task, and Laura was sincerely grateful. At least she'd have something important to keep her busy. She buried herself in the work with enthusiasm, feeling infinitely better already, just knowing she would be contributing to the household.

Although she hadn't accomplished much more her first day at work than a quick perusal of the records and a cursory filing system consisting of numerous stacks of categorized papers, Laura was tired but happy when she finally quit the study and slipped outside.

Her soft slippers made only the barest whispering sounds on the smooth wooden planks of the veranda as she crossed it and gratefully sank down onto the steps. She unhooked the tiny buttons at the collar of her gown and pulled the slightly damp material away from her slender throat, enjoying the cool caress of the evening breeze.

Gingerly she stretched her long shapely legs out in front of her and twisted her shoulders to relieve the stiffness from her hours of work. She leaned back and propped her elbows on the step above, resting her spine lightly against the hard edge of the wood, enjoying the peaceful interlude. The dying sunset painted the puffy undersides of the clouds with soft pinks and oranges and golds. Her head lolled against a walnut column still warm from the day's sun as she proudly considered all she had accomplished.

Through hooded eyes, Laura caught a flicker of movement on the horizon. A tiny figure on horseback was plodding slowly down the road, just barely visible through the deep purple shadows of the twilight.

Blake! Laura's heart sang. She was suddenly eager to discuss her new project, to share her newfound feelings of accomplishment and the pleasing feeling of productivity with someone. She quickly sat up and tucked her skirts around her ankles, wiggling like a small child in anticipation. She could hardly wait to tell him about her day.

Impatiently she watched the elusive silhouette slowly approach, shrouded in shadow against the backdrop of darkening sky. The hazy outline of the man wavered and blended with the deep shadows of the looming trees as he came closer and closer.

Laura's heart thumped painfully against her rib cage as she waited restlessly for him to reach the house. A wide smile on her lips, eyes luminous with the pleasure of his return, she finally threw propriety to the wind and descended the stairs, skirts whipping behind her as she ran down the wide dirt road, eager to share her happiness with Blake.

"I'm so glad you're here. Just wait till I tell you what I've been doing," she called in a breathless voice as her hurrying feet carried her beneath the dark canopy of tree limbs.

The man drew his horse to a halt, and Laura lifted her gaze from the precarious path and then blinked in bewilderment. Her upturned face was a pale oval in the hazy dusk, her mouth a startled round O of surprise. Eyes slightly glazed, she stood still, as if frozen in place, skirts still clutched high in fingers that had grown suddenly numb.

"What a wonderfully warm welcome, Laura, my dear. I can't begin to tell you how glad I am to be here."

"William!" Laura gasped.

In a bewildered haze, Laura drifted through the proper motions of welcoming William—finding a hand to stable his rented horse, making introductions to a rather baffled Anthony, getting William settled comfortably in the room next to Anthony and Maria.

An hour later, when all but Maria were gathered in the parlor before supper, Laura was still in a mild state of shock.

Through cobwebs of confusion, she watched William seat himself on the sofa. She strove to escape the haze of surprise and disbelief that had surrounded her since his arrival. The strange mixture of emotions played across her face.

"Laura, are you all right, my dear?" Anthony asked.

William watched Laura struggle back to reality as her

brother's question finally penetrated her reverie. A small quirk of his aristocratic mouth betrayed his quick perception of her awkward situation. He flicked an imaginary fleck of lint from the sleeve of his impeccably tailored coat and settled himself more comfortably against the soft leather upholstery, waiting with practiced patience to see how Laura would handle herself.

"Why, of course, Anthony. I'm just fine," Laura managed to say. "Why do you ask?"

"You don't seem quite yourself this evening."

"Oh . . . well, it's just that I'm so surprised at William's arrival. I . . . I didn't expect . . . I mean . . . well, I just never dreamed that William would simply ride in one day." She dropped her gaze to her lap, nervously twisting her hanky.

Oh, dear! How could she ever explain to Anthony about the letter and the brazen plea she had made to William? She avidly wished she had mentioned William to her brother weeks ago. But she had never dreamed he would just show up on Anthony's doorstep. Even her wildest daydreams had centered simply around the arrival of a letter requesting her speedy return to the East so that she and William could begin their life of matrimonial bliss.

"Yes . . . uh . . . well, we're certainly glad to have you hear, Mr. Stratford," Anthony finally said, trying to fill the awkward moment of silence.

"Yes. Yes, we are," repeated Laura, turning a radiant smile on the handsome man sitting a polite distance from her. William—her own dear William—was really here! Sitting just inches away from her. If she wanted to, she could reach out her hand and actually touch him! Oh, how very wonderful to see someone from home again.

Home? How very strange, Laura thought. The phrase didn't sound quite right in her mind. Without even realizing it she had begun to consider Texas her home.

The thought of leaving Texas filled her with a regret that startled her.

Well, of course she'd be sad to leave Texas! Leaving Texas meant leaving Anthony and Elizabeth and Olivia—and Blake. She'd been so desperate to escape Philadelphia and the awful predicament she'd been in that she'd simply never considered the fact that she might come to enjoy Anthony's nearness and her new life in Texas so much that it would pain her to leave it.

Laura squared her shoulders at the sobering thought, drawing a deep breath of resolution. Leaving Texas and her new friends might make her sad for awhile but she'd get over it. Everything would work out in the long run. After all, for years and years she'd wanted nothing more than to be with William.

And now, here he was. Instead of simply writing, he'd traveled absolutely hundreds of miles in answer to her letter. What a wonderfully romantic thing for him to do! A woman could hardly ask for more devotion than that! It would certainly be worth giving up her new life and friends for the blissful one she would share with William.

Anthony cleared his throat nervously, still fighting feelings of confusion about Stratford's arrival and Laura's strange behavior. He turned his attention back to William. "I . . . uh, I understand that you've known Laura for quite some time."

"Ah, yes. My family moved to the north side of town about eight years ago—actually just down the street from your uncle's home. I've had the great privilege of watching Laura grow from an adorable child into a lovely young woman."

William smiled in Laura's direction, his pale gray eyes sweeping her with a warm gaze from head to toe. He had expected to find the attractive but reserved girl who had hovered at the edge of his consciousness at the parties and soirees of wealthy Philadelphia society during their young years. But this was a different Laura. Under the warm southern sun she had blossomed into a beautiful, intriguing woman.

William surreptitously perused the satin texture of Laura's skin, gilded a warm apricot by her days on horseback, and the lush curves of her body beneath the softly clinging fabric of her gown. How foolish of him not to have perceived what a beauty Laura was destined to be. What a waste of time and opportunity, he mused, remembering how those innocent blue eyes had watched him with barely hidden admiration over the years.

Perhaps, William thought smugly to himself, his plan would be more pleasure than chore, after all.

"And just exactly what brings you to Texas, Mr. Stratford?" Anthony questioned.

Laura's alarmed gaze flicked to William. Oh, dear! Whatever would she do if he told Anthony the truth? Drat! Everything was becoming so complicated. Why hadn't she spent the last hour formulating a sensible explanation for William's arrival instead of mooning around like a silly schoolgirl?

"Call me William, please. I've heard Laura talk about you so often over the years that I feel I already know you."

"Very well—William," Anthony conceded, shifting uncomfortably and wishing the man would answer his question. He wasn't quite sure how to take the suave, rather patrician-looking man. William seemed nice enough—a trifle dandified for Anthony's taste after his long years on the frontier—but that certainly shouldn't be held against the man.

"When Laura's letter finally caught up with me, I felt compelled to answer her plea."

"Letter? Plea?" Anthony asked tartly.

"Yes . . . uh . . . you see, I wrote to William before I left Philadelphia. He had always been . . . well, I mean—"

"Laura and I have been dear friends for a very long time," William interrupted smoothly. "She wanted advice about the journey she planned to undertake."

Laura threw him a look of pure gratitude for saving her from the embarrassment of owning up to the real contents of the letter. She had no doubt that Anthony would think that proper young ladies did not throw themselves at the feet of their gentlemen friends—not even those headed for the wild frontier to escape an untenable wedding.

"But, alas, I had just left town, and it was only when I returned to Philadelphia that her letter caught up with me. Laura has always been very dear to my heart." Laura's eyes widened in surprise, and a rosy flush traveled up her throat and into her cheeks. "So naturally I felt compelled to see for myself that she had reached her destination safely. After all, a gentleman could do no less."

"Humph! Yes . . . well . . . I see," Anthony muttered, not sure he saw at all.

The soft rustle of satin drew Anthony's attention as Maria entered the room. His face brightened. "Maria! Come in, darling. We have a guest." He took her hand and threaded her arm lovingly through his own. "Darling, this is William Stratford, a very old and dear friend of Laura's who just arrived tonight from Philadelphia. William, may I present my wife, Maria."

William came quickly to his feet, clicking his heels together in cavalier fashion. With a speculative eye he thoroughly scrutinized the petite woman, noting with approval her sultry beauty and flashing dark eyes.

A small smile tugged at the corner of his mouth. With a gambler's uncanny intuition, he instantly cataloged all of

228

Maria's virtues and vices—exotically beautiful, sensuous and fiery, spoiled, ambitious, greedy for all life had to offer—and then filed his assessments carefully away just in case there should come a time when he might turn her weaknesses to his own use.

William knew how to handle women like Maria; and he was smugly sure he could win over the brother, too, given enough time. He could outbluff the best of them.

All he had to do was play his cards right.

This was one game he intended to win. The stakes were too high.

Chapter 21

It didn't take Maria long to react to the new man in the house and put her womanly wiles to work—old habits were hard to break even if there was the worry of a war going on. And, in return, William turned on the sophisticated charm that had woven such a glittering web of beguilement around Laura during her young years.

Laura watched the flirty repartee as if from a far, far distance, not once feeling the stab of irritation she had suffered when Maria had turned those same sultry allurements on Blake. The strange hollowness of emotion tugged gently at the edges of her curiosity, but she finally decided it was simply because she was now more accustomed to Maria's ways.

And besides, Laura argued with herself, hadn't William come all this way just for her, Laura? Such total devotion was surely above such a petty emotion as jealousy.

Laura pushed away the perplexing thoughts and turned her attention back to the conversation just as William was, for Maria's sake, once again going through the reasons behind his trip.

Maria's dark eyes raked William's lean, handsome face while he recited the story in an easy, self-confident voice.

Her shrewd mind took in the cool gray eyes that betrayed nothing, the confident tilt of his aristocratic head, the almost smug curve of his mouth as he turned to gift Laura with another dazzling smile. Whatever William Stratford's reason for coming to Texas, Maria mused, it was certainly more complicated than that silly story they had spoon-fed to Anthony.

Maria glanced quickly at Laura, thinking that perhaps she had misjudged the girl. Maybe her sister-in-law wasn't the simple, sweet innocent she appeared. Still, there was one positive factor to William's arrival. He would monopolize Laura's time, thereby freeing Maria for the more important tasks she would have to accomplish during the next few weeks.

Time was of the essence. Right now, Maria would welcome the devil himself if it would help further her cause.

When William ended his discourse, Maria shrugged minutely and then dutifully expressed the proper sentiments required from a hostess.

Anthony, however, was still a trifle uncomfortable with William's glib recital about his trip. Something about the story didn't ring true.

Why would a man travel halfway across the continent in search of merely a "dear friend?" Anthony's fingers raked nervously through his gray-flecked curls. He could understand a man's acting irrationally in the throes of a deathless passion. After all, he thought wryly, he himself hadn't been quite rational when he fell in love with Maria, had he? But, to Anthony's way of thinking, William's cool demeanor exhibited no signs of such ardent devotion.

Anthony's gaze flickered back and forth between his sister and the stranger. He continued to sift through his perplexed feelings as he studied the two of them. Just what was their relationship? Would William have offered for Laura if Uncle Henry hadn't decided that Laura could be used to advance his own devious desires? From Laura's previous panic-stricken narrative, Anthony's troubled mind conjured up the image of the odious old man who had, all too obviously, been more than happy to trade whatever business concession Uncle Henry hungered for in exchange for Laura's sweet innocence.

But, if William and Laura were truly such dear, close friends—or if William were in love with Laura—wouldn't he have been aware of what was going on? Wouldn't she have told him of her unhappiness about the impending marriage? At which point, wouldn't William have quickly proposed himself?

But Laura had been forced to solve her problem all alone, and by a somewhat foolhardy method. Just where had her dear friend William been when she needed him?

And what about Laura? She was obviously shocked to see William. Why, she'd been practically walking around in a daze since his arrival. And Anthony had been so sure that she was beginning to care for Blake. Or had he just imagined it? Was his mind playing a trick on him now simply because he preferred Blake to William? That really wasn't fair, was it? After all, he'd had a good many weeks to develop a friendship with Blake, and William had only been here a matter of hours.

Or could it be that he was being overprotective of Laura's feelings by slipping back into the "big brother" role he had undertaken years ago when they were orphaned? Laura was much too grown-up to need such coddling now.

Anthony sighed deeply and tossed off his second whiskey of the evening. There was too much to think about now. He would offer his hospitality to Stratford—after all, he could do no less—and then hope things would sort themselves out in proper fashion while he was gone.

Laura was a woman now. Whatever was going on, he had to trust her judgment and allow her to make her own decisions.

Maria stirred restlessly, the stiff fabric of her low-cut black gown rustling in the sudden stillness of the room. "You will excuse me for a moment, *por favor,*" she said to the others. "I must check on supper, to be sure that Juanita has no problems." She rose and crossed the room, stopping momentarily to hover over the grandly laid-out table in the dining room and then on through the door at the back of the room which led to the kitchen.

Grateful for a reprieve from his troubled thoughts, Anthony took the opportunity to dash outside for one last discussion with the ranch hands. Perhaps Miguel had returned from his survey of the far boundaries of the ranch. Anthony needed to talk with him if possible before he left for Austin in the morning. There was no way of knowing how long the responsibility for running the ranch would be on Miguel's shoulders, and Anthony wanted to be sure that his instructions were clear.

With Maria's and Anthony's departure, Laura and William were left alone.

"Well," William murmured softly, as he slid over closer to Laura, "I must say I'm quite taken with your family. And with you, as always." He smiled his perfect smile, and Laura gratefully returned it. "If I had known all these years that you felt the same way I did, we could have saved a great deal of time, my dear."

"W-what?" gasped Laura, positive that she had misunderstood the meaning of William's words.

"But, of course," he assured her warmly, reaching to stroke his long, slender fingers down the satin smoothness of her arm. "I've cared about you for absolutely years. But I never had the slightest clue that you could possibly feel the same way about me."

233

"Oh, William! Really?" Laura asked in astonishment. She was naive enough—and female enough—to reap immense pleasure from William's pretty speech, regardless of the mixed emotions it aroused. What woman wouldn't be thrilled to hear such words of devotion?

But for just an instant Laura wondered how he could possibly *not* have known how she felt. She'd always been sure that her heart was in her eyes every time she looked at him. But, she argued silently, *she* had certainly been unaware of *his* feelings—so how could she even remotely question the same human failing in William?

"My silly little angel," William said huskily. "Why else would I have made such a rigorous trip? No one in his right mind would come to this godforsaken place except in pursuit of someone or something very important."

"Oh," breathed Laura softly, her eyes large and luminous as she contemplated the amazing fact that her girlhood dreams just might become reality.

Saddle leather creaked in protest as Blake shifted his weight again, bracing his hand against the horn to relieve the tension in his back. He'd spent two long, tiring, frustrating days on horseback, and he'd learned absolutely nothing of interest from his long hours in the saddle. Oh, everyone was riled about the war, all right. But Blake certainly hadn't picked up any feelings of sympathy for Mexico.

Maybe the department would have something new for him when he contacted them by telegraph. He certainly hoped so. He could prolong his search for a while longer, but if his next report was still negative, the department might call him back to Washington. And that possibility was something Blake had not been able even to consider of late.

For the first time in his years with the government, he wasn't looking forward with his usual eagerness to a new assignment, a different place, fresh faces, another exciting challenge.

The muffled rhythm of Blackjack's hooves echoed through the warm, still night. The sky was almost cloudless, and the bright aura of the moon bathed the countryside in silver splendor. Blake adjusted his weight slightly as the tired horse topped the final ridge and then descended into the shallow bowl of the valley.

Blackjack snorted in happy anticipation, prancing sideways in his eagerness. Home, thought Blake, Blackjack smells home. The horse tossed his head impatiently and increased his speed, the slow clip-clop of his hooves becoming an eager beat against the earth. Pinpoints of bright golden light beckoned from the distant windows of the house. Blake's heart gave a funny little lurch at the welcoming glow, and he leaned over Blackjack's neck, suddenly as eager as his mount to return to a safe haven, to put the day and all his worries behind him.

They covered the remaining distance at a fast clip, galloping past the house and into the barn like a whirlwind. Blake swung his leg over and dismounted practically before Blackjack came to a halt in front of his stall in the barn. The distant dim glow of a lantern at the far end of the barn danced their shadows across the walls. Blake leaned and uncinched the saddle, turning with one smooth movement to throw it over the rail with a row of other saddles.

Sugar nickered a welcome from her adjoining stall, and Blake reached quickly to pat her velvety nose. He wondered if Laura had been out riding. How had she spent the past two days? Had she missed him at all?

The velvety darkness of Blackjack's skin twitched in nervous anticipation as he eyed the fresh sweet hay and the ration of oats that Blake dumped in his feed bin. He shoved against Blake in his eagerness to enter the familiar security of his stall, knocking the tall man slightly off balance.

Blake laughed in sheer exuberance, feeling the same warm eagerness in his own veins. "All right, boy, go on in. I understand." He slapped the horse lightly on his high, broad rump and stepped aside as Blackjack daintily picked his way over the straw-covered floor and then pushed his long nose into the bin.

He quickly rubbed a cloth across the horse's sweat-stained back and then slipped the latch on the gate of the stall, turning with a feeling of pleasant expectancy toward the barn's wide entryway—and the path leading to the house, to Laura.

Blake whistled a soft little tune as his long legs followed the well-worn byway under the tall sheltering trees. He could see figures moving beyond the small kitchen window at the corner of the house—Rosita and Juanita finishing the supper chores. He smiled in anticipation of one of Juanita's mouth-watering Mexican dishes and the homey comfort of sitting down to a meal with friends to share pleasant conversation.

A narrow vertical line of golden light appeared at the back of the house, widening until it became a rectangle of open doorway. The figure of a man moved from the shadows and hovered at the edge of the light. The man hesitated for a moment, framed against the golden backdrop of the doorway, evidently speaking to someone just out of sight inside the house. Then he descended the steps and melted into the shadows. The door eased shut, and blackness enveloped the back of the house once more.

Blake blinked several times to adjust his eyes to the dark.

"Hello," Blake called. "Who's there?"

No one answered. The fine hairs at the nape of Blake's neck prickled. Someone was still out there, standing very quietly in the black velvet shroud of the night. Why wouldn't he answer Blake's call? And who had he been talking with? Blake hesitated, alert to any sign of danger. His razor-honed instincts sent adrenaline pumping through his veins.

Finally, Blake's pupils adjusted, and the deep shadows of the night took on varying shades of gray and black. He proceeded with cautious steps.

A soft rustling caught his attention—a sound that could be the gentle foot fall of someone moving with care away from the closed door, away from the light that would once again bathe the back of the house when Blake opened the door. For an instant Blake thought he could see a dark gray shape separate from the clinging shadows of the house, a hazy, vague outline against the charcoal backdrop of the sky. Then the shadows flowed together once again and the night was still.

Blake mounted the steps. Then, hand on the knob, he turned to scrutinize the area again. Nothing. No one. How very strange, he thought. Oh well, it was probably one of the hands. Maybe he didn't understand English.

Blake shrugged away his unrest as he pulled open the door and stepped into the small hallway that opened onto the kitchen. Subconsciously he cataloged the thought that there was no one in the hallway and no one in the kitchen except for Rosita and Juanita—and he'd been able to see them through the window while he'd watched the shadow man.

"Ah, Senor Saunders," greeted Juanita happily, looking up from the dish-laden working table. "You return in time for the supper, no?" She grinned broadly, black eyes sparkling with good humor against the bronze of her skin.

"I certainly couldn't pass up one of your fine meals,

237

now, could I?" Blake teased. "You're going to make me fat, Juanita, with all that good cookin'."

Juanita giggled when Blake patted a nonexistent belly. She exchanged a quick appreciative glance with Rosita, each thinking with stoic feminine logic that such a fate would never befall this handsome gringo.

"I'm going to slip up to my room to wash and change. Would you please tell the family that I'll be right down?"

"*Si,* senor," Rosita agreed.

"Thank you," Blake called over his shoulder as he exited through the door into the hallway.

He took the stairs two at a time, hurrying to his room. He was anxious to clean up and get back downstairs. Funny, he'd always been pretty much a loner, but these past two days he'd really missed the family.

Blake's weariness fell away as he stripped off his clothes to stand naked in front of the porcelain washbowl. He quickly sponged off, bathing the dust of the trail from his long, muscular body. He hurriedly pulled a brush through his tousled curls and smoothed the slash of dark mustache over his lip with a quick fingertip. The reflection in the mirror curved in an answering smile as he contemplated seeing Laura again.

There seemed to have been some sort of turning point in their relationship on the night of the dance. There was a strange fluttering in his chest as he thought of the quiet time they had spent together—the pleasurable hour alone under the star-studded sky, dancing, talking, teasing. He had almost wished the night would never end. As long as the music played, he had an excuse to hold her in his arms, listen to the sweet musical tone of her laughter, gaze into the tempting blue depths of her eyes.

All too soon the dance had been over and they had returned to the hotel and bade each other good night, going their separate ways—as they did each night in the house. Over the past weeks it had become sweet agony to

238

lie awake in the velvety darkness and know that Laura was on the other side of the wall, mere inches away.

His reflection stared back at him from the looking glass with wry amusement. What was wrong with him? My God! He was mooning around like a man in love! Deep brown eyes continued to bore into his.

You're a fool if you think you can run away from your feelings.

Who's running away? he retorted mentally.

You've been trying to run away from it for weeks. But it's not working, is it? It's not going to work—no matter what you do.

Don't be an ass! Running away from what?

Why don't you give up and admit how you feel?

Feel? Feel about what? About who?

Dazed, Blake sank wearily onto the bed. He sat there for several immobile minutes. And finally his stubborn mind gave in to the persistent thoughts that swirled through his head and his heart.

He couldn't fool himself. How could he possibly think he could fool anyone else? There was no sense in denying that Laura had become very special to him.

But what to do about it? Should he tell her how he felt? Would she even be receptive to his overtures? Yes, of course she would. Hadn't she gone out of her way lately to be friendly? No, surely her sweet attentiveness was more than simple friendship!

A little slide of apprehension tickled his stomach, and he felt like a callow schoolboy again. He was a little stunned at his own admission of genuine feeling for the girl.

Good Lord! He was thirty-four years old and this was the first time in his life he'd even contemplated such a thing! He'd always scoffed at the thought of settling down and tying himself to one woman! And now, here he was, acting like some lovesick adolescent in the throes of his first infatuation!

But what Blake was suffering from was not some passing folly, and deep down he knew it. There really was no sense in fighting his feelings any longer. They weren't going to go away; they only got stronger by the day.

He'd just have to tell her, that's all. It was suddenly all so simple, so right.

Blake felt a cleansing surge of relief. He pushed himself off the bed with renewed eagerness. He slid his long legs into firm-fitting beige trousers, stuffing the crisp white cotton shirt in with quick, efficient strokes. Shrugging the dark brown jacket across his broad shoulders, he reached for the door handle before the fabric had time to settle along the contours of his rugged frame.

Laura, Laura, Laura. His hurrying footsteps drummed out her name against the smooth polished wood of the staircase and across the parlor floor. He smoothed his hand nervously across the tumble of bronzed curls one more time, and his lips curved up in a broad anticipatory smile as he entered the dining room.

"Evening, everyone. Sorry to be so late," he called out, his gaze going first to Laura and then sweeping around the table, jerking to a halt as it fell upon William. Blake's brow furrowed as he contemplated just who the unexpected visitor might be.

The broodingly handsome dark man casually raised his head and flicked an aloof nod in Blake's direction. Then he nonchalantly raised a slim, white hand and adjusted the cuff of his immaculate silk shirt the barest fraction of an inch beneath the sleeve of his fine broadcloth coat before continuing with his meal.

The man certainly didn't look like any of Anthony's usual acquaintances or neighbors. Perhaps he's someone from Austin, Blake decided, his musings and judgment taking place so quickly that no one but Laura noticed the slight hesitation between Blake's greeting and his move toward the empty chair across from her.

"Blake, glad you could make it." Anthony's voice clearly indicated his pleasure at Blake's return. "Allow me to introduce another guest from the East. This is . . . uh . . . a friend of Laura's, Mr. William Stratford of Philadelphia."

The bottom suddenly fell out of Blake's world. He forcibly kept his face empty of all reaction as he nodded at the man, but an instant spark of displeasure turned the clear brown depths of his eyes to a stormy mahogany.

Butterflies buffeted the walls of Laura's stomach as Blake's eyes seemed to bore into her very soul. Goodness! What had she done wrong now? He had been so nice to her at the dance—and the next morning, too. She swallowed uncomfortably and quickly lowered her gaze beneath a protective brush of lashes, confused and more than a little hurt by Blake's strange hostility.

"This is Blake Saunders, Mr. Stratford," continued Anthony in explanation. "If it hadn't been for his fast thinking, Laura might not be quite as safe and sound as she is today."

"Oh?" said William.

Was there the tiniest hint of condescendence in that bland comment? thought an already irritated Blake as Anthony hurried on with the story.

"Yes, the stagecoach they were riding in was ambushed by a band of renegade Mexicans. Two lives were lost, including Blake's partner's—"

"Antonio, please, not at the supper table." Maria turned censoring eyes on her husband.

"I'm sorry, darling. You're quite right. This is no place for such a conversation. I'm sure Laura will tell you the whole story in good time, William. Anyway, since then

241

we've been pleased to have Blake as our guest while he explores the surrounding land for a potential investment."

"How very interesting," William murmured as he gazed across the polished tabletop, intuitively sizing up the bronze giant of a man as he eased his large frame into the chair. Would he pose any threat to William's plans? He certainly looked very irritated at something. "You must tell me all about your little adventure. The only things I had to worry about on my trip were heat and boredom, which could hardly be considered detrimental to my well-being."

William chuckled dryly at his own joke. Laura winced and lowered her head. Was William implying that Blake's actions hadn't been quite as heroic as Anthony suggested? It certainly sounded that way. Drat! She'd so wanted everyone to get along. What in the world had happened? They seemed to have gotten off on the wrong foot before a word had even been spoken.

Blake's eyes narrowed dangerously in perusal of the offending figure across the table before he turned his attention to the linen napkin beside his plate, snapping it out with such ferocity that the material popped loudly before he drew it across his lap with irritated haste.

Once again Anthony took up the conversation, anxious to soothe the suddenly troubled atmosphere of the room. "Uh . . . how long do you plan on visiting in Texas, William?"

"Well, no longer than necessary to take care of my business dealings—"

"What kind of business?" questioned Blake, struggling to keep the venom out of his voice.

"Umm . . . well, I'd probably better not divulge that information quite yet. My partner stressed the importance of confidentiality. I wouldn't want to betray his trust."

"Of course not," agreed Blake a bit snidely.

"At this point, I'm . . . uh . . . simply awaiting the arrival of some business funds so I can finalize the agreement. Actually, they were supposed to be waiting for me at the bank in Galveston upon my arrival. But there was a muddle of sorts. I suppose my . . . uh . . . my partner was anticipating the transaction being handled with the same expediency we receive back East, and he simply didn't allow enough time."

William gave a small shrug and decided he'd better change the subject since there was no business partner, and he didn't want to keep fabricating a story that might not sound plausible to his host. He raised his glass for a sip of wine. *Egad, is it impossible to get a quality wine in this godforsaken place?* If this was the best these backwoods men had to offer, William would opt for whiskey from now on.

"Interesting wine, Anthony. I don't believe I've ever tasted anything quite like it," remarked William. "Don't you agree, my dear?" he asked Laura.

"I . . . uh . . . I suppose so," she replied hastily, her gaze darting to his face and then back to the untasted food she'd been pushing around her plate since Blake's arrival. "I really don't have your expertise," she finished lamely.

"Ah, yes. I suppose a season on the continent does broaden one's scope somewhat. Too bad you and Cynthia never had the opportunity. I always thought it a shame that Henry was such an old miser about the better things in life."

"You've traveled extensively?" Blake inquired.

"Oh, yes. Paris and London are absolutely delightful this time of year."

"I suppose you've traveled throughout the East as well."

"Well, yes, I have."

243

"Where exactly?" Blake struggled to sound nonchalant. Just who was this man? And what did he want?

"Well, all up and down the seaboard, naturally."

"Ever been to the capital?"

"You mean Washington?" William asked. "Yes, on occasion. However, I find politics rather boring so I generally avoid such areas."

Good Lord, thought Anthony, watching Blake's expression grow even stormier as William continued his discourse. He had to do something quick before Blake completely lost his composure.

"Was there no news for you at the bank in Galveston?" Anthony finally interrupted William, hoping it would alleviate the strain in the atmosphere.

"Actually no. So now I've asked that word be sent to Washington-on-the-Brazos. Quaint the way they call that small village by the same name as our great capital city, isn't it? I suppose I'll hear from them when it's all straightened out. In the meantime, I'm afraid I'll just have to wait. I sincerely hope I won't be an imposition on your generous hospitality."

"No, no, of course not," Anthony assured quickly. "Let me see now . . . You actually came to Texas because of this business deal?"

"Oh, no. I came to Texas because of Laura." William shot Blake a quick warning glance. Hands off. She belongs to me. Blake's eyes sparked black fire in return. "I only agreed to transact the business deal as a favor to my friend. After all, I was coming to Texas anyway, so why not take advantage of the opportunity to combine business *and* pleasure. Anyway, he assured me that he would send the funds immediately. Oh, I'm quite sure they're on the way." William raised his hand as if in pledge.

Blake gritted his teeth. The man was a phony. Couldn't Laura see it? Couldn't Anthony? Or were they so taken with his fancy manners and highfalutin speech that they couldn't see him for what he was? How could they be so blind? It was obvious to Blake that William was spoiled, egotistical, and condescending and up to no good. And, of course, his opinion didn't have a damned thing to do with Laura!

Blake stabbed a piece of meat with his fork and carried it sullenly to his mouth, mulling over William's story as he angrily chewed. There had to be an ulterior motive to William's actions. Despite his pretty speech about friendship and loyalty, William certainly didn't strike Blake as the type of person who would inconvenience himself for anyone, not even Laura. No, there was definitely more to Mr. Stratford than he was divulging.

And just what in hell did he have to do with Laura? Blake's stormy gaze flicked back and forth between the two figures across from him.

Laura squirmed uneasily in her chair. The dark looks she was receiving from across the table made her highly uncomfortable. Why was Blake so angry with her? She hadn't done anything. And why was William acting like such a snob? Was he intentionally trying to antagonize Blake? And whatever for? Oh, why couldn't Blake and William have gotten along? Would that have been so much to ask? Two wicked old tomcats couldn't be more cantankerous than these two were being, sparring with words, sniping at each other in subtle ways. It seemed almost as if William was doing everything he could to point out the vast differences between his own impeccable social standing and Blake's dubious status.

The tense meal finally came to an end, and the group adjourned to the parlor where whiskey and cigars were offered to the men and sherry to the ladies.

Blake slouched morosely in the cushioning depths of a chair, brooding eyes watching each and every move that William made. He frowned in irritated remembrance of

William's quick-footed move to position himself beside Laura on the sofa. Just what in hell was going on?

Friend. Wasn't that how Anthony had introduced Stratford? Where in the world had Laura picked up a *friend* like this pompous ass? And just what was he doing in Texas?

William continued to speak in his secure, indulgent tones, going out of his way—or so it seemed to Blake—to draw Laura into conversations about places and people, with whom only the two of them were familiar. Blake continued to brood about what role William had played in Laura's life before she came to Texas. By what rights did he speak with such easy familiarity?

In exasperation, Blake flashed a dazzling smile at Maria. Two could play this little game. He chatted with Maria about fashions and parties and plays, regaling her with grandiose tales of Washington's glittering society. He'd show Laura and William that he was no hayseed! During his tenure with the department he'd been a guest at some of the most splendid parties imaginable, and he took every opportunity to divulge this information. Blake turned his full attention on Maria, inclining his head in rapt attention, listening with feigned delight to every word she uttered, expressing great interest in the upcoming San Antonio social season—all the while thinking that the war would certainly put a stop to much of the festivities—responding to everything Maria said with a great show of enthusiasm, complimenting her profusely at every opportunity, commenting time and again on how very lucky Anthony was to have such a beautiful and charming wife.

Anthony watched the scene being enacted before him with barely concealed amusement. He was no fool. He felt no threat from Blake's intense attention to Maria. He knew all this sudden interest stemmed not from Blake's enthrallment with Maria but rather as retaliation to the

246

attention William was lavishing on Laura.

And with great curiosity Anthony watched Laura's reactions to Blake's bright banter. The more attention Blake paid to Maria, the more Laura fawned over William. William, on the other hand, seemed oblivious to the whole byplay, basking in the glow of Laura's attention as if by divine right.

The frenzied conversation went on for the better part of an hour. Anthony was finally distracted from his ruminations concerning all three of his houseguests when William suddenly turned from his conversation with Laura and questioned him about the size of the ranch.

"And what type of cattle do you raise?"

"Longhorns," Anthony managed to answer, not sure what else William's question had entailed.

"How interesting. Laura has been telling me a little about your endeavor here. I find it extremely fascinating. Do you have one of the original Mexican grants?"

"No, I came to Texas later than that."

"I was under the impression that cotton was the main source of revenue for Texas farmers. You must have a great deal of faith in this new venture of yours. You strike me as a shrewd businessman, so I suppose there must be a great deal of money to be made."

Anthony resigned himself to answering William's prying inquiry. Stratford certainly didn't appear to be the type of man who would have much interest in cattle or farming, but Anthony tried to answer his queries politely.

"Darling, why not show Mr. Stratford the map of the ranch you have in the study?" Maria suggested.

"Capital idea," William said with apparent delight at her offer.

"Very well," Anthony agreed. "Come along, my dear, and I'll try to answer our guest's questions a little more thoroughly."

Maria accepted his arm, and they escorted William out of the parlor and across the hallway to the room that Anthony used as a combination study and office.

Laura's gaze darted quickly toward Blake. She smiled nervously, very aware that Blake was considerably irritated for some reason, although for the life of her she couldn't fathom what she had done to make him so angry. She searched her mind for something to say, some way to break the uncomfortable silence.

"I . . . uh . . . suppose you had a busy day today."

"Yes, I did," Blake almost snapped. "It appears that *you* had a very busy day, too. Tell me, have you been expecting Mr. Stratford's arrival all along?"

"Well, no . . . I mean yes."

"Which is it?" Blake said with a scowl, thrusting his long legs out in front of him and slumping down even lower in his chair. His brooding eyes raked Laura as he struggled with his temper.

Was he angry with Laura or with himself? He really had no right to be so irritated with her. He had no hold on Laura, no right to place expectations on her—and that was his own damn fault! How was she to know that he'd been toying with the now seemingly ridiculous thought of making some sort of commitment to her this very evening? It was now all too obvious to Blake's wounded pride that she didn't care for him in the same way.

But what about those times he had held her in his arms? What about the way she had responded to him? The way her lips had reached hungrily for his, the way her skin had grown as warm as sun-kissed honey under his searching hands. Would she have responded to him so completely if there was another man in her life?

Maybe. Who knew how a woman's mind worked? Why had he been so stupid as never to consider such a possibility?

Blake's mouth turned down in a sardonic sneer as he remembered how hard it had been for him to admit even to himself that he might care about Laura. How could he expect her to know how he felt when he'd been denying it to himself all along? He chided himself bitterly for his own stubbornness and stupidity.

What a fool he'd almost made of himself! My God! What if he'd made his declaration of undying love tonight and William had shown up tomorrow? Wouldn't *that* have been a humiliating experience! The only thing left for him to do was gather his tattered pride and put the whole foolish notion behind him from here on.

He'd always been perfectly happy to live his life alone and unattached. His obsession with Laura probably stemmed from the simple fact that there had been few other women around. Well, it wouldn't take long to fix that problem once he got to Louisiana! Most probably he was still suffering from the effects of John's death. After all, they'd been very close. It was only normal to transfer some of that feeling to the only other person around at the time. Yes. Of course. That was it. He'd been suffering from a delayed reaction to the loss of his partner. Blake breathed a small sigh of relief. Everything was going to be fine.

He'd walked away from women far more beautiful than Laura; he could damn well do it again. It had never bothered him before. Why should it be any different this time?

Because, you utter ass, not one of them ever reached for your soul and wound it around her little finger with no effort at all. The relentless thought was galling.

Shut up! Just forget it! Forget her! Put the whole thing out of your mind.

"Just what is the point of Mr. Stratford's trip to Texas?" Blake was appalled to find himself asking,

249

despite his stern determination to put the whole humiliating experience behind him.

"He came out of concern for my welfare," retorted Laura, suddenly equally angry at Blake's unfathomable actions during the course of the evening and his present presumptuous tone. What right had he to question her friend's motives?

Blake snorted derisively. "Is that so? How touching! Just how well do you know this man?"

"I know him very well, if that's any of your business!"

Blake snapped to attention. He leaned forward, hands braced stiffly against his knees, face contorted. "Really? And just how 'well' is that?"

"You're insufferable!"

"And you're a foolish young woman who is about to let some lecherous two-bit hustler take advantage of her stupidity. You can't even see that the man is after something—"

"He came here because of me!" she interrupted angrily.

"Oh, I have no doubt that he wouldn't be adverse to sampling your luscious charms . . . that is, if he hasn't already . . ." Blake's insides churned at this devastating thought.

"Oh! You wretched, egotistical . . . you . . . you pompous jackass! How dare you!" Laura jumped up from her chair to stand glaring down at him, hands clenched tightly at her side as she fought to keep her composure. "By what right do you cast slurs on my reputation and on William's?"

"At least I'm not blind to the man's obvious faults. Someone has to open your eyes! Anyone with any brains at all can see that the man is after something."

"Just who do you think you are?" Laura raged, struggling to keep her voice to a whisper so as not to alert the whole household to their bitter argument. "Why do men persist in the ridiculous idea that women have no more sense than a goose! Is it some sort of balm for your monumental egos? Uncle Henry always treated all of us—Aunt Mary, Cynthia, and me—like half-witted simpletons. He made even the most trivial decisions and never bothered to ask our opinion about a thing!"

"What's that got to do with the issue at hand?" Blake demanded.

"Everything! I'm sick of men running my life! I was smart enough to get to Texas without a man's help. I'm sure I can continue to take care of myself just fine! I refused to let Uncle Henry run my life, and I'll be damned if you're going to step in and try to do the same thing!"

"I'm not trying to run your life!"

"Well, it certainly sounds like it to me," Laura replied hotly. "You mind your own business. I'll run my life as I see fit!"

"But you don't understand. I think—"

"I don't care what you think! William's certainly not going to try to do anything you haven't already tried!" Laura hissed at Blake, her face suffused with scarlet.

Blake's mouth snapped shut. How dare she! Was she actually accusing him of some underhanded behavior? Why, he could have taken advantage of her any number of times! Hadn't he always behaved like a gentleman . . . well, almost always? What about that day at the creek? Hadn't he ignored the searing pain of his own passion out of concern for her? My God! What did she expect from him? He was only human! He certainly had never forced himself on her; she'd always been more than eager to participate in the kisses and embraces they'd exchanged. And if he wasn't such a gentleman, he certainly could have had a great deal more than he'd settled for!

"You don't have the slightest idea of what you're letting yourself in for."

"I most certainly do!" she exclaimed, stomping her foot for emphasis. "William is everything I've ever wanted."

"Ha! You don't know *what* you want! How could you *want* your dear William so much when you responded to me the way you did?"

"Oh! What a wicked thing to say. How could you! I'll have you know I love William."

"Love!" Blake spat. "You don't know the meaning of the word! You think those foolish little schoolgirl moonings you've felt for William mean you're in love? You think that simpering, foppish caricature of a man could ever even remotely offer you what you really need? Not likely, my dear Laura! I'll show you what real love between a man and woman is all about!"

Blake uncoiled himself from the chair in a flash, grabbing Laura and hauling her into his steely embrace before she knew what was happening. His mouth slanted angrily against hers; his tongue parted her lips, delving, thrusting with hot, mind-paralyzing strokes. The sweet burning taste of the whiskey he'd downed over the course of the evening set her tender flesh atingle. He raked the soft inside of her mouth with blazing finesse, building a fire in the pit of Laura's belly that threatened to consume her very soul. She struggled for a moment, hands pushing uselessly against his granite-hard chest, then her arms slid around his neck, and she arched her body against his, blindly seeking to lose herself in his heated strength.

The kiss ended as quickly as it had begun. When Blake stepped away from Laura, her knees buckled and she swayed weakly. His hands clasped the soft flesh of her arms until she regained her equilibrium, his breath equally as ragged as hers as they both struggled back to reality. When her lashes slowly swept up and her eyes focused once again on his angry face, he gave her a small exasperated shake and thrust her from him.

Blake and Laura stared at each other, inches that might as well have been miles separating their sweetly tortured bodies. With a soft curse, Blake finally pulled his gaze from her flushed face and stomped to the breakfront to pour another splash of whiskey into his glass. He stood with his back to Laura for a long moment, sightless eyes staring out into the velvet blackness of the night as he wrestled to subdue his desire.

The sounds of approaching footsteps finally penetrated the angry haze enveloping him. He heard the rustling of Laura's gown as she reacted to the return of the others by settling herself quickly back on the sofa. Pulling a deep breath into his laboring lungs, Blake struggled to compose his face.

"Very interesting, Anthony," drawled William as he followed Anthony and Maria back into the parlor.

Blake slowly turned around. "Anyone need a refill?" he offered in a casual voice that he hoped did not betray the emotions still swirling inside him.

"No thanks, old man," replied William.

As Anthony moved forward to replenish his glass, he noted the rigid clinch of Blake's jaw and the ramrod stiffness of his back. Glass in hand, Anthony returned to the sofa and took his place beside Maria. He quickly perceived the stunned look on Laura's face and the vacant way she responded to William's jovial comments about the ranch.

Anthony wondered just what had transpired between Laura and Blake while they'd been out of the room. Maybe it was a good thing that Blake was planning to accompany him to Austin. Otherwise, some real fireworks might well be in the offing.

Finally Blake was at the end of his patience. The air in

253

the room seemed stifling. He tugged distractedly at the collar that, for the last hour, had threatened to choke him. If he stayed in the room with that pompous jackanapes one minute longer, he would punch the self-satisfied smirk right off William's face. If he had to watch William lay his hand caressingly on Laura's arm one more time or watch him lower his head and lean ridiculously close to her to whisper yet another silly inanity—

No, he'd had all he could stand.

"Anthony," Blake choked out, almost leaping to his feet. "I'm sorry. You'll have to excuse me. I'm really tired from the long day. And if we're planning on riding out at daybreak . . ."

"Of course, Blake, you're right. It's time we all retired. Go on up. We'll be right behind you."

"Good night," Blake managed to mutter before he strode from the room, oblivious to the fact that Laura's troubled gaze followed him until he was out of sight.

His long, angry strides carried him quickly to his room. He twisted the doorknob viciously and slipped into the room, slamming the door behind him. He stumbled through the moonlit room, yanking off his coat and throwing it on the bed as he made his way to the dresser. His hand shook when he fumbled for a match, struck it and held it toward the candle.

He was leaning against the dresser, struggling for composure, when the gentle murmur of voices caught his attention. Quickly he extinguished the feeble flame and moved cat-quiet across the room. Very carefully he turned the knob, easing the door open so that he could see just the tiniest sliver of the hallway through the slit. He stood still, his eye fitted against the slender peephole.

Two figures passed his doorway, William's taller bulk almost obscuring Laura's slim frame. All that was visible of her for a moment was the voluptuous swirl of her skirts as they paced slowly down the hallway. Laura paused in front of her door and turned to face William, offering her hand in dainty farewell.

"Good night, William. This evening has been such a pleasure—"

Laura's words were cut off as William quickly bent his head and claimed her lips.

A black rage clouded Blake's eyes. His emotions whirled and fought and protested as he watched the almost unbearable scene being enacted only inches away. He finally pulled his stricken gaze away, turning to press his fevered forehead against the cool wood of the door frame as his fingertips gently pushed the door completely shut.

The tiny, almost imperceptible click of the latch was like a shot to his heart.

Chapter 22

In the misty quiet moments just before dawn, two silent figures readied themselves and their mounts for the long trip ahead. The flickering light of the lantern bathed the men in its feeble glow as they went about their tasks: thrusting bits between the horses' strong, square teeth, fastening harnesses, pulling cinches tight. Blake tossed the heavy saddlebags across Blackjack's broad back and fastened them securely just as Anthony was finishing with his horse.

"Better get on our way," remarked Anthony as he extinguished the lantern and led Dancer out of the shadowed barn.

Blackjack whinnied his protest at being left behind. His halter jingled merrily in the silence of the vast deserted building as he gave his head a spirited shake. He snuffled loudly, prancing sideways to pull against Blake in eager anticipation of the freedom of the trail.

"All right, boy. Take it easy. We're going, too," Blake said softly, running his hand along the big horse's muscular neck to soothe him before gathering up the leads to follow Anthony out into the cool morning air.

Pale butter-colored fingers of sunlight were already reaching into the night sky, chasing away the deep purple shadows, heralding another golden summer day. A soft little breeze soughed through the treetops, stirring the leaves in a dainty dance. Blake scanned the skies, hoping that it wouldn't get too hot before the long day was done.

"Ready?" questioned Anthony.

"Yes," Blake answered, slipping his foot into the stirrup and mounting Blackjack in one swift movement.

Anthony noted a decided lack of enthusiasm in Blake's voice and cast a quick glance back at him. He wondered if Blake was wishing he hadn't volunteered to accompany Anthony to Austin. Even in the deep shadows cloaking the yard, Anthony could see that Blake's gaze was fastened broodingly on the house.

Anthony had no doubt that the object of Blake's morose musings this morning was none other than Laura. He wasn't even too surprised that Blake's black mood from last night was still hanging on. If anything, this morning was worse.

Actually, Anthony sympathized with Blake, feeling that he was removed enough from the situation to recognize what was really bothering Blake: William's arrival. Blake's trip was providing William with a golden opportunity. The thought of all those days he would be alone with Laura must be driving Blake to distraction. William had made it perfectly clear last night that there was more between himself and Laura than mere friendship.

Blake tried to concentrate on the journey ahead, but time and again his gaze was pulled to the window of Laura's bedroom. Was she sleeping? Could she hear the small rustlings and jingles of the horses as they picked their way slowly down the path? Would she even miss him while he was gone? Or would William fill her days and thoughts?

Blake scowled darkly. He didn't like William Stratford—not one little bit. And it was more than Laura's angry declaration of love for William that set Blake's teeth on edge. The man was too smooth. There was something about him, something Blake couldn't quite put his finger on.

Blake's intuition continued to nag; parts of William's story didn't ring quite true. Oh, Stratford had come to Texas for a reason, all right, but Blake would bet everything he had that it wasn't the one Stratford said it was.

Just what did he want? Laura? Did he act like a man so overcome with love that he had followed his sweetheart all these many miles to claim her? No, that was hardly the case. His attitude toward Laura was too smug. He didn't appear to be pleading his suit at all. It was as if he took her acceptance for granted.

But why had he waited until now to pursue Laura's affections? After all, they had lived in the same community for many years, been well acquainted, traveled in the same circles. If Stratford was in love with Laura, why hadn't he spoken up before? What could have compelled him to come all this way at this point in time?

There were ways to find out such things if one had the right contacts, and Blake certainly did. The department was privy to a vast amount of information. Blake had only to ask. If there was anything amiss about Stratford, the department would be able to track it down. Blake had never used his position for personal interest before, but he damn well planned to do so now!

It hurt terribly to think that Laura didn't return his feelings. But, regardless of how things were between them, he owed it to her to make sure that William wouldn't hurt her in any way.

She was so young, so naive. She deserved better than what Blake was very much afraid William had in store for her. And she was blinded by her ridiculous notions of love and loyalty to see William for what he was.

It was up to Blake to set things straight.

Anthony watched Blake closely as they made their way under the canopy of overhanging limbs and past the silent house. Was Blake even aware that he was in love with Laura? If so, he had only recently attained that knowledge. Blake struck him as the kind of man who, with a fervor, would fight settling down. Ah, yes, but those were the very ones who fell the hardest when love caught up with them.

Anthony's voice broke the silence of the dawn. "Are you all right?"

Blake's head whipped around. "Wh-what? Oh . . . uh . . . yes, sure I'm fine." He forced a semblance of a smile. "Gonna be a warm day, isn't it? Good travelin' weather if it doesn't get too steamy. I'm really looking forward to this trip. I'll be interested to see Austin. I've heard a lot about it."

"Sure. I hope you can stay long enough to get acquainted with some of the folks."

"You bet."

Blake continued to ramble about the coming trip while Anthony nodded occasionally in agreement, not even bothering to listen to the conversation as he continued to mull the situation over in his mind. He knew there was little of importance being said—Blake was only trying to get his mind off of Laura. But he wasn't fooling Anthony one bit. He'd been watching Laura and Blake over the past few weeks and suspected their feelings were deeper than either realized.

Anthony liked Blake. Really liked him. He seemed to be a good man, an honest man, a hard-working man. He was the type of man who would provide properly for a woman. Anthony had quietly been hoping that Blake and Laura would come to an understanding and that Blake would not leave Texas after all. Texas needed such men.

His sister needed such a man. And he'd been so sure that Laura cared for Blake—until William showed up.

Anthony sighed deeply and turned toward Blake, very tempted to bring the subject up. Maybe a friendly little discussion would help Blake work through what was bothering him. But, no, that wasn't Anthony's way. He simply couldn't interfere in someone else's life like that. Everyone had a right to make his own choice.

Anthony shifted uncomfortably as he remembered how in past years some of the townspeople had alluded to his relationship with Olivia Moore—dropping small hints about marriage and settling down. Anthony frowned at the disturbing memory.

He wondered if Olivia ever thought of what might have been. If he hadn't made that trip to San Antonio and been swept into that crazy rushing river of emotion by Maria's dazzling charms, he probably would have married Olivia.

Anthony settled his hat more comfortably on his head and sighed with resignation. Life with Olivia would have been very pleasant, no doubt. They thought alike, wanted many of the same things out of life. But would a peaceful, sweet, enduring love have been able to take the place of the fire and passion that Maria offered? Maybe. The thought made him feel disloyal, but sometimes deep down he wondered if a gentle kind of love might not be better.

There was no sense even thinking about what might have been. Anthony would never know. It wasn't that he regretted marrying Maria; he was still wildly in love with her. But there were times—more and more often lately—when he felt they were at cross-purposes. Would he ever *really* know Maria?

Oh, he knew the sweet contours of her body better than his own. He knew the ecstasy of losing himself in her heated embrace. He knew the flash of pride he felt when he looked at her beauty and marveled that she belonged to him. But would he ever know her mind? Was it just because they came from two different cultures that he felt there was a part of Maria he would never know? Would time take care of that strange gap in their relationship?

Damn this war and the pressures it put him under! Anthony felt compelled—even driven—to do everything he could to help his adopted state maintain its freedom. He desperately wanted it to grow and prosper and attain the greatness that he believed Texas and its people were destined for, a destiny he felt in every fiber of his being. But each hour, each day, away from home and Maria was just widening the chasm between them.

Oh, the fire was still there—the physical passion. He still desired her as much as he had from the first moment he'd laid eyes upon her. But he had no greater understanding of her mind, her feelings, her dreams, her soul, than he had the day they married.

Was it this way between every man and wife? When the first blazing of passion began to cool, did everyone find himself facing a stranger? Would Laura and Blake suffer from the same malady even if they did manage to admit their love for one another? Or would they be able to find that feeling of togetherness, which Anthony felt somehow cheated of? What right did he have to interfere, to prod Blake and Laura toward a recognition of their feelings, when he had questions about his own marriage?

Anthony kicked his heels into the soft flanks of his horse, prodding Dancer into a pace that would drive away the uncomfortable thoughts. He had a commitment to the state, he thought grimly. He'd settle that issue first, and when this crazy war was over, he'd do his damnedest to open those secret doors to Maria's feelings. But for right now he was going to put all those troublesome questions behind him and concentrate first on the task ahead.

There was a war to be won.

Blake threw one last glance back at the house and then spurred Blackjack to a gallop so he could catch up with Anthony. The horses broke from under the canopy of trees and into the soft misty light of sunrise. Blake glanced at Anthony and noted the dark look on his face. He wondered what was causing it.

Was Anthony worried about the war? Did he have misgivings about where his loyalties lay? Blake idly wondered just how much influence Maria had over Anthony. Could Anthony be tempted to help Mexico out of loyalty and love for his wife? Just how far would a man go to hold onto the woman he loved?

Yes, how far indeed?

And the drumming of the horses' hooves beat out a tattoo against the hard Texas dirt as the two men, each struggling with his own personal demon, silently searched for peace of mind.

Blake wearily dismounted and threw Blackjack's reins over the hitching post. He placed his hands against the small of his back and stretched his tired muscles. Lord, it felt good to finally climb out of that saddle and know he wouldn't have to mount up again immediately. The trip to Austin had been long and hot. After two whirlwind days, Blake had left Anthony there and continued on his way alone. It had taken many more hours in the saddle to finally reach Louisiana.

He walked from the sunny street into the gloom of the livery stable. "Yo, anybody here?" he called, and his voice echoed hollowly in the vast expanse of the old wooden building.

A wizened little man appeared out of the last stall. "What can I do for you?"

"I need to board my horse for a few days," said Blake.

"Be glad to. I just got this stall cleaned out. You can

put him in here." The little man spit a stream of brown tobacco juice into the dusty straw and wiped his mouth on the sleeve of his shirt.

"I'll be at the hotel across the street for a few days," Blake explained after he'd settled Blackjack into the stall. "Could you direct me to the telegraph office?"

"Go north two blocks. You can't miss the train depot. Telegraph's in the corner office."

"Thanks," Blake said, tugging at the brim of his hat.

Fifteen minutes later Blake was scanning the contents of his message one last time to be sure he hadn't left out anything of importance. No, it all read fine. There was just one odd entry, but Blake knew his contact back in Washington would simply fill the request and not question why Blake wanted to know about one William Stratford.

Yes, thought Blake with a feeling of relief, in just a few days he ought to have some answers.

Blake handed the pages of foolscap to the telegraph operator. The man flicked a quick glance at the long message and then back at his customer's grim face. He shrugged his shoulders and set to work at the telegraph key.

It had been four days since Blake sent his message. Four long days, and four even longer nights while he tried to drown his troubled thoughts in whiskey and women.

He lay on the lumpy hotel bed in the dark hours of the night, hands folded under his head. A small breeze lifted the corner of the lacy curtains bracketing the open window. Blake could hear raucous laughter and the tinkling of a piano from the saloon across the street. But he'd been in no mood for crowds tonight. It was useless anyway.

No amount of whiskey could deaden the yearning he felt. No other woman could drive from his mind the one he really wanted.

Not that he hadn't tried.

The first night he'd accepted the overtures of a saloon girl who was the exact opposite of Laura: blonde, short, luxuriously rounded with an abundance of sweet, willing flesh. But all of her allurements had been for naught when they retired to the privacy of her room above the saloon. Her insipid little giggle had almost driven him to distraction. The abundant flesh had suddenly felt doughy under his hands. His body had refused to respond, no matter how skilled her hands and mouth. He'd finally given up in embarrassment, pleading exhaustion from his arduous trip, and slipped her a bill large enough to still her protests.

The next night he had deliberately sought out a girl with long, brown curls and a slender figure. She'd been warm and willing, quite beautiful by most standards. But, despite the similarities, she hadn't been Laura.

Her hair hadn't been the long, silky length of curls that Laura's was. It didn't feel warm and velvety soft the way Laura's had when Blake had twined his fingers in it that afternoon on the riverbank. And young though she was, her skin didn't feel as fresh and satiny and fine textured as Laura's had under his eager hands. And the harsh rasping sounds she made had not been the soft little mewings that had spilled from Laura's lips when he'd caressed her and trailed kisses down her throat and across her silken breasts.

Once again Blake had dropped a bill on the dresser for far fewer services rendered than he was paying for and returned to his room alone to spend a long, restless night with nothing but aching loins and burning memories to keep him company.

Today, surely today, his reply would come. He turned

his head toward the window and wondered how many hours until morning.

In the long, dark hours of the night he willed the sun to rise, willed the telegraph wires between Washington and this noisy frontier town in Louisiana to hum with the answers to his questions.

Chapter 23

Laura tallied the figures for the fourth time. They still
didn't come out right. It didn't make sense. There was a
great deal of money going out, but the goods simply
weren't listed in the supplies inventory in Anthony's
journal. She threw the pen down on the desk and pushed
the irksome books out of the way. There had to be an
answer somewhere. Perhaps whoever had checked the
supplies in had made a mistake. Yes, of course, that made
perfect sense.

It must have been one of the Mexican hands, and
they'd probably forgotten to notify Maria or Anthony
when the goods were received. Or perhaps they were
simply having a difficult time translating the long rows of
figures from English to the Spanish that they were used
to dealing with. There was simply nothing left to do but
check the storerooms herself.

Determined to solve the problem that afternoon if at
all possible, Laura grabbed up the journal and the pen
and ink pot, then hurried out of the study and across the
broad entry hall. She almost collided with Rosita when
she pushed through the doorway into the dim back hall
off of the kitchen.

"Oh, good. I was just coming to look for you, Rosita.

Do you know where the extra household supplies are stored? Medicines, bolts of cloth, linens—that kind of thing."

"Some in that closet," Rosita replied, pointing toward a door on the far side of the hall. "Others out in the storeroom behind the barn."

"Thank you. Could you fetch a light? I want to check something in here." Laura pulled the door to the pantry open and poked her head into the dark recesses of the large closet. Shelves lined the walls on three sides, from the ceiling to the floor.

Rosita scurried back from the kitchen with a small lamp, her hand cupped protectively over the flickering flame. "Here, senorita." She handed it to Laura.

"Thank you." Laura lifted the light high and stepped inside the enclosure, turning slowly so she could view the contents of each shelf, top to bottom. She cleared a spot on a plank of convenient height for her light and journal. Pushing the little ink pot to the back so that it wouldn't spill, she opened her ledger to the proper page and began to count the supplies on the shelves against the numbers scribed in the book.

Rosita watched with perplexed interest as Laura ran her tallies. She tried to be helpful by reaching every once in a while to push a bolt of cloth or a cluster of containers and bottles out of the way so the ones behind would be visible to Laura.

Laura frowned at the book. "Why, there's not nearly as much in here as the inventory shows. Drat! The orders don't match the inventory ledger, and the inventory ledger doesn't match the actual count," she muttered as she finished her survey.

Rosita shrugged. "Perhaps the rest is in the store-room."

"Yes, I suppose so. Well, there's no sense wasting any more time in here. Those supplies have to be somewhere.

And I'm not giving up until I find them."

"*Si*, senorita," Rosita intoned gravely, although she had little understanding of what Laura was babbling about.

Laura handed the lamp back to Rosita and then gathered up her paraphernalia once again. When they had both stepped out of the pantry, she closed the door with a loud bang. "Thank you, Rosita. Ummm . . . do you happen to know if Miguel is down at the barn?"

"No, senorita, I do not know. I haven't seen him this morning. He does not come often to the house."

"Well, I'm going down there anyway. Maybe there'll be someone who can show me the storeroom."

"*Si*, senorita."

Laura was just about to reach for the knob on the back door when she heard William call her name. She sighed in exasperation and considered slipping out without answering him. She was almost instantly ashamed of the thought. How could she even consider being so rude to dear William? He'd been the epitome of attentiveness ever since his arrival; she owed him no less than her undivided attention whenever possible.

After all, it *was* because of her that he was in Texas—and evidently bored to distraction. If he'd said it once, he'd said it a million times: Texas certainly couldn't hold a light to the glamor and activities of even the smallest towns back East, and how did anyone stand all this solitude and silence day after day without going balmy.

She knew William was used to the bright lights and hectic schedule of Philadelphia, but surely he'd known he couldn't expect such diversions here in Texas. Laura hated to admit it, even to herself, but lately his monotonous complaints were beginning to grate on her nerves.

She sighed again and dropped her hand from the knob. Yes, of course, the inventory could wait. She certainly

268

owed William more consideration than that. It was just that she so desperately wanted to complete the task before Anthony returned. He'd be so proud of her efforts, as well as relieved that the problem had been solved—*if* she ever managed to find enough time to do so! But, good heavens, did William have to make it so difficult?

He seemed to monopolize her every moment. Sometimes she felt as though she couldn't breathe! The only opportunity she had to devote to her challenging task was during the morning when both William and Maria slept late. At least those hours—if nothing else—were still her own.

"Yes, William. I'm coming." She forced a cheerful smile onto her face. With measured footsteps she crossed the kitchen and made her way into the parlor.

"There you are, darling!" William came quickly to her side, looking as handsome as ever. He leaned to bestow a tender kiss on her lips.

"Oops! Watch out for the inkhorn," Laura admonished as the small bottle was jostled precariously. She slipped quickly out of his arms to keep it from spilling ink down her dress.

"Where have you been? I looked in the study, fully expecting you to be closeted away in there, since you've practically locked yourself in that dreary room every day."

"I was checking the inventory."

"Really, Laura, why do you insist on continuing with this nonsense? It's not a woman's place. Look." He grabbed her right hand and surveyed it darkly. "Ink smudges on your lovely fingers. Hardly proper at all."

"William, really!" Laura pulled her hand gently from his grasp. She felt as if she were trying to explain something to a petulant child. "Please try to understand and be patient. I've told you before. I promised Anthony

269

that I would do the work—and I intend to. If you'd just let me finish the work, I could devote my full time to you. Besides, I must admit that I'm rather enjoying the challenge."

William shook his handsome head sadly. "What a waste of that pretty head, spending hours shut up in that dank old room pouring over those boring journals."

"William," she admonished again, a hint of irritation creeping into her voice. "It's not a dank old room. Actually it's quite sunny for the better part of the day and very pleasant. And the books are not boring. Surely you've experienced the enjoyment of solving some perplexing problem?"

"Well . . . uh . . . of course I have, dear," replied William, who in actuality had done everything in his power to avoid every initiation into the business world that his father had ever tried to provide over the years.

Such boring pursuits weren't in his realm of interest. William scoffed at the thought of worrying about such mundane endeavors when he had a juicy inheritance due on his next birthday. With a little luck and a great deal of skill, once he got his hands on that trust fund he should be able to support himself and his habits in the grand style to which he was accustomed. All he had to do was obtain enough funds to tide him over until that time.

No doubt about it, the thought of taking Laura for his wife was becoming more appealing, especially when she might come endowed with a tidy bundle of cash herself.

It was time to lay his cards on the table.

How lucky for him that Laura had turned out to be such a delectable little morsel. The thought of possessing her was becoming a burning obsession with him, and he fully intended to have that pleasure, no matter what. Perhaps that growing desire had even helped tip the scales toward his final decision. But he had to admit that the main attraction of her brother's wealth was what had truly sweetened the pot. It had been almost painless to come finally to the conclusion that—with a little guidance—Laura would make a properly obedient wife.

William was smugly delighted that his hunch had been right. It was all too obvious that Anthony had a great deal of money and the promise of even greater riches in the future. Surely such a prosperous man would be more than willing to share a little of that wealth with his only sister—and her devoted husband.

"Then I simply don't understand why you complain about what I'm doing."

"Ummm?" William pushed aside his fanciful musings and turned his attention back to Laura. "Because such things are a man's responsibility. I just don't understand your interest in figures and inventories." Heaven forbid that she should get it in her head that she would have a say in their financial affairs! No, he needed to nip this unseemly inclination in the bud immediately!

With growing determination, William gingerly removed the hampering journal and writing apparatus from her arms and placed them on the table. He gathered her tenderly into his arms and brushed a feathery kiss at her temple.

"Darling, I don't want you cluttering your pretty little head with such things. I have more suitable plans in store for you."

"You do?" Laura whispered. Her mind whirled expectantly at the serious tone of William's voice. Was this the moment she had waited for all these years? She prepared herself for overpowering jubilation.

"My silly little angel, why else would I have come to Texas? It's an absolutely barbaric place. There had to be an extremely important reason behind my actions. Surely you know that."

"Oh," Laura breathed softly, not sure if the strange twinge of emotion that rippled through her was because

271

of his slur on the land she had come to love or because of the possible portent of William's words. "Well, I suppose . . . I mean . . ."

He gazed lovingly at her, his eyes ablaze with smoldering calculation. "But how silly of me! Even if you do have a clue to my motives, I should have remembered that women like all the little embellishments. I'm terribly sorry, darling. I've been so caught up in the relief of having found you safe and sound that I've forgotten the importance of such formalities."

Where were the butterflies? Why wasn't her head swimming with delight? She was numb, simply numb. Yes, that was it! Of course she was numb. She was so overjoyed after all these years that her mind simply couldn't comprehend the wonderful thing that was about to happen.

"William—"

"Hush, my dearest." He pressed a trail of restrained little kisses across her cheek. "Let me tell you how beautiful and adorable you are, how very much I respect and love you, how deeply honored I would be if you would consent to be my wife."

There. She could hardly believe it. After all these years, he'd finally said it. Laura waited for the bells and banjos. Nothing. Oh, Lord! How long was she going to suffer from this strange lethargy?

"William, I—"

"I know, Laura, darling. You're overcome with emotion. I quite understand. I am, too."

William captured Laura's lips in a fevered kiss, forcing her lips apart to poke and probe with his rapier tongue. He ran his hands down her arms and captured her wrists, lifting her leaden limbs to place them around his neck. He never for a second relinquished possession of her mouth during this maneuver, and when it was completed he wrapped his arms securely about her slender body once more.

Laura forced her arms to respond, to tighten their hold around shoulders which seemed somehow insubstantial—the breadth and bulk weren't quite right. She splayed her fingers in the ruff of dark hair on the back of his neck. It felt strange to her touch, straight and silky fine. Deep in her troubled mind a memory flared and flamed—the feel of Blake's tousled hair under her hands, curly and fairly springing with the same rich vitality as the man himself. Desperate to extinguish the thought, she strained to press her body against William's, crushing her breasts against his chest.

It didn't feel right! Oh, God! It didn't feel right! What was wrong with her? The angle of the embrace, the tilt of their heads, the texture of the mouth slanted across her own—they all felt wrong! With a sob she tore herself from his embrace and turned to bury her face in her hands.

William was filled with a crowing satisfaction at her display of emotion. He fairly preened at his ability to trigger such a heated response in Laura.

It wouldn't take him long, he thought smugly, to break down the fragile barriers of maidenly restraint. And thank goodness for that! His body ached for physical relief, while his unprincipled mind cataloged the certainty that a physical uniting would surely bond Laura to him, come what may.

Always eager to stack the cards in his own favor, he knew such a move would give him an extra measure of assurance.

"There, there, darling." He patted her arm soothingly. "Don't take on so. I know the depth of feelings you're experiencing is a little frightening for one so innocent, but it's perfectly normal for two people in love. You just need a little time to get used to it. Everything will be wonderful, I promise you."

273

Laura stifled another sob. "Yes, yes, I'm sure you're right," she managed to reply. "W-will you excuse me, William?"

"Of course, darling." He placed a properly reverent kiss on her cheek.

Laura whirled and ran from the room.

Up the stairs she went as fast as her feet would carry her, wanting only to reach the safety and privacy of her own room. Once inside its haven, door shut securely against the rest of the world, she threw herself across her bed and wept.

It was all her fault! If she'd only waited for William before sampling the tantalizing fruits of passion. She didn't deserve his love and devotion. She had betrayed his trust time and again with Blake. Oh, why had she ever let Blake kiss her, touch her? The overwhelming responses he had awakened should have blossomed because of William's embrace. Now, all her muddled mind seemed able to do was compare the two men—with William coming up a poor second!

When she had cried herself out, she turned on her back, arms outflung, eyes fixed unseeingly on the ceiling. She desperately wanted to understand why she felt like she did. She'd responded to Blake in the way she'd always dreamed about feeling with the man she loved. But that man was William.

It was all so confusing! If she *didn't* feel anything when William kissed her and held her, did that mean she no longer loved him? And if Blake's caresses set her body on fire, could that possibly mean that she cared for him?

Or was she simply a fallen woman, falling prey to her own wicked desires? All the whispered speculations she'd shared with Cynthia over the years seemed to point with terrifying certainty to that conclusion.

The only honorable thing to do would be to tell William the truth. He deserved a pure and unsullied love—and heaven above knew she was no longer worthy of him. But how could she do that after he'd bared his soul to her and asked her to be his wife? It would break his heart!

The man had displayed his boundless love and devotion by traveling over endless miles for long, hard days just to be with her. To cruelly dash William's hopes after all he'd been through on her behalf would be unforgivable.

All too well she remembered the longing, the fears, the sometimes utter misery of loving someone who might not, for any number of reasons, return her affection. She simply couldn't subject another human being to that heartache.

If it took every ounce of strength she possessed—and all the rest of her days—she'd master her rebellious emotions and become the loving woman William deserved.

She could do no less.

By morning the despair Laura felt had frozen into a small, nagging ache in her heart, momentarily subdued and appeased by her firm conviction to atone for her past transgressions. Firmly cloaked in a righteous resolution of emotional metamorphosis, she once again set out to solve the mystery of the missing inventory.

The path to the barn was splashed with daffodil-bright sunshine. She stopped long enough to turn her face into its brilliance for a moment, willing its warmth to soothe away the weariness of her long, sleepless night. The southerly wind that tickled her nose and tugged playfully at her hair carried the spicy aromas of abundant grassses and fecund soil. A tiny stab of regret pierced her mind when she realized that all this beauty and serenity would soon be lost to her.

Then, irritated at herself for once again allowing such perfidious emotions to surface, she purposefully pushed the troublesome thought away. Such reflections could no longer be allowed to intrude upon the proper scheme of things. She squared her shoulders with virtuous conviction and proceeded down the path.

Luck was with her. Miguel was just about to mount up and ride out when he spied Laura. Quickly he dismounted and led his horse back to the corral, looping the reins over the top rail. With eager, fluid strides he hurried to greet her.

"Senorita Laura," he said with a small nod of his regal head, a smile of pleasure tilting the corners of his sensuous mouth. Obsidian eyes gazed at her with barely concealed delight. She looked so fragile, so beautiful. The armload of books she clasped to her breast pulled the pale material even tighter against the sweet curves. His face was inscrutable, the only evidence of his emotion a small pounding vein at his temple.

He frowned with displeasure when he noted the smudge of dark shadow under her beautiful eyes. With granite determination he restrained his hand from reaching to touch her cheek, his arms from reaching to enfold her. He smothered his longing once again. He could wait. He'd become very good at waiting over the years.

No, he dared not touch her yet. The moment was not right. He needed the time to paint a picture of a life so splendid, so glorious, that she would be unable to resist its temptation.

Lord! He'd wanted her from the first moment he'd seen her. At first it had been merely the physical attraction of a man for a maid. But each time he'd seen her the desire had grown stronger. And now he wanted to know more than the sweet succor of her body. He wanted her to come willingly into his arms. He wanted to see her eyes light up with pride and awe and love when she gazed at him. And she would. Oh, yes, she would. The time was almost right for him to make his move.

The dream had always come first, above and beyond everything. Now that it was almost within his grasp, he could allow his yearnings to surface. Oh, how he longed to share the fruits of that dream with her. He had grudgingly shared his quest with others less worthy throughout the years because of his desperate need for their help. But now, what he wanted, what he needed, was the perfect woman to stand by his side when the dream was finally fulfilled. Laura.

What fools the two gringos were! He pushed Blake and William contemptuously from his mind. Neither of them would have her. Neither of them could hope to offer her what she deserved. But he could. Soon. Very soon.

Miguel was aware of the conflicts in the big house. There was always a servant or two willing to gossip about the occupants. He also knew that those conflicts could be used to further his own cause. He would ply Laura with gentle attention now, gain her confidence, and when the time was right, he would show her what a true man had to offer.

"I need your help, Miguel."

Her statement brought a wild flutter of exaltation to his heart. "Yes, of course. What can I do?"

"Would you show me where the storeroom is? I'm checking the inventory books."

A brooding blackness extinguished the small flame of hope that had burned so brightly in his chest. Fool! She was quite unaware of his fantasies—as she should be. Patience. Patience. "Certainly. It is behind the barn. If you will follow me . . ."

"Do you have a key?" Laura eagerly fell into step with him.

"Yes, I know where one is kept. Anthony carries the

only other one," he replied, his voice kept in strict control.

Laura's foot tangled in a creeping vine at the edge of the path, and she stumbled. Quickly Miguel reached out to steady her, placing his hand solicitously under her elbow. He simply nodded when she expressed her thanks, basking in the opportunity to inhale the sweet feminine scent that was uniquely Laura's. Pulses beating wildly from the tantalizing contact, he left his hand where it was as they made their way toward the storeroom.

They stopped in front of a small planked structure, and Miguel reluctantly released his hold, allowing himself the tantalizing pleasure of trailing his fingers along the soft flesh of her arm in the process. He secured the key from its hiding place and bent to turn it in the lock. The door creaked in loud protest when he swung it open.

"Can I do anything to help you?" he asked Laura, eager to grasp at any opportunity that might prolong his time with her.

"I think I'll need a lantern."

The shack was fairly large and crowded with a confusing jumble of goods. Laura placed her books on top of a barrel and waited for Miguel to strike a match and light the lamp that was set on a ledge just inside the door. When the feeble flame finally caught and held, she could only stare morosely at the mounds of merchandise. With a sigh, she pushed up her sleeves and started counting.

"Well, that's the last of it," Laura said tiredly, closing the final book with a soft thud. She dusted her hands together and pushed a stray lock from her forehead with a dejected sigh.

"Is something wrong?" Miguel had watched her studiously for the last hour, wondering at the purpose behind her endeavors. In the time he'd been working for

Anthony, no one had ever paid much attention to the storeroom or its contents.

Laura slid her fingers beneath the wealth of rich brown hair that tumbled down her back to massage the tired muscles at the nape of her neck—and Miguel instantly wished it was his own hand providing the relief.

"I don't know," she said. "I just can't seem to get these figures to match up."

"What do you mean? What figures?"

"There seems to be a lot of things missing. They've been ordered, and some are even marked into the inventory book, but they're nowhere to be found. And there's no record of how the supplies were dispersed. It just seems that far too much has been ordered, even for a ranch this size."

Miguel didn't reply. He simply watched her pace the floor restlessly while he tried to decipher the importance of this latest development.

Laura finally stopped, a tantalizing arm's length away from him. Miguel's fingers curled convulsively at his sides.

"Miguel, who has access to this room? Who decides what to do with the supplies—who gets them, when to order, how much to order?"

"Senor Nichols."

"No one else?"

"No. Maria simply buys whatever he tells her. She has no liking for such things. She would never be able to keep track of it all. Senor Nichols must tell her what to do."

"But what about the times when Anthony is gone?"

Miguel gave an eloquent shrug of his broad shoulders. "Then he tells me before he goes. I simply follow his orders."

Laura considered this statement for a long moment, one arm clutched at her waist, her chin propped against the knuckles of the other.

279

"Would there ever be a time when goods were dispersed without Anthony knowing about it?"

"Possibly."

"Like when?"

"Oh, if a neighbor had an emergency and came here for help rather than going into town." Miguel shrugged as if to say that the whole situation was really not that important. There were much more critical things to do on a ranch than juggle useless columns of figures.

Laura gathered up her books. "Thank you for your help."

"You are not satisfied?"

"No, I'm not. But I don't know what to do. If Anthony is the only one who makes such decisions, I guess I'll just have to talk with him about it when he returns from Austin. There's no doubt the books are incorrect, for one reason or another. But perhaps I can help him work out a proper system before I leave."

Miguel straightened swiftly as alarm raced through him, his attention riveted on Laura. "Leave? What do you mean? Surely you are not going. But this is your home."

Laura gave a small, forlorn laugh. "No, I'm afraid it's not. I'll be returning to Philadelphia in a few weeks."

"So soon? But you mustn't."

"Oh, but I'm afraid I must." Laura's voice was small and almost sad.

Miguel bit back the torrent of words that threatened to escape his lips. It would do no good. He must have time to think this dilemma through.

He swung the door shut and snapped the lock into place before escorting Laura to the front of the barn. After she'd thanked him again and turned away, he slumped against the barn.

Fighting feelings of frustration at this unexpected turn of events, he watched her walk to the house. His mind was awhirl with a rage of emotions. The careful timetable he'd laid out was useless now. All his plans would have to be changed.

Angered, driven, Miguel quickly swung up into the saddle and spurred his horse into a wild mind-numbing gallop.

Chapter 24

Anthony retraced his trail under the relentless heat of the Texas sun, back to Washington-on-the-Brazos with hopeful news of the war. Once again a crowd, anxious to hear information that was days, weeks, and sometimes months old, gathered on the weathered boardwalk in front of the hotel.

Nat quickly provided a sturdy crate from his storeroom, and Anthony climbed atop it to deliver his message. The heavy summer heat pressed against him, intensified by the crush of bodies.

"First of all, you'll be glad to hear that Taylor pulled off a great victory at Palo Alto in May—"

There was a round of cheers. When the crowd quieted down again, one man called out, "Ain't that inside the disputed territory? Inside Texas? I thought they was gonna keep the fighting out of the state."

Anthony dragged his dust-covered hat from his head, paused to swipe his sleeve across his sweat-beaded brow, and then replaced it to better shield his eyes from the bright rays of the afternoon sun.

"For the most part they are. And they're doing a good job of it. After Palo Alto, Taylor pushed the Mexicans back to Resaca de la Palma and whipped them there, too."

282

More cheers and applause filled the steamy air.

"What about losses? Are casualties running high?" called another voice.

"We're holding the line there. Mexican losses are reported to be seven times as high as ours. But I've got some bad news, too. Most of you've heard of Sam Ringgold and that newfangled flying artillery of his." The crowd murmured assent. "Well, there's no doubt it stacked the odds in our favor at Palo Alto, but I'm sorry to say that Ringgold was severely wounded at the battle and died a few days later."

A collective sigh went up from the shuffling mass of people.

Anthony continued. "There's good men who served under him to take over, although it might slow things down a mite. But maybe not. Last I heard, they were doing all right. Why, at one battle Taylor's troops beat that ol' Arista so severely he plumb forgot to take his solid silver dinner service along with him when he tucked tail and ran away!"

A roll of laughter helped ease the tension of the growing crowd as they jostled and pushed for a better view.

"Do they need more men, Mr. Nichols?" asked young Ben Tucker earnestly, his voice cracking in a high-pitched squeak from the excitement.

Ben's diminutive mother aimed an angry slap at the gawky youngster who stood a full head taller than herself and fiercely whispered, "You hush that nonsense up right now, Benjamin Tucker! I don't want to hear another word! Do you hear me?"

Ben muttered a quick "yes'm" as he easily ducked the blow. He gingerly inched away from his mother's grasp, blushing blood red clear to the tops of his ears when the crowd crowed in delight at the exchange. Despite his mother's distraught reprimand, his young eyes still held the fever of anticipated feats of glory on the battlefield.

"You best stay put, Ben," Anthony was quick to say in hopes of soothing the boy's wounded ego as well as subduing his rash eagerness. "We need all our men at home right now. Besides, volunteers are still arriving at the Mexican border in large numbers. In fact, the camps are getting so crowded they're beginning to have a problem with dysentery and yellow fever. I've heard that disease is taking as many lives as the battles."

Concerned murmurs rippled through the assembly. Mrs. Tucker blanched with renewed fear at this terrible thought and clutched at her husband's arm with trembling fingers.

"The best news I've got is that Taylor's using Matamoros as a staging ground to make his move deeper into northern Mexico. He has every intention of pushing the Mexicans all the way back to Mexico City!"

Again the people bellowed their support.

Anthony waited for the cheers to cease before continuing. "The worst news I have is that Santa Anna is back in Mexico—"

"What!"

"I thought he was in exile!"

"How did that happen?"

Anthony held up his hands, trying to quiet the flood of questions. "I don't really know. Seems that he was allowed to slip through the blockade. Some even say the federal government had something to do with it."

"You mean President Polk knew about it?"

"Why'd he do a thing like that?"

"Preposterous!"

Again Anthony waited for the shouts and questions to fade away. "I don't even know if the rumor's true. But if it is, I'm sure Polk had a good reason. We'll just have to wait and see what happens. But the word is out that Santa Anna's back at his old tricks, trying to raise troops again. I guess we'll find out soon enough what's going on."

"We whupped that one-legged bastard afore and throwed him out of the country, we can damn sure do it again!" Oscar Fields declared loudly in his ancient, scratchy baritone.

The crowd roared with approval. Eli White cackled loudly at his crony's remark and brazenly poked Miss Coggin's tightly corsetted ribs with a bony elbow. She emitted an outraged gasp and then pressed her thin spinster lips even tighter together, all aquiver in righteous indignation.

"You bet we can!" Anthony joined in the anxiety-cleansing laughter that followed the cantankerous old man's remark. He answered a few more questions, then finally pleaded weariness.

The crowd slowly dispersed, the old men back to their place in front of the general store, others to their homes or businesses, while a stubborn few hung around in groups of threes and fours to mull over the startling news of Santa Anna's return.

"Now, you come on in here," Nat insisted, taking Anthony's arm in a stranglehold and steering him into the cooler interior of the hotel. "It's plain to see that you're bone tired. I'm not about to let you get back on that horse without some good strong coffee and a decent meal. Why, 'Lizabeth'd skin me alive!"

"All right, I'll go peacefully," Anthony agreed with a weary laugh, following Nat through the familiar swinging doors leading to the dining room. "It'd probably do me good to rest a bit. Say, have you heard any news from the ranch?"

"Pedro was in a week or so ago to pick up a few things at Henderson's." Nat lowered his bulk onto the chair across the table from Anthony.

Within minutes Matilda scurried to set steaming mugs

of dark brew and plates heaped with food before them. "Miz Lizbeth, she say she be right out jest soon's she finishes in the kitchen."

"Fine," replied Nat, digging his fork into a mound of beans. "As I was saying, you know how Pedro is—he never has much to say. But he did tell Henderson that everyone out at the ranch was doing fine."

Anthony let out a little sigh of relief. "I'm sure glad to hear it. Blake been through yet?"

"Nope."

"Ummm, he must still be in Louisiana. I was hoping he'd beat me home."

"Well, even if he didn't stop in town we'd probably have heard about it from Amos." Nat chuckled. "Nobody's gonna get anywhere near that ferry without him knowing about it, that's for sure!"

"Howdy, Anthony." Their plates were half empty when Elizabeth's voice interrupted their conversation. She slipped through the kitchen door, wiping her hands on the tail of her apron. "Glad you made it back. I hope you brought us good news from the capital."

"Well, I suppose I did. Everybody in Austin is still pretty optimistic. The fighting's been mostly confined to the border, and Taylor's about ready to make a big push on into Mexico."

"Well, good! The sooner all this fightin' is over with, the better I'll like it," she stated firmly.

Anthony smiled warmly at her as she settled into the chair between the two men. "I know how you feel, Elizabeth. Lots of us are wishing for a speedy conclusion to this mess."

"Enough of this depressing talk. Did you tell him about the big doin's?" Elizabeth asked Nat.

"Haven't had a chance yet."

"What big doin's?" Anthony asked.

"Come Sunday, Cletus is having a big shindig for

286

Olivia's birthday. Says he's going all out. Barbecue, horse racing, a little dancin'. You name it."

"That man sure sets a store by that girl of his." Nat shook his big shaggy head.

"She's a fine lady," commented Anthony softly, resolutely pushing away the small memories of times with Olivia that persisted in deviling him.

Elizabeth shoved a straggling lock of brown hair back behind her ear. "Well, of course Cletus has always enjoyed doing such things for Olivia, but I kinda have a feeling that the war has something to do with this party, too. Don't you, Nat?"

"Yes, I do."

"What do you mean?" Anthony's gaze flickered back and forth between his two friends.

"Oh, everybody's been so restless, kinda tense and nervous like. I think a big party's just what we need to take the edge off everyone's nerves for a while," Elizabeth replied.

"Yeah, lots of the younger fellas been spoutin' talk about volunteering. Their blood's getting hot to get on down there and join in the battle before they miss out on all the fun."

"Yes, I know. I heard Young Ben, same as you. He's raring to go. Mrs. Tucker came real close to boxin' his ears good out there this afternoon."

"Mrs. Tucker's not the only mother about to have a fit over the war."

"Well, let's pray it doesn't come to that." Anthony was filled with sadness at the thought of the young men of the town riding off to do battle, maybe even losing their lives in the process.

Nat shrugged. "Maybe Cletus is afraid it just might come down to that. Maybe he thinks this could be the last time for all of us to get together for quite a spell."

Anthony's cup rattled against his plate as he lifted it

287

for a sip before replying. "I hate to say it, but he might be right—although I'm hoping the regular army can handle this miserable situation, and the whole state won't be pulled into the fighting."

"Let's hope so," murmured Elizabeth fervently.

Anthony placed his cup back on the table with careful deliberation. "Well, anyway, the party sounds like a fine idea to me," he declared emphatically. "I'm sure Maria and Laura will be happy to hear about it. Ummm, gonna have horse racing, did you say?"

"Yep, they sure are. You gonna run Midnight?" Nat's eyes were bright with interest.

"I just might do that. I guess it's time to see if he's got what it takes."

"I heard that Pennington is bringing over that big bay stud of his. And every other young buck in the area is begging his pa for the best horse on the place. Looks like we got the makings of a fine racing day."

"Nothing like the excitement of a little contest or two to take everyone's mind off this war business!" Anthony said with a laugh as he pushed his empty plate away. "Thanks Elizabeth, that was delicious, as always. Guess we'll see you out at the Moore's then. Right now, I'm headed for home. It'll be nigh on to midnight before I get there, and I've been gone way too long!"

Anthony's mouth quirked up in a wicked little grin in answer to Nat's deep, suggestive chuckle.

The house was dark and still when Anthony entered it. He crept up the stairs, staying close to the banister, being extra careful to avoid the center of the next to the top step that always creaked in protest. With a growing sense of anticipation, he traversed the darkened hallway and eased open the door to his bedroom. The broad windows had been left open, the heavy drapes thrown back to admit a teasing little breeze.

A patchwork of silver and shadow draped Maria's sleeping form in the high four-poster bed. She sighed deeply and turned over, snuggling further into the feather pillows at the whisper of Anthony's steps across the floor. His heart began the trip-hammer beat her sultry beauty always triggered.

He peeled his clothes off and dropped them in a heap at his feet, then padded naked to the bed. It rustled in gentle protest and then dipped under his weight as he stretched out beside his sleeping wife and gathered her into his arms. She mumbled grumpily, like a small petulant child about to be stirred from its soothing slumber.

Anthony's strong blunt fingers teased a trail across Maria's shoulders, pushing aside the lacy ruffle of her silken gown to bare creamy skin to the lustrous glow of moonlight. With tender deliberation his hand moved back to the front of her gown where he pulled one trailing length of tiny satin ribbon, tugging softly until the loop of the bow slipped the imprisoning knot and released its protective hold on the deep vee opening of the gossamer garment. With hungry fingers he whisked the fabric aside, freeing a dusky rose-tipped breast from its confines. His lips closed gently over the peak, tugging and suckling with gentle persuasion.

Maria's eyelashes fluttered weakly in response and then fell back against her shadowed cheeks. She mumbled a few words in irritated Spanish and fought to remain in the sheltering cradle of deep sleep. Anthony ran his hand softly down the small, voluptuous form and tugged the hem of her gown gently upward. Under his slow ministrations a spark flared and then flamed brightly, flowing through Maria's veins to carry an insistent heat throughout her sleep-drugged body.

The peevish mutterings became soft sighs and whispered urgings as her body responded with wild abandon. Gone and forgotten were the protests, which had at first clouded her mind. All that was important now was to appease the growing inferno raging in every cell of her being.

And the fact that her whole future might well depend on Anthony's continued addiction to her charms easily quenched whatever small feelings of disloyalty she might have felt at first.

"Anthony!" Laura squealed in delight, dropping Sugar's reins in her excitement. She ran toward her brother. He caught her and swung her up with equal exuberance. "I'm so glad you're home! I've missed you." Her happy words tumbled over each other in excitement.

Miguel gathered up Sugar's lines and stood silently between the restless horses, watching the two people through brooding eyes. A fiery determination swept through him. One day soon she would greet him, Miguel, with such abandoned joy!

Laura clasped Anthony's hand in both of hers and pulled him back toward the horses. "Miguel and I were going riding. You'll come with us, won't you?"

A small flicker of anger surged through Miguel. He did not want to share the few hours he had with Laura with anyone else. The only opportunity he'd had to put his secret plan to win Laura's heart into action had been during the early rides they had shared the last few mornings. He was determined to have her, no matter what the cost. No one was going to stand in his way.

But he wanted her to come willingly. And that would take some doing. He had so little time to gain her confidence. Things were moving very fast now. He needed every moment alone with her that he could manage. There was never an opportunity to speak in private, to tempt her fantasies, to win her approval, at any other time—always there were Maria and William hovering in the background, jealous of every small word or gesture that Miguel might try to share with Laura. After one very uncomfortable evening at the big house, Miguel was careful to pursue his interest only when he could get Laura away from their probing eyes.

"Where's William? Why isn't he riding with you?" Anthony questioned.

Laura gave an irritated flip of her head. "Oh, he complains so much about the heat and the dust, I simply don't ask him anymore. He'd rather sleep late anyway. Please say you'll go."

"I'm afraid I can't, honey. I have a hundred things to do. You and Miguel go ahead. But make it a short ride today, will you? In a little while I need to talk with Miguel about something."

"Oh, Anthony," Laura muttered, her voice laced with disappointment. "I wish you'd come. Or maybe I should just postpone my ride until tomorrow. I don't want to hamper your work or take Miguel away just when you need him—"

"No, it's fine for you to go, honey. I still have things to do back at the house. I just wanted to let you know I was back home." He patted her arm affectionately. "I know there's little enough diversion around this place for a young lady; I'm not going to take this small pleasure away from you."

"Well . . ." She frowned as she contemplated his words, tiny lines etching her fair brow.

She glanced toward Miguel as if seeking some sort of confirmation. His black eyes bored into hers, and he gave a minute shrug of his broad shoulders. Laura brightened a little. If Miguel wasn't worried about the situation, then Anthony really must not mind. After all, a good employee would hardly jeopardize his standing with his boss over such frivolity unless he was sure it wouldn't create a problem. "All right, I'll go, if you're sure."

"I'm sure." Anthony bent to give her a leg up onto Sugar's broad back. She smiled fondly down at her brother, noting with another small stab of worry that he already looked tired at this early hour of the morning. She wished he could slow down, relax a little. He had too many worries, too many responsibilities. They were taking far too heavy a toll on her beloved brother.

"Is everything all right?"

"Everything's fine, honey. The war news is good. Now you quit worrying that pretty head of yours." He turned to the dark man who'd stood silently during the entire discourse. "Miguel, you take good care of her. I'll meet with you in a couple of hours."

"*Si*, senor. You can rest assured that I will take excellent care of Senorita Laura." Her name rolled melodically off his lips. He swung his tall, lean frame easily into the saddle and lightly flicked the reins against Poco's neck.

"Bye. We'll be back soon, I promise," called Laura over her shoulder as Sugar eagerly broke into a gallop to follow Miguel's horse across the dew-kissed field.

Anthony watched the spectacle with a wry grin as the heavy thud of horses' hooves faded away. Laura was becoming quite a horsewoman. She looked so vibrant, so alive atop her mount, back straight and proud, chestnut curls streaming behind in riotous disarray. As he turned toward the house, the silvery cascade of her delighted laughter floated back to Anthony.

At the base of the road leading over the rim of the broad valley, Miguel reined in and waited for Laura to catch him. The horses settled into an easy, swaying pace as they worked their way slowly, side by side, up the red dirt trail. Their ascent up the hill's gentle incline allowed the riders to enjoy the view and carry on a conversation.

"I'm so glad Anthony's back," Laura said, reaching a

slim hand up to brush an errant wind-tossed curl from her forehead. "I want all the time I can possibly have to visit with him before I leave."

"You still persist in this idea, senorita?" Miguel's hooded eyes were barely successful in concealing the inner turmoil he suffered each time she brought up the subject of leaving.

"I have to."

"But why? Senor Nichols will be very disappointed if you go. Besides, it is not safe to travel with this war going on."

Just then Sugar aimed a playful nip at Poco, causing Miguel's leg to bump softly against Laura's. His heart leapt in his chest, and he gripped the saddle horn tightly with both hands to keep from reaching for her.

"That's exactly why William says we should leave as soon as possible. What if the Mexicans manage to take over Galveston? William says we have to go while it's still possible to book passage on a ship."

"Perhaps I am being too forward, senorita, but I fail to see why Senor Stratford should have such influence on your plans." There was a tinge of irritation in his black-velvet voice.

Miguel knew Laura had left Philadelphia because of some sort of dispute with her guardian. Household gossip had provided him with that much information, although he had as yet been unable to find out exactly what Stratford had to do with the situation. Too many things still didn't make sense. If Laura had run away from the uncle, why would she consider returning? Especially when she seemed so happy here with her brother.

A small sneer of contempt tugged at Miguel's mouth. Had Laura's uncle sent William to find her? Perhaps the uncle had offered William a finder's fee—a bounty—for Laura's return. Such a man as Stratford would no doubt be more than happy to accomplish this feat—if the price was right.

No, there was more to it than that. But meanwhile Miguel had to find a way to dissuade Laura from her foolish plan.

"I do not understand, Senorita Laura. I was under the impression that you planned to stay with Senor Nichols for a much longer period of time."

"Well, I did at first . . . but that was before William arrived. He's very anxious to return home. I . . . I really have no choice."

A brilliant blue dragonfly flitted by Sugar's ear. The mare cocked her ear forward and then tossed her head with a loud snort, setting her harness to jingling.

Miguel shifted his weight, his brooding black eyes raking her face. "But it seems a very simply choice to me. Stay here. Let Senor Stratford return if he wishes."

Her smile was almost sad as she gazed back into those dark eyes. "I wish it were so simple." She shook her head slowly. "But you see, William has done me the great honor of asking me to marry him and I've agreed—"

"Marry!" The word exploded from Miguel's mouth. "You can't possibly mean that! It will spoil everything!"

Laura laid a gentle hand on his arm. "Thank you, Miguel. It's very sweet of you to be so concerned about me."

Miguel searched for a reason that would convince Laura to change her mind—any reason but the real one. "But you don't understand. Senor Nichols needs you here. He has many worries. This I know! He has been much happier since your arrival. You can be of so much help to him—"

Laura made a wry face. "Well, I don't know how much help I can be. After all, I wasn't able to solve the mystery of the supply inventory." She gave a small sigh. "Miguel, I know you're concerned about the ranch's success and about Anthony's well-being, and I appreciate that concern very much. But maybe it's for the best that I leave."

"No, senorita. That is not true. Senor Nichols will be very upset—"

"Oh, I know Anthony might be a little disappointed when I leave, but I'm sure he'll understand. And perhaps it will be better for him and Maria if I'm not under foot all the time. I really don't think Maria's very fond of me. I have no doubt she'll be glad to see me go."

Miguel turned eyes that snapped with fire and thinly concealed anger on Laura as he seized upon a possible reason for her decision. "Maria! If that woman has said anything to you to make you feel that you must leave, I vow I will—"

"No, no, Miguel! It isn't like that at all. I simply meant Maria and I had not become the best of friends since my arrival. But she's been perfectly . . . uh . . . perfectly lovely to me. Really."

Laura flinched inwardly when she uttered the lie. But it was necessary to soothe Miguel. She had no intention of letting bad feelings develop between Maria and her cousin. She of all people knew family was too important to let some silly feud develop, especially over someone who would soon be gone. And the truth of the matter was, Maria really had nothing to do with Laura's decision to leave, despite her frequently less than congenial attitude since Laura's arrival.

If Laura hadn't been burdened with a crushing sense of loyalty and obligation toward William, she could easily continue to ignore Maria's snippy temperament as she had over the past few months. For the life of her, Laura hadn't been able to figure out what she'd done to cause Maria to dislike her so. But she had finally ceased worrying about it. Besides, the wonderful freedom of the ranch and Anthony's love and appreciation more than made up for Maria's occasionally hateful disposition.

But none of that mattered now. She had a duty to William, and nothing and no one was going to prevent her from fulfilling that duty. Echoes of her own previous misery and loneliness were still too sharp even to consider refusing William's devoted offer.

Laura reached to lay a reassuring hand on Miguel's arm. "Thank you for your concern. You've been very kind to me—"

Miguel quickly grasped her hand, snaring it beneath his strong fingers like a small bird that threatened to escape. "Laura, listen to me. You must reconsider. There is so much you don't know yet. There's a bright and glorious future waiting for you right here. You must simply be patient. If I could only tell you of the splendor that could someday be yours—"

"Miguel, please," Laura whispered, easing her hand from beneath his grasp. "I know you're only trying to help, but there's really nothing left to discuss. I've given my word to William. Would you have me break my promise?"

Miguel bit back a heated retort. Vows! Promises! What did they matter when compared with what he could soon offer her? But it was impossible for him to say more than he already had. One slip to the wrong person and everything could be ruined.

Time. Time was of the essence. He must wait just a little longer.

His face once again became a closed bronze mask. In a tense, aloof voice he said, "We should return now. Senor Nichols will be waiting for me."

"Yes, of course," Laura answered softly, and she ducked her head as tears gathered on her lashes and threatened to spill down her cheeks.

What was wrong with her? Why did her whole life suddenly seem to be in such a muddle? She should be gloriously happy now. Her wedding to William should be the happiest moment of her life. Why did she feel so forlorn and sad when she should be celebrating her good fortune? She had considered Miguel her friend, and she hated the strange defensive barrier that had suddenly materialized between them.

What had she said, what had she done to cause such a reaction? What did he know about the ranch or Anthony that she didn't know? Why did he feel so strongly about her leaving?

Confused and unhappy, Laura watched the straight proud back of the man as he moved away from her. With a forlorn sigh she shifted the reins alongside Sugar's neck and turned her mount to follow Miguel back to the house.

Chapter 25

The deepening shadows of night cloaked Anthony's serene little valley in thick, velvety pools of black, purple, and indigo blue. Blake stood in a small patch of silvery moonlight, back propped against the weathered trunk of a lightning-struck tree. The bare, twisted limbs above him cast long, bewitching shadows across the crest of the small hill on which he stood. With mixed emotions he viewed the deeper black shadows that marked the location of the house snug in the center of the valley.

There was still that wonderful, heady sense of elation when he considered the information the department had managed to garner for him about William Stratford. All Blake had to do was tell Laura about William's shady past, and his problems would be over.

Blake had resented William's intrusion from the first. But, much as he'd hoped for information from Washington that would help him persuade Laura she was making a mistake, he'd never in his wildest dreams imagined the tantalizing tidbits that fate had tossed his way.

The long report on William's excessive gambling, frequent womanizing, and his rather embarrassing habit of occasionally skipping out on hotel bills would surely persuade Laura that she'd made the wrong choice in suitors. The fact that Stratford currently owed a very sizable sum in gambling debts to the nefarious Mr. Theodore Franklin—who was, according to a very reliable source, searching high and low for William at this very moment—would simply be icing on the cake. That choice piece of information went a long way in explaining Stratford's sudden arrival in Texas.

Well, Blake was going to make damn sure that Laura didn't suffer at the hands of that small-time, petty hustler. Now that he had in his hands the unvarnished truth about William, he was going to set things straight. Laura couldn't possibly continue to harbor her misguided feelings of loyalty for the man after learning such condemning facts.

But the joy Blake felt as he considered his possible reconciliation with Laura was all but obliterated when he remembered the rest of the message he'd received. The department's contact in Mexico had verified that the man behind the rumored uprising was a well-respected local gentleman whom no one would ever suspect of such wicked double-dealing.

They still had no name for this wily adversary, but it was known that the man had excellent connections with the state officials in Austin. Connections good enough that time and again he was able to pass along important information to his contacts in Mexico, information that was privy to only an elite few. And if he continued passing that vital information to his cohorts across the border, it could very well spell disaster for Texas in the war's outcome.

But there was one perplexing situation that didn't seem to fit the normal scheme of things. The man behind the scenes in Texas had not been inclined to help President Paredes when his troops rebelled and overthrew his government after the humiliating defeats at Palo Alto and Resaca de la Palma. Nor did he seem to be throwing his support Santa Anna's way now that he had escaped exile in Cuba and returned to Mexico. It was almost as if this strange, unknown foe had some other reason for mounting his rebellion—perhaps even a very personal reason.

Blake bent restlessly and picked up a handful of pebbles. One by one he tossed them at the dark silhouette of a large boulder, which sat snug against the bend of the road. Each click of contact echoed loudly in the still night air as Blake contemplated the dilemma in which he found himself.

The information Blake had received about their shadowy adversary was driving him to near distraction. Try as he might, he could think of no one who fitted the description any better than Anthony Nichols.

Blake was sick at heart at the mere thought of such a possibility. The bond of friendship and respect he felt for Anthony made it very difficult for him to consider the possibility that there might be even a shred of truth to this alarming deduction. He didn't want Anthony to be the culprit—not only because of his own personal feelings for the man but also because of what such news would do to Laura.

Why did fate have to be so fickle? Blake had been fortuitously handed the means to force William out of the picture. But hand in hand with the good news he'd been faced with the fact that any opportunity to gain Laura's affections would be dashed beyond hope if he were compelled to unmask her brother as a traitor to his country.

A slow war of emotions had raged within Blake every step of the way as he crossed the border into Texas and made his way back to Washington-on-the-Brazos. For the first time in his life he was ready to throw over his career—call it quits and never go back to Washington. It would be so easy. All it would take was one telegraph to the department saying he was resigning his commission. The department could send someone else to shoulder Blake's responsibilities. Someone else could be the recipient of Laura's wrath if Anthony turned out to be the traitor.

Before he left Louisiana, Blake had considered sending such a telegraph. And time and again during the long days on the trail he had battled the compulsion to turn around and return to that little office at the train depot. Just a few words and he'd be free. Free to return to Texas, tell Laura the truth about William, and then declare his own feelings.

The thought of sharing a small snug house with Laura for the rest of his life was a thought that was becoming more tempting every day. He'd saved enough money during his time with the department to buy a sizable tract of land and a small herd of cattle. They could have a wonderful life. Maybe even have a couple of babies. The temptation was almost overwhelming. He was so close to just walking away from it all. With Laura as the prize it would be worth it.

Blake had almost convinced himself that he could do it. Let someone else worry about Anthony's guilt or innocence. Let someone else be the bad guy if Anthony turned out to be the one they'd been looking for. All Blake wanted was to marry Laura and spend the rest of his days enjoying a blissful life with her.

He was tired of war, tired of spying, tired of playing all these games. For once he wanted to be himself—to not have to watch every word he said, every move he made.

Yes, if he walked away from the problem now, he could probably claim Laura for his own. He was positive that the worry of William was about to cease; his little cache of information would see to that. Everything he'd been dreaming of was within his reach. All he had to do was reach out his hands and take it.

Blake threw the last rock. It ricocheted off the boulder and bounced away into the dark.

Walking away sounded so easy. But what about John? What about the honor and duty he'd believed in, lived for—died for? If Blake walked away now, it would be like turning his back on everything John had stood for—and everything that Blake had always believed in. If he gave in to this compulsion, would he be any less a traitor than the mysterious man they'd been searching for all these months? Just what would that make him?

Blake must choose: Laura or his honor. Which would it be? If she ever found out that he suspected her brother of such a despicable thing, she'd never forgive him. But if he simply abdicated his duty, could he ever live in peace with himself, or would that spoil the very love he'd be sacrificing that duty and honor for?

Dear God! There had to be a way to accomplish both goals! There had to be a way for him to win Laura's love and fulfill his duty to his country. If he could just find out enough information to either condemn or exonerate Anthony, then he could turn it all over to someone else and resign his position. Someone else could do the dirty work—make the arrest, testify at the trial.

Yes, of course! That would be perfect. If he handled it that way, Laura need never know that Blake was the one who triggered the whole thing.

But would it work? Could he *make* it work? Was he capable of finding the information they so desperately needed soon enough without tipping his hand?

Blake slumped wearily against the tree, chin tucked despondently against his chest. He didn't know. He just didn't know, but it was the only chance he had. He sighed and pushed himself away from the gnarled trunk. Blackjack nickered softly, raising his head from the patch of lush grass he'd been nibbling while Blake searched his heart and soul.

"It's all right, boy. Let's go home." Blake bent to gather the reins. Giving in to utter weariness and worry he leaned his forehead against Blackjack's muscular neck, as if to draw additional strength for the ordeal ahead.

He finally raised his head and with great deliberation squared his shoulders. The pale silver moon played across a face etched with determination. Placing his foot in the stirrup, he swung into the saddle. Blackjack began a slow descent into the valley.

Blake paced the floor just inside his doorway. For the tenth time in as many minutes he stopped and searched the hallway through the small crack of open doorway. It was still deserted. He frowned and ran his fingers haphazardly through his already tousled curls, then returned to his endless pacing.

Pale-gold fingers of sunlight plucked at the heavy drapes bracketing the open window, then crept their way across the polished floor. The house was still quiet, but with the sun climbing fast in the brilliant blue sky it wouldn't be long before its occupants woke and began to stir.

Blake had risen just as the soft pink and coral streaks of dawn stained the eastern sky. He'd shaved and dressed quickly and then taken his position near his slightly ajar door, pacing the room ever since like a tawny mountain lion preparing to stalk its unsuspecting prey.

He made three more circuits of the room before the moment he'd been anxiously awaiting finally came. He stood still when he heard the creak of Laura's door. His mouth went dry, and he swiped suddenly damp palms against his trousers.

Quickly he covered the few steps to the closed portal and pulled it open, stepping in front of Laura and

303

blocking her way just as she was about to pass his room.

"Blake!" Laura cried with a start, placing her hand over her heart. Her eyes were wide with alarm, and a sudden rosy glow stained her cheeks. "You startled me. I didn't know you were back. You must have come in very late. I didn't hear a thing."

"Yes, it was late. I'm glad I didn't disturb you. I tried to be quiet." His gaze devoured her. It felt like years rather than weeks since he'd last seen her. She was so beautiful, so desirable. Her pale-blue dress hugged her bosom most enchantingly; the full skirt accentuated a waist so tiny that he felt sure he could span it with his hands, which by sheer willpower he held rigidly at his sides.

Laura gifted him with a small nervous smile, and then her eyes shifted quickly from his face. "Well, you succeeded. I promise I didn't hear a thing."

"Good."

"I was just on my way to breakfast. Are you coming down?"

He shifted his weight from one foot to the other and cleared his throat nervously. So much depended on the next few minutes. "Yes, of course, but first I need a moment of your time."

"Oh? What for?" Her fingers traced jittery patterns against the fabric of her skirt.

"It's something very important. Would you mind stepping in here for just a minute? What I have to say won't take long, but I think some privacy would be best." He reached to swing the door to his room open and stood aside so she could enter.

Laura frowned in consternation. She really didn't want to be alone with him. But why was Blake being so serious? Was there a problem about Anthony?

"Well . . . all right. I suppose it won't hurt for just

304

a moment."

Her gown swished softly as she edged past him to enter the room, the hem of her skirt barely brushing against his legs. She was very careful to keep as far from him as the small doorway allowed so that there would be no body contact between them.

The room assailed her senses. It spoke of Blake in a dozen different ways. The familiar spicy scent of the cologne he always wore hung faintly in the air. There was a soft cotton shirt thrown carelessly over the back of a chair. His brush and toilet articles were laid out on the dresser.

She turned and, unbidden, her gaze flew to the large, ornately carved bed that dominated the room. Although Blake had taken the time to spread the covers, the soft feather bed had not been properly patted and plumped. It still held the faint indention of his form. She could almost see his long, lean body stretched out on its cushioning surface.

Laura clasped her hands tightly together in front of her. It suddenly seemed very important to get this strange confrontation over with, to get out of the room and back to safety.

Her chin came up. Her eyes hardened with a grim determination. "Now, Blake, what can I do for you? Is it something about Anthony?" Her voice held more than a touch of concern.

Blake winced inwardly. What would she say if she knew just how much problem there *was* about Anthony? She'd be horrified, that's what. No, he didn't dare dwell on those worries just yet. He had to forget about Anthony and that particular predicament for now. He could only handle one dilemma at a time. And right now he had to dispense with William.

"I suppose you know I went to Louisiana to contact

305

my . . . uh . . . office—"

"Yes, of course."

"Well, I took the opportunity to ask for some additional information . . . a simple thing to do actually since we have access to a great many sources about any number of things."

It was clear from the look on her face that she was perplexed. "What are you talking about?"

"There are some things you need to know about Stratford . . ."

Anger flashed in her eyes. "I should have known! You're up to your old tricks again."

Regardless of the growing feelings of doubt she herself had felt concerning William over the last few weeks—or maybe because of them—she felt compelled to defend him to Blake. Feelings of guilt washed over her. Guilt because she subconsciously doubted her love for William, and guilt because of the crazy feelings she still felt for Blake regardless of how often she denied them. These troublesome feelings only fired her determination further.

Blake's jawline tightened and a tiny angry tic began to beat in his temple. "They're not tricks! Everything I have to say is the truth. Now, if you'll just listen to me—"

Her eyes snapped blue fire. "I have no intention of listening to you. I told you before and I meant every word of it. My life is none of your business. Stop interfering. Stop making your ridiculous accusations about William—"

"They are not ridiculous!"

Blake started toward her, and she responded quickly by backing further away from him. She dared not let him touch her, for it would surely mean her downfall.

"Why do you insist on persecuting the poor man? He's never done anything to you!" With each step he took

306

forward, she took another backward. Her back finally bumped painfully against the carved edging of the chest. She was trapped against its solid front, and Blake was still advancing.

"The hell he hasn't!" Blake slammed his hand down on the chest's smooth polished top. The china pitcher rattled dangerously in its bowl. "He's trying to take something that belongs to me!"

"What are you talking about?"

In a flash Blake closed the small space still separating them. Relentlessly his strong hands gripped the soft flesh of Laura's upper arms. "You know very well what I'm talking about. You can't keep denying your feelings—"

"I've never denied my feelings about William," Laura retorted hotly.

Blake gave her an angry little shake. "I'm not talking about Stratford, and you damn well know it!"

"I have no idea what you're talking about!" Laura struggled to free herself. "Let go of me!"

Blake pulled her even closer, looming over her until her head fell back, and all she could do was stare up into the deep brown depths of his angry eyes. "Please," she whimpered.

"God, Laura! You're driving me mad! No one before has ever been able to create these crazy wild feelings in me. All I have to do is just get close to you, and my head quits working. My wits simply dissolve. Why? Why do you affect me this way?"

"I don't know," she whispered. "I haven't done anything—"

"No, you don't have to *do* anything at all. All you have to do is tilt your head a certain way, smile that special little smile, or simply walk into a room. It's crazy, I know. I can't explain it. I've fought it. It doesn't do any good."

"Blake, listen to me—"

"No, you listen to me. I have something to tell you that's going to change everything. There are things you don't know about the man—"

"I don't want to hear this. Please let me go." Her voice was thick with emotion as she looked at him beseechingly with eyes the stormy blue of the ocean depths. Inwardly she struggled as desperately with herself as she did with Blake. Her resolve was fading fast. She had to get out of his arms, away from the tantalizing sound of his voice.

"No, I'm not going to let you go . . . not now, not ever." Suddenly his lips descended and captured hers.

Heat rushed through her body in the same familiar way it always did when Blake touched her. She melted against him, all logical thought gone. He wrapped his arms tightly around her slim body and drew her even closer.

Unconsciously her hands slid up the granite hardness of his chest until her fingers were twined in the riotous golden curls at the nape of his neck. Her body was consumed with molten fire. Her heart was doing crazy little flip-flops in her chest, beating like a caged wild bird against her ribs.

His lips burned kisses across her jawline and down her slender throat. Mindlessly her head fell back to allow him even greater access to the tender flesh. With nimble fingers he brushed aside the tumble of chestnut curls laying on her shoulder. He nuzzled the tender spot just behind her earlobe and she moaned softly. Once again his lips made the slow tortuous trip back to her mouth, where his tongue prodded and plundered with infinite skill. She strained against him, almost desperate to feel the pressure of his body against her own.

The force of Blake's mouth softened just the tiniest bit, and he breathed his words gently against her lips, their very breaths mingling sweetly. "You're mine. Always. I'll never let him have you."

Shame flooded through Laura at the reference to William. Good Lord! What was she doing? She was engaged to another man! How could she possibly have let this happen?

She wrenched herself from Blake's arms. Her hands flew to her mouth, where trembling fingertips tried to wipe away the memory of his kiss. Fat teardrops of humiliation welled in her eyes.

"Please, Blake. We must stop this—"

"We can't. Don't you know that? We've both tried. It's never worked."

"It has to work. I can't go on like this. William doesn't deserve this kind of treatment—"

"William deserves anything he gets—"

"Don't say that! You don't know him. How can you judge him like that?" She turned her back on him. It was the only way she could keep herself from flying back into his arms.

"I know enough to clear your conscience about your feelings for me."

"It's too late. Don't you understand?" She turned and looked at him imploringly. Her hands were clenched tightly at her sides. "I've agreed to marry William. We'll be leaving very soon to return to Philadelphia."

Blake reeled under the impact of her words. How could she have agreed to such a thing? He *knew* she cared for him. She had to! How could she not when he cared so very much for her? He gave his great tawny head a shake to clear the mists of hurt and shock. He mustn't give up! The engagement might make things more difficult, but it still wasn't too late. When she learned of William's past, she'd break off with him, and she wouldn't have to suffer any feelings of betrayal or wrongdoing about it.

"Laura, listen to me. I have to tell you something about Stratford—"

"Please, Blake." She held a slim hand up as if to ward off his words. "I don't want to hear any more. If you care anything for me at all, please do as I ask. Please. I'm asking you—no, I'm begging you to let me do what I have to do. If you care about me even the slightest bit, you'll never bring this subject up again." Her voice was the barest whisper.

Blake was stunned. If he didn't tell her, he'd lose her. And if he persisted in having his say regardless of her plea, it would as good as deny his love for her after what she'd just said.

He held out his hands one more time as if in supplication, praying that she'd surrender to her feelings and come to him. But she didn't. The tears in her eyes pooled and spilled, and she ducked her head in misery.

He dropped his hands and stepped aside. With heartsick eyes he watched her run from the room.

It was a long time before Blake left his room. He descended the stairs and with reluctant steps made his way into the dining room. The sun-splashed room was empty except for Rosita, who was busy clearing away the remains of breakfast.

"Good morning, senor," she said brightly.

Her cheery greeting grated on his frazzled nerves, but he managed to force a semblance of a smile. "Morning, Rosita."

"I will fix you some breakfast right away."

"No, please, don't go to any bother. All I really want is a cup of coffee."

"*Si*, senor." Hands laden with dirty dishes, she scurried through the door leading to the kitchen, returning in seconds with a mug of steaming liquid.

"Thank you." Blake accepted the cup and then wearily

lowered his large frame into a chair. Elbows braced on the table as if to support a burden far heavier than a mere coffee cup, he sipped morosely until the mug was empty. Rosita poked her head through the door to inquire if he needed anything else. Blake shook his head and asked, "Where is everybody?"

"They are all down at the corral with the big black horse." Her dark eyes sparkled with excitement. "Senor Nichols, he is making plans for the big race."

"Race, what race?" asked Blake in confusion.

"The one to be held at the big party."

Making little or no sense of Rosita's heavily accented answers, Blake shoved the mug away and pushed himself out of the chair. With a few long strides he was out the back door and traveling the sun-dappled path to the barn. The trail looped through a thick stand of trees and then out across an open patch of ground, finally allowing Blake a clear view of the corral.

At the sight of Laura's slim figure bracketed between Anthony and William in front of the fence, Blake fought the urge to turn around and go back to the house. He didn't know if he could handle seeing Laura again so soon, especially with William snug at her side. And even his usual pleasure in seeing Anthony was tainted by the suspicions that had plagued him since Louisiana.

Gathering his courage, he finished his journey. As he neared the group, he mumbled a quick hello to everyone, being very careful to do no more than glance in Laura's direction.

As for Laura, she kept her eyes straight ahead as if mesmerized by the magnificent horse trotting nervously around his enclosure. She had sensed Blake's approach long before she heard his footsteps. She gripped the rough surface of the log fence with both hands and concentrated hard on the huge black animal in the corral,

311

hoping that sheer determination would still the butterflies that battled in her stomach.

Suddenly Midnight charged at the fence, then reared high, forelegs slicing through the air. Laura jumped and backed away from the fence, her heart beating in her throat. The stallion had always aroused a curious sense of unease in her, and now his wild, excited behavior was intensifying those strange feelings.

"Are you all right, dear?" asked William solicitously when he noticed her unease.

"Yes, I'm fine." She squeezed her eyes shut for a long moment, drawing small, even breaths until the curious tingling in her stomach eased a little.

Anthony greeted Blake warmly, reaching to shake his hand with a firm grip. "Glad to have you back. Hope you had a good trip."

"Thanks. It's good to be back. Yes, everything was just fine. No problems at all."

Blake experienced a twinge of guilt when he grasped Anthony's hand. He found it difficult to meet his host's open, steady gaze, so he quickly turned his attention to Midnight.

"I take it there's some excitement afoot? Rosita said something about a big race, but I didn't quite catch it all. What's going on?"

"Cletus Moore's holding a big shindig tomorrow. An all-day affair to celebrate Olivia's birthday. Put a few Texans together and you just naturally get a little horse racing." Anthony gave a quick nod in Midnight's direction. "Miguel and I were just discussing our strategy."

"He is in top form, Senor Nichols," assured Miguel, reaching to rub the velvety nose that Midnight thrust over the fence. "He should run the endurance race with excellent results."

Blake just barely managed to listen to the rest of their discourse. In the back of his mind he was wondering if he could divulge to Anthony what he'd learned about William and seek his help in convincing Laura to give up her insane scheme to marry the wretched bounder.

Blake quickly cast aside that idea. If she wouldn't listen to him, she probably wouldn't listen to her brother either. Besides, he was certain that she'd view his telling Anthony as just another way of refusing to honor her plea.

"Well, I for one am looking forward to tomorrow. I always did enjoy a good race," William said with enthusiasm. "Are you going to ride Midnight yourself, Anthony?"

"No, I'm afraid I'm getting a little old for all that particular type of lunacy. Cletus has a three mile course laid out, and it goes through some pretty rough spots. I guess I'll just have to let Miguel have the pleasure. In all honesty, he can handle Midnight better than I can anyhow."

Miguel accepted the compliment with a barely perceptible nod of his head.

"Well, you've certainly got a fine horse," said William with a sage nod of his head in Midnight's direction. "I wouldn't mind the opportunity for a ride on such a magnificent animal myself."

"You really think *you* could handle a horse like Midnight?" Blake shot back at him without thinking, all the pent-up frustration he was feeling ready to burst forth at the slightest provocation.

William turned a jaded eye on Blake. "Where *I* come from, any gentleman worth his salt is taught to handle good horseflesh in the course of everyday education during his younger years."

The implication that Blake's background was not quite

313

up to William's hung heavy in the air.

A slow burning kindled in Blake's stomach. He took a small menacing step toward William, fighting the desire to knock the cocky little smile William wore right down his throat. And suddenly a wild scheme took form in Blake's mind.

"I don't suppose you'd like to back up that statement, would you?"

"You looking for a wager, Saunders?" William took a step closer to Laura, laying one hand possessively against the small of her back.

"Why not? Don't tell me you're adverse to a small bet now and then." There was a derisive tone to Blake's quiet words as he struggled to ignore William's proximity to Laura.

Hound-dog alert, Miguel watched the growing animosity between the two men.

"William, maybe you shouldn't . . ." Laura began in a small apprehensive voice.

"Now, my dear, you mustn't worry. This might be rather amusing."

"Then you're game?" goaded Blake.

"Nothing I'd like better," William replied with aplomb. He quickly considered the cache of bills tucked away in his money belt. It should be more than sufficient to meet any amount Blake might care to bet. All thought of caution disappeared; he ached to put Blake in his place once and for all. It would serve Saunders right if he lost every dollar he possessed.

Anthony felt the sudden tension in the air. He gave a nervous laugh and stepped between the two men. "You two will have plenty of opportunity to bet tomorrow. If there's anything a Texan likes better than a horse race, it's betting on one."

"Just name your terms, Saunders," said William in a mocking voice, totally ignoring Anthony's attempt to soothe their growing antagonism.

Blake could almost see the dollar signs clicking behind those clear gray eyes. There was nothing to lose and everything to gain by going ahead with his foolhardy plan. And it just might work—if he could keep William angry enough to accept the unconventional terms he had in mind.

Voice edged with sarcasm, Blake said, "I'd be real interested in seeing a demonstration of that equestrian skill you so proudly boast about."

William's mouth gaped open. "You mean you're challenging me to a race?"

"Only if you're man enough to accept."

William's gaze flickered quickly to Laura. There was a strange worried look in her eyes. Was she afraid he'd refuse? Not hardly! He couldn't afford to lose face in front of her now. Besides, his pride was sufficiently injured by Blake's insulting remarks to make him accept any challenge Blake might throw his way.

"I'd be delighted to have the opportunity to whip you severely—as you deserve," William replied with far more confidence than he actually felt.

Anthony shuffled nervously, eyeing the two men in confusion. There was a strange undercurrent to the conversation that he didn't understand. "Gentlemen, please . . ."

Blake's eyes never left William's. "Any problem for us to join that big race you've been talking about, Anthony?"

"Well, no, of course not. They're all open to anyone who wants to ride."

"Fine. Then it's settled?"

"Yes," agreed William. "All you have to do is name the amount of your bet."

Blake smiled a smug little smile that never reached the icy depths of his eyes. "Why don't we leave the details

315

until later, Stratford? I want this friendly little wager to be real interesting." He drawled the words out slowly, mockingly. "Besides, I wouldn't want to offend the lady's sensibilities by discussing such things in front of her."

William shrugged. He had no idea what Blake had up his sleeve, but he wasn't about to turn back now. "As you wish."

Chapter 26

The wagon swayed slightly as it topped a hill and rolled down the gentle incline on the other side. Laura caught the side of the seat to balance herself and then leaned forward to peer around Maria as she continued her conversation with Anthony.

"I was able to tabulate all the totals and get the books brought up to date, but I simply couldn't find the goods themselves—or any record of when or where they were dispensed. I can't make heads or tails of the whole matter, Anthony. All I know for sure is that you've paid out a lot of money for items that don't seem to exist. I'm afraid you'll have to spend some time with me to go over everything if you want to get those inventory records corrected."

"I'll try to find some time to do that, Laura, but I really don't know what good it will do. Since I've been so busy at the capital, I've left all that up to Maria and Miguel."

"But Miguel said—"

"Antonio," snapped Maria, her heavy Spanish accent becoming even more prominent when she was angered. "I told you at the very beginning I was not brought up to have to worry about such things. We had servants for such mundane tasks. It was unfair of you to expect me to take over such responsibilities!"

"Now, honey, don't get yourself all riled up."
Anthony cast a quick glance of supplication toward
Laura. If Maria lost control of that fiery temper of hers
now, it would ruin the whole day for sure. "What say we
forget about all this for now, Laura? Let's just have a
good time at the party. All right?"

Laura was reluctant to drop the subject, especially
since there was a definite contradiction between what
Miguel and Anthony said. But she was smart enough to
realize that a few more words might be all that was needed
to set Maria off. It would be better to forget the whole
thing than cause bad feelings between her brother and his
wife. Besides, what did it matter anyway? Even if she
managed to straighten up the records now, she'd soon be
gone, and within months it would all be for nothing.

Laura pushed the troublesome questions out of her
head and turned her attention to the road ahead. It was a
glorious day for the party. The Texas sky was painted a
clear, bright cornflower blue. What few clouds could be
seen were great white cottony billows edged with a silver
glow by the splendid morning sunshine. A brisk little
wind was blowing, just enough to take the burn out of the
day's heat.

Laura had mixed emotions about the big event they
were traveling toward. She was pleased that it would give
her an opportunity to visit with the friends she had made
during her stay in Texas—perhaps for the last time if
William's determination to leave as soon as possible
prevailed. She had quite run out of excuses for
postponing their journey. Besides, since she had chosen
to make her future with William, it was probably time to
put all this behind her and get on with her life. There
was nothing to be gained by staying any longer. Each day
only intensified her feelings of doubt and unhappiness. It
certainly wouldn't be fair to enter into a marriage still

plagued with such incertitude. Since it was obvious she couldn't overcome her feelings while in close proximity to Blake, she had no choice but to remove herself from the temptation.

It appeared William had been right all along. It was time to leave. Tonight after the party she'd tell him she was ready.

The sun had just hit the mid-morning mark when the wagon rolled into the large, open meadow behind Cletus Moore's big weathered house.

There was an impressive jumble of buckboards and carriages parked in the field. It looked like the whole town had turned out, as well as everyone within riding distance. A couple of flatbed wagons had been set up with refreshments. A holiday feeling flowed through the crowd that jostled and moved through the hodgepodge of vehicles. The large corral at the side of the barn was filled with milling horses. Dogs slept fitfully in the shade of the wagons, and small children chased each other through the crowd with wild whoops of unbridled pleasure.

Anthony guided their wagon carefully through the maze of humanity and reined in in an area that had been roped off from a large section of the flat, grass-covered pasture land surrounding Cletus's house.

Just as Laura turned to accept Anthony's help down from the wagon, two lathered horses with low-hunched riders thundered past on the other side of the barrier. A roar of encouragement went up from the crowd as the horses galloped past the finish line.

Laura mumbled an absentminded "thank you" to her brother and hurried to the head of the wagon so she could view the exciting event closer.

"Anthony, Maria! Glad you could make it." Cletus pushed his way through a wall of humanity to greet the newest arrivals. "And Miss Laura. Olivia will be so glad to see you. She's talked of little else since that night

319

in town."

"That's very kind of you to say. I've looked forward to seeing her, too. This is so exciting. I've never been to anything quite like this." Laura's eyes were large with wonder as she soaked up the sights and sounds.

Olivia was just seconds behind her father in greeting their guests. After a few exchanged pleasantries, she led the women off and left the men to their conversation.

"Your other two guests arrived with Miguel an hour or so ago," Cletus informed Anthony.

"Good." He glanced around the field.

"I think they're all at the barn checking the horses. Midnight's doing fine. Pedro stayed with him all night. Good thinking to send him over yesterday. He should be plenty rested for the race."

"I'll have to admit it wasn't my idea. Miguel seems very determined to win this race. He was the one who wanted Midnight here overnight so he wouldn't wear himself out on the ride over today. By the way, who else is running the point-to-point?" Anthony asked.

"Pennington sent his bay over last night, too. Ol' Sam Duffy's boy Herman will probably ride that gray of theirs. Guess that'll be all."

"No, it won't." Anthony sidestepped a little redheaded boy who was running full tilt over the broken ground in pursuit of his older brother.

"What do you mean?"

"Blake and Stratford decided to enter the race yesterday. I'm not sure just exactly what's going on. Nobody really *said* anything, but I have a funny feeling that it's some sort of grudge match."

"What would those two fellows have going on that would rile them up so much?"

"I haven't figured it out for sure, but I suspect it's Laura."

"Ah," said Cletus, nodding his head in understanding.

"Well, I don't know that Stratford fellow, but Saunders struck me as a right nice guy the times I've been around him."

"Yeah, I kinda favor Blake myself. But it's out of my hands; Laura apparently has already made up her mind."

"Is that so?"

"Yep. She says she's going to marry Stratford."

Cletus cocked his head to one side and eyed his friend. "Kinda sudden like, ain't it?"

"I don't know," Anthony answered with a shrug of his broad shoulders. "They say it's been in the plans for a long time. Anyway, he came all the way to Texas from Philadelphia after her, so I guess he'll be good to her. That's all that's important to me."

"Well, sure it is. I know you just want her to be happy. They staying in Texas?"

"No, she's going back to Philadelphia with him."

"Olivia's gonna be plumb disappointed to hear that Laura's leaving so soon. She was sure looking forward to having someone nearer her age to visit with." Cletus shook his shaggy head.

"I'm gonna hate to see her go, too. I haven't had near enough time with her, what with this damn war and all. And now she says she's leaving."

"But how did this lead to Blake and Stratford entering the race?"

"Beats me. But they're both determined. Blake is taking Blackjack over the course and I'm going to let Stratford use Dancer—"

"*Your* favorite horse?" Cletus asked incredulously.

"I don't really have much choice. I feel kinda obligated to provide him with a good mount—because of Laura, you know?"

"Yeah, I know how it is. It sure ought to be a hell of a race!" Cletus threw a meaty arm over Anthony's shoulders. "Come on, boy. Let's go see that stud of yours.

Take your mind off all this other stuff. Life's too short to let it get you down!"

Anthony knew his friend was trying hard to cheer him up. He forced a grin in answer to the friendly teasing. "Sure thing, Cletus. You're right. Let's go see what everybody's up to."

They disappeared toward the barn. Inside they found Miguel, William, and Blake, all busy seeing to their respective mounts. The air was charged with tension. William and Blake continued to dig at each other at every opportunity. As usual, Miguel kept to himself.

"Well, boys, they all look good," remarked Cletus as he stomped across the hay-strewn floor, "but I'm afraid I'll have to put my money on Miguel and Midnight."

"Speaking of money, Saunders, when are you going to be ready to state your wager?" William's mouth turned down in a rather mocking manner. "You're not going to turn yellow now, are you?"

Blake gave William the same kind of look he might reserve for a skunk. "Not on your life, Stratford. You better worry about yourself. Just see to it that *you* don't try to welch on our agreement."

"A gentleman would never do that, Saunders."

"That's what I'm counting on."

Anthony listened to the conversation and then shook his head. He still couldn't figure out what was going on between the two men.

"Well, when are you planning to divulge your little secret?" prodded William.

"Keep your shirt on, Stratford. I think you'll eventually appreciate the fact that I waited to discuss it in private." Blake deliberately turned his back on William and nonchalantly walked away.

"And just what do you mean by that?" called William angrily.

Blake ignored him. He wanted him good and mad when

he finally told him the terms of his wager.

An hour later, five riders and their respective entourages were gathered in the shade of the wide front veranda of the house to hear Cletus enumerate the rules of the race.

"The distance is approximately three miles around four points. Each rider must stay to the course, passing the named points on the far side of each. No cutting across. You will be on your honor. The first point is that large oak tree on the far side of the field." He stopped long enough to thrust a finger in the proper direction. "Then onward to where the creek makes a double loop in the bottom land and up the embankment of the other side." His arm continued to trace the course. "The third point is the abandoned cabin on the far side of those woods. And finally back to the finish line." An edge of excitement began to creep into his voice. "Everyone understand?"

They all said yes.

"Then I reckon that's all. Get your horses ready and be at the starting line in thirty minutes."

The porch cleared quickly. Cletus and Anthony descended the steps to join Oliva and Laura, who were chatting with Nat and Elizabeth. Young Pennington and Herman Duffy hurried away with their fathers. Maria beckoned to Miguel, and they quickly melted into the crowd, leaving William and Blake alone for the moment.

"I'm still waiting, Saunders." William's voice held a touch of sarcasm.

Blake leaned casually against the post at one corner of the veranda, knee bent, the heel of his boot hooked on the rim of its base. "I have news from a friend of yours . . ."

William's eyebrows rose mockingly. "Really? And just who might *that* be?"

"Theodore Franklin."

The color drained from William's face. "You . . . you must be mistaken. I-I never heard of the man."

"Oh, I think you have. Matter of fact, he's very interested in finding you right now. I suppose the gentlemanly thing for me to do would be to let him know where he might be able to locate—"

"Now listen, Saunders, I don't know how you managed to find out—"

"No, *you* listen. I'm going to propose a little wager to you that I don't believe you can afford to turn down. We're not going to pay any attention to who comes in first in this race. All that matters is you and me. Agreed?"

"Y-yes."

"Good. Now, if you win, I'll forget all about telling Mr. Franklin where he might find his dear lost friend."

There were beads of sweat on William's forehead and a pinched white look to his nostrils. "Is . . . is that all?"

Blake pushed himself away from the post to loom over William. "Not quite. If I win, you're going to tell Laura that you just remembered you're not free to marry her after all. I don't care what kind of story you tell her. It shouldn't really be a problem for the likes of you. From what I've heard, you're pretty good at embroidering the truth whenever it suits you. Just make it sound good, so good that she won't even want to question your motives. And then get the hell out of Texas." Blake ground out those last words with deadly determination.

William swallowed convulsively. Laura was his last chance. He'd counted on her being able to cajole Anthony out of a sum of money sufficient enough to get them both back to Philadelphia *and* pay off Franklin. His hands worked at his sides, clenching and unclenching in desperation. He still needed that money. There was no way he could let Blake win this race.

"And . . . uh . . . if I win, you'll back off and leave us alone?"

Blake shrugged. He didn't intend to let William win. Everything he wanted for the rest of his life depended on this. He could think of no other way to stop Laura from going through with her foolish plans. She had already made it very clear to him that she intended to marry Stratford despite anything Blake might say. Blake knew the only way to stop the marriage was to force William to call it off. "Yes, I'll leave her alone."

"I have your word as a gentleman?" William asked petulantly.

"Sure, why not. An honorable agreement between two upstanding and honest gentlemen." Blake gave a small bitter laugh and walked away.

Excitement buzzed through the crowd as the five riders moved toward the starting line. Final instructions were given, and then the men on foot melted back into the mass of humanity that pressed against the barrier separating the race course from the spectator's area. Finally, Cletus was left alone on the track to start the race.

Laura and Olivia leaned hard against the rope restriction, catching the fever of anticipation that grew with each moment. The two young women were drawn together by a strong bond of friendship and silent understanding. Each sensed in the other something of the unspoken sorrow that tinged her own life.

"I guess I don't have to ask who you'll be cheering for." Olivia cut her clear gray eyes at Laura. "Father told me about your betrothal. I . . . I suppose I should offer my congratulations."

"Thank you."

"I'm afraid I'd be less than honest if I didn't tell you that I'm very sorry to hear that you're leaving."

Laura's smile didn't quite reach her eyes. "Thanks,

Olivia. There are times when I wish I wasn't leaving. I really do love it here. But this is the culmination of something I've dreamed of for years." She sighed deeply. "I wish I could explain all of this to you. But I'm not sure I understand it myself."

"I get the feeling that there's some sort of problem. I know we haven't known each other for very long, Laura, but if I can do anything to help—"

"You're very kind. I'm afraid there's nothing that anyone can do right now. Sometimes you just have to make the best of life . . . even if things don't turn out like you thought they would. Do you know what I mean?"

Olivia's eyes unconsciously searched the crowd lining the racetrack, hesitating for a long moment when she spotted Anthony. When she realized what she was doing, she quickly ducked her head. Long seconds later, she raised her eyes to Laura again, a small forlorn smile on her lips. "Yes, I know exactly what you mean."

Laura would have had to be blind to have missed the melancholy tone of Olivia's voice—or the direction of her sad-eyed gaze. She reached to give Olivia's hand a comforting squeeze.

"Olivia, I'm so sorry. I wish things were different."

Olivia shrugged softly. "We do the best we can, don't we?"

"Yes. Yes, we do." Laura nodded in quiet agreement.

A ripple of excitement traveled through the crowd. Voices got louder, and the people began to shift and push even harder against the fragile barrier separating them from the beaten dirt track. Laura and Olivia once again turned their attention to the course and the cluster of restless horses and men.

Duffy's gray shied nervously, rearing up on his hind legs. The boy on his back fought for control and finally brought the big horse back to the line. Miguel was keeping a tight rein on Midnight, leaning forward to pat

326

his neck and whisper gentle Spanish words in his ear while the huge black stud pranced and pawed at the ground. Pennington's boy seemed to have his big bay well under control for the moment.

To Blake, the others might as well have been invisible. He didn't care who won the race. All he wanted to do was beat William. He knew it would take one hell of an effort if Stratford were any kind of horseman at all. Although not the horse that Midnight was, Dancer had stamina and strength. But William had never ridden him before. Blake's familiarity with Blackjack's ways after many weeks of companionship had to be a plus on his side. He knew his horse's strong points and weaknesses, but he knew Dancer had heart—and often that could be the deciding factor.

Blake shot a quick glance William's way. Stratford's nervousness was already transmitting itself to his horse. Dancer was sweating in shiny dark patches on his shoulders.

"Quiet! Attention, folks. We're just about ready here. Let's have some quiet!"

Cletus waved his hat over his head, and his booming voice finally silenced the mutterings of the crowd from a roar to a persistent buzz. The riders gave him their undivided attention.

"Hold them steady, men!"

Dancer tossed his head and William sawed at the bit. "Damn you, you nag!" Dancer crabbed, bumping softly against Blake's leg. Quick to place the blame on anyone but himself, William's head snapped up and he snarled at his enemy. "Keep your goddamn horse under control!"

Blake only smiled in that slow maddening way and gently edged Blackjack a few inches away. He was glad to see Stratford all anxious and keyed up. It was highly possible that William would be so tense that he'd make a major mistake during the race. Blake was praying for just

327

such a blunder.

"Steady . . . steady," Cletus said softly, hand held high over his head as if to hold the massive beasts at bay.

For one split second they were all in line. Cletus swiftly dropped his hand.

"Go!" he bellowed.

The formation broke, and a cloud of dust billowed up and over the course before sifting slowly over the hysterically screaming spectators.

The riders eased into a free-swinging canter, not yet ready to push their horses. It was a long course, a hard course. They didn't dare expend too much energy immediately; too much would be needed later for the rough terrain ahead.

As they neared the first marker the gray pulled slowly away, the boy on his back forgetting his father's terse instructions in the heady excitement of the moment.

Good, thought Blake. The gray would break a path for the rest of them through the thick stands of grass. He could afford to reserve Blackjack's strength until it was really needed.

They rounded the far side of the massive lone oak that stood sentinel in the wide field. William lay against Dancer's neck and cut his turn as close to the ancient trunk as he dared. His swift passage through the low-hanging foliage whipped it into a frenzy. One slim branch snapped back, and the tip of a slender limb flicked a long thin gash in Blake's cheek. A drop of bright red blood welled in the cut and then trickled over his jawline to mingle with the sheen of sweat already soaking into his shirt.

On they raced toward the low-lying marshy area that bordered the creek. The echo of hoofbeats softened as they reached the spongy ground of the bottomland. Clods of rusty red mud flew from the horses' hooves as they thundered on.

Miguel eased into the lead, expertly working Midnight through the thick tangled brush that bracketed the swiftly running water. The gray was beginning to tire and was fast falling behind to last place when Midnight splashed into the creek. A raccoon jerked upright at the edge of the wide stream, casting frightened bandit eyes in their direction before dropping to all fours and scuttling away from the terrifying onslaught.

Young Pennington thrashed his way through the water in hard pursuit of Miguel. William maintained his third place, confident enough to cast a quick glance back at Blake.

"Give up, you bastard!" he gasped. "You're not going to win, goddamn you!" He dug his spurs into Dancer's flanks, raking the tender flesh unmercifully while urging the big bay harder and harder.

Blackjack's gait altered as he felt the ground soften beneath his hooves. Blake angled off to the left to avoid an obvious mud hole, easing up on the reins a bit to allow Blackjack to pick his own way across the boggy ground. Finally back on firm ground, Blackjack bunched his great muscles and cleared a stand of low brush. He landed soundly and then arched his neck even harder against the pressure of the bit, each long stride eating up great chunks of distance.

William turned to check Blake's whereabouts again, his face an ashen white blur just yards ahead of his adversary. Blake was so close he could see the grim lines of determination bracketing William's pinched mouth and the raw panic in his eyes.

As Blake drew closer, a scalding fury washed over William. He applied the whip against Dancer's sweat-soaked flank. Dancer lunged and landed on a scattering of loose rocks. His hooves scrabbled for purchase on the treacherous ground. He slithered and slid, stumbling almost to his knees. By the time the big bay had regained his footing, Blake was fast upon them. They hit the water at almost the same instant, throwing up a shimmering veil of droplets that sparkled like diamonds in the golden sunlight.

"Damn you! Damn you!" William almost sobbed, not at all sure whether his oaths were cast at his mount or at the tormenter who'd suddenly drawn up beside him.

Miguel had worked Midnight up the steep embankment on the far side of the second loop of the creek with a series of zigzag backtracking moves that had brought him to the top a good distance to the rear of where he had begun at the bottom. He reached the rim and straightened Midnight out just as Blake and William left the water and reached the bottom of the steep bank.

Pennington's bay was right behind Miguel but the boy was pushing too hard. It wouldn't be long until his mount tired and lagged behind. Miguel eased up on the reins, allowing Midnight's pace to slow just enough to let him catch his second wind for the leg ahead. Duffy's gray had fallen far behind and was just now reaching the first loop of the creek.

From his vantage point atop the rim, Miguel could look almost straight down on Blake and William as they rode knee to knee, vying for the lead position up the steep trail. What happened next took only a split second of time, but it seemed to play in slow motion before Miguel's eyes. Pennington's boy had already pushed ahead of Miguel and broken through the brush that crowned the narrow ridge they were on, and Duffy was too far back to see what happened. But Miguel had a bird's-eye view of the whole incident.

Desperately afraid that Blake was going to reach the trail to the top first, William pulled hard on the reins and crashed Dancer into Blackjack. When that didn't throw Blake off his pace enough to allow William an advantage, he did the only thing left he could think of.

Hooking the toe of his boot under Blake's instep, he gave a sudden, vicious lift of his leg. Blake's foot slipped from the stirrup, and the momentum of William's unexpected attack threw him sideways. He grabbed for the saddle horn, almost caught his balance, then lost it again. He flew through the air and then hit the curve of the embankment on his shoulder and rolled wildly down its rock-strewn slope.

Without Blake's guiding hand, Blackjack slid and panicked, rearing and plunging down the shallow spit of land that lined the creek. In just a matter of feet the wildly flying reins tangled and caught on a spiny scrub bush. Blackjack whinnied once, gave a frightened yank at the lines and then settled down to stand docilely.

Blake staggered to his feet, dirt and bits of grass clinging to his clothes. The cut on his cheek had opened even further, and blood was running in steady cascades down his neck to soak in widening crimson stains on his once white shirt. He stumbled as he ran for his horse. "The bastard! The dirty bastard!" He grabbed up the reins and propelled himself atop the horse once again, twisting the lines savagely until Blackjack was once again aimed at the treacherous cliff.

William had already reached the top and was vainly trying to catch Miguel across the open field leading to the deserted cabin that served as the third marker. Miguel's mind was whirling like a dervish. He could hardly believe the cowardly thing William had done.

Young Pennington reached the cabin first, but he tried too tight a turn around the far corner. His horse lost footing, stumbled, and they tumbled head over heels in the long prairie grass. They both scrambled up, remarkably unhurt, but the cinch on the big bay's saddle had snapped. They were out of the race.

With every fiber of his being, Blake urged Blackjack on. "Come on, you beauty! Come on! You can do it." The words rasped out between his harsh gasps for air. The valiant horse's great shoulders pulled forcefully, massive strength lunging into each stride.

As they cleared the turn around the cabin, Blake was gaining on William. Blackjack was pouring heart and soul into his effort.

"Look! They're coming!" cried Olivia, jumping up and down in excitement as the thundering echo of hooves rolled toward them.

Laura's heart was in her throat. "Who's leading? I can't tell. They're too close together!" She stood on tiptoe and shielded her eyes against the glare of the sun, desperately trying to identify the riders atop the galloping horses.

The crowd surged against the rope, threatening to escape its confines and burst across the crudely marked finish line.

Cletus ducked under the rope and ran down the line. "Stay back! Get out of the way!" he shouted to the milling throng when they became even more inflamed as the riders came closer and closer.

In a tight pack the three remaining horses crossed the finish line. Miguel led by a length. Blake and William were desperately jockeying for second place, but as they passed the stakes marking the final length of the course, Dancer pulled away from Blackjack, leading by a head.

The riders astride their lathered steeds were almost lost in the dust that billowed up from the thundering hooves. As soon as they cleared the finish line, the crowd broke through and spilled over the course, waiting for the riders to slow their mounts' momentum and return for the celebration.

As each rider guided his weary mount back to the edge of the group and then dismounted, they were quickly surrounded by dozens of babbling well-wishers, each trying to express his congratulations louder than the person next to him.

William swaggered through the milling throng. He caught Blake's contemptuous look across the bobbing heads. Impulsively William sought out Laura, eager to place the stamp of his ownership on her in full view of Blake.

"Congratulations, William," she shouted to him over the noise of the crowd. To her surprise and acute embarrassment he threw his arms around her, pulled her onto tiptoe and gave her a resounding kiss on the lips right in front of everyone!

"William, please!" Laura shrieked, placing her hands against his chest to push him away. She blushed all the way to the roots of her hair at his unseemly display. Heedless of her chagrin, the crowd roared its approval of William's actions.

William shot Blake one last spiteful look, threw back his head and laughed at her discomfiture. "Now, Laura, I won that kiss, fair and square! Didn't I, fellas?" He challenged the surrounding assemblage with a wicked smirk and a questioning little quirk of his eyebrow. They swiftly shouted their endorsement of his boldness.

Miguel was oblivious of the attention he received for winning. He was too busy trying to contain the irritation that burned within him at the sight of William's treatment of Laura. He wondered morosely if Laura had even noted that he'd won the race. It was galling to be the victor and have the woman he wanted standing at William's side rather than his own.

Miguel longed desperately for the time when his charade could end. It was all he could do to continue to smile and murmur the proper replies to the people who came to congratulate him.

Caught up in the revelry of the moment and in his own smug satisfaction at having bested Blake, William soon forgot that Laura was even there. He strutted about from

333

group to group, soaking in the praise from all who offered it.

Blake stayed at the edge of the crowd, exchanging a few words with those who offered him condolences and assurances that he'd run a great race despite his loss. He kept up a happy facade as long as the people were there. When they finally faded away to again join the groups around Miguel and William, he sagged against Blackjack with weariness. He placed his arms around the heaving horse's neck for a moment, resting his own dirty sweat-streaked cheek against the tired flesh of his brave mount.

"We did our best," he whispered to the spent animal. "We did our best." He gathered up the reins and started to lead Blackjack back to the barn.

"Blake!"

Reluctantly he turned to find Laura standing there, worry lines etching her pale face.

"You're hurt," she whispered. She raised her hand and touched the ruby blotch that covered one side of his shirt. "Let me help you—"

"What are you doing here? Why aren't you with William? Just had to rub it in, did you?" Blake flinched away from her touch. "Well, go on back to William. He's the one you're supposed to be congratulating."

"How can you be so horrid? You know that's not what I intended—"

"Then what do you want?" he asked with a strange, intense calmness.

"I just wanted to be sure you were all right. Any friend would do the same."

"Friend?" he repeated mockingly. "You're still living in fairy tales, my dear."

"Blake, that's not fair—"

"There's a lot about life that isn't fair. But I'm afraid you're going to have to find that out the hard way. I've given up trying to save you from yourself."

"How can you talk to me like that! Something must be terribly wrong with you—"

"Something wrong with me, Laura?" he scoffed. "Good heavens, no. I'm fine, never been better. Can't you tell?" He sounded bitter, remote, aloof, and yet there was an aura of subdued anger in his eyes, in the clench of his jaw, in his very stance.

"Blake, please—"

"No, Laura. No more." There was a poignant vulnerability in his voice now, and the hard edge of a man who'd been pushed too far. "Go on back to your precious William. Leave me alone. Just, please, leave me alone."

He turned away from her. With slow, weary steps he walked away.

Chapter 27

The Moores had thrown open the double doors between the parlor and the dining area in their big comfortable house. The furniture had been pushed back to the walls or cleared from the rooms so that there would be plenty of room for dancing. The air held the pungent aroma of hot candle wax, cigar smoke, and good food.

The room was filled to overflowing with a boisterous, good-natured crowd. They shuffled about while waiting for the fiddler to strike up the first tune, enjoying the opportunity to visit with seldom-seen friends. William, with Laura close at his side, accepted proffered hand-shakes and claps on the back with expansive gestures and a broad, self-satisfied smile. He eagerly recounted the events of the race to anyone who would listen.

Laura soon grew uncomfortable from William's continued preening. She found herself wondering why he was so ecstatically happy. After all, he'd only come in second. She shrugged mentally and pasted a bright smile on her face in response to yet another loud discourse by William. Why was it all such an effort? Everyone else seemed to be enjoying themselves, but Laura's mood was tinged with a strange despondency she didn't really understand.

Throughout the long evening Laura's gaze was drawn time and again to the front entryway. Each new arrival would inexorably attract her attention. And each one always brought a curious sense of disappointment.

It took her a while before she realized that she was looking for Blake. Somewhat shaken by this discernment, she quickly assured herself that it was perfectly normal to be concerned about him. From the way he'd looked after the race, she had every right to worry. What if he were really hurt—despite his denial and Anthony's later assurances? She just wanted to know that he was all right. That's all.

But as the evening progressed and Blake still didn't appear, the ache of apprehension and disappointment she felt became more acute.

She tried her best to keep her attention on William, to smile at the right times, to make the correct replies when people stopped by to chat with them and discuss the festivities. But underneath the bright facade of happiness she presented to the other party guests, she kept wondering where Blake was. She hadn't seen him since he'd walked away from her with that curious sad look on his face after the race. Something had been drastically wrong; she was sure of it.

Where could he be? If only he'd come to the dance, she'd find some way to talk with him and perhaps discover what it was. But the evening dragged on and on, and Blake never came.

Miguel watched Laura's forced enthusiasm from a secluded corner of the parlor. He even noted the fleeting look of something akin to relief that flickered across her face when William, with even more pomposity than usual, shooed her off to dance with Nat. Perhaps no one else noticed her troubled expression, but Miguel was certain she was feeling a touch of embarrassment because of William's continued boastings.

337

Except for the few times Maria had managed to slip away from Anthony to share a word with him, Miguel had stayed unobtrusively to himself. He effectively fended off one ambitious mother with her simpering homely daughter in tow by claiming to be still wearied from the race. He had more important things to do. He was looking for just the right opportunity to approach Laura.

Fate, in the guise of a boisterous group of card enthusiasts, answered his silent prayers.

"Come on, Stratford, join us for a hand or two," Ed Harrison cajoled loudly. "It's not often the womenfolk are busy enough that we can sneak off for a while."

James Duffy joined in. "Just a couple of hands. Come on, what do you say?"

William's face was flushed. He'd long ago lost count of the number of drinks he'd downed as the evening progressed.

"Well, why not?" he agreed expansively. "It looks like today is my lucky day, gentlemen. Maybe I better take advantage of it."

Without as much as a backward glance in Laura's direction, William laughed at his little joke and followed the three other men to a back room.

Miguel intently watched Laura and her partner finish the reel they were dancing; and when the music ceased, he slipped from his shadowed corner and moved silently to her side. Panther quiet in his approach, he startled Laura when he leaned close to her ear and asked her for a dance.

"Oh!" She gave a little jump, and her hand flew to cover her fluttering heart.

Miguel's gaze followed the unconscious movement to rest hungrily on the silky sheen of bosom displayed above the ruffled bodice of her rose-colored gown.

"Miguel! I didn't hear you come up." Her eyes searched the room for some sign of William.

338

Sensing what she was doing, Miguel was quick to inform her of his whereabouts. "Senor Stratford left the room with several gentlemen a few minutes ago."

"Well, in that case . . ." She shrugged her bare shoulders in the most tantalizing manner and gifted him with a dazzling smile of acceptance. "I'd be delighted to dance with you."

Miguel tucked her hand possessively through his black linen-clad arm and led her out to the center of the floor, where he gently enfolded her in his arms as the fiddler drew his slender bow across his instrument in the first sweet note of a waltz.

Miguel danced beautifully, effortlessly guiding Laura in a series of flowing steps and turns that had almost every pair of eyes in the room watching them. More than one person remarked about what a handsome couple they made. Miguel's raven-winged hair and ebony eyes were a subtle complement to Laura's vibrant honey-and-cream beauty.

Miguel gloried in the opportunity to hold Laura in his arms, to feel the gentle swell of her breasts against his chest as they turned and swirled to the lilting music.

"Have you enjoyed yourself today, Laura?" Her name always sounded so lyrical on his lips. His obsidian eyes glowed with pleasure as he smiled down at her.

"Yes." She smiled up into his eyes, a hint of dimple appearing in one velvety cheek as his tender solicitations helped soothe the troublesome worries she'd been plagued with all evening. "Yes, of course, it's been a lovely day. Oh, and congratulations on winning. You ran a splendid race."

"It was nothing." Miguel had the good grace not to preen as William had been wont to do. "Midnight is magnificent. Anyone could have won with him."

"You're too humble, Miguel. If I know nothing else about you, I do know what an excellent horseman you

339

are." She tilted her head to look up at him, her countenance very serious as she softly rebuked him for belittling his accomplishment.

The gesture provocatively arched her slender throat. Miguel could see the tiny pulse beat of her heart in the tender hollow at its base, and he longed to place his lips against it. He felt the quickening of his loins, and with great effort he forced his eyes back to her face.

"Ah, Laura, that has been my saddest disappointment." His voice was husky with hidden emotion. "We have not had near enough time to get acquainted. You have no idea how difficult it is to be a stranger, cut off from one's country, removed from friends and family."

"Oh, Miguel, I'm sure it is."

Her heart filled with a sudden compassion for the man. This was the first time she had considered the thought that Miguel's aloofness might actually be a defense mechanism against the loneliness he suffered because of his exile.

She forced a bright smile. "But you must remember that you haven't lost your whole family. You still have your cousin Maria as well as a bright future here with Anthony. You know how much he depends on you. I'm sure it's only a matter of adjustment. It will all get easier as time goes by."

"Yes, you're right. There's always Maria." There was a fleeting bitter downturn to Miguel's sensual mouth before he continued. "But you are the first person in a long time that I have wanted to share anything of myself with. I have so been hoping that you would grant me the privilege of getting to know you better. Perhaps in the next few weeks I will be able to do so." His tone was lightly teasing, but there was a definite vein of seriousness below the surface.

"How very sweet of you to say that, Miguel. I'm really very sorry we won't have the opportunity to do so,"

340

Laura said gently, her gaze searching the deep hidden depths of his eyes. "I know I would be proud to count you as a friend . . ."

Miguel turned on a smile that would melt the coldest heart. "Then what is stopping us?"

"I won't be here. William and I will be leaving at the end of the week."

Miguel's stomach gave a sickening swoop. So soon! It would be impossible to accomplish his plan if she left that quickly. He *had* to stop her. All he needed was another couple of weeks. By that time his elaborate scheme would be in motion, and there would be no further need to continue his charade.

He searched his mind for a solution to the dilemma. How could he stop her from leaving? Damn Stratford! If not for him she wouldn't be considering such foolishness. She had no business going off with that man! He was despicable. He didn't deserve her!

But wait! That was it! If he told her what he'd seen Stratford do to Blake, she'd realize what a blackguard he was. No matter how sweet and loyal Laura was, she couldn't possibly continue with this mad scheme, knowing that damning truth about William. Miguel quickly made up his mind.

Ebony eyes bored into Laura's, his handsome bronze face a study in seriousness. "I must talk with you in private. It is something very important. Please. Your whole future depends on it."

She frowned, trying to make sense of Miguel's sudden peculiar statement. Her teeth worried at her bottom lip. Whatever could it be?

"I don't understand . . ."

"I must tell you something of great importance. Something I only discovered today."

"Very well, Miguel. I'm listening."

His gaze swept the room. There was no privacy here.

341

Anyone could overhear their conversation. To make matters even worse, Anthony and Maria were standing just at the edge of the floor talking with Nat and Elizabeth, only a few feet away from where Miguel and Laura were dancing. With intense aggravation, Miguel noted that Maria was already scowling darkly in his direction.

When Miguel didn't answer her right away, Laura glanced quickly at his face. Noting the pinched look around his mouth, she traced the direction of his brooding gaze—straight to her brother. Anthony! It had to be something about Anthony!

Oh, Lord, did she really want to know? What could she do if it were something quite terrible? How could she help her brother if she were back in Philadelphia? She knew it would be almost impossible to talk William into another postponement of their trip. She felt Miguel's hold on her tighten as he continued some inner contemplation.

After a long moment Miguel finally responded. "We must talk, but not here. There is too much noise, too many people. We need some place where we can talk quietly, without interruption. You are not going to like what I have to tell you."

Laura tried to ignore the worrisome little flutter in her stomach. "Well, where would you suggest?"

"Come, we will take a little walk outside. No one will consider that anything is amiss."

"Very well," she agreed. "Let's go."

Miguel released his hold on her and turned toward the door, working his way carefully through the clusters of dancers and onlookers. Laura gathered her voluminous skirts up, stopping only long enough to assure young Ben and James Duffy's boy that she would indeed save them a dance. Then she hurried after Miguel and out the front door.

Flickering lanterns cast scattered patches of yellow

light across the wide veranda. The echo of their hurried footsteps was almost lost in the music wafting through the wide-open windows. In her haste to catch Miguel's retreating form, Laura almost collided with a shadowed figure.

"Howdy, Miss Nichols." Amos Hall quickly doffed his hat and bobbed his head politely in Laura's direction. "You remember the missus?" He shoved his plump little wife forward.

"Yes, of course," Laura managed to reply. She smiled at Amos's stern-faced wife. "How are you, Mrs. Hall. So nice to see you again."

Laura fidgeted through five minutes of polite conversation about the weather, the party, the war, her fears looming larger and larger with each second that passed. She finally managed to excuse herself from the Halls and rejoin Miguel, who was waiting in the deep shadows at the bottom of the porch steps.

Miguel grabbed her hand and pulled her along behind him as he crossed the broad field surrounding the house and ducked behind a large stand of trees.

He came to such an abrupt halt that Laura bumped into him, almost losing her balance. He quickly reached out to steady her, his hands gripping her arms possessively. They stood silent in the pale silver moonlight for a long minute.

Laura finally drew a ragged breath and, in a voice she hoped didn't betray her fears, said, "Now, Miguel, just what is this all about?"

"He is not worthy of you, Laura. I cannot allow this to go on."

"But what has he done?" Laura dreaded what was to come, but she had to know.

"There is no honor in the man. He cheated rather than depend on his own abilities."

The words Miguel spoke made no sense to Laura. She

was so prepared to hear bad news about Anthony that their real meaning did not register. "But how? When? I don't understand."

"During the race."

Laura blinked in confusion. Anthony? The race? "What are you talking about? What could he possibly have done?" she questioned, thoroughly perplexed by the whole conversation.

"He purposely caused Blake to fall from his horse. I have little doubt that Senor Saunders would have come in second if not for that accident."

"But how could Anthony have done that? He wasn't anywhere near the riders—"

"Anthony?" Miguel said in surprise. "I'm not talking about Anthony, I'm talking about Senor Stratford!"

"William?" Laura said blankly.

"Yes, William. He cheated and caused Blake to fall!"

"But surely you don't mean that. William would never do such a thing on purpose."

"I wish I could agree with you, but that is not the case. I was above them on the ledge of the embankment. I could see everything very clearly. William caught Blake's foot deliberately and caused him to lose his balance. There was absolutely no way to mistake his intentions."

"But . . . why? Blake could have been badly hurt! Hurt worse than he was. Good heavens! He had blood all over him after the race—"

"He was very fortunate that he only received a few cuts and bruises. Luckily he was still at the bottom of the escarpment when it happened. If he had been a few feet further up the embankment, it could have been a very dangerous fall. As it was, Senor Saunders was badly shaken up, but it certainly could have been much worse."

"But, Miguel, surely you're mistaken about it being on

purpose. Couldn't they have just collided . . . or something?"

"No, there is no doubt in my mind, Laura. I saw everything. Now you can understand why you must not marry such a man. He is not honorable. To have cheated like that simply to win a mere horse race is unthinkable! Who knows what he might do under other circumstances—what he might be capable of under really drastic pressures? No, Laura, you must listen to me, please."

He pulled her up against him, his fingers tightening on the tender flesh of her arms. She had to listen to him, she had to!

"Laura, you must realize the importance of what I have said. You cannot possibly commit yourself to a future with such a man."

The almost desperate look on his face frightened her. "Miguel! You're hurting me," she protested, twisting fruitlessly in an effort to free herself from his steely hold.

"I'm sorry, Laura." He snatched his hands away as if he'd been burned. The bland, aloof mask he usually wore slipped into place again. He drew a long breath and forced the anxiety from his voice. "I didn't mean to. It is only that I'm very concerned."

Unconscious of her actions, she gently rubbed the place his fingers had bruised. Her mind spun with a thousand questions and a thousand excuses concerning Miguel's accusations against William. Awash with feelings of confusion, she turned away from Miguel and paced slowly up and down beneath the sheltering boughs of the trees, passing from shadow to moonlight and back again.

Miguel closely watched her every move, searching her face each time she passed him, finding it devoid of expression, strangely calm and masklike. He hadn't a clue as to what she was thinking. He shuffled from one foot to the other as the long minutes ticked away. Had his ploy worked? He waited nervously for some sort of reaction from Laura.

In direct contradiction to her outer calmness, Laura's mind scurried and scampered like a small trapped animal as she explored the endless questions racing through her mind. Was she too eager to escape her bond to William? Was that the reason she tended to believe Miguel's tale? If she were loyal to the man she was supposed to love, she would never have listened to such a story in the first place—much less considered that it might be true. If she truly loved William, she should believe in his innocence with no reservations.

It bothered her greatly that it was more difficult for her to believe in William than to accept what Miguel had said as truth. To her, that somehow seemed very unfair. She should be on William's side no matter what. Shouldn't she?

But what he'd done— No! She mustn't think like that! What he'd been *accused* of doing was so unforgivable.

Blake's vision seared across her mind. The look in his eyes—the sadness, the dismay. Is that why he'd looked at her like that? Because he knew what kind of man William really was? What was it he'd said about giving up trying to save her from herself?

She had sensed that something was terribly wrong with Blake after the race. Could this possibly be the reason? But he should have told her!

Her mind retorted bitterly, And have you refuse to listen to him just like you did before?

But this is different!

Different? How so? How do you know what he was trying to tell you that other time? You never gave him a chance.

The battle within her continued. Weary from the inner turmoil, she finally stopped her pacing in front of

Miguel's tall form, her head slumped dejectedly. He reached out with infinite tenderness and placed one strong finger under her chin, lifting until her eyes met his.

"I know this is a difficult thing for you to face, Laura."

The moonlight bathed the planes of her face in silver; velvet shadows sharpened the angles and hollows. "Yes, Miguel, it is, but I'm very much afraid it must be done."

He felt a great weight lift from him. At least she had believed him. Now all that remained was for her to confront William with the truth. His fears were well on their way to being dissolved.

Laura's eyes glittered like small pools of sapphire, hinting at the tears that threatened to form. Her mouth turned up in a small trembling smile. "I guess it's time to go back in before everyone misses us."

"Yes," Miguel answered with great reluctance. "I suppose it is."

He wished she'd tell him what she intended to do. But he argued with himself that he should be happy to settle for what he had achieved so far. It wouldn't seem reasonable to her if he pushed too hard for a further response.

It was all he could do to restrain himself from pulling her into his arms. He wanted desperately to cradle her head against his shoulder, to kiss away the wounded look of bewilderment that played across her face. But there would be time now—time to heal the hurt and disillusionment, time to introduce her to pleasures so intense she would soon forget she'd ever cared at all for William Stratford.

"I must wait for the right time to talk with William," Laura said with sudden conviction. "Tomorrow . . . yes, tomorrow. I simply couldn't face it right now. Not with all those people around. It's going to be difficult enough as it is."

"I think you've made a wise decision."

Miguel clasped her hand reassuringly, twining their fingers together as they began their slow walk back across the field. His touch was soothing, reassuring, and she was flooded with a sense of appreciation for his kindness and unselfish concern for her well-being.

Although reluctant to give up the small measure of contact he had with her, Miguel knew he must do so before they reached the house. He gave her fingers a firm little squeeze of encouragement just before they stepped into the pool of light bathing the porch stairs and then released his hold on her hand.

He consoled himself with the thought that in the not too far future he would have the opportunity to do more than hold her hand. Soon he could sate himself with the heady feel of her flesh under his hands. The thought was intoxicating.

"Laura! We've been so worried about you." Anthony's concerned voice rose above the raucous noise emanating from the house. "Maria was afraid something was wrong."

Maria's eyes glittered like black diamonds as her gaze flickered back and forth between Laura and Miguel. "You shouldn't disappear like that. People can only think the worst."

"The worst of what, my dear Maria?" Miguel questioned in a deceptively calm tone.

Her chin came up defiantly. "Well . . . that Laura might be sick or something. She should not worry her brother in such a manner."

"Oh, I'm sorry, Anthony," Laura was quick to explain. "I didn't mean to cause you concern. I . . . I just got a little warm, that's all. Miguel was kind enough to accompany me while I sought a cooling breeze. We must have lost track of time."

"Ah, Maria, always so kind and concerned for others.

How very thoughtful of you, my dear, to be so worried about your sister-in-law." The mockery in Miguel's eyes went unnoticed by Laura and Anthony, but Maria looked ready to spit fire.

"It must be a trait that runs in the family, dear cousin. After all, *you* were the first to show your concern for Laura."

"Yes, thanks for looking after her, Miguel. I get so caught up in all these worries about the war that I sometimes forget the needs of others. Shall we go back inside?" Anthony offered his arm to Maria, who shot Miguel one last look of pure venom before smiling adoringly up at her husband.

Laura was given the opportunity to confront William much sooner than she desired. The dining room at Anthony's was strangely deserted the morning after the big party. Blake was still nowhere to be found, and Anthony had elected to stay in his cozy bed with Maria rather than rise at the crack of dawn as was his normal habit.

For a few blessed moments Laura thought she'd been given a reprieve, that she could finish her morning meal and escape to the barn for a ride on Sugar. She still needed time to digest the distressing news she'd heard from Miguel, and as yet she'd come to no conclusion on how to broach the touchy subject to William. But her hopes for a respite were dashed when William entered the room just as she emptied her cup of the last drops of coffee.

He looked slightly haggard, no doubt the result of his copious consumption of alcoholic beverages the night before.

"Good morning, Laura, dear," he muttered, bending to aim a quick kiss at her forehead before sinking into a chair. "Coffee, Rosita!" he called loudly and then momentarily cradled his head in his hands.

Rosita scurried through the doorway with a large steaming mug. "Would you like some breakfast, Senor Stratford?"

"Good heavens, no!" William snapped, his stomach revolting at the mere idea of food.

Rosita backed away from him, lips compressed in a tight disapproving line in response to his unnecessary gruffness. "*Si*, senor," she said with barely concealed irritation. Head tilted at a proud angle, she stalked from the room. Laura heard a smattering of dark Spanish muttering as the door closed behind the plump little woman.

Laura cast apprehensive eyes toward William. Should she say something now? Perhaps it would be better to leave William alone for the time being. He looked to be in a terrible mood. Surely this was not the right time to bring the subject up.

Coward, mocked her conscience.

She fidgeted with her empty cup, gave a loud sigh, and finally turned toward William, who was slumped like a rag doll in his chair. There was a dark shadow just under his jawline where he'd missed a small patch of whiskers while shaving that morning—the result of a none too steady hand perhaps? Laura never remembered seeing William in such a condition before. He'd always been so well turned out, all spit and polish.

Or was it that she'd never looked at him with clear eyes before?"

"W-William," she said and her voice cracked with nervousness. She stopped, cleared her throat and began again. "I need to ask you something."

"Well, would you mind making it quick? I do believe I'm going back upstairs and lie down for a bit. I have a rather nasty headache, and the coffee hasn't helped at all." He raised slim fingers to massage his temples gingerly.

"I . . . I'm sorry you aren't feeling well . . . but this is important. I would very much like to hear your side of the story—"

"Story?" William came bolt upright in his chair. "My side of *what* story?"

"Well, something I heard. I really don't want to believe it, but I'm terribly bothered by the implications, William. It's very important that we discuss this now. I don't think I can let it go unresolved in my mind any longer."

"I knew that son of a bitch Saunders wouldn't keep his mouth shut! I should never have trusted him," William snarled.

He shot out of his chair and began to pace the perimeters of the room.

"Well, it isn't true! Not one word of it. I never heard of Theodore Franklin. I don't care what Saunders says—I don't owe Franklin anything and especially not any gambling debts! It's all lies. Saunders has taken a simple little misunderstanding about a small business deal and blown it all out of proportion."

Laura's mouth dropped open in surprise. Franklin? Gambling? What on earth was William talking about?

"But, William—"

"Now, listen, Laura." William scowled down at her fiercely. "I would hardly call it loyal of you, my dear, to listen to such gibberish! What right did that man have to pry into my private dealings, anyway? Don't tell me you're going to listen to those lies. It's just that I had a little bad luck on a business deal."

"But—"

"It's really very simply to understand. I didn't learn about the problem before I left the East, or I would have taken care of everything then. Franklin has his story all

351

mixed up, and Blake is just twisting things to suit himself—"

Laura's brows knitted in consternation. "But, William, I thought you said you didn't know this Mr. Franklin."

"What? Oh! Well, yes, I mean I don't know him very well. He's just a remote business acquaintance, and I certanly have no idea why he's saying these things about me!"

"I don't understand any of this."

"No need for you to, my dear. Just put your mind at rest. I intend to have a little talk with Mr. Saunders at the first opportunity. He has no right to go around telling you such things!"

"William, Blake didn't tell me anything."

"What?" He whirled to face her. "But you said—"

"I didn't say anything. You didn't let me finish. Blake has never told me a thing about you. Oh, he wanted to one time, but I wouldn't listen to him. Perhaps . . . perhaps I made a big mistake."

"Now, Laura." William quickly returned to the table, pulling his chair close to hers and clasping her hand in a coaxing manner. "This is absurd. There's nothing to get upset about. I can explain everything."

"All right. Can you explain about the race and what you did to Blake?"

William's eyes narrowed dangerously. "I thought you said he never told you anything."

"He didn't. Someone else who was in the race saw what happened and told me."

"It's all lies!"

"Like the story about Franklin is a lie? When do I find out how to tell which is the truth and which is a lie when it concerns you, William? I seem to have been suffering under a vast misconception for a very long time. I thought I knew you—knew what kind of man you are—

but it appears that I've been very wrong."

"Now, listen to me, Laura. This whole thing can be worked out. It was really nothing, just a little joke between Blake and me. You needn't worry your pretty little head about it. Just trust me. Everything is going to be fine. Why, when we get back to Philadelphia—"

"I'm not going with you, William," Laura said softly, suddenly realizing that her obligation to William was over at last. Relief surged through her.

"You can't mean that."

"I do mean it, William. For the first time in my life, I see you as you really are. I've been in love with a fantasy, but now it's over. I'm really sorry for my part in your problems. I should never have written you that letter. It was wrong of me, and I apologize. But I'm not going to pay for one silly mistake for the rest of my life."

Quick as a snake, William was up and around the edge of the table. He grabbed Laura's wrist, jerking her viciously out of her chair. "You're not going to get away with this. You owe me! You teased me along. I gave up everything back East to follow you because of your promises. You *have* to come with me."

"Let go of me!" Laura pulled at the fingers wrapped tightly around her fragile wrist. "I don't *have* to go anywhere, and I am *not* going with you—not now, not ever!"

"I can't let you get away with this. Too much depends on it. I would advise you to reconsider."

"And I would advise you to take your hands off my sister, Stratford." Anthony's deadly voice cut through the room.

William jumped as though he'd been shot. Quickly he released his hold on Laura's wrist and gave a nervous little laugh. "Anthony, old man, I didn't hear you coming."

"That's obvious."

"Uh . . . we were just having a little lover's quarrel. You know how it is." William stammered his way lamely through the excuse. "If you'd be so kind as to allow us a little privacy, I'm sure we can settle this quickly."

"I think not, Stratford. I believe Laura said she wasn't going with you. Is that right, Laura?"

"Yes, Anthony," she answered gratefully, gently rubbing the bruised places on her wrist.

"In that case, Stratford, I think it's time you got your things together and got the hell off my land!"

Chapter 28

Laura threw back the tangled sheets and propped herself up on her elbow to pound the pillow into submission one more time. She lay down again, turning first one way and then another. It was no use. Although it was far past midnight, sleep still eluded her.

She was simply too keyed up from the events of the day. William had finally left just before lunch—but not without more bitter words and recriminations. Laura's cheeks burned hot at the memory of some of his accusations. It was almost impossible for her to reconcile the angry man who'd stormed out of the house today with the charming person she'd always thought William to be.

How could she have been so wrong? Guilt lay heavily upon her heart. Guilt for almost more reasons than she could number. After all, it was her fault that William had come to Texas in the first place. If she'd behaved like a proper lady, none of this would have happened!

But, her mind retaliated, if you'd behaved like a proper lady, you'd be married to that disgusting Bernard Arbuckle now.

She shuddered at the thought. No, almost anything was better than that!

Still, she did feel bad about the way things had turned

out. Why did life have to be so cruel? Why were people so foolish and blind to reality?

And, much to her shame, it appeared she'd been foolish not once, but twice! She'd held on to her belief in William in the face of some pretty damning evidence—simply closing her eyes and refusing to see the truth that had been right under her nose. That was bad enough. But to top it off, she had spurned Blake's attempt to set her straight on the matter.

What an utter fool he must think she was!

Laura had to admit that she'd suffered very little upon William's departure, considering the years she had invested in adoring him. In fact, she was almost ashamed to admit that she'd been filled with a curious kind of exhilaration when he finally disappeared over the horizon—as if she'd been saved from some horrendous fate.

No, William's absence was not a problem. But Blake's certainly was.

She knew it was useless even to consider that Blake might forgive her. How could he possibly do so after the way she'd treated him? No man would. And certainly not a proud man like Blake.

Hadn't he made himself perfectly clear after the race? He was through worrying about her. He'd told her so in no uncertain terms. Whatever feelings he'd had for her were gone—extinguished by her own stubbornness and stupidity.

She mustn't dwell on what might have been. She didn't dare. For, if she did, she would surely cry until her heart broke. How could any one person be so absolutely foolish? She'd thrown herself at the feet of a man who wasn't worth a single hair on the head of the man she'd spurned.

Yes, she assured herself, she certainly deserved all the misery she was suffering. She'd brought every ounce of it down upon her own head.

"Fire and damnation!" she whispered in the darkness, reaching to swipe an escaped tear from her cheek. Somehow the brazen, uncharacteristic words bolstered her resolve a bit.

With a loud sigh she flopped over in the bed and reached to pull the sheet back into place. Lying on her side, one arm under her pillow, she restlessly watched the dark shadows of the leaves dance in a patch of moonlight outside her open window.

She knew she must give up all thought of what might have been with Blake. At this point it was very doubtful that she'd ever even see him again. He had not returned to the ranch since that awful confrontation after the race.

He might never return. Why should he? After all, it would be a simple matter to write Anthony and ask that his belongings be forwarded. And who would blame him? If Laura were in his position, she wouldn't want to subject herself to any further hurt either.

At least she was honest enough with herself to admit that it might even be easier on her if he didn't return. Maybe never seeing him again would eventually make forgetting him less of a problem. It was too late to admit she loved him, too late to make up for all the misery she'd caused.

She tried to resign herself to this depressing thought, but a small niggling phrase kept whirling in her head. If ever in her life she'd owed someone an apology, it was Blake. If only she could tell him how sorry she was, maybe then she could put the whole miserable episode behind her and get on with her life.

There just might be one last chance to ease her conscience. She could at least write him and ask his forgiveness.

Laura frowned in the darkness. Write him? Yes, of

course, but where to send her apology? She searched back through the past months and was shocked to realize just how little she knew about Blake.

Had he ever mentioned an address? Even a city, other than Washington, D.C.? What about his family? She could recall no comment about his mother or father. She didn't even know the name of his company or any of his business acquaintances. Except for John—and John was dead.

How strange—and she thought she'd known him so well. But they had always talked of the present, with very little reference to the past or the future.

But surely Blake would write to Anthony. He wouldn't abandon all his clothes and personal articles. She'd have to wait until they heard from him. He'd have to give Anthony a forwarding address. Then she could send her letter.

With that somewhat encouraging thought, she settled down a little. Her eyes were getting heavy when she thought she heard something in the hall. She listened drowsily. Nothing. It was only the house creaking, she finally told herself. Her eyes drifted shut again.

But wait, there it was again! Her eyes flew open. It couldn't be—but, yes, it was. There were small noises coming from Blake's room.

Relief flooded through her. She'd have a chance to tell him how sorry she was, after all! She refused to allow herself to think any further than that. An apology, just an apology. That's all she hoped to be able to do. Tomorrow. Yes, tomorrow she'd seek him out and have her say.

She felt better already—until the small noises continued for far longer than necessary for Blake to ready himself for bed.

What was he doing? Oh, surely he couldn't be packing! Did he mean to just slip in, get his things, and slip out again without a word to anyone?

Would you blame him? her guilty conscience taunted.

With each passing second she became more positive that that's exactly what he was doing. Now she'd never be able to tell him how she felt. He'd be gone by morning, and there'd be no letter claiming his belongings—no way to forward her message.

Why, any second now he could slip from his room and disappear into the night, and she'd never see him again! She couldn't let that happen. She just couldn't.

Being exceptionally careful not to make any more noise than necessary, Laura eased out of bed. She padded barefoot to the wardrobe, planning to quickly don a dress. Grasping the tiny ribbon straps of her gown, she started to pull it over her head. There was a loud creak from Blake's room. Was that his door opening? Her heart beat wildly against her rib cage. Her trembling fingers released their hold on the silky material, and it slithered back down her body.

Oh, Lord, there wasn't time to worry about such things. He could be gone any minute! She grabbed up her wrapper and shoved her arms through the sleeves. The sash went ignored as she scampered for her door and hurriedly pulled it open.

The hallway was dark. She tiptoed nervously down its shadowed length. There was a tiny narrow strip of light under Blake's door. Her heart gave a lurch of relief. He was still there!

She paused in front of his door for a long moment, watching the thin sliver of light at her feet. Every once in a while an inky shadow would chase across the golden glow, and her heart would give a little *ka-thump* against her breast.

It was now or never. She could stand there like a ninny for the rest of the night, or she could get this thing over with. She might even be able to get a decent night's sleep

359

if she could clear her conscience.

She swiped her damp palm against the side of her robe. Drawing a deep breath, she raised her hand and timidly knocked on the door. There was no response for a long time. Her courage was fading fast, and she was just about to snatch up the skirt of her gown and run back to her room when the door was thrown open.

Blake loomed over her, a golden giant in the soft velvet shadows of the room. He was clad only in trousers that rode low on his lean hips. His naked torso shone like burnished brass in the flickering candlelight. The silky hairs that covered his corded arms and the broad expanse of his chest looked as if they'd been sprinkled with gold dust.

Laura froze, oblivious to her own state of dishabille. Her tongue stuck to the roof of her mouth and stubbornly refused to work at all. Her frightened eyes sought his for some small signal of encouragement on his part. His eyes glittered darkly, revealing not one iota of feeling. When, after a long, agonizing moment his stern expression changed not a whit, she dropped her gaze in confusion.

How could she even attempt to talk to him when he looked at her in such a way? He didn't want to hear what she had to say. He didn't even *care* what she might have to say.

As she contemplated her situation, the satiny fabric of the wrapper she had clutched so desperately to her throat slipped unheeded through her fingers to lay like a second skin against the soft curves of her body. Her arms dropped to her sides in weary defeat. It was useless. She might as well forget this whole wild scheme and go back to her room now, right now, while she still had a few shreds of dignity left.

But her body refused to obey her commands. She stood frozen in place. The tip of her tongue darted out nervously to moisten her dry lips, and still she could say nothing. She raised her eyes, large and full of emotion, to his again. The glow of the candle flame was reflected as twin pools of light in the dark blue orbs. A tiny accelerated pulse beat visibly in the soft hollow of her throat.

Blake's fingers tightened on the doorknob. How could she come to his room looking like that in the middle of the night! Was she determined to drive the last sliver of sanity from his mind?

They stood like graven images, each filled with remorse and dread—and longing. Their eyes devoured what their hands and lips refused to seek.

In a voice almost too weary for words, Blake finally spoke. "What do you want, Laura?"

She took a small step forward. Her wrapper fell open. Shadows danced across the ivory swell of bosom above the silken gown, gliding, flicking, licking at the sweet, secret valley that dipped beneath the low-cut bodice. The pouty tips of her high, firm breasts pushed against the fragile fabric, their delectable darker crowns teasingly revealed by the golden flame of the candle.

Blake swallowed convulsively and forced his eyes back to her face.

"Could . . . could I talk with you?" Her voice was breathy, like the rustle of flower petals in a soft summer breeze.

"I don't think there's anything left to discuss, Laura." He was desperate to get her out of his room. A giant fist closed around his chest, making every breath a monumental effort.

"Yes, there is . . . please," she whispered throatily.

Blake finally released his stranglehold on the doorknob and stepped back into the room, almost as if to escape her nearness.

Laura took another step forward. "I . . . I came to

361

apologize. I should have listened to you."

Blake smiled wryly. "Don't you think we've played this game long enough? I can't take any more. You belong to William. I've accepted it. Why do you persist in torturing me?"

"But I don't."

"Oh, yes, you do." His voice was husky with emotion. "The thought of you tortures me night and day." He moved back a few more inches, desperate to keep her out of reach.

A scarlet flush bathed her face and crept down her bared bosom. Oh, sweet heaven, could he possibly still care?

She moved toward him, drawn like a moth to a flame, and again he retreated. He stumbled against the corner of the bed and swiftly moved around it. He stopped in the center of the room, hands clenched at his sides, and he glared at her.

"That's not what I meant." She could hardly lift her voice above a whisper.

"What then?" He was in agony. His eyes were relentlessly drawn to the one delicate chestnut curl that lay on the sweet slope of her breast in the most beguiling manner. His hands itched to touch it, to twine the silken strands around his finger.

"I mean, I don't belong to William. You were right all along. I never did. I never will."

"I don't understand—"

"He's gone."

"Gone?" Blake repeated huskily.

"Yes. Gone forever. I sent him away."

Blake's mind refused to digest this startling piece of news. He stood in stunned silence for a long time before finally turning away from her. He needed space—space to breath, space to think.

With slow, measured steps he crossed the room to the

362

ornately carved chest. He leaned his hands upon its smooth surface, head bowed, keeping his back to her as if to gain enough strength for what was still to come. The whipcord tendons along his arms tensed; the muscles across his back and shoulders bunched and slid under the gilded skin as he fought a battle within himself.

He finally raised his head and looked into the mirror. He could see her shadowed figure in its reflecting surface, and he drank in her beauty like a starving man.

"But why?" he managed to finally say.

"Because he wasn't what I thought he was. Because he wasn't what I wanted."

With slow deliberate steps she moved to the center of the room. Blake hungrily watched her reflection, still holding himself back with steely determination. She was so beautiful, her hair in splendid disarray. The tousled curls hung like a misty halo around her pale face, caressing her cheeks, stroking her shoulders, tumbling over the tempting flesh he longed to touch.

The pale-blue wrapper hung open, and the filmy gown beneath it did little to shield her body from his eyes. The golden candlelight draped her with a gentle glow, throwing soft purple shadows beneath the sweet heavy weight of her breasts, gently nuzzling the flat plane of her belly, highlighting the dark velvety delta of her womanhood through the gossamer fabric.

Blake pulled a ragged breath into his laboring lungs and turned slowly to face her. She saw the raw hunger in his eyes and felt the sweet pulse of echoed desire in the pit of her stomach.

His voice was ragged with restrained passion. "If you have any doubts—any doubts at all—you'd better leave. Now."

And she knew what he meant. It wasn't why she'd come, but it no longer mattered.

"No."

The word was a velvet caress. It enveloped him, stoking the fire within. The embers of desire flamed and became an inferno in his belly. Sweet heat flowed through his veins.

With slow, deliberate steps he crossed the room to stand before her, his eyes holding hers every step of the way. Her head tilted back on her slender throat as he drew nearer and nearer, as if she were loath to break the bond of their gaze.

At last he stood only inches away, almost touching— but not quite. His warm breath stirred the wispy curls at her temple. His eyes were hooded, leaving only burning, narrow slits of glittering black fire that threatened to consume her.

Every muscle in his body was tense, thrumming with an exquisite agony as he postponed touching her for as long as he could. Then slowly, slowly his hands reached out and cupped her arms. His fingers slid across the sweet slope of her shoulders, flickered like a butterfly up the beguiling column of her throat, teased with utter tenderness at the feathery tendrils surrounding her face, and finally threaded their way into the tumbled curls to cup her face between his palms with infinite tenderness.

He tilted her head up, dipping his slowly until there was but a breath between him. With tantalizing slowness he ran his tongue across her bottom lip, exalting in her sweet taste. The fine silken hairs of his mustache teased at her mouth. And still their bodies did not touch.

Laura's nipples pebbled and hardened, aching to be crushed against the granite strength of his chest. And the ache grew and whispered its way through her very soul until her whole body cried out with need. She could feel her hammering heart beat in every pulse point: Blake, Blake, Blake, it called.

Ever so gently he covered her mouth with his own, using the tender pressure of his fingers to slant her head until he could possess her lips completely. For a long moment he simply gloried in the feel of her. Then his mouth began a slow sweet ravishment of hers. His teeth nibbled along the edges in tiny teasing bites. His tongue traced the rim of her lips and then laved the slick inner lining with infinite care before gliding deeper.

At the thrust of his tongue, her stomach did a slow heart-stopping roll. She moaned softly, and her arms went around him, hands splayed against the hard muscles of his back. Her fingers ventured wonderingly over the ridges of muscle, caressing the tiny knobs of bone up the center of his spine, whisking over the sharp thrust of his shoulder blades and the rounded contours of brawn and sinew to finally bury themselves in the tawny golden mane at the nape of his neck.

Her touch released all the pent-up emotion he'd been holding back. He finally allowed himself the luxury of pressing his body to hers. His right hand slid around to cup the back of her head and press her mouth even harder against his own. His left hand slid down the nape of her neck, down her slender spine, down the soft swell of her buttocks. His fingers flexed on the tantalizing mound of flesh and cupped her to him, pulling her tight against his body until his loins were cradled against the sweet heat of her femininity.

Long minutes later, he broke their kiss to gulp for air, their breaths mingling, warm and sweet. Just before he seared their lips together again, she heard him murmur brokenly, "Laura, sweet Laura. My God, what you do to me!"

She twined her arms around his head, dragging him down to her, straining to press her lips tighter to his. His right hand dropped to join his left, and he palmed the sweet plump flesh of her buttocks and pulled her up on tiptoe, rocking against her in a pulsating rhythm that made her want to sob with desire.

His arms slowly fell away, and he stepped a mere breath away from her.

"No!" The vehement protest escaped on a soft, ragged sigh when his warmth was taken from her.

"Hush, my darling," he consoled. "Let me look at you."

He placed his hands on her shoulders and gently grasped the edges of her robe. With a tormentingly slow movement he drew the garment down her arms until it slipped from his fingers to fall in a silken pool on the floor. With trembling fingers he took hold of her gown. He hesitated, his gaze burning into her eyes, waiting for her protest. When she swayed toward him, his heart soared, and his questing fingers began their work again, drawing the tiny ribbon straps over the flame-bathed shoulders and down her slender arms.

For one tormenting moment the fabric hung tauntingly on the coral-crested tips of her breasts. It finally surrendered, continuing its journey down her lush body. His breath caught in his throat as the gown pooled at her feet, and her full beauty was at last revealed to him.

She bent her head, and her hair fell like a curtain across her face. He longed to reach out and brush it aside, but he held himself back. Then Laura raised her eyes to his and bravely tossed her head, sending the chestnut curls flying to tumble down her back. Her spine stiffened, her shoulders squared, and she pulled herself up straight and proud before his gaze.

His heart threatened to burst through his chest. God! She was splendid. The tiny candle flame tinted her flawless skin the color of old ivory. Her breasts were full and firm and taut with desire. Her waist was small, almost fragile looking, before it flowed into the lush swell of her hips. The smooth flat expanse of her stomach was broken by the tantalizingly tiny dimple of her navel.

His eyes feasted on her beauty, traveling over every

inch of her in silent awe. He fervently vowed that his hands and his mouth would have the same pleasure before the night was over.

One step forward, and she was in his embrace once again. He swept her up and cradled her against his broad chest. Her arms went about his neck, and she buried her face in the curve of his shoulder, her senses bedeviled by the exotic, spicy smell that was Blake's alone. He covered the distance to the bed in quick long strides, bending to place her on the bed with a gentleness befitting a fragile piece of crystal.

"My God, you're beautiful. Never in my life have I wanted a woman as much as I want you," Blake murmured. Laura's heart sang with joy in response to his words.

Slowly Blake's hands went to the fastening of his trousers. In the twinkle of an eye he slid them down his lean, long legs and stepped free. Laura gasped at the magnificence of his hard, muscular body.

"Blake," she whispered longingly, and her hands reached out for him.

The bed dipped under his weight, and he stretched the length of his body close to hers, wrapping her in his arms until every possible inch of their bodies was touching. His breath was ragged and hot upon her bare skin, and he rained kisses in the tender curve of her neck, across the wildly beating pulse in her throat and down the gentle slope of her throbbing breasts. When he gently took one nipple in his mouth to suckle, she thought she would die of pleasure. The silken pull of his lips set up an answering pulsation in the pit of her stomach. And when his strong fingers traced a heated trail down the satin smoothness of her belly to finally dip into the secret warm recesses of her soul, she sobbed out his name.

He prolonged the sweet pleasure as long as he could, needing her to want him as much as he wanted her. Only when she cried his name over and over did he lift himself over her to slip gently between her thighs. He brushed a loving kiss across her lips and eased himself into her sweet depths. The thrust of his tongue matched the thrust of his body, muffling the small cry of pain that escaped her throat.

"Shh, my darling," he breathed against her lips, holding back his desire. "It's all right. The hurt is over. Relax, relax, trust me, my sweet." He tangled his fingers in the cascade of hair spread on his pillow and peppered kisses over her face and throat.

Slowly the white heat of desire began to build again, and her body moved of its own accord, tiny pulses at first, testing, teasing, searching for the answer to a timeless question. And his body began to match the beat; blending, thrusting, arching, joining the two of them in an ecstasy beyond his wildest dreams.

Laura's breath caught sharply in her throat. She was lost to reality, completely caught up in the tumultuous reactions of her body. There was a tensing in every cell of her being, and then a strange little ripple that began at the center of her womanhood. It grew and grew and grew, moving through her body like concentric circles on a pond.

Her arms went tight around Blake's neck, drawing his head down to lay against her own. Her body arched, her legs lifting to wrap tightly around his. Sensing the imminence of her release, he increased the rhythm of his thrusts. Each bold stroke drew a tiny sob from her lips until he gave one mighty final stroke and joined her in sweet release.

The candle had long since burned itself out. The room was cast in black velvet except for the patch of moonlight that splashed across the bed to bathe their sweat-sheened bodies in pale silver.

The tremors racking their bodies peaked and finally

ebbed away until they were but small aftershocks. Their heartbeats gradually slowed to normal.

Blake lifted his head and gazed in amazement at the woman beneath him.

"My God, Laura, you're unbelievable . . . so beautiful, so giving. I didn't want to hurt you—you know that, don't you?"

"It doesn't matter," she whispered back. "I quite forgot about it later." She blushed furiously at her bold statement and then offered him a small tremulous smile.

Blake chuckled. "You're wonderful! You don't know how I've longed to hold you like this. But even in my dreams I didn't expect such sweetness—"

Laura raised her head to meet his lips. She whisked a kiss over his sensuous mouth, teasing the tip of her tongue over the feathery softness of his mustache, remembering the feel of it on her body with deep satisfaction. She purred deep in her chest, contented beyond measure.

"I love you, Laura," Blake whispered in wonder.

Her heart soared in delight at his declaration. "And I love you, my darling," she whispered back. Her fingers lovingly traced the contours of his face.

"I don't ever want to be separated from you again."

"I feel the same way."

"I thought I'd lost you for good. I almost couldn't bear it. I didn't know what I was going to do, where I was going. I just knew that something precious had escaped me."

"Shh," she soothed, running gentle hands over his broad back. "I'm here. I'll always be here for you . . . for as long as you want me."

"I'll always want you. I want you to be my wife. I want to spend the rest of my life with you. Will you marry me, Laura?"

"Yes, Blake, yes, my darling." Tiny tears of joy pooled

in her eyes.

With great reluctance Blake gently eased down beside Laura, and then pulled her securely against him. She snuggled happily into his warmth. Soon they were sound asleep, arms and legs holding, clinging, intertwined in sweet contentment.

Chapter 29

Laura woke just before dawn, coming slowly back to reality as the pale pink fingers of the coming day probed delicately at the ebony sky. She stretched gently and then nestled blissfully back against Blake's enveloping warmth, head cushioned comfortably on his shoulder. Somewhere in the back of her mind she knew she should be embarrassed at waking up in his bed—but she wasn't. There was something so wonderfully comforting about the feel of Blake's hard male body next to hers that she couldn't imagine being sorry for what had happened.

She studied his slumbering face in the pale, misty light of promised day and was filled with such a sense of well-being and happiness that she had to swallow a sudden lump in her throat. Her hand rose to brush gently across the silky dark slash of his mustache; then she gave in to temptation and dipped her finger into the tiny intriguing cleft in his chin before tracing the strong curve of his jaw. He mumbled sleepily and flicked his hand at the tickling sensation her touch produced.

Laura smothered a giggle and then slowly leaned forward to rain soft little butterfly kisses across his bare chest. He mumbled again and flung his unencumbered arm out across the pillow. With devilish delight she flicked her warm pink tongue out and bestowed a quick little caress on the tantalizing copper nodule nestled in the midst of the forest of tawny fur. Blake's reaction was instantaneous. In the space of a heartbeat Laura was clasped in his embrace, staring up into sleepy, mirth-filled eyes.

"Woman, just what do you think you're doing?" he growled with mock ferocity as he settled his weight more comfortably upon her before capturing her lips with sweet savagery.

"Me?" she squeaked between kisses. "I don't recall having done a thing."

"Maybe I need to stimulate your memory." The silky tuft of his mustache dusted across her throat and down the slope of her breasts to capture one pert, coral-capped tip.

"That's not my memory you're stimulating, sir," she managed to gasp as his nimble fingers worked their way down the satin texture of her belly.

"Fancy that," he murmured and his lips sought hers again, his warm breath mingling with hers. "How could I have made such a mistake."

"Well, far be it from me to dissuade you from learning through trial and error. Some people can only profit by making their own mistakes." Her voice was a mere teasing whisper in his ear. "How very lucky for me that you seem to be that type of person." With innocent eagerness she returned his kisses, experiencing a sense of overwhelming self-satisfaction at the growing signs of his passion.

Blake was delighted with the open, unhesitating way she returned his lovemaking. He had been almost afraid that the cold morning light would bring tears and bitter recriminations. But Laura simply responded with un-bound affection and acknowledged need once again. None of his past experience had prepared him for such a total and unselfish response from a woman, especially one so innocent until a few hours ago.

To have been the one to bring her to womanhood made Blake's heart fill with tenderness. To have her respond to him with the same joy he himself felt this morning was almost beyond his understanding. He gloried in her response, knowing he was, indeed, a lucky man.

In the quiet moments after their loving, Blake was content to just lie beside Laura in the tangled bed linens. Her hair was fanned over his arm in smoky disarray, her head nestled against the hollow of his shoulder. Her soft breath stirred the amber curls on his chest in the most tantalizing manner. One warm, rounded leg was thrown, knee bent, over his loin, and her slender calf was insinuated most intimately between his thighs. Blake would have been content never to move again.

He still wasn't sure what strange hold this girl had over him, but there was no resistance on his part any longer. He knew without a doubt that he wanted to spend every night of the rest of his life holding her sweetness in his arms.

Laura nestled contentedly in his arms, her happy thoughts fluttering distractedly from one thing to another. A smile tugged at her mouth when she suddenly remembered Aunt Mary's uncomfortable and almost indecipherable effort to prepare her for the forthcoming rigors of marriage with Bernard Arbuckle: the confused, rambling, and infinitely meaningless instructions that dealt with vague references to a wife's "duty" to her husband and learning to "endure" and "think of other things." Poor Aunt Mary—she obviously didn't know what she was missing!

A delicious little feeling of wickedness flowed through Laura's veins. She'd *endure* Blake's attention anytime! Never in her life had she felt so gloriously happy.

Blake could almost feel the treacherous sun inching its

way back into the blue Texas sky. He knew he should get Laura back to her room quickly, but he kept putting it off. Too great was the temptation to enjoy one more minute of blissful snuggling. And then it was too late.

The spark of his desire was fanned by the soft contented little murmurs she made when he touched her. When her arms went tightly about his neck and her warm lips turned up to his in complete surrender, the flames burned past all hope of control.

After only a few minutes of soft touching, gentle stroking, warm kisses, they were both beyond reason. Young bodies arched, longing, crying for surcease, and they came together again.

When her small muffled cry of fulfillment echoed in his ear, he captured her mouth again and tightened his arms about her, dreading their imminent separation. She delighted in his weight, wrapping her arms and legs tightly about him to hold him as close as possible. She purred her contentment deep in her throat and rocked her heated center against him.

"Oh, no, you don't, you little vixen." Blake chuckled at her wantonness. "You tempt me almost beyond reason, but I've got to get you out of here."

"No." Laura made a small moue and cuddled even closer.

"Listen here, girl, I only have so much willpower and it's fast slipping away." He rolled to her side and then eased off the bed. "I'm not ready to battle Anthony over your honor. There're infinitely better ways to handle this—"

"But, Blake . . ." she pouted.

Blake stooped and gathered her gown and robe from the floor. "Now, be a good girl." He clasped her hands and pulled her into a sitting position. She giggled and went limp the minute he let go in order to lift the gown over her head. "Laura, stop acting like a child!"

374

"Oh," she purred up at him, "do you think I'm a child?"

"You know darn well I don't," he said. He made a concerted effort to sound stern and wound up grinning down at her instead. "But you've got to cooperate. Anthony could be awake any time now. Can't you imagine how angry he'd be to find you in here?"

Blake certainly didn't want to find out! What he wanted was time and the opportunity to ask for Laura's hand in marriage properly. And that meant keeping up normal appearances until he had Anthony's approval.

"Ummm," Laura replied absently, thoughts of Anthony far from her mind. Blake looked absolutely delicious—buck naked and magnificent in the pale pink light of morning: arms akimbo, standing sternly over her with her fragile silken gown clasped tightly in one fist.

Laura smiled sweetly and let her gaze wander provocatively. The results were instantaneous. She quickly pressed her hands over her mouth to still the cascade of delighted laughter that threatened to pour forth.

"Laura Nichols, you'd better behave or I'm going to spank you!" Blake whispered menacingly, quickly bringing his clenched fists forward from their resting place on his naked hips so that her gossamer gown offered a smidgen of cover.

"But I didn't *do* anything," Laura said in a strangled little voice. The laughter bubbled forth again. She stretched luxuriously and the sheet slipped provocatively. Blake cursed softly.

Laura had never felt so wonderful in her life. The knowledge that she affected him so completely fed her contentment. To share such glorious intimacy, to see the naked desire in his eyes again only moments after being bedded, intoxicated her much more than mere wine could ever do.

Her eyes burned a bright blue as she contemplated the magnificence of the man before her. "Are you sure you want me to leave?" she whispered.

"Ah, Laura, dear Lord, you're going to be the death of me!" He sank onto the edge of the bed and gathered her in his arms again. "If I had my way you'd never leave my sight, but we have to be reasonable. It won't be for long, I promise. I'll speak with Anthony at the first possible opportunity. We'll be married as soon as we can make the arrangements. Then we'll never have to be separated again."

"Oh, yes, Blake. Yes, yes." She hungrily returned his kisses.

An alarm went off in Blake's head. He jumped up and backed away. "Oh, no, you don't! Put this on." He thrust the gown toward her. "And get back to your room, you insatiable little hussy." When she finally climbed from his bed, he leaned over to deliver a soft little spat to her delectable derriere for further emphasis.

She made a face at him and then slipped the gown over her head. He grabbed up the trousers he'd discarded last night and slipped them back on.

"I always heard that men lose interest after they've had their way with a woman," Laura said, pouting prettily as she retrieved her robe and eased her arms into it.

Blake growled and pounced, pulling her into his arms with mock ferocity. She squealed in delight. "I'll show you 'lose interest' if you don't watch out! Now, get out that door before the whole house is awake!" Shirtless and barefoot, he pushed her gently toward the door.

"I'll miss you," she murmured, raising on tiptoe to nip at his earlobe.

"Good Lord, I'll miss you, too. But I'll see you at breakfast. Now behave yourself!"

Blake returned her smile with an equally delirious one of his own and then opened the door carefully. He poked his head slowly through the crack and peered up and down the still dark hallway before escorting Laura quickly back to her room.

She blew him a little kiss just before her door closed between them. A smile wreathed his face, and he took the time for a deep calming breath. Hands in the pocket of his pants, Blake almost swaggered back to his room.

He felt as though he could lick the world.

"Good morning, Anthony."

Anthony looked up from his plate as Laura sailed happily into the dining area. Her eyes held the sparkle of diamonds, her cheeks were flushed with rosiness. The hem of her pale apricot gown swished merrily against the polished floor with each bouncy step. She looked so vibrant and alive that he had to smile in response.

"Isn't it the most glorious morning you ever saw?" She threw her arms around his neck and planted an exuberant kiss on his forehead before plopping into her chair.

"Morning, senorita," said Rosita, entering with a steaming cup of coffee for Laura. "You would like some breakfast?"

"Oh, yes, please! I'm famished!"

Rosita scurried off to prepare a plate, returning shortly with a heavily laden dish.

"Yum! Everything looks wonderful. Thank you, Rosita." Laura dug in with great enthusiasm.

Anthony marveled at his sister. Could this possibly be the same girl who'd been moping around for weeks? Good heavens, if he'd known Stratford had had that much negative effect on his sister's happiness, he'd have thrown him out ages ago.

Laura had barely started on her enormous breakfast when Anthony heard the clump of boots down the stairs and across the parlor floor. Uh-oh, he thought. Blake must have finally gotten over his animosity about the race enough to come home. Anthony fervently hoped Blake's mood wouldn't be as gloomy as it had been at the Moore's just before he'd disappeared. He really didn't want anything to spoil Laura's happiness this morning.

"Good morning, Anthony, Laura," said Blake with an unexpectantly broad smile as he entered the room. He quickly crossed to the table and took the chair beside Laura's. Rosita soon had a cup of coffee setting on the table before him.

"Morning, Blake," Anthony quickly replied.

"Why, good morning, Blake." Laura dimpled devilishly, cutting mischievous blue eyes his way. "How are you this fine morning?"

"Couldn't be better," he replied, a matching twinkle in his eye.

"I do hope you slept well," Laura purred.

Blake choked on his coffee. He coughed and spluttered until Anthony finally reached over and pounded him on the back a few times.

"Are you all right?" Anthony asked, concern apparent in his voice.

"Yes, fine, thank you, just fine," Blake finally managed to gasp.

They all settled back down, and Anthony and Laura resumed their meals. Rosita brought Blake a plate, and he raptly turned his attention to its contents. Between bites Blake and Laura carried on a seemingly meaningless little conversation, with occasional remarks addressed Anthony's way, all of it punctuated at great frequency by small laughs and almost idiotic smiles.

Anthony watched the curious banter between Laura and Blake with great interest. Ummm. William was gone, and suddenly Blake and Laura were both deliriously happy. Anthony cocked one eyebrow and gave them a

378

thorough appraisal.

Well, what do you know! It appeared that he'd been right about those two, after all. Blake must have heard in town that William left yesterday, so he'd hightailed it back to the ranch this morning. Well, well! Anthony smiled smugly.

Anthony quickly made up his mind to do everything he could to promote a relationship between the two. He'd decided long ago that Blake was a good man—just the sort of fellow that Laura needed. What harm could a little brotherly pushing do? Might even get these two to admit their feelings for one another.

Anthony's intentions were also colored by the fact that he really wanted Blake to stay in Texas—preferably around Washington-on-the-Brazos—and settle down. He'd always been outspoken about the need for more good men in the state, and as far as Anthony was concerned, Blake fit the bill perfectly. Well, no time like the present to get the ball rolling.

Laura listened attentively as Anthony told Blake about some land for sale just south of his own spread.

"It's a good place, lots of water, plenty of grazing. You ought to ride over and take a look at it today."

Laura slowly eased her foot out of her slipper. She pushed it from under the voluminous skirt and edged it sideways toward Blake.

"How far did . . . oh!"

"What?" asked Anthony, looking up from his plate.

"Uh . . . how far did you say it was?" asked Blake, finding it suddenly very hard to concentrate on the conversation. He flashed Laura a warning look, and she smiled demurely back at him before genteelly stabbing the last bit of sausage on her plate and popping it into her mouth with a rapt expression.

"Couple of hours. If you started out pretty soon, you could have a good look-see and be back before supper,"

Anthony prompted. "Uh . . . how about taking Laura along? I'm sure she'd enjoy a chance to get out. I don't think she's been over to that part of the country yet. Be good for her." There! That was certainly subtle enough, wasn't it? Anthony was smugly pleased with the ingenuity of his impromptu plan to throw the two of them together.

"Why, Anthony, what an interesting idea," Laura exclaimed sweetly. She turned to Blake and batted her eyelashes. "Would you mind very much if I came along for the ride, Blake?" Her toes traveled up his ankle.

He tugged at his collar, sudden heat flowing through his body. "Why . . . uh . . . not at all, Laura. I'd be happy for some company."

"I'll have Rosita pack a nice lunch so you two won't have to rush back." Anthony smiled expansively. Why, matchmaking was really quite easy. Studying their innocent, beaming faces, he was sure they didn't suspect a thing!

"I really ought to feel guilty," murmured Blake as he nipped teasingly at Laura's earlobe.

"But you'd have hurt Anthony's feelings if you hadn't brought me along," Laura was quick to assure him.

"Yes, but I don't think this is exactly what he had in mind when he made his suggestion."

"Well, you shouldn't be so hard on yourself," Laura drawled. "It *is* the inevitable conclusion of his little matchmaking scheme. We just moved our timetable ahead of his a little bit."

"Somehow I think Anthony would have sandwiched a preacher in there somewhere before we got to this part," Blake commented wryly. "I'm going to talk to him . . . tomorrow morning, or tonight if I get a chance." He brushed a lingering kiss on her mouth. "I want you to be mine—"

"I am yours." She gave a little sigh and twined her arms tighter about his neck.

"Legally."

She smiled softly, teasingly, her gaze bonded to his. "If you insist."

"I certainly do. Do you think I'm going to take a chance on losing you again? I think I'd better tie you down while I've got you believing that I'm the man you love."

"Ummm, I certainly do believe that!" she whispered emphatically.

He lifted his weight from her and rolled to his side. She shifted position, turning to settle her head comfortably against his chest, fingertips trailing playfully through the thick mat of hair. The sun streaming through the wind-kissed leaves danced a dappled pattern of light and shadow over their sated bodies. The warm Texas air caressed their damp skin, and they drifted into blissful sleep.

Chapter 30

"Well, of course you have my blessings!"

Laura and Blake stood inches apart in front of Anthony's easy chair. They shot a quick glance of relief and happiness at each other as Anthony jumped up and hurried toward them to pump Blake's hand in an enthusiastic handshake.

"I couldn't be happier with your choice, Laura." He hugged his glowing sister exuberantly. "Right, my dear?" Anthony asked, turning back to Maria who, in slight shock from the sudden turn of events, still lingered in her place on the sofa.

"But, of course, Antonio, *mi amor*. I am thrilled to hear this news." Maria even sounded like she meant it—and, actually, she did.

Mentally she was congratulating herself on the fact that the little problem about Miguel's foolish interest in Laura had been neatly solved—and all without a turn of her own hand. She could now discard the numerous plans she had desperately been toying with the past weeks.

Although this hadn't been the first time Maria had found it necessary to temper Miguel's hot blood, his infatuation with Laura hadn't seemed quite as transient as the ones in the past. She'd even been afraid that Miguel was actually beginning to fancy himself in love with the little snip. Maria had grown increasingly worried as his interest grew and threatened to become more than a passing physical attraction.

But Laura and Blake's news had flooded her with relief. Her worries were over. And there was no way Miguel could even remotely blame her for interfering. Laura and Blake had been obliging enough to take care of the situation all by themselves.

Now that Laura had been removed as a threat to Miguel's continued loyalty, Maria could almost like the girl. She rose languidly from the sofa and majestically made her way to the center of the room where the others were still hugging and backslapping.

"I wish you much happiness, Laura, dear." Maria pressed her smooth cheek against her sister-in-law's. "I'm positive you are doing the right thing. We must make plans for the wedding immediately. Surely you don't intend to wait?"

Laura almost blushed. "Well, no, we had thought we might go ahead with the ceremony before too long."

"Yes," agreed Blake, nodding his tawny head. "A few weeks perhaps. Just enough time to let Laura make the necessary preparations . . . and let me wrap up my business obligations. I want to be able to settle down and not worry about my . . . uh, partners back East. I'll make arrangements to telegraph them my final recommendations and put in my resignation just as soon as possible."

"Wonderful!" boomed Anthony. "Anything you want, you just let us know. Why, we can have the ceremony right here at the house. How would that be, Laura?"

"That would be lovely, Anthony," Laura agreed quickly, moving closer to Blake and slipping her hand into his.

Once upon a time she'd dreamed of a fairy-tale wedding with billowing white dress and long trailing veil. Now she no longer cared about such things. In her newfound maturity she realized that the happy moments in life would not come from such material things, but from the bonds of love and friendship and trust she would share with Blake. She was more than willing to forgo all those trivialities for the privilege of spending each and every day with him.

She was as frustrated as he in trying to snatch a few moments alone. It would be bliss not to have to hide their love from the rest of the world any longer.

"Now, I want you to know that you're more than welcome to stay here with us as long as you need to," Anthony assured them.

Blake grinned in appreciation of the offer. "Thank you. I'm hoping to make arrangements to buy that land we looked at yesterday as soon as possible. Of course, it'll take time to put a house up, but at least we'll have something to look forward to."

"Well, it won't take much time to put up a starter cabin. The local neighbors are always glad to pitch in and help. You know Texans," said Anthony with a loud laugh. "Always looking for an excuse to celebrate, and we sure do a powerful lot of celebrating after a house-raising!"

Blake grinned self-consciously, indulging himself with mental pictures of a small, secluded cabin where he and Laura could lock themselves away from the rest of the world.

"I don't know what to say."

"Don't need to say anything. Just name the date for the wedding, and I'll take care of the rest," Anthony assured him.

"Yes, we must make it soon," urged Maria, wanting to

384

get the ceremony over with before anything else could go wrong. "We can send Pedro into town tomorrow with a message for Reverend Crawley."

"Splendid," agreed Anthony, smiling benevolently. He couldn't help but gloat to himself just a little over the results of his matchmaking. Why, if it hadn't been for him and his tricky maneuverings, the two of them might never have realized how they felt. He rocked back on his heels and beamed at the others with genuine self-satisfaction.

Maria tilted her head, eyeing Laura intently. "I do believe we could make over my wedding gown for you."

"Why, Maria!" Laura exclaimed with shock at Maria's unexpected generosity. "How very sweet of you to offer. I never dreamed of such a thing. But, really, I couldn't. Wouldn't you prefer to save it?"

Maria waved her hand. "No, no. It's a beautiful dress. It should be enjoyed. I think it will fit for the most part. We will need to add another flounce to lengthen it, but that shouldn't be much problem for Miss Coggins."

"Well, thank you. I really don't know what to say." Laura cast a glowing look at Blake. Perhaps the heavens were going to be doubly kind to her. She'd have Blake *and* a beautiful wedding. What more could a girl ask for?

"Come," ordered Maria, almost imperiously. "We will go up to my room so you can try the dress on. Rosita can pin it, and we will send it to Miss Coggins when Pedro goes to town tomorrow." She swept from the room, fully expecting Laura to obey.

Laura looked at Blake, gave a small shrug of her shoulders and did just as Maria expected, leaving the men to continue their discussion on purchase arrangements for the land Blake planned to buy.

*   *   *

385

"You're lying—"

"I am *not* lying!" Maria spat at Miguel, stomping across the small clearing to follow him to the edge of the ridge. Their tethered horses whinnied and shied away at the sound of her angry voice. "I'm afraid you're just going to have to resign yourself to the fact that this is one conquest you won't be able to make."

Miguel spun around, his face a bronze mask of fury. "Don't push me too far, Maria. You might regret it."

She stamped her foot and cocked her hands on her hips. "Don't you dare tell *me* what to do! After all I've done for you—"

"I never forced you to do anything."

"No! I did it all for love! I have lied for you, stolen for you, even given myself to a man I do not love—all for you!"

"Come, come, my dear," Miguel said with a wicked smirk. "Surely you admit that greed and ambition have played their part in your sacrifices."

"And why shouldn't I be rewarded for my efforts? I have earned my right to rule at your side," she hissed at him. "Have I not stood behind you all these years and dreamed your dream with you? Have I not done everything I could possibly do to help you fulfill that dream?"

Miguel cast a derisive look over his black-clad shoulder and went back to studying the azure Texas sky.

Maria was infuriated with his continued disregard. "I have turned my back on your little infidelities in the past, but I will *not* stand by and let you make a fool of yourself over the sister of the man you forced me to marry!"

Miguel spun and grabbed her arms, jerking her up against his rock-hard body. "I forced you to do nothing! You formulated the plan as much as I did. In fact, it was you who sent word to me about the great and rich Senor Nichols who had fallen so madly in love with you. It was you who said the ranch would be a perfect cover! And you were the one who thought of introducing me as your cousin. I would have been content to stay in Mexico and raise volunteers for the revolution!"

"Yes, and no matter how many men you could talk into joining your fight, you'd still be sitting there trying to get the necessities to begin the revolution if it weren't for me! You could never have raised the money or gotten your hands on all those supplies you have hidden at Sunfire Valley without my help."

"Robbery works as well in Mexico as it does in Texas, Maria. I've managed to attain quite a bit in that manner, my dear, in case you forget. I could have obtained the rest of it without your help. It just might have taken a little longer."

"What about all the supplies that we took from the ranch? It would have taken you years to accumulate such large amounts!"

"Yes, I'll have to admit that was a brilliant idea on your part. But don't fool yourself, I would have managed by myself."

"But it was my marriage to Anthony that gave you the opportunity you needed."

"You've never protested having to marry Anthony. I certainly haven't seen you turning down any of the baubles and fancy dresses he's showered on you. In fact, I do believe you've enjoyed playing the grand lady living in your fancy house—while I sleep in the workers' quarters!" His look was scathing.

"Why should I turn anything down?" Her eyes sparked black fire. "You know I've earned everything he's given me! Don't you see? The sooner we begin the revolution, the sooner we can take our rightful place in the palace in Mexico City!"

"Then quit crying that you've been so mistreated. You knew what you were getting into from the first."

"Yes, I did, but I didn't know it was going to take so long. I'm tired of all of this! I want to go back home!"

"You're being ridiculous! It has taken time to obtain the supplies and then smuggle them down into Mexico. We're just about finished with that. There's only a small amount left at the valley. The plan has worked perfectly so far. Don't spoil things now!"

"Me! Spoil things!" she shrieked, struggling to free herself from his iron grip. "*You're* the one who's ruining our plans. If you hadn't kept delaying things, we'd already be on our way back to Mexico."

"It was necesary. We had to have enough guns and ammunition to arm the people who wait for our return, not to mention medicine and clothing. How do you propose to fight a revolution without the proper supplies, you stupid woman?"

"Ha! You can't fool me! You forget that I know you better than anyone. It's not the supplies. You've been delaying because of Laura! I know it. Don't try to lie to me! It's time to get the last of the materials loaded up and get back to Mexico. Now!"

"You know nothing!" Miguel ground out furiously. "And what I do is none of your business! I will make the decision when to strike! I *alone*, do you hear me?"

"No! You should already have alerted the men in Mexico. Now Santa Anna is back, and it will be that much harder to recruit enough men to overthrow the government. You should have gone back when Paredes was in power. He was weak. Look how easily he was overthrown! You will never succeed if Santa Anna gets a stronghold on the people again!"

"I *will succeed!* Don't ever say that I won't! Mexico *will* rise to greatness again—under my rule!" He flung her violently from him, and she stumbled and fell to the soft, cushioning grass. Her hair came loose from its pins and fell about her shoulders in a glorious dark cloud.

Enraged, she scrambled back up and flew at him, tiny fists beating uselessly at his brawny chest. "How dare you treat me like this!"

"I dare anything!" he said darkly. He grabbed her wrists and pinned them behind her, their bodies pressed tightly together. His black eyes seared into hers. "And it's time you realized that."

She grew quite still when she recognized the sudden spark of passion in his eyes. Her breath came more quickly as the old familiar hunger grew, and she felt the growing urgency of his desire. Her heart beat faster as they continued to glare at each other.

At last his lips captured hers in a savage kiss, his tongue stroking, probing, thrusting until she could no longer breathe. "I always like you best when you're full of fire, Maria," he whispered. "I think it's because we're two of a kind."

She melted against him, her knees suddenly turned to liquid. A white-hot fire raged through her veins.

"Miguel," she breathed, arching against him. "Please."

They dropped to the ground, tearing at each other's clothing until their hungry hands and eyes and mouths could seek their fill.

Sullenly watching as Blake rode out across the pasture, Miguel was in a black mood and had been ever since Maria had so spitefully delivered her message of Laura's impending marriage. Maria was smugly sure that the issue was closed. But it was far from settled as far as Miguel was concerned. He had no intention of giving

389

Laura up.

Laura was the one he wanted, and he intended to have her. No matter what. Maria was becoming too much trouble. She'd served her purpose. It was time to get rid of her.

He watched Blake grow smaller and smaller as Blackjack galloped across the field. There had to be a way to get rid of him, like he'd gotten rid of Stratford. Just what was it Blake was up to, anyway? He rode out every day and sometimes didn't come in until dark. Perhaps it would be wise to follow Blake and see how he spent his time.

Miguel glanced toward the house and then back at Midnight's corral. He knew the big black stud would be able to catch Blake. Midnight could outrun the best of them—as he'd proven time and again. Anthony didn't much like Midnight being ridden for every-day use—not even by himself. He pampered the stallion and worried over him, wanting to save him for the races and for breeding. But this wouldn't be the first time Miguel had slipped off with Midnight. Anthony had never been the wiser. Miguel wasn't too worried about his finding out this time.

With long, angry strides he crossed to the barn and retrieved Midnight's saddle. In mere moments he was saddled up and on his way after Blake.

For the rest of the day Miguel followed Blake at a safe distance, watching his every move, wondering about the purpose behind his seemingly random ride. Each time Blake stopped to talk with ranch hands or field workers, Miguel would watch from afar, debating with himself as to what Blake was trying to accomplish.

After Blake rode away, Miguel would sometimes ride down and talk with the men himself—especially if they were his countrymen. It was easy to trade a few jokes, comment on the weather or ask about families, and then ask what the big gringo had wanted. The men were more than eager to repeat their conversations with Blake.

Little by little a pattern began to form. Blake was looking for information, and the clues pointed more and more toward the fact that he was looking for information about Laura's brother. He continued to ask small, meaningless questions about Anthony's comings and goings of one group, and then ask another group of men if they'd ever noticed any strangers on Anthony's land, and had the senor ever been seen with them.

Blake never said enough to alert any of them to the peculiarity of his interrogation, but Miguel began to piece the clues together, and they all continued to point toward a very strange interest in Anthony. He puzzled about this curious turn of events as he waited in the shadows of a stand of trees for Blake to put some distance between them, his mind flitting from one random memory to another.

Suddenly he slapped his forehead with the flat of his hand. *Madre Dios!* Why had he never made the connection before? Laura had been on the stagecoach that he'd raided last spring—the time when they'd been forced to shoot that man who carried papers identifying him as a United States agent. Miguel was positive of that; he'd never forgotten that first glimpse of her. It had been the beginning of his desire for the beautiful *Americana.* For a long time he'd been terribly worried that she might recognize him. But she hadn't.

His strong, lean fingers rubbed his temple in confusion. None of this made any sense. There'd been only one man on that stagecoach. Blake hadn't been there, Miguel was sure of that.

No, wait! Miguel knew that Laura and Blake knew each other before coming to the ranch but he'd never paid much attention to the matter. He assumed they'd met in town. As far as Saunders was concerned, Miguel only knew that Blake was supposed to be looking for land to buy. But somewhere in the deep recesses of his mind Miguel was remembering a random comment or two. What was it about Blake's partner having been killed during their journey to Texas?

Could that possibly mean that the agent had been Blake's partner? Dear God! What a thought! Miguel didn't know for sure, but resolving this sudden fear was much more important than following Blake for the rest of the day.

He turned Midnight in the direction of the house and slapped the reins hard against the black-velvet neck. The horse lunged forward. Maria would know the whole story.

And this time he'd listen!

The soft, warm night surrounded Blake and Laura. He reached to pull the sheet over them and snuggled her into the crook of his arm. They had tried time and again to stay away from each other—but it never worked. One or the other would come tiptoeing in the middle of the night to claim a few moments of rhapsody.

Just a few more weeks and they could stop these silly games. There'd be no more sneaking around in the wee hours of the morning to appease the fires that raged within. They longed for the time when they could climb into the big bed together every night and wake up every morning in each other's arms.

Blake sighed with contentment. They'd come so close to losing each other. It made what they shared now even more precious. "Ummm," he breathed against the crown of her head.

392

"What?" she asked softly.

"Happy, that's all. I was just thinking how foolish I was. I did some pretty stupid things—"

"So did I."

"Yeah, I won't argue that point. But I really almost finished us off when I went in to town after that damn race. I was so mad I didn't care if I ever saw you again." He gave a soft chuckle.

Her fingers drew a pattern through the soft whorls of hair on his chest, brushing lightly over his sensitive nipples. He sucked in a harsh breath.

She turned her face toward his, searching his eyes in the pale moonlight. "Would . . . would you ever have tried to contact me if you'd stayed gone?"

His arms tightened around her. "I don't think I could have helped myself."

"I'd already decided I was going to write you . . . that I wasn't going to give up until I could at least apologize for my behavior."

"Well, that's nice to know."

"But, you know what, Blake?" She frowned as she remembered. "When I was trying to decide what to do, I realized I didn't even know where to write you or how to get ahold of you."

Blake shifted uncomfortably.

"I still don't know. How strange that I'm soon going to be your wife and I really don't know anything about your past—"

"Uh, Laura . . ." It was time, time to tell her something, part of the truth, anything. He couldn't spend the rest of his life lying about his past. He didn't have to tell her everything. That certainly wasn't necessary. Heaven forbid she ever found out about Anthony's implication in his assignment!

But he was almost positive now that Anthony wasn't

393

involved. He couldn't be! Blake had finally made a decision. In the absence of any real evidence, he was going to go with his gut feeling and believe that Anthony was innocent. He intended to leave for Louisiana in a day or two and send one final message. He'd clear Anthony's name and turn in his resignation at the same time.

"I . . . uh . . . think I'd better explain a little something to you." He swallowed hard.

"What?" She turned her trusting face to his.

"I came to Texas on assignment."

"Assignment? What kind of assignment?"

"For the government."

"The government? I don't understand."

"I know." He brushed his fingers through his tousled hair. "That's who I work for. I was sent out here to scout around . . . uh . . . President Polk wanted to know how the people felt about the possibility of war with Mexico."

Laura shifted, sitting up in bed and turning so she could watch Blake as he continued his explanation. The moonlight tipped her pert nipples with silver. He found it very hard to concentrate on what he was trying to say.

"But why didn't you tell anyone?" Laura asked.

"It's easier to get a real feel for what's going on if people don't know you work for the government."

"Oh." She nibbled at her bottom lip.

"Yeah, that's why I had to go to Louisiana—to telegraph the department about what I'd found out."

"And what did you find out?"

"Well, that everyone is loyal to the United States and willing to fight in the war."

"Was the president pleased?" She giggled softly. "My goodness, to think you know the president! I'm very impressed."

"Well, don't be. I'm way down the ladder. I've never even met the man. All I do is pass the news on to my superior, and he handles the rest."

394

Her eyes grew worried. "It still sounds rather exciting. You . . . you won't mind giving all that up to stay here with me?"

"No," he replied, his voice husky with emotion. "No, I won't mind at all." He cupped her shoulders and gently pulled her back against him, wrapping her carefully in his arms like a precious jewel.

Chapter 31

Miguel waited for just the right moment. He was too smart to try to get to Laura about Blake the same way he'd handled the situation with William. Two serious talks would be just too much for coincidence. No, what he had to do was plant the seeds of suspicion in her mind so that she'd never realize he'd planned it that way and let human nature take its own course.

Maria had confirmed his worst fears about Blake, but he felt sure he'd found a way to solve the problem. Miguel knew how strong Laura's feelings were for her brother. Just a hint that he was in danger because of Blake would be all it would take. And, on the outside chance that this plan didn't work, Miguel had no compulsion about shooting Blake in the back while he was out on one of his little excursions. Either way, the situation was well in hand.

It took almost a week for the right opportunity to present itself, but Miguel's patience finally paid off.

Laura ambled down to the barn just at sunset to sneak Sugar an apple as she did on occasion. It was warm in the house and rather boring with only Anthony and Maria. She was restless because Blake was quite late getting home today, so she sought diversion with a walk. It was very quiet along the path. The ranch hands had evidently gone to their quarters. The chirp of the crickets, the occasional call of a bird was all that broke the heavy silence. Laura was alone as she entered the barn.

Miguel had been waiting for just such a chance. It was so very easy for him to casually enter the barn on pretext of a chore, pretend surprise at finding Laura there, and then spend a few minutes in relaxed conversation. Miguel was even smug enough to offer congratulations on Laura's forthcoming marriage—a perfect way to divert any suspicions on her part later—before he nonchalantly moved across the barn and began to sort through the tack.

"Why, thank you very much, Miguel," she replied, genuinely pleased that he would take the time to express his good wishes. Sugar nibbled daintily at Laura's palm, seeking more treats. She laughed and rubbed briskly between the mare's ears and scolded her. "My, you're so greedy tonight!"

"I am sure you and Senor Saunders will be very happy. He appears to be a fine man," Miguel continued smoothly, looking up from his work to smile slightly as Sugar bumped Laura's shoulder insistently with her head.

"Yes, so he is." Laura turned and leaned comfortably against the stall, Sugar's curious nose draped over her calico-clad shoulder. The pungent sweet smell of fresh hay filled the air. Dust motes danced in the last sunbeams.

"Tell me" said Miguel casually, "does he still plan to buy some land and raise cattle as I have heard him speak about before?"

"Yes, I think he's made a final decision about that land to the southeast. It's a lovely place. I think we'll be very happy there. Why do you ask?"

Miguel turned his dark eyes upon her. "I was just

wondering. The men have been talking . . ."

"Talking? About what?"

Miguel flicked a hand absently. "Oh, it's nothing. Perhaps I shouldn't even mention it."

And now Laura's curiosity was piqued. Anything that had to do with Blake, she wanted to know about. She pushed away from the rough planking of the stall. With a few quick steps she was beside Miguel. He continued to check the harnesses hanging on the wall, intent on finding any that might need repair. She raised her hand and laid it gently on his arm.

"Now, Miguel, you know a lady doesn't like to be kept in the dark. What did they say about Blake?" She turned her face up to his, an enticing smile wreathing her mouth.

Miguel continued his inspection as if nothing were amiss. "Oh, it was something unimportant, I'm sure. Some of the men have just mentioned that he asks a lot of questions about Senor Nichols. They thought perhaps he was going to stay here and be his partner.

Laura frowned. "Well, no. Actually we'll stay here until we can get a house built, but they certainly haven't discussed being partners. At least, not that I know of." Now her curiosity was really aroused. "What kind of questions was he asking?"

"Oh, things like how much time Senor Nichols spends out on the range, how often he's gone, and how many supplies are used." Miguel grew still, frowning as if trying to recall some random tidbit. "Oh, yes, I think he asked some questions about strangers being seen around here . . ."

"Strangers?" asked Laura in a bewildered manner.

Miguel shrugged. "Perhaps he's afraid someone else is going to buy the land. It's nothing, I'm sure."

"Ummm," Laura mused, trying to decipher this odd

bit of information.

"And there is always the chance that the men did not understand him too well. You know, the English. Some of them still have a great problem with it, and Senor Saunders does not speak very much Spanish."

"But why would he be asking such questions about Anthony? What purpose would it serve?"

Miguel draped two worn harnesses over his arm and prepared to leave. "I'm sure I wouldn't know. It's bound to be some sort of misunderstanding . . . nothing to worry about. I probably shouldn't have brought it up."

"Yes, you're probably right," Laura agreed, but the conversation continued to bother her.

Miguel tipped his head in Laura's direction. "Good night, Senorita Laura. Pleasant dreams." He was filled with self-satisfaction. The seeds had been planted.

In the twinkle of an eye he was gone, and she was left alone. Sugar nickered softly, begging for another apple. The horse in the last stall shuffled and turned, rustling the straw.

Laura's fingers went unconsciously to the tumble of curls over her shoulder, winding and unwinding one long chestnut strand as she tried to make sense of what Miguel had said. She finally gave Sugar an absentminded pat on her soft velvet-smooth nose and wandered out of the barn.

A little breeze teased at her cheeks as she walked over to Midnight's corral and leaned against the high log fence to enjoy the solitude and cool air for just a few more minutes. In the back of her mind, she was still pondering Miguel's strange remarks.

Suddenly Midnight was taken with one of his spirited displays of energy. He reared and charged the fence, turning sharply right in front of her to thunder back across his corral like a black whirlwind. Laura gave a small scream and jumped back.

That damn horse! Something about him had always frightened her. He was too spirited, too wild. And he looked too much like the big black horse the leader of the ambush had ridden.

No—he looked *exactly* like the horse the leader had ridden! But it couldn't be. Laura's eyes grew large and frightened as she stood rooted to the spot, watching the huge steed plunge and rear, kicking his heels high in the air with nervous energy.

As she watched, a scene began to play itself in her mind—those horrifying minutes of the ambush.

She could see it so clearly: the place, the restless stamping horses held by the tall, thin bandido, the fat man who'd touched her with his grimy fingers. A shiver ran up her spine. She cringed as if his hands were actually violating her again.

And she heard the harsh Spanish words of the leader atop the big black horse. Words she didn't understand, but their meaning had been obvious. He had made that horrible man leave her alone.

Why? It was obvious that the passengers meant nothing to them. The bandidos wanted only the money. John had warned her that their lives hung by a thread. Men as ruthless as those thought nothing of killing.

And John had been right. Just one provocation was all it had taken for John to lose his life. They'd shot him down without blinking an eye. What had it been? Something about the papers he carried in his wallet. Had they realized he was an agent—just like Blake? She wasn't sure. All that remained in her mind was the memory of a sudden explosion of gunfire and the horror of John sprawled in the dust, his life's blood seeping slowly into the ground. She'd expected to feel the impact of a bullet at any minute.

Then suddenly the leader had whispered his harsh instructions and the men had quickly obeyed, riding away and leaving her alone—but alive. She remembered how the dark man had reined in his horse at the top of the hill to turn and gaze at her for one last, long minute before galloping after his men.

Why had he protected her? Why had he intervened and saved her from his men and from death? Who was he?

She didn't even know what he looked like. His face had been shadowed almost completely by the bandanna and his broad-brimmed black hat. She couldn't even judge his size or height; he had looked enormous atop that wild black horse.

That horse—Midnight! She forced her frightened eyes to focus on Anthony's favorite horse.

Oh, God! Anthony's favorite horse. The phrase rang again and again in her mind. He never let anyone ride that horse. He had even been reluctant to let Miguel ride Midnight in the race at the Moores'.

She backed slowly away from the corral as if to back away from the ugly thought that was creeping into her mind. Surely it couldn't have been Anthony leading that raid! Why? Why would he do such a thing? Her mind refused to accept the insidious thought. It didn't even make sense.

But then she remembered: A lot of things didn't make sense. The missing supplies, for one. Why were so many things ordered? Where did they go? Miguel and Maria had both said that Anthony took care of all the disbursements. Why would they lie?

And what about the times Laura had tried to talk to Anthony about it? He'd always managed to sidestep the issue. He always promised he'd take the time to go over the books with her—but he never had. He had avoided any discussion on the subject. And she reluctantly remembered that he'd tried to talk her out of the work in the first place.

But why? her mind cried. Why would Anthony do such a thing? For Maria? Could he possibly be so enamored of his Mexican wife that he would betray his country? For what purpose?

Granted, he'd never spoken badly about the Mexican people. He seemed to want what was best for Texas. Was it possible that he thought Mexican rule would be best for the state? Then why would he spend so much time in Austin?

And then Laura realized in horror that the only proof she had that Anthony ever went to Austin was his word. He simply said he was going, disappeared for days or weeks, and then returned. What about the time Blake brought news of the raids on the supply trains from town? Hadn't Anthony been gone then?

Laura clutched her hands tightly together. A chill swept through her, and her flesh shivered and puckered despite the warmth of the evening. It couldn't be! It just couldn't be. There was an explanation for all of this. Anthony wasn't guilty of such horrible things. She *knew* he wasn't! No one could ever convince her that he was.

But why was Blake asking such strange questions about Anthony? He'd admitted to being an agent for the government. He was supposed to be checking the mood of the state regarding the war with Mexico. Why would he be making inquiries about Anthony unless—unless he, too, was worried about her brother's involvement somehow?

Laura paced restlessly in front of the barn. The bright orange ball of the sun sank closer and closer to the horizon, and night prepared to drape its velvet cloak across the land. The crickets continued to chirr. A mockingbird called a shrill, sharp note that hung in the hazy air. But Laura heard nothing and scarcely noticed the waning light.

Her mind was in turmoil. There were too many confusing elements to make any sense of the situation—and too much emotional involvement on her part for her to be able to think rationally. She loved Blake and she knew he had a job to do. But Anthony was *family*. He was her *brother*, for God's sake! How could Blake even have considered that Anthony might be implicated?

Her hands flew to her face, trembling fingers pressed against her lips. Anthony was *her* brother, and *she* was guilty of thinking the same horrible things!

And then she remembered the loving older brother who had kissed away her childish tears, who'd mended toys and played games, who'd sat by her bed many a night after their parents' death and told her beautiful stories so she could fall asleep.

No! She was wrong. She had to be. About everything. If Blake had even considered such a thing, he'd have told her. He wouldn't hide something that important from her.

But he hid the truth about who he was, didn't he? her mind said mockingly.

Yes, but—

But nothing. He only told you the truth after you questioned him. Would he have ever told you if you hadn't forced the issue?

Of course, he would have!

Are you so sure? What else has he lied about?

Nothing!

Did he lie when he said he loved you? Was he using you to get to Anthony? Did he plan this whole thing? Plan it long ago? After all, he knew your name and that you were going to your brother's before the stage ever

403

left Galveston. If Anthony was his target even back then, that would have given him the perfect opportunity. What more could he ask for? All he needed to do was win your trust.

"Laura . . ."

Laura uttered a small, startled cry as Blake's voice shattered the stillness of the dusk. In her anxiety, she hadn't heard his approach.

He swung down from Blackjack and walked toward her. He looked so happy to see her. He was tired and dusty from his ride, and his shirt was sweat circled under the arms, but he was still so handsome it made her heart ache. "I'm sorry, darling. I didn't mean to frighten you." He smiled and reached a hand toward her.

She backed away.

"What's the matter?" His brow furrowed, and the smile dropped quickly from his lips. "Laura, what is it? What's wrong?" He quickly looped Blackjack's reins over a tree limb.

Her voice quivered with emotion. "Answer one question for me . . . just one."

"Yes, of course. What is it?" His boots whispered through the tall grass as he moved toward her.

"Did you come to Texas looking for a specific person?"

His mouth dropped open. She had only to look into his eyes to see the guilt, to know the answer. "Who was it, Blake?"

"Laura, listen to me. I don't know what you're thinking—"

"Have you been asking questions about Anthony?"

"Yes, but—"

"Because you suspected him? Because you were sent to search for him?"

"I was sent to look for a man, but—"

404

"No," she whispered, shaking her head from side to side as if in agony. "If you can't tell me that you never suspected my brother of any wrongdoing, I don't want to hear anything you have to say."

"But, Laura—"

"Can you honestly tell me that?"

He raked his fingers haphazardly through his hair. "Listen to me. It's not what you think. I admit I did suspect him for a while, but I've checked everything so thoroughly. I've come up with nothing. I'm going to telegraph Washington and tell them that I've found nothing! No one!"

"But *if* you'd found any kind of evidence against Anthony . . . would you have turned him in?" She held her breath, waiting for the answer.

"Laura," he pleaded. His eyes were full of misery, begging her to understand. "It's my job . . . my country. What kind of a man would I be if I could turn my back on a traitor?"

Her eyes grew wide in dread. "You'd have done it, knowing he's the only family I've got? Knowing what it would do to me?"

"Please try to understand. It won't happen. There's no evidence. It's over with. I'm quitting. I'm through. We'll have our lives together. None of this will touch us again."

And she was torn with fear, because she was very much afraid there *was* evidence. If she was right about Midnight— No! She couldn't think about that. No one in the state had any suspicion about Anthony. She was the only one.

There was just one problem: Blake. She had to get him as far away from Anthony as possible. He'd never be able to put this totally from his mind. There was still John's death to avenge. If he ever found out about her fears,

405

there'd be no stopping him until he tracked down the truth.

And what if—oh, dear God—what if there was some truth to her fears! No matter how much she didn't want to believe her brother was capable of such a thing, she couldn't quite shake the terrible fears from her mind. For Anthony's sake, she couldn't take that chance.

And she knew without a doubt that she couldn't spend the rest of her life afraid that she'd say something, do something to betray her own brother. No matter how much she loved Blake, it would be impossible to live like that. His honor would never let him keep silent if he found out the truth. And she could never live a happy life with him as long as this horrible suspicion was eating away at her heart. She'd never know a moment's peace. That ugly creeping fear would despoil and tarnish everything they had.

It would be better to live with the memory of Blake's love than to have him realize one day that she had chosen to protect her brother at the possible cost of his own honor.

She swallowed back the scalding tears that threatened to break free. "It's over, Blake." Her voice was so soft that he wasn't sure he understood.

"Yes, I know, darling. It *is* over. We can forget the whole thing now—"

"No, I mean us."

"Laura, you can't possibly—"

"Yes, I can." She had to find a reason—something that sounded logical enough so that he would honestly believe that her love for him was dead. "You lied to me, and I can't forgive you for that. There could never be any trust between us after that." She wrung her hands. "We can't build a marriage—a life together—without trust. How would I ever believe that you really loved me? That you weren't just using me to get to Anthony?"

It hurt her to say those words because in her heart she couldn't bear to believe such a thing. Belief in Blake's love was all she'd have left. But she also knew that Blake would expect her to feel that way.

"How can you say that? You're not being fair." He moved toward her, reaching to pull her into his strong arms.

She stepped aside quickly. "Don't touch me. Not now. I couldn't bear it." If he touched her, she'd never be able to do what she had to do.

Blake's arms dropped to his sides. He was filled with pain at the thought that his touch was repugnant to her.

"I could never live with you, knowing what I know." Her words were spoken sincerely. But she meant one thing and he heard another.

"Laura . . ." The lump in his throat made speaking almost impossible. There was such utter finality in her voice that he knew he'd lost her. There was nothing left to say. The pain in her eyes told him that the hurt he'd inflicted upon her was too great for forgiveness.

She shook her head sadly, tears finally welling and spilling down her cheeks.

Blake's shoulders slumped. He looked at her with such raw hurt that she thought her heart would break.

Unable to bear the pain a moment longer, Laura sobbed and ran for the house. She stumbled and almost fell as she scrambled up the stairs, seeking the sanctuary of her room. She locked herself in for the rest of the evening, responding only that she was ill when Anthony came to check on her.

The pale, pinched face he glimpsed through the tiny crack of the door seemed to confirm her statement, and Anthony finally went away, vowing to send for the doctor if she didn't feel better in the morning.

Laura cried until she was exhausted, finally falling into a deep, oblivious sleep.

In the morning, Blake was gone.

The vase hit the wall and shattered into a million pieces. "That lying little bitch! She's tricked me again." Maria was furious beyond reason. "I won't let her get away with it. I won't!"

She whirled, looking for something else to throw. Her lacy dressing gown swirled about her bare feet. She snatched the brush from her dresser and hurled it after the vase.

She'd barely been able to control her temper when Anthony told her the news that Blake was gone. Thank God he'd left immediately to ride into Washington-on-the-Brazos to see if he could locate Blake and find out what had happened to make him leave so suddenly.

Blake had left a message with Rosita that he'd leave Blackjack in town for Anthony to pick up—no other explanation, nothing. Anthony had hurried up the stairs, worry lines etching his face, with curt instructions that Maria should be extra sweet and consoling to Laura until he could return from town.

Sweet! He'd think sweet when she got through! There was no way she was staying here another day—no way she could let Miguel stay with Laura here and Blake gone. She was tired of waiting. She'd fix it—she'd fix everything!

She tore off the expensive ruffled dressing gown, dropping it to the floor like a rag and kicking it out of her way as she hurried to the wardrobe to pull out a riding skirt and shirtwaist. She dressed quickly, stopping only long enough to pull her hair back and tie it with a ribbon and jam her feet into a pair of dark leather boots.

Maria pounded down the stairs and out the back door,

passing Rosita without a word. Rosita called after her, but Maria simply ignored her, hurrying to the barn, where she sharply instructed Pedro to saddle up her horse.

He barely had the saddle cinched before she was climbing atop the gentle roan. She kicked the horse savagely in the flanks and rode for Sunfire Valley.

Chapter 32

Miguel pulled his horse up in alarm, watching the cloud of dust grow larger and larger against the leaden gray of the sky. Who would be coming from that direction? No one went to Sunfire Valley! Could there be a problem with the small band of men he had left there to guard the last cache of rifles and ammunition taken in the supply-train raid? He had repeatedly warned his men never to venture in the direction of the ranch. They wouldn't dare disobey him!

His stomach gave a sickening lurch. Surely no one had discovered their hiding place! He quickly pushed that disturbing notion from his mind. The valley was difficult to reach, and the people of the area had a healthy respect for the old Indian burial grounds and the superstitious legends that surrounded it. Besides, he had lookouts posted who would shoot any stranger who dared to breach their security.

Apprehension sat heavy in his belly as he watched the approaching rider. Who could it be? He felt in his bones that trouble was coming. Why did it have to happen now? His plans were almost complete. He couldn't afford a mishap at this late date. He was almost ready to take the few men left in hiding in the valley and return to Mexico, where he would call his volunteers to arms.

The figure drew nearer and nearer and began to take shape in the plume of red dust. Miguel recognized Maria's horse before he could actually make out her face. He scowled darkly. What could she be doing coming from that direction?

He glanced at where a bright yellow sun should be hanging in the Texas sky, but all he saw was the growing mass of dark, tumultuous clouds, piled high like dirty cotton against the gunmetal-colored firmament. Even without the sun's confirmation, he knew it was still very early in the morning—much too early for Maria to be up and about under normal circumstances. Something must be dreadfully wrong.

He kicked his horse into a gallop and rode to meet her, reining in so hard that Paco reared up and then crabbed sideways.

"What's wrong?" he demanded as soon as Maria halted beside him. "What are you doing out here?" His voice was tinged with accusation and just a touch of anxiety.

"I've been to the valley to give warning," Maria replied breathlessly, her full breasts heaving from her hard ride.

"Warning? Why? For what reason? Surely no one has discovered our hiding place!"

Maria's hair had long ago lost its ribbon. It floated wild and free about her shoulders. A sudden gust of hot wind whipped it savagely across her face. She tossed her head to clear her eyes.

"Not yet. But I'm very afraid that there's going to be trouble." Her eyes were large and stormy with anxiety. In truth, there was no imminent problem, but she didn't dare tell Miguel what was causing her vexation. She had

411

to get him moving—and quickly—before he could discover the real reason behind Blake's sudden departure.

"What kind of trouble?" Miguel prodded.

"Blake has gone to town. I fear he has discovered something. I . . . uh . . . something that Laura said makes me think this is so. I have already alerted the men. They will be prepared to leave as soon as we can get back."

"Leave?" Miguel asked blankly. "Why?"

Maria was highly agitated and her mount sensed it, tossing its head and curling its upper lip back to nip at Miguel's horse with big yellow teeth. Miguel slapped at the offender angrily and prodded Paco a few inches out of harm's way.

Maria shot him a look of pure exasperation. "Back to Mexico, of course! We must leave before we are caught. Blake could return at any time with help from town. The men will be ready soon. We must hurry to join them. It's time to pursue our cause, Miguel! We don't dare wait any longer or all could be lost."

Miguel's strong arm whipped out and secured a hold on the bridle of Maria's fidgety horse. "Just a moment, Maria. You're making no sense. What does Blake know? What did Laura say?"

Her gaze slid away from his. Damn! She should have known he wouldn't simply accept her word in the matter. She should have thought her story out better. He wasn't reacting the way she'd hoped. He should be eager to leave right now, desperate to protect his precious cause! Why did he have to be so pigheaded when speed was so essential? What was wrong with him? Had he lost sight of their goal?

"Miguel," Maria insisted. "There isn't time for all of this now. Please. You go on to the valley and help the men get ready. I'm going to ride back to the house and pack a small bag. I'll even stop at your quarters and get your things so you won't have to return."

Heat lightning flickered in the distance, casting a greenish tinge across the sky. The dark clouds, heavy with moisture, loomed higher and higher against the horizon. Small gusts of wind picked up bits of grass and twigs and dirt, twirling it into the ominously heavy air.

Miguel's voice was deadly quiet. "So you took it upon yourself to issue the orders to leave?" It was obvious from the quiet fury of his voice that he was angry at her usurpation of authority. "Why didn't you come to find me when you learned of this problem? Why did you go straight to the valley yourself? I warned you before. I will decide when we will leave."

"I-I did try to find you. I thought you'd already gone out there. So I knew I had to find you and tell you the news—before it was too late."

She laid a beseeching hand against his rock-hard thigh. He could feel the almost imperceptible trembling of her fingers.

Something was very wrong. Miguel could sense it. Maria was as nervous as a cat. It showed in the agitated flicker of her eyes—the way she couldn't quite meet his gaze—and the way her free hand fiddled with the reins. It was just as obvious that she wasn't going to tell him the truth. He'd have to find out for himself.

Knowing how stubborn and devious Maria could be at times, Miguel pretended to believe her. It would be easier to check out the story for himself if she was off guard.

If there was any truth to her tale and there really was danger of discovery, the proper safety measures had already been taken. The men had been alerted and would be prepared to leave as soon as he arrived in the valley. But first he intended to return to the ranch—for a very important reason. Regardless of what Maria thought, Miguel had no intention of leaving without Laura.

"Maria," Miguel said soothingly, cupping his hand over hers where it lay on his thigh and giving it a little

413

squeeze. "You must calm yourself. Everything appears to be under control. You were very wise to handle the situation as you did."

Maria breathed a sigh of relief. She could hardly believe he was yielding so easily.

"But I still must return to the ranch," Miguel continued in a voice as smooth as glass. "I have some money hidden away in the storeroom. We will need it for the revolution. I will not leave without it."

He quietly noted the swift look of disappointment that flickered through her eyes. She wasn't very happy with the turn of events, but she didn't dare question his actions again.

"Now, Maria, tell me. When did Blake go into town?"

"He left perhaps two hours ago," she replied almost sullenly.

"And where is Anthony?"

"He went to town also."

Yes, there was definitely something else going on here. Both of the men were gone. There was no way they would have left Laura alone at the house if they suspected anything. If they'd had even an inkling of the truth, they would have taken her with them to ensure her safety. They had no way of knowing whether or not the ranch hands were also involved in Miguel's scheme.

Miguel was now more sure than ever that it would be safe to return. None of the ranch workers suspected a thing. He had been very careful not to involve any of them for fear someone would let slip what was going on. It had been infinitely better to keep everyone connected with the ranch in the dark, except for Maria. And Maria had never dared reveal the truth—because she herself was too deeply involved.

"Listen carefully, Maria. You go on back to the house so no one will suspect anything. It will take me an hour or so to secure the money and be prepared to leave. So you will have plenty of time to pack and sneak out. No one will suspect a thing if we act normal. I do not think Blake or Anthony can possibly return from town before we can escape."

She cut a quick glance at him from under the thick brush of her lashes, knowing that to argue further would surely cause him to question her motives. "Well, all right," she finally agreed.

She knew Blake had no intention of returning. And, knowing Anthony, he wouldn't easily give up trying to change Blake's mind about leaving—if and when he found him. It might even be nightfall before Anthony returned. By then she and Miguel could be miles away.

Her plan could still work. She had simply wanted to keep Miguel away from the ranch. But if he was busy recovering the hidden money, he wouldn't have time to do anything else. Besides, she knew she had pushed Miguel as far as she possibly could.

Her naturally selfish inclinations surfaced as she considered an additional implication of his instructions. If she was forced to acquiesce to Miguel's authority, she might as well put the time to good use. Another hour or so would give her a chance to pack a few more things. Anthony had given her some very beautiful jewels. There would come a time in the not too distant future, when she took her rightful place at Miguel's side as ruler of Mexico, she would need such regal adornments.

After all, why should she abandon *everything?* She'd earned it all. She deserved to keep as much as she could! And there was no sense in leaving *all* of her pretty clothes. With a little more time to prepare, she could choose a suitable wardrobe to take with her.

Greed glittered in her eyes. "If we have to return, then I want you to prepare the wagon so we can take it. I would prefer to travel that way rather than by horseback for such a long journey."

"Of course, whatever you wish," Miguel agreed quickly, knowing all the while that he had no intention of doing any such thing.

Maria smirked inwardly. This little delay in leaving might well be to her benefit after all. Who knew what the circumstances would be, once they reached Mexico? Who knew how long it would be before she could replace the extensive wardrobe she was being forced to leave behind? At least now she could take *some* of her things along.

"Good. I agree with the rest of your plan," she said with a small smile of self-satisfaction.

As if you had any choice, my dear, Miguel thought to himself. He barely managed a warm smile in her direction.

"Very well. We will ride back. When we get near the ranch, I will fall behind so that no one will know we have been together. You return to the house quickly. I will do what I have to do. Then I will signal you when it is time to leave."

"How?" she demanded.

"I will simply give Rosita a message for you. I will tell her that I need to speak with you on matters concerning the ranch. Since Senor Nichols is away, she will think nothing of the request. Then you will come to the barn."

"What about my things?"

"Just have them packed. I will see to their loading myself," Miguel snapped.

Maria nodded her head in agreement. She jerked at the reins, turning her horse toward the ranch. Miguel cracked the ends of his reins against his horse's neck and set off beside her.

The hot wind gusted and whipped about them as they rode. Deep warning rumbles of thunder sounded in the distance.

*   *   *

Maria followed Miguel's instructions perfectly. He stayed in the shelter of the woods while she continued to the barn and then ran for the house. As soon as she disappeared up the back steps, he proceeded with his careful plans.

Inside the barn, he quickly unsaddled his horse and shooed him into an empty stall. He then moved to the sheltered doorway and peered out. There was no one in sight.

With swift, catlike strides he traveled the path to the house. He crouched low and eased up under the kitchen window. Sure enough, Rosita and Juanita were busy with the usual preparations for the noon meal. He could hear their incessant chatter distinctly through the open windows.

Just like two old magpies, Miguel thought wryly. He could always count on them to be discussing the latest happenings in the house. They never knew how much information he'd gleaned from their ramblings in just this manner.

It didn't take him long to obtain an explanation for Maria's sudden irrational behavior. Blake's leaving had nothing to do with any suspicions concerning Miguel. Rosita and Juanita were indulging in their usual gossip, only this time the topic was the speculated cause of Laura and Blake's final argument. Obviously, Maria's panic upon hearing the news that Blake had left triggered her actions.

Miguel hunkered down to contemplate the portent of what he had heard. He absentmindedly pulled a tuft of long grass, twirling it aimlessly in his fingers while he mulled the matter over. What he'd overheard from the two chattering women confirmed his fears. He could no longer trust Maria in any way. He would be forced to leave before she could spoil everything he had worked so hard for.

He had no more time to win Laura's trust and love. He

would have to convince her to come with him in some other way. Once he had her away from Texas, he could win her love. He was sure of it. What woman could possibly turn down the glorious future he was going to offer Laura?

The blades of grass fell from his fingertips, and he rose quickly to glance in the window again. The two women would not be moving from the kitchen for awhile, which meant that the front of the house should be deserted.

Miguel eased away from the window and crept around the house. No one saw him enter and sneak up the grand staircase.

He knew which room belonged to Laura. He'd watched her delectable shadow on the drawn curtains enough times. When he reached the landing at the top of the stairs, Miguel quickly checked the other hallway. Empty. Silently he made his way to Laura's door.

His hand gripped the knob, turning it softly, slowly, and then easing the door open. In a fraction of a second, he was inside.

Laura was seated before the mirror, listlessly brushing her hair. Although she'd risen from bed at a very late hour that morning, plum-colored shadows under her eyes bespoke the sleepless night she'd spent. At the sound of the door she glanced up, gasping in surprise at Miguel's sudden appearance.

"Miguel! What are you doing here?" she asked in a startled voice, turning around on the small bench to face him. She unconsciously crossed her arms to clasp her robe more securely about her body.

"Shh," Miguel said, positioning his finger over his lips. "I have a message from Senor Nichols—"

"Anthony?" Fear flooded through her, and her heart began a crazy trip-hammer beat. "What is it? What's wrong?"

Miguel moved across the floor on cat feet. "He has sent

418

me to fetch you."

"But why?"

She stared up at him with wide, frightened eyes as he loomed over her. His hands reached down and gripped her arms, pulling her gently to her feet.

"We must be very quiet," he whispered. "He says there is danger to his life. You must come quickly. He wants no one to know that I am taking you to him. No one . . . not even Maria. Do you understand?"

She nodded mutely.

"Good," he breathed, his warm breath fanning across her flushed cheeks. "Put on your riding clothes and then come out to the barn. I will be waiting for you."

Again, she nodded.

"You must not let anyone see you," he cautioned again. "Can you manage that?"

"Yes, but—"

Miguel quickly pressed his fingers against her lips. "There's no time for explanations now. You must trust me, Laura. Your brother's life may hang in the balance. Will you do as I ask?"

"Yes." Her lips formed the words, but no sound escaped the fright-induced stricture of her throat.

Miguel backed away from her. "I will be waiting for you in the barn. Hurry, but do not take any chances. Go out the front door and around the far side of the house. You must stay off of the path. Keep to the shelter of the trees."

"I will," she managed to say.

With one last penetrating look, Miguel was gone.

Laura was consumed with a cold dread. She had no idea what was going on. She knew only one thing: If Anthony needed her, she had to go.

She was shaking so hard she could hardly peel away her nightclothes and choose a dress. With fumbling fingers, she finally managed to clothe herself and take the

419

first faltering steps toward the door.

Laura cringed as the door creaked slightly when she opened it, holding her breath until she was sure that no one was in the hallway. She slipped out and pulled the door gently shut behind her, then tiptoed down the hallway. At the edge of the landing she leaned carefully over the banister and peered down into the entryway. She could see no one. There was no noise coming from the front of the house either.

Laura took a deep breath and eased down the stairs, her hand gripping the railing so hard that her knuckles turned white. A quick look into the parlor and she was out the door and across the porch. Hugging the shadows of the house, she finally reached the back corner. She dashed for the sheltering trees and then quickly worked her way along the edge of the path to the barn.

There was a stitch in her side by the time she entered the dark entrance. Miguel reached out and grasped her arm, hauling her into the interior. She blinked to adjust her eyes to the dim light.

Miguel's inscrutable bronze face showed nothing of his inner turmoil. His flat black eyes were indecipherable. "Everything is ready. The horses are saddled. Hurry, we must leave quickly."

He led Laura to where Sugar stood patiently waiting and then bent over to give her a quick boost into the saddle. Once Laura was safely up, he pulled Midnight's reins free of the restraining knot around the support post and quickly vaulted onto his back.

Miguel and Laura broke the cover of the barn at a gallop just as Rosita opened the back door to empty a pan of dirty water.

The water sloshed alarmingly as Rosita paused in her endeavor to peer at the retreating pair. She watched with mild interest as they headed north. Giving a shrug, she finally turned her attention back to the task at hand, turning the pan over to thump the last drops from it.

Miguel and Laura were halfway across the broad field surrounding the house by the time Rosita reentered the house.

The fast pace of the horses gave Laura no chance to ask even one of the dozens of questions spinning in her head. She had only to catch a glimpse of Miguel's grim face from time to time and she would choke back her words and prod Sugar to even greater exertion.

Once they were far out of sight of the house, Miguel slowed their mad dash. The horses were going to have to carry them over a long distance. He didn't dare expend all their energy before even reaching the valley.

Lightning sizzled across the horizon, and Sugar shied with fright, spinning and fighting against the bit. Miguel whipped Midnight around and quickly returned to Laura's side.

"It's all right," he called to her when she finally got Sugar calmed down. "The storm is still far away. Just keep a tight hold on the reins. We'll slow down a bit since she's so nervous."

Laura was grateful for the opportunity to catch her breath and even more thankful that she would at last be able to ask for an explanation.

"Miguel, can you tell me what's going on now?"

"I'm sorry, Laura, but I can't. Senor Nichols would prefer to explain everything to you himself."

"But surely you can tell me something—"

"I gave my word."

"But—"

"It is not far, Laura. Be patient, please. Soon everything will be clear to you."

"All right," she said with a sigh of resignation. She turned her attention to the front, eyeing the brooding storm with trepidation. She glanced quickly at Miguel as thunder rumbled ominously again. He didn't seem disturbed by the threatened violence of the elements, although Laura felt sure the storm was closer than he'd stated.

The sky continued to darken, taking on a dark and brooding patina. The air fairly sizzled with turbulence as Laura continued to plod blindly across unfamiliar ground after Miguel. The land gradually changed from lush prairies blanketed with deep grass to a rougher terrain, pockmarked by barren, scraggy patches of brush and jumbled rock.

Long minutes passed as the wind's strength increased, plastering their clothes hotly against their bodies, stinging their eyes with fine particles of dirt. Miguel finally called a halt, turning his horse's rump into the wind. Laura followed suit.

"Here," he said, passing her a large silken handkerchief. "Put this on so it will shield your eyes."

She left the square of fabric unfolded, fighting the erratic gusts to place it on her head and tie it in a double knot under her chin. She pulled the flapping triangle down low over her eyes and lowered her head to the wind's brunt.

Miguel tied a faded bandanna across his nose and tugged his black hat lower on his forehead. They urged the horses around and started out again.

Spears of lightning came ever closer, flashing and flickering their jagged paths through the roiling clouds. The smell of ozone was heavy in the air.

Miguel edged in front of Laura and began an ascent up a steep hill. Sugar fell into step, head lowered so that Midnight's flank partially blocked the violence of the wind.

"Miguel," Laura called loudly over the wail of the wind. "How much farther? Will we make it before the storm hits?"

Just as Miguel glanced back over his shoulder to reassure Laura, a tremendous flash of lightning lit up the sky. Miguel's silhouette was thrown starkly against the sooty skyline, searing his visage across her mind: the large, dark figure atop the mammoth horse, the hat and bandanna shielding all but his black, brooding eyes.

Terror slammed through Laura.

She knew who he was.

Chapter 33

When Maria failed to come downstairs for the noon meal, a concerned Rosita went looking for her. She rapped at Maria's door, then waited a bit impatiently for an answer. When none was forthcoming, she tried the knob. She huffed in irritation when she found the door locked and began to knock even louder.

The door was suddenly flung open, and Maria confronted Rosita with a scowl on her face. "Yes, what is it?"

"I was worried when you did not come down to eat," Rosita replied, not the least intimidated by Maria's bad moods. She had weathered all degrees of them in the years since she had taken charge of her as a tiny babe.

She had devoted her life to lavishing love and care on Maria, trying to make up for the death of her mother and the negligence of a father who never recovered from the loss of his beloved wife. Maria's father had showered her with all that money could buy as she grew, but Rosita's love had never been able to make up for a father's withdrawal from the child's life.

Rosita's fondest dream would come true the day she could take charge of Maria's children. She longed often for a rosy-cheeked, smiling little girl with black ringlets: a perfect, tiny replica of Maria, the child Rosita had loved as her own for over twenty years.

Rosita was willing to concede that Maria might be a little spoiled and willful, but her love for the girl had long ago blinded her to the true ruthlessness of Maria's personality. Having no children of her own, she had lavished all her motherly affections on Maria throughout her life.

Once again, as she had done hundreds of times over the years, she sought to cajole Maria out of her bad mood.

"Now, my lamb, you know you should eat. You must remember your health. Someday you will want babies, and you will be glad that I fussed at you."

"Babies," spat Maria. "Not I! I have better things to do with my life than change soiled diapers and wipe snotty noses. Now, go away and leave me alone. I am busy."

Ignoring the command, Rosita pushed the door wide open and bustled her way into the room despite Maria's fit of pique. Maria stamped her foot in irritation and then turned her back on the stout little woman. Time was too short to spend any portion of it arguing with Rosita. She stomped over to her wardrobe and withdrew a dress.

Rosita's mouth dropped open in shock as she viewed the room. There were piles of clothing and scattered pieces of luggage on the bed, and the floor was littered with colorful pools of dresses. As she watched uncomprehendingly, Maria quickly perused the dress she was holding and then dropped it to the floor with the others.

"Good heavens! What are you doing?" Rosita exclaimed, aghast at the havoc Maria was creating.

"I'm deciding what to pack," Maria retorted, discarding still another dress.

Rosita scrambled to pick up some of the clothes, clucking and shaking her head all the while.

"Maria," she said sternly, "there certainly is no necessity to make such a mess. Senor Nichols will be most displeased to find the room in such a condition. Now, if you will tell me how long you and the senor will be gone, I will pack for you."

By now Rosita had an armful of rumpled clothes, and she scurried to the big bed to lay them carefully on the foot of it before she began smoothing and folding. Maria ignored her, finally selecting a garment and hurrying over to stuff it in one of the bags.

Rosita propped her knuckles against her plump hips in exasperation. "Maria, my lamb, if you will tell me where you and Senor Nichols are going, I will help you select the proper clothes—"

"I'm not going anywhere with Anthony," Maria told her with a defiant flip of her head.

"But what do you mean? Is there danger of some sort? Is he sending you to town so you'll be safe?" Rosita was filled with concern for her ward.

"I'm going home," Maria declared, "and don't you dare try to stop me!"

"Home!" shrieked Rosita. "You mean Mexico?" Her hand clutched fearfully at her abundant bosom. "My angel, you can't do that. There is a war going on! Senor Nichols would never allow it."

"Senor Nichols," Maria replied mockingly, "will not know until it is too late to stop me." She stuffed a lacy chemise into the bag.

"Maria, why would you do such a thing? You cannot go running off like this. This is your home now. You must behave like a proper lady. Think of your poor husband. It would worry him so and he is so good to you—"

Maria whirled, her face contorted with fury. "This is not my home! And I do not care what Antonio thinks or does. I am leaving."

Rosita recognized that blazing glint of stubbornness in Maria's eyes and felt dismay spiral through her. "But,

426

how will you get there? Who will look after you? Who will take care of you? You mustn't do this." She reached to touch Maria's arm. "If you insist on such madness, I will come with you."

"If you tell me I *mustn't* do something again, I will scream." Maria's voice was deadly quiet. "I don't need you to go with me, Rosita. You forget I am no longer a child. Miguel will take care of me—"

"Miguel!" Rosita's face darkened with indignation. She clasped her hands tightly together atop the slight mound of her belly and drew herself up imperially. "I knew that nothing good would come of him following you here. I should have told the senor the truth about Miguel at the very beginning."

Maria ignored her, hauling a handful of clothes out of one bag and stuffing it in another. Rosita was wringing her hands, berating herself mentally and verbally for not having foreseen the possibility of such a disaster.

"I kept hoping that you would learn to appreciate Senor Nichols's kindness and affection, that you would realize how lucky you are to have a good man to love you. If I had but told him the truth, that Miguel is not your cousin, then he wouldn't have given him a job in the first place."

"If you had ever opened your mouth, old woman, I would have sent you packing!"

"Maria! My lamb, how can you say such things to me? I have cared for you all of your life."

"If you care for me so much, why do you try to stop me from being with the man I love?" Maria's black eyes blazed defiantly.

"He is no good for you. There is something strange about Miguel . . . something I do not trust. He will come to no good, I tell you. There is nothing but hurt for you in the future if you pursue this madness. He cares for no one but himself!"

427

"You're wrong. He loves me! There are many things you do not know. One day you will be sorry you said such things about him. Miguel is going to be a great man. And when he achieves his dream, I will be the one to stand by his side!" Maria retorted haughtily.

Rosita pursed her lips together in a thin, angry line. "And if he loves you so much, little one, why is he with Senorita Laura this very moment?"

The breath hissed out of Maria. Her eyes went wide and wild. "What?"

"You heard me," Rosita said smugly. "I saw them leave."

Maria clutched Rosita's arms and shook her. "You didn't! You're lying to me. You just want to stop me from leaving!"

"I am not lying. I saw them ride off together at noon."

Maria gaped at her. A slow insidious fear began to form in her tormented mind. "What direction did they take?"

"They went north." The tone of Rosita's voice went from triumphant to concerned when she saw the shock blossoming on Maria's face.

Maria slowly released her hold on Rosita, dropping her arms to her sides. She swayed slightly, and Rosita quickly placed an arm around her shoulders and led her to the side of the bed.

"Sit down, my lamb. There, there. Everything will be fine." She sat down beside Maria, patting and rocking and soothing the stunned girl just as she had done so many times when Maria was a small child.

Neither knew how long they sat like that: Rosita feeling thankful that she had been able to stop Maria's wild plan; Maria trying desperately to comprehend what had happened.

Little by little, Maria's emotions thawed, and a white-hot hatred began to flow through her veins. "That bastard!" Maria whispered vehemently. Her long nails

428

dug into her palms. Her mind darted to and fro like something demented, searching for a means of revenge.

Fate delivered her a vehicle for retaliation.

Downstairs, a strong gust of wind caught the front door just as Anthony opened it, crashing it against the wall. Anthony peered into the dark interior. No candles had been lit, despite the coming storm. The house seemed deserted. A tremor of apprehension went through him.

"Where is everybody?" he called loudly.

His shout was easily heard by the two women upstairs.

"It's Senor Nichols!" Rosita said with alarm. "Quick, my angel, run down and delay him. I will clean all this up, and he will never know."

Maria looked at her blankly.

"Hurry, Maria. You can think of some way to keep him downstairs for awhile. Tell him—"

"Tell him?" Maria repeated. Her mouth turned up in a strange little smile. Fire sparked in her eyes. Her voice grew stronger, a note of hysteria building in it. "Tell him. Yes, yes! I'll do just that!"

She jumped from the bed, almost flinging herself through the open doorway. If she heard Rosita's last desperate call, she ignored it. Her clothes were in disarray, her hair a wild ebony cloud of tangles that streamed behind her as she fled down the staircase.

"Anthony!" she cried, a sob in her voice and tears in her eyes. "Thank God you got home in time! Something terrible has happened!"

Alarm flowed through Anthony at the sight of his hysterical wife. "My God! What is it, Maria? What's wrong?"

She fell sobbing into his arms. He caught her, supporting her weight until she could control her crying enough to talk. She turned her tear-stained face up to his. "It's Laura . . ." she said in a strangled voice.

"What about Laura?" he demanded, fear radiating

through him. She sobbed even louder. "Dammit, Maria, tell me!"

"Miguel took her! He forced her to leave with him. He's the one who's been stealing the supplies! I tried to stop them, but it was no use."

Anthony's mouth gaped open. "But why?"

"I don't know!" she wailed. "You must stop him. He deserves to be punished for betraying me like this!" She clutched spasmodically at his lapels, her voice rising in desperation.

"Where did he take her?"

"To Sunfire Valley!"

"Sunfire Valley? The old Indian burial grounds?" Anthony repeated in a stunned tone.

"Yes! He even bragged about what he'd done, that he'd been stealing to help the Mexicans win the war. He's been hiding the supplies in the valley until he could move them secretely to Mexico. You must punish him, Antonio! He has betrayed me! I can't let him get away with it! He must pay!"

"But, Laura . . . what about Laura? Will he harm her?" Anthony demanded.

"Harm?" A mad light glinted in her eyes. "Yes . . . yes! He threatened to kill her once he got to Mexico. You must stop him!"

"Maria, child! No, don't—" Rosita's desperate plea from the landing above went unheeded. She scurried down the stairs. "Senor Nichols, you must listen—"

"I know all about it, Rosita. Maria told me. Here, try to get her under control." He pushed Maria tenderly into Rosita's arms. "I must hurry."

Anthony ran into his office. He buckled on his gun belt and then quickly gathered all the ammunition he had in the house, stuffing his pockets full. In just moments he was back in the foyer.

"Senor Nichols, please . . ." Rosita protested.

Anthony paused at the door for just a moment. "Take care of her, Rosita," he said with a nod in Maria's direction, knowing full well he might never return. And then he whirled and was gone, pounding down the steps, shouting at the top of his voice for Pedro to ride to Cletus Moore's for help.

Maria gave a strangled sound—something between a laugh and a sob—and ran up the steps. Rosita hesitated, battling within herself whether to follow Anthony and tell him the truth before he left or to see to Maria's needs. A loud, anguished wail from Maria's bedroom swayed her decision. Rosita wearily began to climb the stairs. As always, Rosita's concern lay first and foremost with Maria.

Blake peered moodily out the window of Thomas Matthews's office. The old law man watched with sympathy. Something was sure eating at the young fellow's guts—and it was much more than what he'd just told the justice of the peace.

Somehow Matthews hadn't been too surprised to learn that Blake worked for the government. His sudden appearance in town, his superior knowledge of political maneuverings, the quietly intense way he seemed to absorb everything that went on around him—all of these things had triggered more than a few questions in Matthews's mind over the past weeks. And now Blake had finally explained the whole situation.

While making his last anguished trip into Washington-on-the-Brazos that morning, Blake had decided to stop by the justice of the peace's office before leaving town to tell Matthews everything—everything except for Anthony's possible involvement. That he could not do. Whether for Laura's sake or because of his own beliefs, he didn't know. He'd only known, when he sent Anthony away earlier, that he could not besmirch the reputation of such a man.

When Anthony had tracked him down at the hotel that morning, Blake had been afraid the coming confrontation would be bitter. At best, he expected a long argument about his actions. He knew how much Anthony loved Laura and wanted her to be happy.

But, once again, he appeared to have sold Anthony short. Blake had been almost pathetically relieved when Anthony had quietly listened to what he had to say and then accepted it as final.

Blake had told him the only thing he could: that he was absolutely convinced that Laura would never be happy with him, that he had to leave in order to give her peace of mind.

Anthony's gaze had bored into his, as if searching Blake's very soul for the truthfulness of the sad statement. Finally, his shoulders had slumped, and the hope had gone out of his eyes.

"I'm really sorry," he'd murmured before offering his hand to the man he knew his sister loved. "Good-bye, Blake. We won't forget you." And he'd climbed back on Dancer and ridden away.

"When will that damn stage get here?" Blake muttered, turning away from the window to pace the floor.

Matthews's mouth turned up in an ironic little smile. "I would think you, of all people, would know the delays that can plague such a trip."

Blake ran his fingers distractedly through his already tumbled curls. He gave a small, wry laugh. "You're right. I'm just ready to get on with things—get back to Washington, *my* Washington, and get my life back in order." His footsteps continued to echo across the weathered plank flooring. "Things have been all jumbled and confused since . . . since John's death," he finally

432

filled in lamely. But his heart was saying "since Laura."

"You might as well relax," Matthews urged him. "It'll take them awhile before they're ready to leave again, anyway. They'll have to change teams, unload any shipments or passengers. And, besides, I'm sure Max won't leave until he fills up on some of Elizabeth's home cooking."

"Yeah," Blake grinned in return. "I guess it would be hard for anyone to pass up a piece of Elizabeth's berry pie."

"Have you eaten yet?" the old man asked with concern. "It might do you good to get a hot meal under your belt before you start out. It's a far piece to the next stopping point."

"How well I remember."

The familiar sounds of an arriving coach filled the air. "Well, it appears your wait is about over," said Matthews, pushing his dilapidated chair away from the scarred desk to stand up.

"Yeah, I guess so." Now that it was almost time to leave, Blake felt an almost overwhelming reluctance. He was going to miss this town, these people. It was going to be very hard to let go of his dream. Would he ever again feel the desire to own his own land, to settle down with a woman and live a normal life? Or would the loss of Laura forever condemn him to the loneliness of the life he'd always lived?

Matthews crossed the room to take Blake's hand. His other hand gripped Blake's upper arm with genuine affection. He hated to see Blake leave. He would have made a fine addition to the community. Someday soon, Matthews knew, he would have to retire. Time was catching up with him. He regretted that Blake wouldn't be around to maybe take his place when that time came.

"You take care of yourself, Blake."

"I will."

433

"Maybe someday you'll be out this way again."

Blake's dark eyes were glazed with sadness. "Sure . . . maybe I will." And he was filled with utter remorse at the thought that it could never happen.

"Excuse me, gentlemen," a voice said from the doorway. "I just arrived on the stage. I was told I would find the justice of the peace here." The man was big and rather burly under his dandified clothing; his eyes were clear and sharp.

"Yes, sir. That's me. What can I do for you?" Matthews replied.

"I need directions to the ranch of Mr. Anthony Nichols. I have a very important official notice for a gentleman who's staying with him. I may need your help."

Blake snapped to attention. "Are you looking for me?" he almost growled.

"That, sir, depends entirely on who you are," the man answered warily.

"Blake Saunders," he barked in irritation. His heart was thudding painfully against his rib cage. Something very special was happening. The department *never* contacted the agents in the field—unless there was an absolute emergency.

"Mr. Saunders," the man said with a smile, reaching to pump Blake's hand enthusiastically. "My name's Jess Emerson. Glad to meet you finally. I've heard a lot about you—"

"Cut the crap!" demanded Blake. "What's the message?"

Emerson cut his eyes toward Thomas Matthews.

"He's all right. He knows about it," Blake was quick to reassure. "Now tell me what's going on."

"Well," Emerson drawled, "our man in Mexico finally got a breakthrough. He found out that the man we've been looking for is a Mexican national who's been working for Mr. Nichols. What's worse, it seems that Mrs. Nichols is his accomplice."

"Miguel! And Maria!" Blake spat out the names. Suddenly everything fell into place.

Of course their foe had been able to send top secret information about the doings in Austin! Maria could easily find out from Anthony—he trusted his wife implicitly—and then she, in turn, passed the news on to Miguel. No wonder everything pointed to Anthony! Anthony had been a dupe, guilty only of loving and trusting his wife. Miguel was well respected in the community. Why shouldn't he be? He worked for one of the most prominent men in the area. In such a position, he would naturally be above suspicion. He could be anywhere, at anytime, and no one would think anything of it. With Anthony gone much of the time, Miguel and Maria would have been able to do anything they wanted. There was no one to stop them. After all, most of the ranch hands were Mexican.

Dear God! How many of them were in on this scheme? And Laura was alone out there right now!

". . . And when we found out—" Emerson was still rambling on.

"Never mind all that now!" Blake said frantically. "I've got to get back to the ranch immediately. Laura and Anthony could be in grave danger."

"Certainly, I'll go with you as soon as I can get a horse—"

"No! That wouldn't be safe. I have to go alone." Blake's mind was whirling as he discarded one desperate plan after another. "Tom, you round up everyone you can. We may have a hell of a fight on our hands out there, depending on how many of Miguel's people are at the house."

"All right. What are you going to do?"

"They're used to seeing me there. It won't cause any

alarm if I show up alone. I can warn Anthony and Laura. I'll try to get them out of the house before anyone realizes what's going on. Then we'll head back for town."

Matthews nodded in agreement. "Sounds good."

"Give me enough time to get them out of the house. I hope to have them out and be on the way back to town before you ever get close. Maybe we can meet on the road between town and the ranch. Bring someone who can take Laura on into town. And then we'll go back and get that traitorous son of a bitch!"

Maria sobbed as if her heart would break. Nothing Rosita said could console her.

"Why? Why?" she would cry, pounding the pillows and kicking her feet as she lay facedown across the big bed she had shared with Anthony. "He'll be sorry! He'll learn that he can't do this to me!"

"Maria, darling," Rosita pleaded. "You must stop this. You are going to make yourself sick." She knew she had to prevail upon the girl to gather her strength. Someone was going to die out in that valley, and Rosita fervently hoped it wouldn't be Senor Nichols. It was vital to Maria's future well-being that she muster her reserves and prepare herself for what was to come.

Maria finally flopped over on the bed, arm thrown over her swollen eyes. "He'll come crawling back to me, begging my forgiveness. Just you wait and see."

Rosita was filled with dread at Maria's words. She didn't even realize what was going to happen out there! Did Rosita dare force her to see the truth? Yes, she must! It would be better for her to face the possibility of Miguel's death now than when Senor Nichols returned. Perhaps then they could rebuild their lives. After all, he need never know of Maria's deceit.

"Maria, please. You must realize that Miguel is gone.

436

Whatever happens, you must put him out of your life. Even if the senor does not kill him—"

"Kill him?" Maria repeated in a frighteningly bewildered voice. "But, of course, Antonio won't kill Miguel. He's just going to stop him from taking Laura. Then Miguel will see how much he needs me! Everything will be as it should be—"

"No, no, Maria. You must listen to me. You can't honestly believe that Senor Nichols will simply allow Miguel to go free after what you told him."

The girl stared at her blankly. "But I only wanted Antonio to stop him . . . to punish him for betraying me. Just a small punishment. He mustn't harm Miguel."

"Maria, darling, there's every chance in the world that Miguel will die out there. No one would blame Senor Nichols for such an act. He's trying to protect his sister."

Maria sat up, alarm in her eyes. "But that can't be. That's not what I want at all—"

"Come," Rosita prodded gently. "Wash your face. Come downstairs with me. I'll fix you some nice hot cocoa. It will soothe your nerves."

Twisting her hands together nervously, Maria repeated dully, "Cocoa? How can you think of such a thing now? Do you think I can stay here while Miguel is in such danger? I must warn him—" She tried to rise, a wild look in her eyes.

"Dear child, you can't do that!" Rosita grabbed at Maria, trying desperately to hold her down. "Listen to me. You're ill. You don't know what you're doing. Please—"

Maria twisted out of the old woman's grasp. "You can't stop me. I'm going to the valley. I've got to stop Antonio . . . to warn Miguel. I must!"

Blake's stomach knotted even tighter as he viewed

Anthony's house from the rim of the saucer-shaped valley. It looked forlorn and deserted under the growing masses of dark clouds scudding across the sky. The wind whipped at his clothes. He could detect no movement in the house, no welcoming glow of candlelight.

Pulling a deep, troubled breath into his lungs, he squared his shoulders and pasted what he hoped was a normal look on his face. He clucked at Blackjack, feeling gratitude once again that Anthony had neglected to reclaim the horse from the livery stable where Blake had left him that morning.

"Let's go, boy," he said softly and began the descent into Anthony's valley.

His alarm continued to grow as he neared the house. Something was wrong. The front door stood wide open to the whirling dust and debris. Blake swallowed hard and dismounted. He had to force himself to walk slowly up the porch stairs. What he really wanted to do was run all the way to Laura's room and gather her in his arms.

The entryway was dark and deserted, he thought, until he saw Rosita's huddled form on the bottom step of the massive stairway. She was hunched over as if in pain, her apron pressed against her face.

Blake touched her shoulder with tender concern. He was filled with a sickening dread. "Rosita, what is it? What's wrong?" he asked in a gentle voice.

She raised her head and looked at him, eyes glassy and hopeless. A final tear trickled down her brown face. "My baby. She has gone."

"Gone? Who? Where?" Blake hunkered down so that he was on the same level with the despondent little woman.

"Maria. She's gone to warn Miguel." Rosita's voice was resigned, almost devoid of emotion. "I begged her not to go, but she wouldn't listen." She shook her head sadly.

438

Blake sighed heavily. "How did she find out we were coming for him?"

"You?" Rosita repeated in confusion. "No, not you. Senor Nichols."

"Anthony? But why?" Blake gripped her lifeless fingers. "Rosita, you must tell me what's going on. Where's Laura? Upstairs?" He breathed a silent prayer that her answer would be yes.

"Senorita Laura is with Miguel. He has taken her to Sunfire Valley. Senor Nichols went after him. I know he will try to kill Miguel. And Maria followed to warn Miguel."

"Goddamn!" The oath exploded from Blake. He was too late. Now what did he do?

"The valley's to the north, isn't it?"

She nodded.

"Is Anthony alone?"

"*Si*. But he sent Pedro to Senor Moore's for help. They can cut across the far corner of the ranch and get to the valley. They may already be there. If so, Senor Nichols will have help, but my poor Maria will have no one." Rosita shook her head sadly, tears pooling in her eyes again.

"Listen to me, Rosita. There are people on the way here. When they arrive, tell them where I've gone." He gave her a little shake. "Do you understand me?"

"*Si*, senor."

"Good. Maybe I can still get there in time—"

"Time?" Rosita muttered. "Time to help Maria? Oh, Senor Saunders, will you help my baby? Please, senor! She did not mean to cause this trouble. It's just that she needs love . . . you must understand." Her trembling fingers plucked at his arm.

"Rosita," he said with infinite patience, feeling a terrible sorrow for the old woman's pain. "I'm leaving now. Please, be sure to send the men after me. I may need all the help I can get. Will you do that?"

"*Si*, senor."

He left her still huddled against the banister and ran for his horse. In seconds, he was whipping Blackjack into a gallop, asking his faithful mount for a supreme effort.

They thundered across the meadow, into the eye of the storm, as though the very devil were on their heels.

Chapter 34

The two riders, bent against the onslaught of the turbulent wind, followed a dimly marked trail through the desolate, narrow end of the shallow valley that cradled the ancient Indian burial grounds. As they neared the far end, the barren ground gave way to a heavily wooded area. A tangle of trees and bushes and vines twined over and around the haphazard piles of tumbled rocks and boulders along the last mile of their passage. The leader stooped under the low-hanging branches at the edge of the thicket and then threaded his way to a small clearing, with the other rider following closely.

"Tell the men to get ready to leave immediately," Miguel snapped at the lone man beside the sheltered campfire. He continued across the clearing, leading Laura to the far side, where a rundown shack, door hanging from one broken hinge, leaned drunkenly against the surrounding tall oaks.

To follow their progress, the young man stopped stirring the simmering pot of beans that hung over the low fire. "But what about the storm?" he asked in very broken English, eyeing the leaden sky with obvious apprehension.

"That's precisely why we must hurry! Do you think the lady can travel in the rain, you fool? Now do as I say!" Miguel commanded in a voice loud enough to be heard distinctly above the wild thrashing of the leaves high in the trees.

"*Sí,*" replied the youngest of Miguel's men, scrambling to obey his orders. He was far more afraid of angering his volatile leader than of facing the raging elements. He hesitated only long enough to cast a quick appreciative glance Laura's way before jamming his battered hat on his head and scurrying away.

Miguel continued to hold Sugar's reins tightly as he dismounted. Then he stepped between the two weary mounts and carefully pulled Laura from her saddle. She struggled as her feet touched the ground, trying to break Miguel's velvet-steel hold on her wrist while his attention was turned to looping the lines over a low limb.

"Please don't fight me, Laura," he pleaded. "I don't want to hurt you in any way. That is the last thing in the world I would ever want to happen."

"Why are you doing this to me? I thought you were my friend!" she entreated.

He shook his head almost sadly. "I want nothing more than for you to be happy. I know that is hard to believe at this point, but you will come to know the truth soon enough. If you cooperate, you will come to no harm."

"Cooperate?" she asked with a frightened catch in her voice. "How could I possibly do that? You . . . you're a bandit! A common outlaw!" She continued to tug against his iron grip.

"You will because you must," he replied simply, his eyes full of a strange, proud sorrow. "And I am no common bandido, Laura. I fight for the freedom of my country. You must understand; I do not fight your country. I'm going back to Mexico to free her from the

442

oppressions she has suffered under the fools who have ruled for the last decade. I want only to bring Mexico back to the power and glory that once belonged to her. Tell me, is that such a bad thing?"

"I . . . I don't know," she finally said, tears of frustration sheening her eyes. She ceased her useless struggles. "But how can you justify the things you've done, the people you've hurt? What about Maria? And Anthony? How could you betray their trust like that?"

Miguel held himself rigid against her taunts. "I never betrayed Maria. She has been a part of the scheme since the very first."

Laura gazed at him in shock. "But . . . but that means—"

"Yes, it was her idea to use Anthony and the ranch as a cover."

"She . . . she betrayed her own husband?" Laura gasped. "She *had* to know that Anthony might be blamed for the things you've done. And yet . . . my God! How could she do such a thing?"

Laura's mind whirled with the impact of this bitter news. No wonder Blake had suspicions about her brother! Of course everything pointed to Anthony's guilt. *Anyone* would have thought the same thing. Maria and Miguel had set the trap well.

"But . . . how could you do such things? What about the people you've hurt? The deaths?" Laura turned stricken eyes upon her captor. "Oh, Miguel, I remember the stagecoach ambush . . . John's death. I know it was you! You can't deny that fact."

A peculiar zealous fire burned in his eyes. "I don't deny it. I only tell you that such things were necessary in order to accomplish my goals."

Miguel retained his grasp on her slender wrist, urging her with great gentleness toward the entrance of the shack. A hodgepodge of supplies littered the floor of the small building.

"Please, Laura, make this easy for both of us. I know I don't have much to offer you at this time, but I promise you that one day I will be able to make up for our less than noble beginning."

"What do you want from me?" she asked, trying hard to keep the tremble out of her voice.

"I want you to accompany me to Mexico. When the present regime has been overthrown and I take power, you will stand at my side." His absolute belief in his dream was expressed in the rapt expression on his handsome face, in the fiery glow of his eyes, in the strong conviction of his voice.

"You . . . you can't be serious!" Laura managed to say. "I'm not going to Mexico!"

"Oh, but you are," said Miguel in a satin-edged voice. "Someday you will be grateful that I took you with me."

"Miguel," she pleaded, "you can't possibly believe that I could ever feel that way."

Miguel gave a slow, proud smile and shrugged his broad shoulders. "Oh, but I do. I do not intend to argue the matter with you now, Laura. Time will prove me right."

She watched the steely determination of his face for a long minute and managed to bite back the arguments that formed on her tongue. They would do no good. Obviously she couldn't reason with him.

Filled with inner frustration, she buried her face in her trembling hands, her desperate mind exploring and discarding one useless plan of escape after another. Perhaps it would be best now to at least appear to acquiesce. There was no sense wasting her energy in arguing with a man who only heard what he wanted to hear. She dropped her hands from her face and drew a deep breath, offering him a small tremulous smile. She had to get him off guard. It was just a matter of waiting now, waiting for an opportunity to escape.

"Good," Miguel commented, delight flooding his face. "I knew you'd understand. Now rest, my dear. It will be a long trip, and you will need all your strength."

Anthony crouched behind a large boulder, his eyes searching the shallow valley spread out before him. There were bound to be lookouts posted. But where were they? So far, he had been unable to detect any movement. Perhaps they had abandoned their posts and taken shelter from the promised storm.

Again he surveyed the lay of the land, noting each pile of rocks, each sheltering bush. There were plenty of places for Miguel's men to hide. It would be almost impossible to cross the barren stretch of ground between the natural entranceway and the heavily wooded section without being detected.

His eyes went to the thick stand of trees that covered the fat teardrop-shaped end of the valley. It was the only place he could see that would shelter a good-sized group of men. Because the Indians had long ago been banished from the surrounding areas and the white man had continued to avoid the area, over the years the brush had grown tall and tangled. It would provide a perfect screen for any number of people.

Anthony's only hope was to continue to watch the valley entrance. If Miguel had wagons to take out with him, it would be impossible for him to get them up the steep grade of the land that rimmed the thick copse of trees where Anthony believed they were hiding. They would *have* to come out this way.

If the marauders didn't try to leave before Cletus man-

445

aged to get there with his men, perhaps there would be a chance to rescue Laura. They could set up an ambush just this side of the narrow opening and attack Miguel and his men in surprise when they came through.

Anthony ducked back behind the rock. He didn't dare take a chance on being seen. The last thing he wanted to do was alert Miguel to his presence. If he only knew how many men Miguel had with him! God! He wished he'd thought to ask Maria if she knew.

If there was just one or two, he might take a chance on working his way into the woods. But he didn't know, and he didn't dare take a chance on endangering Laura's life by doing such a foolish thing. No, he had to wait for Cletus.

Cletus Moore's weathered face was grim with determination as he led his men across the broad, grass-covered prairie leading to Sunfire Valley. He wondered if they'd lost too many precious minutes before calling his men to arms. Trying to decipher Pedro's almost incoherent chattering had been time consuming and frustrating.

He still didn't know the whole story. All he knew was that Anthony was in trouble and Laura was in grave danger—and it all seemed to center around Miguel. What on earth had caused Anthony's foreman to do such a thing as force Laura to leave with him? For what purpose? Pedro had rambled something about stolen supplies and the war, but it had made little or no sense to Cletus.

He cast an apprehensive eye at the pewter-colored sky, tugging his hat even more securely over his forehead. It wouldn't be long. No sense worrying about it now. Time would tell.

"Let's go, men!" he shouted, kicking his horse's flanks. "Yehaw!" His shout was almost lost in the demonic wail of the wind.

Blake stood in the stirrups and shielded his eyes against the swirling dust. Yes! It *was* a horse and rider far in the distance. The murky light made it hard to pick out any details, but the direction was right. It had to be Maria! He sank back down against the punishing leather of the saddle and spurred Blackjack into a gallop.

Thunder rolled and rumbled in the distance. The wind took on a slight chill as it tugged and teased at his clothing. Lightning danced across the sky in shimmering waves of light that bathed everything in a ghostly white glow and then quickly plunged the world into near darkness again.

Anthony could feel the approach of the riders in the small tremors that echoed the heavy beat of hooves through the ground and into his supine form. He prayed that it was help, feeling thankful for the roar of the wind that would muffle their arrival. At least Miguel would not be warned. Being very careful to keep his head down, he pushed himself up from his prone position behind the rock and ran in a half crouch back to where he'd tied Dancer.

He was flooded with relief when he recognized Cletus and a dozen men from the Moore ranch. Anthony ran madly across the field, waving his arms to draw their attention. He had to stop them before there was any chance of their being spotted from the valley. Cletus reined up just inches from his friend, dismounting in almost the same instance.

"What the hell's going on?" Cletus demanded.

His men hurried to dismount, holding their wind-

447

battered hats to their heads. They quickly gathered around to hear what Anthony had to say. Mouths agape, they listened in shocked silence to his story.

"Son of a bitch," murmured Cletus when Anthony was finished, stroking his chin in consternation. "What do we do now?"

Anthony shook his head. "The only plan I can come up with is to wait and try to surprise them as they leave the valley. Maria was positive they're going to leave today, just as fast as they can."

"And you haven't seen anyone yet?" Cletus prodded.

"Not a soul. They have to be holed up in that stand of trees on the far side. We don't dare rush them; they'd have a clear shot at us, and we'd never even be able to see where they were firing from."

"Yeah, you're right about that," Cletus said morosely. "I guess we'll just have to wait. If they want to get out of there before that storm hits," he said, casting a baleful eye at the roiling mass of clouds overhead, "they'll have to move quickly."

Anthony directed the men to find shelter, and then he and Cletus hunkered down, sitting on their heels in the lee of the big rock he'd been using for cover.

"Olivia rode on to your place," Cletus informed him once they were settled as comfortably as possible.

"Damn, Cletus! Why'd she do that? She shouldn't be out in this weather."

Cletus shrugged his massive shoulders. "She thought she might be of assistance, that Maria . . . or some-body . . . might need help. You know Olivia. She used to drag home every stray she could find as a youngun . . . always doctoring and fretting over something. What makes you think I can change the way she is now?"

Anthony smiled a gentle smile. "Yeah, I know."

Just then Anthony looked up and spotted a distant

figure, galloping wildly toward them over the rough terrain. He frowned and placed his hand on his gun, ready to draw if it proved to be one of Miguel's men.

"My God! It's Maria!" he said, a mixture of surprise and anger flowing through his veins when she drew near enough for him to recognize her.

When the disheveled figure slowed to pass their vantage point, Anthony ran to grab her reins and pull her to a stop. "What are you doing, Maria? It could be dangerous here. I told Rosita to take care of you!"

"I came to warn—"

"I don't need a warning!" he shouted in vexation. "I know what I'm up against. Now get off that horse and get under shelter. All hell's gonna break loose around here any minute!"

When she refused to dismount, Anthony reached up and hauled her off the horse. Maria spat and kicked like some wild animal as Anthony tried to guide her, his hand clamped over her mouth to silence her screams and the bitter Spanish invectives she hurled his way. Mouths agape, the men watched from their sheltered positions.

Anthony dragged her to the sheltered side of a large tumble of boulders. "Pedro, you and George get over here and see that she stays put!"

"*Si*, senor!" The two men scampered to obey.

"Maria, honey, you stay here! It's for your own good. Don't you understand?" Anthony asked, forcing her into a natural corner between two large rocks. He positioned the men in front of it, effectively blocking Maria inside the narrow space. "Keep her out of the way until it's safe," he instructed the two men.

They mumbled an agreement.

"No! Don't make me stay here!" Maria begged.

"This isn't a game, Maria! Do as you're told."

"Anthony, please!" she called after him as he walked

449

away. "Let me talk with Miguel. I can convince him to let Laura go. I know I can. Please!"

"No, dammit! Do you think I'm going to let my wife go into danger like that? You don't know what he'd do. Hellfire, that would just give him another hostage. I can't take that chance with your safety!"

The wind snatched away her answering argument as he stalked back to where Cletus waited.

"Appears that somebody else is coming," Cletus muttered just as Anthony got settled down again.

"Dammit! Who is it now?" Anthony demanded. His jaw bunched in anger as he watched the rider approach. A wave of relief washed over him when he recognized Blake.

Blake waved frantically when he spotted Anthony and Cletus, swerving Blackjack in their direction at a dead run. It took but a few seconds for Blake to dismount, throw Blackjack's rein over a limb and run to where Anthony and Cletus waited.

"Any news?" he asked the minute he was within hearing distance.

Anthony shook his head and then proceeded to explain his plan. A fat solitary raindrop fell on the crude map he was drawing in the dirt. All three faces turned up to the sky; all three muttered curses at the worsening weather.

"I can't just sit here, Anthony. Laura's in worse danger than you realize. There's . . . there's something that you don't know about yet." His eyes flickered toward Maria, who was watching him with fear in her eyes, and then he looked back at Anthony's worried face. Did he have time to explain everything? What kind of help would Anthony be in the fight ahead if Blake told him of his wife's betrayal? No, it wasn't worth the risk. "Never mind. There's time for all that later. But right now, I'm going after Laura."

"Hell, man, that's suicide!"

"No, I have a plan."

'What are you going to do?" Anthony probed.

"At least I can work my way around the back and find out what they're planning to do—see if they're packing up to leave, or what. Maybe I can spot Laura or get some idea on how to reach her. You can keep watch here just in case they decide to leave before I get back. If it looks like they're going to be holed up for awhile, then I'll come back here and we'll decide whether to wait or rush them."

"All right," Anthony and Cletus agreed, both at their wits' end for any better idea. At least somebody'd be *doing* something, instead of just sitting.

Blake prepared to rise. Anthony reached out suddenly and clamped a strong hand on his arm. "Good luck," he said in a husky voice. "Be careful."

"Sure. You, too."

In seconds Blake was up on Blackjack and riding back the way he'd come. Anthony watched him make a wide turn and begin to circle around, noting that he was being very careful to stay out of sight as he worked his way toward the far side of the heavily wooded ridge at the back of the valley. Anthony watched until Blake was out of sight, praying that he'd return with good news.

Having tied Blackjack at the crest of the ridge, Blake slipped and skidded down the steep incline. Thank heaven for the crazy wail of the wind, the incessant booming thunder in the distance. The small rocks that were dislodged by his boots rolled almost silently to the bottom. He would never have dared such a move in normal weather. Bird-dog alert, he worked his way through the dense trees. Inch by inch, foot by foot, he

451

drew nearer to Miguel's camp.

The blood rushed to Blake's head in a surge of white-hot anger when the small clearing that held the shack and the milling bandidos finally came into view. What he *wanted* to do was rush in, guns blazing, and take back what was his. What he *had* to do was bide his time until he could find out where Laura was and how many men Miguel had.

He quickly crouched down behind a thick shrub, oblivious to the small thorns that plucked at flesh and fabric alike when he reached both hands into its foliage to create a small tunnel for viewing.

He counted seven men besides Miguel and one youngster who could hardly be dry behind the ears. From his hiding place, he couldn't see Laura. A time or two he had a real clear shot at Miguel, and his trigger finger itched to put the wretch out of his misery. But that would still leave eight others to contend with: far too many for one man alone. Besides, before he did anything, he had to know that Laura was safe. He prepared himself for a long wait.

The wind whipped the upper branches of the trees in a frenzied dance. Laura jumped as they rattled and thumped loudly against the roof of the shack. Her last hope of being able to slip from the ramshackle building had been dashed when Miguel's men appeared. She watched as they began to remove the last supplies from her place of imprisonment. There were too many of them. She'd never be able to escape.

When the last item was loaded, Miguel came for her. His strong hand clasped her elbow in the most solicitous manner as he escorted her across the clearing.

Blake's heart thudded with relief when he saw Laura step from the shadows of the ramshackle hut. Jealousy consumed him when she stumbled at the edge of the clearing and Miguel's strong arms caught her and steadied her in the most tender manner. Blake longed to smash Miguel's face for daring to look at the woman he loved with such covetous eyes.

Mouthing a silent curse, Blake fought to control his bitterness. Where was Miguel taking her? He watched in agony as Laura disappeared around a bend. In seconds the clearing was deserted, the men having all followed Miguel and Laura. Blake slipped from his hiding place and followed behind, staying at a very discreet distance.

There was no way Blake was going to turn back now. Anthony would just have to figure things out for himself. Blake wasn't going to let Laura out of his sight again, not even if it meant his life!

A loaded wagon waited in a shallow half-moon clearing at the side of the thicket. Blake watched as Miguel gently boosted Laura up. A few scattered raindrops peppered down, making small wet circles on Laura's blouse. She glanced up at the ominous sky, baring the slender lines of her throat to Blake's view. She was heartbreakingly close—and yet so far out of his reach!

Miguel rounded the back of the wagon, checking the knots that secured Sugar and Midnight to the back of the wagon, before climbing up and taking his place beside Laura on the wagon seat. The rest of the band mounted their horses. Miguel flicked the reins, and the wagon began to roll slowly around the edge of the thicket.

At the entrance to the valley, one of Cletus's men spied movement. He squinted his eyes against the sting of the wind, watching closely, waiting to sound the alarm until he was sure of what was happening. A wagon began to materialize out of the hazy distance, a cluster of men just beginning to fan out around it as they angled toward the mouth of the valley.

"Pssst! They're moving out," hissed old Tom Parker,

pointing and wagging his head until the word had been passed all the way down the line.

"Can you make out Laura?" Anthony called in a carefully modulated voice.

"Not yet. Let them get a little closer," Tom replied.

"Be careful! We don't want to alert them. Stay down! Wait till they get abreast. And for God's sake, watch out for Laura!"

Everyone's attention was riveted on the approaching wagon as it laboriously made its way. It hugged the perimeter of the woods, working diagonally toward the dim wagon trail that cut straight across from the entrance to the center of the woods. The closer they came to the trail, the clearer the figures became.

Deep in the shadows of the woods, Blake paralleled the progress of the wagon and the scattered men, keeping abreast of them every foot of the way despite the clutching thorns that tore at his clothes and the treacherous roots that lay in wait at his feet. Twice he stopped long enough to draw a bead on Miguel, and twice he dropped his gun, frustrated and afraid to fire. Laura was between him and Miguel. Each jolt of the wagon sent her bobbing and wobbling on the high plank seat. He couldn't take the chance. He might hit her instead.

Anthony watched intently from his sheltered position. "Laura's in the wagon! It looks like she's all right." He breathed a sigh of relief and then turned his attention back to the more important task of counting opponents. "Looks like about nine or ten of them. Pay attention! Have your guns ready when they come through between those two big boulders," he instructed.

Rapt attention pinned on the approaching enemy, the men drew their pistols or leveled their rifles, each lining up on a likely target and following his progress with deadly intent.

The two men guarding Maria were caught up in the tension of the moment. Anxious to see what was going on, they shuffled and craned their necks. The temptation was just too great. Step by step they edged away from the boulder, trying to get a clear view of their adversaries.

Maria had been waiting for just such an opportunity. With tiny, careful steps she edged across the face of the boulder and then down its side. Her heart beat so loudly that she was afraid the men would hear. Once she was out of their view, she let her breath out with a whoosh of relief, snatched up her skirts and began to run.

The first Anthony was aware that Maria had managed to slip away was when she broke from cover, running pell-mell across the rough ground, her wildly flying hair a dark smudge against the gray-black sky. Damn! What was she doing? Fear coursed through him. No matter how much she wanted to help him, to help Laura, she had no business putting herself at such risk! He had to stop her!

Anthony knew he had little chance of catching Maria before she reached that terrifyingly barren stretch of ground, but he had to try. Praying that he could succeed, he raced after her.

Maria seemed to sense the danger from behind. Her face was pale with fear when she hazarded a quick glance over her shoulder. Anthony was gaining on her. Desperation gave her one last surge of strength. Her legs pumped harder, and she covered the last few yards to the bleak, open plain.

The land was flooded with light as a jagged flash of lightning stabbed at the ground. "Oh, my God!" whispered Blake as he recognized the two figures racing madly toward the wagon.

"Miguel! Miguel!" Maria screamed with every breath as she continued her mad flight.

Anthony knew it was too late, but still he ran on.

Miguel was bound to see them any second, but he had to protect Maria.

All chance of a surprise attack was gone. Quickly Cletus commanded his men forward, knowing that Anthony's only hope was the quick destruction of the enemy.

The wayward wind carried Maria's anguished cries to Miguel. His head snapped up. Wild black eyes searched the dark horizon. Another flash of lightning sizzled through the air. Miguel's face darkened with fury as he realized what was happening.

Sunfire Valley erupted in a whirlwind of fury. Cletus's men poured through the entrance and out onto the plain.

Miguel screamed his fury at Maria for playing Judas and leading his enemies to the valley. Legs braced against the rocking of the wagon, he stood and leveled the long barrel of his gun at his betrayer. The retort of his shot echoed through the air. Maria stumbled and fell, a small broken doll in the dust.

Laura screamed at the sight and stood up, hands pressed against her cheeks.

Blake stepped from the woods and steadied his gun, praying for a clear shot.

"Maria!" Anthony cried in anguish, throwing all caution to the treacherous wind as he ran to kneel over his wife's lifeless body.

The sound of gunfire challenged the rumble of the thunder, filling the air with a wild cacophony of sound. Horses screamed and bolted. Lightning flashed and danced across the sky as men fell and died.

Oblivious to everything but his own hatred and desire for revenge, Miguel stood impervious against the onslaught of man and nature alike. Once again he raised his gun and took aim. Horror suffused Laura's face as she realized his intent. Her agonized cries rent the air, and she threw herself at Miguel in desperation, knocking his arm up just as the shot rang out.

Anthony stumbled, his hand going instinctively to his shoulder. A small trickle of blood seeped through his fingers where Miguel's bullet had grazed his flesh.

When Blake realized that Anthony was only slightly wounded, he quickly turned his attention back to the wagon. Laura had saved her brother's life, and in the process she had given Blake the opportunity he'd been praying for. Her wild assault on Miguel had carried her over the seat and into the bed of the wagon. And now Miguel stood alone, silhouetted like a black devil against a sky being ripped by lightning flashes.

Blake's finger tightened on the trigger. The sound of the blast was snatched away by the roaring wind. Mortally wounded, Miguel sagged and tumbled from the wagon.

Heedless of everything but the thought of reaching Laura, Blake bolted from his hiding place and charged for the wagon. One leap and he was aboard. Kneeling on the hard wooden planking of the wagon bed, he pulled her to her knees, caging her gently between his legs, wrapping her tightly in his embrace.

All around them, the last moments of the drama were enacted. The gunfire ceased, and the few survivors of Miguel's band threw down their empty weapons and surrendered. The heavens rumbled deeply, then opened to pour forth a cleansing rain. The heavy beat of raindrops washed away the signs of strife and bitterness and then slowed to a warm, gentle shower that soothed, caressed, and purified the earth.

Laura's whole body sang with the depth of her response to Blake's joyous embrace. She pressed herself tighter against him, seeking to lose herself in the safety of his arms. The depth of feeling that was in each of them blossomed and flowed between them. Explanations and apologies were unnecessary as Blake kissed the raindrops from her sweet mouth. Words could not have enhanced the soft reassuring touches or the rapturous embrace of commitment that they exchanged.

They were still kneeling thus when the rain ceased as suddenly as it had begun, and the clouds rolled back to bathe the earth with sweet blessings of golden sunfire.

Epilogue

1848

The carriage jingled to a stop in front of the homey, two-story frame house. Anthony tenderly helped Olivia alight, keeping his arm gently around her waist as he escorted her up the porch stairs to the open door where Blake and Laura waited.

"Came to check on that nephew of mine," Anthony explained with a sheepish smile. "Where is the little feller?"

Blake threw back his head, and his clean, happy laughter filled the air. "The minute I heard a buggy, I told Laura it was you. Gonna get some 'papa practice' in, huh?" he teased.

Olivia blushed sweetly, her hands fluttering protectively over the almost imperceptible blossoming of her pregnancy. She turned adoring eyes on her husband. "I do believe the man's going to be an utter fool about this child."

"Well, no harm in that. Come on in. Little Blake Anthony's in his cradle, just where he should be, but I'm sure you can convince Laura to fetch him for a bit of showing off."

"I won't be a minute," Laura said as she hurried to the nursery.

The others settled themselves in the parlor and waited for her return. When she entered the room, there was a tiny taffy-haired bundle of energy clasped in her arms. Blake's heart filled with such joy that he thought it would burst. His wife. His son. He marveled at the blessings he'd received.

"There's my big boy," Blake cooed at the baby as they all gathered around.

"Say, little feller," Anthony said to the baby. "We just heard some very special news in town. The war is over. Mexico and the United States signed the Treaty of Guadalupe Hidalgo on the second of February—"

The silver crescendo of Laura's delighted laughter rang out. "Good heavens, that's the same day little Blake was born!"

"Yeah," said Anthony with a grin as he watched the baby wrap his tiny hand around Blake's proffered finger.

"Quite a birthday present, isn't it, little one?" Laura crooned to her son.

The baby blinked his big brown eyes and blessed them all with a happy chortle and a wide toothless grin.

Now you can get more of HEARTFIRE right at home and $ave.

Preview
Four Brand New
ZEBRA
Heartfire
Romance Novels...

FREE for 10 days.

No Obligation and No Strings Attached!

♥

Enjoy all of the passion and fiery romance as you soar back through history, right in the comfort of your own home.

Now that you have read a Zebra HEARTFIRE Romance novel, we're sure you'll agree that HEARTFIRE sets new standards of excellence for historical romantic fiction. Each Zebra HEARTFIRE novel is the ultimate blend of intimate romance and grand adventure and each takes place in the kinds of historical settings you want most...the American Revolution, the Old West, Civil War and more.

<u>FREE</u> Preview Each Month and $ave

Zebra has made arrangements for you to preview 4 brand new HEARTFIRE novels each month...FREE for 10 days. You'll get them as soon as they are published. If you are not delighted with any of them, just return them with no questions asked. But if you decide these are everything we said they are, you'll pay just $3.25 each—a total of $13.00 (a $15.00 value). **That's a $2.00 saving each month off the regular price.** Plus there is NO shipping or handling charge. These are delivered right to your door absolutely free! There is no obligation and there is no minimum number of books to buy.

TO GET YOUR FIRST MONTH'S PREVIEW...
Mail the Coupon Below!